PRAISE

THE MORTAL INSTRUMENTS

"The new queen of fantasy." *The Wall Street Journal*

"The Mortal Instruments series is a story world I love to live in. Beautiful."
Stephenie Meyer

"A tale edged by lightning, driven by power and love."
Tamora Pierce

"Cassie's writing makes my toes curl with envy. She is the rare writer who can write fast-paced dramatic fantasy with gorgeous language and memorable characters that you grow to love and worry about, as well as really funny bits that will make you honestly laugh… It is rare to find someone who can do any one of those things well; to find someone who can do them all is just dangerous."
Holly Black

"Hold on tight for a smart, sexy thrill ride." Libba Bray

"Clare's atmospheric setting is spot-on… Werewolves, vampires, angels and fairies all fit in this ambitious milieu. At the core, though, this is a compelling story about family secrets and coming-of-age identity crises. Fans of the smart/chic horror typified by *Buffy the Vampire Slayer* will instantly fall for this series."
Publishers Weekly

"The story's sensual flavor comes from the wealth of detail: demons with facial piercings, diners serving locusts and honey, pretty gay warlocks, and cameo appearances from other urban fantasies' characters… Lush and fun." *Kirkus Reviews*

Also by Cassandra Clare

THE MORTAL INSTRUMENTS

City of Ashes

City of Glass

City of Fallen Angels

City of Lost Souls

THE INFERNAL DEVICES

Clockwork Angel

Clockwork Prince

Clockwork Princess

THE MORTAL INSTRUMENTS

· Book One ·

City of Bones

CASSANDRA CLARE

WALKER
BOOKS

For my grandfather

This is a work of fiction. Names, characters, places and incidents are either the product of the author's imagination or, if real, used fictitiously. All statements, activities, stunts, descriptions, information and material of any other kind contained herein are included for entertainment purposes only and should not be relied on for accuracy or replicated as they may result in injury.

First published in Great Britain 2007 by Walker Books Ltd
87 Vauxhall Walk, London SE11 5HJ

This edition published 2013

2 4 6 8 10 9 7 5 3

This book has been typeset in Dolly

Printed and bound in Great Britain by Clays Ltd, St Ives plc

British Library Cataloguing in Publication Data:
a catalogue record for this book
is available from the British Library

ISBN 978-1-4063-4961-0

www.walker.co.uk

I have not slept.
Between the acting of a dreadful thing
And the first motion, all the interim is
Like a phantasm, or a hideous dream:
The Genius and the mortal instruments
Are then in council; and the state of man,
Like to a little kingdom, suffers then
The nature of an insurrection.
—William Shakespeare, *Julius Caesar*

Part One

Dark Descent

I sung of Chaos and Eternal Night,
Taught by the heav'nly Muse to venture down
The dark descent, and up to reascend...
—John Milton, *Paradise Lost*

1

Pandemonium

"You've got to be kidding me," the bouncer said, folding his arms across his massive chest. He stared down at the boy in the red zip-up jacket and shook his shaved head. "You can't bring that thing in here."

The fifty or so teenagers in line outside the Pandemonium Club leaned forward to eavesdrop. It was a long wait to get into the all-ages club, especially on a Sunday, and not much generally happened in line. The bouncers were fierce and would come down instantly on anyone who looked like they were going to start trouble. Fifteen-year-old Clary Fray, standing in line with her best friend, Simon, leaned forward along with everyone else, hoping for some excitement.

"Aw, come on." The kid hoisted the thing up over his head. It looked like a wooden beam, pointed at one end. "It's part of my costume."

The bouncer raised an eyebrow. "Which is what?"

The boy grinned. He was normal-enough-looking, Clary

thought, for Pandemonium. He had electric blue dyed hair that stuck up around his head like the tentacles of a startled octopus, but no elaborate facial tattoos or big metal bars through his ears or lips. "I'm a vampire hunter." He pushed down on the wooden thing. It bent as easily as a blade of grass bending sideways. "It's fake. Foam rubber. See?"

The boy's wide eyes were way too bright a green, Clary noticed: the color of antifreeze, spring grass. Colored contact lenses, probably. The bouncer shrugged, abruptly bored. "Whatever. Go on in."

The boy slid past him, quick as an eel. Clary liked the lilt to his shoulders, the way he tossed his hair as he went. There was a word for him that her mother would have used—*insouciant*.

"You thought he was cute," said Simon, sounding resigned. "Didn't you?"

Clary dug her elbow into his ribs, but didn't answer.

Inside, the club was full of dry-ice smoke. Colored lights played over the dance floor, turning it into a multicolored fairyland of blues and acid greens, hot pinks and golds.

The boy in the red jacket stroked the long razor-sharp blade in his hands, an idle smile playing over his lips. It had been so easy—a little bit of a glamour on the blade, to make it look harmless. Another glamour on his eyes, and the moment the bouncer had looked straight at him, he was in. Of course, he could probably have gotten by without all that trouble, but it was part of the fun—fooling the mundies, doing it all out in the open right in front of them, getting off on the blank looks on their sheeplike faces.

Not that the humans didn't have their uses. The boy's

green eyes scanned the dance floor, where slender limbs clad in scraps of silk and black leather appeared and disappeared inside the revolving columns of smoke as the mundies danced. Girls tossed their long hair, boys swung their leather-clad hips, and bare skin glittered with sweat. Vitality just *poured* off them, waves of energy that filled him with a drunken dizziness. His lip curled. They didn't know how lucky they were. They didn't know what it was like to eke out life in a dead world, where the sun hung limp in the sky like a burned cinder. Their lives burned as brightly as candle flames—and were as easy to snuff out.

His hand tightened on the blade he carried, and he had begun to step out onto the dance floor when a girl broke away from the mass of dancers and began walking toward him. He stared at her. She was beautiful, for a human—long hair nearly the precise color of black ink, charcoaled eyes. Floor-length white gown, the kind women used to wear when this world was younger. Lace sleeves belled out around her slim arms. Around her neck was a thick silver chain, on which hung a dark red pendant the size of a baby's fist. He only had to narrow his eyes to know that it was real—real and precious. His mouth started to water as she neared him. Vital energy pulsed from her like blood from an open wound. She smiled, passing him, beckoning with her eyes. He turned to follow her, tasting the phantom sizzle of her death on his lips.

It was always easy. He could already feel the power of her evaporating life coursing through his veins like fire. Humans were so stupid. They had something so precious, and they barely safeguarded it at all. They threw away their lives for money, for packets of powder, for a stranger's charming smile. The girl was a pale ghost retreating through the colored smoke. She reached the wall and turned, bunching her skirt up in her hands, lifting it as she grinned at him. Under the skirt, she was wearing thigh-high boots.

He sauntered up to her, his skin prickling with her nearness. Up close she wasn't so perfect: He could see the mascara smudged under her eyes, the sweat sticking her hair to her neck. He could smell her mortality, the sweet rot of corruption. *Got you*, he thought.

A cool smile curled her lips. She moved to the side, and he could see that she was leaning against a closed door. NO ADMITTANCE—STORAGE was scrawled across it in red paint. She reached behind her for the knob, turned it, slid inside. He caught a glimpse of stacked boxes, tangled wiring. A storage room. He glanced behind him—no one was looking. So much the better if she wanted privacy.

He slipped into the room after her, unaware that he was being followed.

"So," Simon said, "pretty good music, eh?"

Clary didn't reply. They were dancing, or what passed for it—a lot of swaying back and forth with occasional lunges toward the floor as if one of them had dropped a contact lens—in a space between a group of teenage boys in metallic corsets, and a young Asian couple who were making out passionately, their colored hair extensions tangled together like vines. A boy with a lip piercing and a teddy bear backpack was handing out free tablets of herbal ecstasy, his parachute pants flapping in the breeze from the wind machine. Clary wasn't paying much attention to their immediate surroundings—her eyes were on the blue-haired boy who'd talked his way into the club. He was prowling through the crowd as if he were looking for something. There was something about the way he moved that reminded her of something...

"I, for one," Simon went on, "am enjoying myself immensely."

This seemed unlikely. Simon, as always, stuck out at the club like a sore thumb, in jeans and an old T-shirt that said MADE IN BROOKLYN across the front. His freshly scrubbed hair was dark brown instead of green or pink, and his glasses perched crookedly on the end of his nose. He looked less as if he were contemplating the powers of darkness and more as if he were on his way to chess club.

"Mmm-hmm." Clary knew perfectly well that he came to Pandemonium with her only because she liked it, that he thought it was boring. She wasn't even sure why it was that she liked it—the clothes, the music made it like a dream, someone else's life, not her boring real life at all. But she was always too shy to talk to anyone but Simon.

The blue-haired boy was making his way off the dance floor. He looked a little lost, as if he hadn't found whom he was looking for. Clary wondered what would happen if she went up and introduced herself, offered to show him around. Maybe he'd just stare at her. Or maybe he was shy too. Maybe he'd be grateful and pleased, and try not to show it, the way boys did—but she'd know. Maybe—

The blue-haired boy straightened up suddenly, snapping to attention, like a hunting dog on point. Clary followed the line of his gaze, and saw the girl in the white dress.

Oh, well, Clary thought, trying not to feel like a deflated party balloon. *I guess that's that.* The girl was gorgeous, the kind of girl Clary would have liked to draw—tall and ribbon-slim, with a long spill of black hair. Even at this distance Clary could see the red pendant around her throat. It pulsed under the lights of the dance floor like a separate, disembodied heart.

"I feel," Simon went on, "that this evening DJ Bat is doing a singularly exceptional job. Don't you agree?"

Clary rolled her eyes and didn't answer; Simon hated trance music. Her attention was on the girl in the white dress. Through the darkness, smoke, and artificial fog, her pale dress shone out like a beacon. No wonder the blue-haired boy was following her as if he were under a spell, too distracted to notice anything else around him—even the two dark shapes hard on his heels, weaving after him through the crowd.

Clary slowed her dancing and stared. She could just make out that the shapes were boys, tall and wearing black clothes. She couldn't have said how she knew that they were following the other boy, but she did. She could see it in the way they paced him, their careful watchfulness, the slinking grace of their movements. A small flower of apprehension began to open inside her chest.

"Meanwhile," Simon added, "I wanted to tell you that lately I've been cross-dressing. Also, I'm sleeping with your mom. I thought you should know."

The girl had reached the wall, and was opening a door marked NO ADMITTANCE. She beckoned the blue-haired boy after her, and they slipped through the door. It wasn't anything Clary hadn't seen before, a couple sneaking off to the dark corners of the club to make out—but that made it even weirder that they were being followed.

She raised herself up on tiptoe, trying to see over the crowd. The two guys had stopped at the door and seemed to be conferring with each other. One of them was blond, the other dark-haired. The blond one reached into his jacket and drew out something long and sharp that flashed under the strobing lights. A knife. "Simon!" Clary shouted, and seized his arm.

"What?" Simon looked alarmed. "I'm not really sleeping with your mom, you know. I was just trying to get your attention. Not that your mom isn't a very attractive woman, for her age."

"Do you see those guys?" She pointed wildly, almost hitting a curvy black girl who was dancing nearby. The girl shot her an evil look. "Sorry—sorry!" Clary turned back to Simon. "Do you see those two guys over there? By that door?"

Simon squinted, then shrugged. "I don't see anything."

"There are two of them. They were following the guy with the blue hair—"

"The one you thought was cute?"

"Yes, but that's not the point. The blond one pulled a knife."

"Are you *sure*?" Simon stared harder, shaking his head. "I still don't see anyone."

"I'm sure."

Suddenly all business, Simon squared his shoulders. "I'll get one of the security guards. You stay here." He strode away, pushing through the crowd.

Clary turned just in time to see the blond boy slip through the NO ADMITTANCE door, his friend right on his heels. She looked around; Simon was still trying to shove his way across the dance floor, but he wasn't making much progress. Even if she yelled now, no one would hear her, and by the time Simon got back, something terrible might *already* have happened. Biting hard on her lower lip, Clary started to wriggle through the crowd.

"What's your name?"

She turned and smiled. What faint light there was in the storage room spilled down through high barred windows smeared with dirt. Piles of electrical cables, along with broken bits of mirrored disco balls and discarded paint cans littered the floor.

"Isabelle."

"That's a nice name." He walked toward her, stepping carefully among the wires in case any of them were live. In the faint light she looked half-transparent, bleached of color, wrapped in white like an angel. It would be a pleasure to make her fall… "I haven't seen you here before."

"You're asking me if I come here often?" She giggled, covering her mouth with her hand. There was some sort of bracelet around her wrist, just under the cuff of her dress—then, as he neared her, he saw that it wasn't a bracelet at all but a pattern inked into her skin, a matrix of swirling lines.

He froze. "You—"

He didn't finish. She moved with lightning swiftness, striking out at him with her open hand, a blow to his chest that would have sent him down gasping if he'd been a human being. He staggered back, and now there was something in her hand, a coiling whip that glinted gold as she brought it down, curling around his ankles, jerking him off his feet. He hit the ground, writhing, the hated metal biting deep into his skin. She laughed, standing over him, and dizzily he thought that he should have known. No human girl would wear a dress like the one Isabelle wore. She'd worn it to cover her skin—all of her skin.

Isabelle yanked hard on the whip, securing it. Her smile glittered like poisonous water. "He's all yours, boys."

A low laugh sounded behind him, and now there were hands on him, hauling him upright, throwing him against one of the concrete pillars. He could feel the damp stone under his back. His hands were pulled behind him, his wrists bound with wire. As he struggled, someone walked around the side of the pillar into his view: a boy, as young as Isabelle and just as pretty. His tawny eyes glittered like chips of amber. "So," the boy said. "Are there any more with you?"

The blue-haired boy could feel blood welling up under the too-tight metal, making his wrists slippery. "Any other what?"

"Come on now." The tawny-eyed boy held up his hands, and his dark sleeves slipped down, showing the runes inked all over his wrists, the backs of his hands, his palms. "You know what I am."

Far back inside his skull, the shackled boy's second set of teeth began to grind.

"*Shadowhunter,*" he hissed.

The other boy grinned all over his face. "Got you," he said.

Clary pushed the door to the storage room open, and stepped inside. For a moment she thought it was deserted. The only windows were high up and barred; faint street noise came through them, the sound of honking cars and squealing brakes. The room smelled like old paint, and a heavy layer of dust covered the floor, marked by smeared shoe prints.

There's no one in here, she realized, looking around in bewilderment. It was cold in the room, despite the August heat outside. Her back was icy with sweat. She took a step forward, tangling her feet in electrical wires. She bent down to free her sneaker from the cables—and heard voices. A girl's laugh, a boy answering sharply. When she straightened up, she saw them.

It was as if they had sprung into existence between one blink of her eyes and the next. There was the girl in her long white dress, her black hair hanging down her back like damp seaweed. The two boys were with her—the tall one with black hair like hers, and the smaller, fair one, whose hair gleamed like brass in the dim light coming through the windows high above. The fair boy was standing with his hands in his pockets, facing the punk kid, who was tied to a pillar with what looked like piano wire, his hands stretched behind him, his legs bound at the ankles. His face was pulled tight with pain and fear.

Heart hammering in her chest, Clary ducked behind the nearest concrete pillar and peered around it. She watched as the fair-haired boy paced back and forth, his arms now crossed over his chest. "So," he said. "You still haven't told me if there are any other of your kind with you."

Your kind? Clary wondered what he was talking about. Maybe she'd stumbled into some kind of gang war.

"I don't know what you're talking about." The blue-haired boy's tone was pained but surly.

"He means other demons," said the dark-haired boy, speaking for the first time. "You do know what a demon is, don't you?"

The boy tied to the pillar turned his face away, his mouth working.

"Demons," drawled the blond boy, tracing the word on the air with his finger. "Religiously defined as hell's denizens, the servants of Satan, but understood here, for the purposes of the Clave, to be any malevolent spirit whose origin is outside our own home dimension—"

"That's enough, Jace," said the girl.

"Isabelle's right," agreed the taller boy. "Nobody here needs a lesson in semantics—or demonology."

They're crazy, Clary thought. *Actually crazy*.

Jace raised his head and smiled. There was something fierce about the gesture, something that reminded Clary of documentaries she'd watched about lions on the Discovery Channel, the way the big cats would raise their heads and sniff the air for prey. "Isabelle and Alec think I talk too much," he said, confidingly. "Do *you* think I talk too much?"

The blue-haired boy didn't reply. His mouth was still working. "I could give you information," he said. "I know where Valentine is."

Jace glanced back at Alec, who shrugged. "Valentine's in the ground," Jace said. "The thing's just toying with us."

Isabelle tossed her hair. "Kill it, Jace," she said. "It's not going to tell us anything."

Jace raised his hand, and Clary saw dim light spark off the knife he was holding. It was oddly translucent, the blade clear as crystal, sharp as a shard of glass, the hilt set with red stones.

The bound boy gasped. "Valentine is back!" he protested, dragging at the bonds that held his hands behind his back. "All the Infernal Worlds know it—I know it—I can tell you where he is—"

Rage flared suddenly in Jace's icy eyes. "By the Angel, every time we capture one of you bastards, you claim you know where Valentine is. Well, we know where he is too. He's in hell. And you—" Jace turned the knife in his grasp, the edge sparking like a line of fire. "You can *join him there.*"

Clary could take no more. She stepped out from behind the pillar. "Stop!" she cried. "You can't do this."

Jace whirled, so startled that the knife flew from his hand and clattered against the concrete floor. Isabelle and Alec turned along with him, wearing identical expressions of astonishment. The blue-haired boy hung in his bonds, stunned and gaping.

It was Alec who spoke first. "What's this?" he demanded, looking from Clary to his companions, as if they might know what she was doing there.

"It's a girl," Jace said, recovering his composure. "Surely you've seen girls before, Alec. Your sister, Isabelle, is one." He took a step closer to Clary, squinting as if he couldn't quite believe what he was seeing. "A mundie girl," he said, half to himself. "And she can see us."

"Of course I can see you," Clary said. "I'm not blind, you know."

"Oh, but you are," said Jace, bending to pick up his knife. "You just don't know it." He straightened up. "You'd better get out of here, if you know what's good for you."

"I'm not going anywhere," Clary said. "If I do, you'll kill him." She pointed at the boy with the blue hair.

"That's true," admitted Jace, twirling the knife between his fingers. "What do you care if I kill him or not?"

"Be-because—" Clary spluttered. "You can't just go around killing people."

"You're right," said Jace. "You can't go around killing *people*." He pointed at the boy with blue hair, whose eyes were slitted. Clary wondered if he'd fainted. "That's not a person, little girl. It may look like a person and talk like a person and maybe even bleed like a person. But it's a monster."

"*Jace,*" said Isabelle warningly. "That's enough."

"You're crazy," Clary said, backing away from him. "I've called the police, you know. They'll be here any second."

"She's lying," said Alec, but there was doubt on his face. "Jace, do you—"

He never got to finish his sentence. At that moment the blue-haired boy, with a high, yowling cry, tore free of the restraints binding him to the pillar, and flung himself on Jace.

They fell to the ground and rolled together, the blue-haired boy tearing at Jace with hands that glittered as if tipped with metal. Clary backed up, wanting to run, but her feet caught on a loop of wiring and she went down, knocking the breath out of her chest. She could hear Isabelle shrieking. Rolling over, Clary saw the blue-haired boy sitting on Jace's chest. Blood gleamed at the tips of his razorlike claws.

Isabelle and Alec were running toward them, Isabelle brandishing a whip in her hand. The blue-haired boy slashed at Jace with claws extended. Jace threw an arm up to protect himself, and the claws raked it, splattering blood. The blue-haired boy lunged again—and Isabelle's whip came down across his back. He shrieked and fell to the side.

Swift as a flick of Isabelle's whip, Jace rolled over. There was a blade gleaming in his hand. He sank the knife into the blue-haired boy's chest. Blackish liquid exploded around the hilt. The boy arched off the floor, gurgling and twisting. With a grimace Jace stood up. His black shirt was blacker now in some places, wet with blood. He looked down at the twitching form at his feet, reached down, and yanked out the knife.

The hilt was slick with black fluid.

The blue-haired boy's eyes flickered open. His eyes, fixed on Jace, seemed to burn. Between his teeth, he hissed, *"So be it. The Forsaken will take you all."*

Jace seemed to snarl. The boy's eyes rolled back. His body began to jerk and twitch as he crumpled, folding in on himself, growing smaller and smaller until he vanished entirely.

Clary scrambled to her feet, kicking free of the electrical wiring. She began to back away. None of them was paying attention to her. Alec had reached Jace and was holding his arm, pulling at the sleeve, probably trying to get a good look at the wound. Clary turned to run—and found her way blocked by Isabelle, whip in hand. The gold length of it was stained with dark fluid. She flicked it toward Clary, and the end wrapped itself around her wrist and jerked tight. Clary gasped with pain and surprise.

"Stupid little mundie," Isabelle said between her teeth. "You could have gotten Jace killed."

"He's crazy," Clary said, trying to pull her wrist back. The whip bit deeper into her skin. "You're all crazy. What do you think you are, vigilante killers? The police—"

"The police aren't usually interested unless you can produce a body," said Jace. Cradling his arm, he picked his way across the cable-strewn floor toward Clary. Alec followed behind him, face screwed into a scowl.

Clary glanced at the spot where the boy had disappeared from, and said nothing. There wasn't even a smear of blood there—nothing to show that the boy had ever existed.

"They return to their home dimensions when they die," said Jace. "In case you were wondering."

"Jace," Alec hissed. "Be careful."

Jace drew his arm away. A ghoulish freckling of blood marked his face. He still reminded her of a lion, with his wide-spaced, light-colored eyes, and that tawny gold hair. "She can see us, Alec," he said. "She already knows too much."

"So what do you want me to do with her?" Isabelle demanded.

"Let her go," Jace said quietly. Isabelle shot him a surprised, almost angry look, but didn't argue. The whip slithered away, freeing Clary's arm. She rubbed her sore wrist and wondered how the hell she was going to get out of there.

"Maybe we should bring her back with us," Alec said. "I bet Hodge would like to talk to her."

"No way are we bringing her to the Institute," said Isabelle. "She's a *mundie*."

"Or is she?" said Jace softly. His quiet tone was worse than Isabelle's snapping or Alec's anger. "Have you had dealings with demons, little girl? Walked with warlocks, talked with the Night Children? Have you—"

"My name is not 'little girl,'" Clary interrupted. "And I have no idea what you're talking about." *Don't you?* said a voice in the back of her head. *You saw that boy vanish into thin air. Jace isn't crazy—you just wish he was.* "I don't believe in—in demons, or whatever you—"

"Clary?" It was Simon's voice. She whirled around. He was standing by the storage room door. One of the burly bouncers who'd been stamping hands at the front door was next to him. "Are you okay?" He peered at her through the gloom. "Why are you in here by yourself? What happened to the guys—you know, the ones with the knives?"

Clary stared at him, then looked behind her, where Jace, Isabelle, and Alec stood, Jace still in his bloody shirt with the knife in his hand. He grinned at her and dropped a half-apologetic, half-mocking shrug. Clearly he wasn't surprised that neither Simon nor the bouncer could see them.

Somehow neither was Clary. Slowly she turned back to Simon, knowing how she must look to him, standing alone in a damp storage room, her feet tangled in bright plastic wiring cables. "I thought they went in here," she said lamely. "But I guess they didn't. I'm sorry." She glanced from Simon, whose expression was changing from worried to embarrassed, to the bouncer, who just looked annoyed. "It was a mistake."

Behind her, Isabelle giggled.

"I don't believe it," Simon said stubbornly as Clary, standing at the curb, tried desperately to hail a cab. Street cleaners had come down Orchard while they were inside the club, and the street was glossed black with oily water.

"I know," she agreed. "You'd think there'd be *some* cabs. Where is everyone going at midnight on a Sunday?" She turned back to him, shrugging. "You think we'd have better luck on Houston?"

"Not the cabs," Simon said. "You—I don't believe you. I don't believe those guys with the knives just disappeared."

Clary sighed. "Maybe there weren't any guys with knives, Simon. Maybe I just imagined the whole thing."

"No way." Simon raised his hand over his head, but the oncoming taxis whizzed by him, spraying dirty water. "I saw your face when I came into that storage room. You looked seriously freaked out, like you'd seen a ghost."

Clary thought of Jace with his lion-cat eyes. She glanced down at her wrist, braceleted by a thin red line where Isabelle's whip had curled. *No, not a ghost,* she thought. *Something even weirder than that.*

"It was just a mistake," she said wearily. She wondered why she wasn't telling him the truth. Except, of course, that he'd think she was crazy. And there was something about what had happened—something about the black blood bubbling up around Jace's knife, something about his voice when he'd said, *Have you talked with the Night Children?* that she wanted to keep to herself.

"Well, it was a hell of an embarrassing mistake," Simon said. He glanced back at the club, where a thin line still snaked out the door and halfway down the block. "I doubt they'll ever let us back into Pandemonium."

"What do you care? You hate Pandemonium." Clary raised her hand again as a yellow shape sped toward them through the fog. This time, though, the taxi screeched to a halt at their corner, the driver laying into his horn as if he needed to get their attention.

"Finally we get lucky." Simon yanked the taxi door open and slid onto the plastic-covered backseat. Clary followed, inhaling the familiar New York cab smell of old cigarette smoke, leather, and hair spray. "We're going to Brooklyn," Simon said to the cabbie, and then he turned to Clary. "Look, you know you can tell me anything, right?"

Clary hesitated a moment, then nodded. "Sure, Simon," she said. "I know I can." She slammed the cab door shut behind her, and the taxi took off into the night.

2

Secrets and Lies

***The dark prince sat astride his black steed, his sable cape** flowing behind him. A golden circlet bound his blond locks, his handsome face was cold with the rage of battle, and...*

"And his arm looked like an eggplant," Clary muttered to herself in exasperation. The drawing just wasn't working. With a sigh she tore yet another sheet from her sketchpad, crumpled it up, and tossed it against the orange wall of her bedroom. Already the floor was littered with discarded balls of paper, a sure sign that her creative juices weren't flowing the way she'd hoped. She wished for the thousandth time that she could be a bit more like her mother. Everything Jocelyn Fray drew, painted, or sketched was beautiful, and seemingly effortless.

Clary pulled her headphones out—cutting off Stepping Razor in midsong—and rubbed her aching temples. It was only then that she became aware that the loud, piercing sound of a ringing telephone was echoing through the apartment.

Tossing the sketchpad onto the bed, she jumped to her feet and ran into the living room, where the retro-red phone sat on a table near the front door.

"Is this Clarissa Fray?" The voice on the other end of the phone sounded familiar, though not immediately identifiable.

Clary twirled the phone cord nervously around her finger. "Yeees?"

"Hi, I'm one of the knife-carrying hooligans you met last night in Pandemonium? I'm afraid I made a bad impression and was hoping you'd give me a chance to make it up to—"

"SIMON!" Clary held the phone away from her ear as he cracked up laughing. "That is so not funny!"

"Sure it is. You just don't see the humor."

"Jerk." Clary sighed, leaning up against the wall. "You wouldn't be laughing if you'd been here when I got home last night."

"Why not?"

"My mom. She wasn't happy that we were late. She freaked out. It was messy."

"What? It's not our fault there was traffic!" Simon protested. He was the youngest of two children and had a finely honed sense of familial injustice.

"Yeah, well, she doesn't see it that way. I disappointed her, I let her down, I made her worry, blah blah blah. I am the *bane* of her *existence*," Clary said, mimicking her mother's precise phrasing with only a slight twinge of guilt.

"So, are you grounded?" Simon asked, a little too loudly.

Clary could hear a low rumble of voices behind him; people talking over each other.

"I don't know yet," she said. "My mom went out this

morning with Luke, and they're not back yet. Where are you, anyway? Eric's?"

"Yeah. We just finished up practice." A cymbal clashed behind Simon. Clary winced. "Eric's doing a poetry reading over at Java Jones tonight," Simon went on, naming a coffee shop around the corner from Clary's that sometimes had live music at night. "The whole band's going to go to show their support. Want to come?"

"Yeah, all right." Clary paused, tugging on the phone cord anxiously. "Wait, no."

"Shut up, guys, will you?" Simon yelled, the faintness of his voice making Clary suspect that he was holding the phone away from his mouth. He was back a second later, sounding troubled. "Was that a yes or a no?"

"I don't know." Clary bit her lip. "My mom's still mad at me about last night. I'm not sure I want to piss her off by asking for any favors. If I'm going to get in trouble, I don't want it to be on account of Eric's lousy poetry."

"Come on, it's not so bad," Simon said. Eric was his next-door neighbor, and the two had known each other most of their lives. They weren't close the way Simon and Clary were, but they had formed a rock band together at the start of sophomore year, along with Eric's friends Matt and Kirk. They practiced together faithfully in Eric's parents' garage every week. "Besides, it's not a favor," Simon added, "it's a poetry slam around the block from your house. It's not like I'm inviting you to some orgy in Hoboken. Your mom can come along if she wants."

"ORGY IN HOBOKEN!" Clary heard someone, probably Eric, yell. Another cymbal crashed. She imagined her mother listening to Eric read his poetry, and she shuddered inwardly.

"I don't know. If all of you show up here, I think she'll freak."

"Then I'll come alone. I'll pick you up and we can walk over there together, meet the rest of them there. Your mom won't mind. She loves me."

Clary had to laugh. "Sign of her questionable taste, if you ask me."

"Nobody did." Simon clicked off, amid shouts from his bandmates.

Clary hung up the phone and glanced around the living room. Evidence of her mother's artistic tendencies was everywhere, from the handmade velvet throw pillows piled on the dark red sofa to the walls hung with Jocelyn's paintings, carefully framed—landscapes, mostly: the winding streets of downtown Manhattan lit with golden light; scenes of Prospect Park in winter, the gray ponds edged with lacelike films of white ice.

On the mantel over the fireplace was a framed photo of Clary's father. A thoughtful-looking fair man in military dress, his eyes bore the telltale traces of laugh lines at the corners. He'd been a decorated soldier serving overseas. Jocelyn had some of his medals in a small box by her bed. Not that the medals had done anyone any good when Jonathan Clark had crashed his car into a tree just outside Albany and died before his daughter was even born.

Jocelyn had gone back to using her maiden name after he died. She never talked about Clary's father, but she kept the box engraved with his initials, J. C., next to her bed. Along with the medals were one or two photos, a wedding ring, and a single lock of blond hair. Sometimes Jocelyn took the box out and opened it and held the lock of hair very gently in her hands before putting it back and carefully locking the box up again.

The sound of the key turning in the front door roused Clary out of her reverie. Hastily she threw herself down on the couch and tried to look as if she were immersed in one of the paperbacks her mother had left stacked on the end table. Jocelyn recognized reading as a sacred pastime and usually wouldn't interrupt Clary in the middle of a book, even to yell at her.

The door opened with a thump. It was Luke, his arms full of what looked like big square pieces of pasteboard. When he set them down, Clary saw that they were cardboard boxes, folded flat. He straightened up and turned to her with a smile.

"Hey, Un—hey, Luke," she said. He'd asked her to stop calling him Uncle Luke about a year ago, claiming that it made him feel old, and anyway reminded him of *Uncle Tom's Cabin*. Besides, he'd reminded her gently, he wasn't really her uncle, just a close friend of her mother's who'd known her all her life. "Where's Mom?"

"Parking the truck," he said, straightening his lanky frame with a groan. He was dressed in his usual uniform: old jeans, a flannel shirt, and a bent pair of gold-rimmed spectacles that sat askew on the bridge of his nose. "Remind me again why this building has no service elevator?"

"Because it's old, and has *character*," Clary said immediately. Luke grinned. "What are the boxes for?" she asked.

His grin vanished. "Your mother wanted to pack up some things," he said, avoiding her gaze.

"What things?" Clary asked.

He gave an airy wave. "Extra stuff lying around the house. Getting in the way. You know she never throws anything out.

So what are you up to? Studying?" He plucked the book out of her hand and read out loud: "*The world still teems with those motley beings whom a more sober philosophy has discarded. Fairies and goblins, ghosts and demons, still hover about—*" He lowered the book and looked at her over his glasses. "Is this for school?"

"*The Golden Bough?* No. School's not for two weeks." Clary took the book back from him. "It's my mom's."

"I had a feeling."

She dropped it back on the table. "Luke?"

"Uh-huh?" The book already forgotten, he was rummaging in the tool kit next to the hearth. "Ah, here it is." He pulled out an orange plastic tape gun and gazed at it with deep satisfaction.

"What would you do if you saw something nobody else could see?"

The tape gun fell out of Luke's hand, and hit the tiled hearth. He knelt to pick it up, not looking at her. "You mean if I were the only witness to a crime, that sort of thing?"

"No. I mean, if there were other people around, but you were the only one who could see something. As if it were invisible to everyone but you."

He hesitated, still kneeling, the dented tape gun gripped in his hand.

"I know it sounds crazy," Clary ventured nervously, "but..."

He turned around. His eyes, very blue behind the glasses, rested on her with a look of firm affection. "Clary, you're an artist, like your mother. That means you see the world in ways that other people don't. It's your gift, to see the beauty and the horror in ordinary things. It doesn't make you crazy—just different. There's nothing wrong with being different."

Clary pulled her legs up, and rested her chin on her knees. In her mind's eye she saw the storage room, Isabelle's gold whip, the blue-haired boy convulsing in his death spasms, and Jace's tawny eyes. *Beauty and horror.* She said, "If my dad had lived, do you think he'd have been an artist too?"

Luke looked taken aback. Before he could answer her, the door swung open and Clary's mother stalked into the room, her boot heels clacking on the polished wooden floor. She handed Luke a set of jingling car keys and turned to look at her daughter.

Jocelyn Fray was a slim, compact woman, her hair a few shades darker than Clary's and twice as long. At the moment it was twisted up in a dark red knot, stuck through with a graphite pen to hold it in place. She wore paint-spattered overalls over a lavender T-shirt, and brown hiking boots whose soles were caked with oil paint.

People always told Clary that she looked like her mother, but she couldn't see it herself. The only thing that was similar about them was their figures: They were both slender, with small chests and narrow hips. She knew she wasn't beautiful like her mother was. To be beautiful you had to be willowy and tall. When you were as short as Clary was, just over five feet, you were cute. Not pretty or beautiful, but cute. Throw in carroty hair and a face full of freckles, and she was a Raggedy Ann to her mother's Barbie doll.

Jocelyn even had a graceful way of walking that made people turn their heads to watch her go by. Clary, by contrast, was always tripping over her feet. The only time people turned to watch her go by was when she hurtled past them as she fell down stairs.

"Thanks for bringing the boxes up," Clary's mother said to Luke, and smiled at him. He didn't return the smile. Clary's stomach did an uneasy flip. Clearly there was something going on. "Sorry it took me so long to find a space. There must be a million people at the park today—"

"Mom?" Clary interrupted. "What are the boxes for?"

Jocelyn bit her lip. Luke flicked his eyes toward Clary, mutely urging Jocelyn forward. With a nervous twitch of her wrist, Jocelyn pushed a dangling lock of hair behind her ear and went to join her daughter on the couch.

Up close Clary could see how tired her mother looked. There were dark half-moons under her eyes, and her lids were pearly with sleeplessness.

"Is this about last night?" Clary asked.

"No," her mother said quickly, and then hesitated. "Maybe a little. You shouldn't have done what you did last night. You know better."

"And I already apologized. What is this about? If you're grounding me, get it over with."

"I'm not," said her mother, "grounding you." Her voice was as taut as a wire. She glanced at Luke, who shook his head.

"Just tell her, Jocelyn," he said.

"Could you not talk about me like I'm not here?" Clary said angrily. "And what do you mean, 'tell me'? Tell me what?"

Jocelyn expelled a sigh. "We're going on vacation."

Luke's expression went blank, like a canvas wiped clean of paint.

Clary shook her head. "That's what this is about? You're

going on vacation?" She sank back against the cushions. "I don't get it. Why the big production?"

"I don't think you understand. I meant we're all going on vacation. The three of us—you, me, and Luke. We're going to the farmhouse."

"Oh." Clary glanced at Luke, but he had his arms crossed over his chest and was staring out the window, his jaw pulled tight. She wondered what was upsetting him. He loved the old farmhouse in upstate New York—he'd bought and restored it himself ten years before, and he went there whenever he could. "For how long?"

"For the rest of the summer," said Jocelyn. "I brought the boxes in case you want to pack up any books, painting supplies—"

"For the *rest of the summer*?" Clary sat upright with indignation. "I can't do that, Mom. I have plans—Simon and I were going to have a back-to-school party, and I've got a bunch of meetings with my art group, and ten more classes at Tisch—"

"I'm sorry about Tisch. But the other things can be canceled. Simon will understand, and so will your art group."

Clary heard the implacability in her mother's tone and realized she was serious. "But I paid for those art classes! I saved up all year! You promised." She whirled, turning to Luke. "Tell her! Tell her it isn't fair!"

Luke didn't look away from the window, though a muscle jumped in his cheek. "She's your mother. It's her decision to make."

"I don't get it." Clary turned back to her mother. "Why?"

"I have to get away, Clary," Jocelyn said, the corners of her mouth trembling. "I need the peace, the quiet, to paint. And money is tight right now—"

"So sell some more of Dad's stocks," Clary said angrily. "That's what you usually do, isn't it?"

Jocelyn recoiled. "That's hardly fair."

"Look, go if you want to go. I don't care. I'll stay here without you. I can work; I can get a job at Starbucks or something. Simon said they're always hiring. I'm old enough to take care of myself—"

"No!" The sharpness in Jocelyn's voice made Clary jump. "I'll pay you back for the art classes, Clary. But you are coming with us. It isn't optional. You're too young to stay here on your own. Something could happen."

"Like what? What could happen?" Clary demanded.

There was a crash. She turned in surprise to find that Luke had knocked over one of the framed pictures leaning against the wall. Looking distinctly upset, he set it back. When he straightened, his mouth was set in a grim line. "I'm leaving."

Jocelyn bit her lip. "Wait." She hurried after him into the entryway, catching up just as he seized the doorknob. Twisting around on the sofa, Clary could just overhear her mother's urgent whisper. "... Bane," Jocelyn was saying. "I've been calling him and calling him for the past three weeks. His voice mail says he's in Tanzania. What am I supposed to do?"

"Jocelyn." Luke shook his head. "You can't keep going to him forever."

"But Clary—"

"Isn't Jonathan," Luke hissed. "You've never been the same since it happened, but Clary *isn't Jonathan.*"

What does my father have to do with this? Clary thought, bewildered.

"I can't just keep her at home, not let her go out. She won't put up with it."

"Of course she won't!" Luke sounded really angry. "She's not a pet, she's a teenager. Almost an adult."

"If we were out of the city..."

"Talk to her, Jocelyn." Luke's voice was firm. "I mean it." He reached for the doorknob.

The door flew open. Jocelyn gave a little scream.

"Jesus!" Luke exclaimed.

"Actually, it's just me," said Simon. "Although I've been told the resemblance is startling." He waved at Clary from the doorway. "You ready?"

Jocelyn took her hand away from her mouth. "Simon, were you eavesdropping?"

Simon blinked. "No, I just got here." He looked from Jocelyn's pale face to Luke's grim one. "Is something wrong? Should I go?"

"Don't bother," Luke said. "I think we're done here." He pushed past Simon, thudding down the stairs at a rapid pace. Downstairs, the front door slammed shut.

Simon hovered in the doorway, looking uncertain. "I can come back later," he said. "Really. It wouldn't be a problem."

"That might—" Jocelyn began, but Clary was already on her feet.

"Forget it, Simon. We're leaving," she said, grabbing her messenger bag from a hook near the door. She slung it over her shoulder, glaring at her mother. "See you later, Mom."

Jocelyn bit her lip. "Clary, don't you think we should talk about this?"

"We'll have plenty of time to talk while we're on 'vacation,'" Clary said venomously, and had the satisfaction of seeing her mother flinch. "Don't wait up," she added, and grabbing Simon's arm, she half-dragged him out the front door.

He dug his heels in, looking apologetically over his shoulder at Clary's mother, who stood small and forlorn in the entryway, her hands knitted tightly together. "Bye, Mrs. Fray!" he called. "Have a nice evening!"

"Oh, shut *up*, Simon," Clary snapped, and slammed the door behind them, cutting off her mother's reply.

"Jesus, woman, don't rip my arm off," Simon protested as Clary hauled him downstairs after her, her green Skechers slapping against the wooden stairs with every angry step. She glanced up, half-expecting to see her mother glaring down from the landing, but the apartment door stayed shut.

"Sorry," Clary muttered, letting go of his wrist. She paused at the foot of the stairs, her messenger bag banging against her hip.

Clary's brownstone, like most in Park Slope, had once been the single residence of a wealthy family. Shades of its former grandeur were still evident in the curving staircase, the chipped marble entryway floor, and the wide single-paned skylight overhead. Now the house was split into separate apartments, and Clary and her mother shared the three-floor building with a downstairs tenant, an elderly woman who ran a psychic's shop out of her apartment. She hardly ever came out of it, though customer visits were infrequent. A gold plaque fixed to the door proclaimed her to be MADAME DOROTHEA, SEERESS AND PROPHETESS.

The thick sweet scent of incense spilled from the half-open door into the foyer. Clary could hear a low murmur of voices.

"Nice to see she's doing a booming business," Simon said. "It's hard to get steady prophet work these days."

"Do you have to be sarcastic about everything?" Clary snapped.

Simon blinked, clearly taken aback. "I thought you liked it when I was witty and ironic."

Clary was about to reply when the door to Madame Dorothea's swung fully open and a man stepped out. He was tall, with brown skin, gold-green eyes like a cat's, and tangled black hair. He grinned at her blindingly, showing sharp white teeth.

A wave of dizziness came over her, the strong sensation that she was going to faint.

Simon glanced at her uneasily. "Are you all right? You look like you're going to pass out."

She blinked at him. "What? No, I'm fine."

He didn't seem to want to let it drop. "You look like you just saw a ghost."

She shook her head. The memory of having seen something teased her, but when she tried to concentrate, it slid away like water. "Nothing. I thought I saw Dorothea's cat, but I guess it was just a trick of the light." Simon stared at her. "I haven't eaten anything since yesterday," she added defensively. "I guess I'm a little out of it."

He slid a comforting arm around her shoulders. "Come on, I'll buy you some food."

***

"I just can't believe she's being like this," Clary said for the fourth time, chasing a stray bit of guacamole around her plate with the tip of a nacho. They were at a neighborhood Mexican joint, a hole in the wall called Nacho Mama. "Like grounding me every other week wasn't bad enough. Now I'm going to be exiled for the rest of the summer."

"Well, you know, your mom gets like this sometimes," Simon said. "Like when she breathes in or out." He grinned at her around his veggie burrito.

"Oh, sure, act like it's funny," she said. "*You're* not the one getting dragged off to the middle of nowhere for God knows how long—"

"*Clary.*" Simon interrupted her tirade. "I'm not the one you're mad at. Besides, it isn't going to be permanent."

"How do you know that?"

"Well, because I know your mom," Simon said, after a pause. "I mean, you and I have been friends for what, ten years now? I know she gets like this sometimes. She'll think better of it."

Clary picked a hot pepper off her plate and nibbled the edge meditatively. "Do you, though?" she said. "Know her, I mean? I sometimes wonder if anyone does."

Simon blinked at her. "You lost me there."

Clary sucked in air to cool her burning mouth. "I mean, she never talks about herself. I don't know anything about her early life, or her family, or much about how she met my dad. She doesn't even have wedding photos. It's like her life started when she had me. That's what she always says when I ask her about it."

"Aw." Simon made a face at her. "That's sweet."

"No, it isn't. It's weird. It's weird that I don't know anything about my grandparents. I mean, I know my dad's parents weren't very nice to her, but could they have been *that* bad? What kind of people don't want to even meet their granddaughter?"

"Maybe she hates them. Maybe they were abusive or something," Simon suggested. "She does have those scars."

Clary stared at him. "She has what?"

He swallowed a mouthful of burrito. "Those little thin scars. All over her back and her arms. I *have* seen your mother in a bathing suit, you know."

"I never noticed any scars," Clary said decidedly. "I think you're imagining things."

He stared at her, and seemed about to say something when her cell phone, buried in her messenger bag, began an insistent blaring. Clary fished it out, gazed at the numbers blinking on the screen, and scowled. "It's my mom."

"I could tell from the look on your face. You going to talk to her?"

"Not right now," Clary said, feeling the familiar bite of guilt in her stomach as the phone stopped ringing and voice mail picked up. "I don't want to fight with her."

"You can always stay at my house," Simon said. "For as long as you want."

"Well, we'll see if she calms down first." Clary punched the voice mail button on her phone. Her mother's voice sounded tense, but she was clearly trying for lightness: "Baby, I'm sorry if I sprang the vacation plan on you. Come on home and we'll talk." Clary hung the phone up before the message ended, feeling even guiltier and still angry at the same time.

"She wants to talk about it."

"Do you want to talk to her?"

"I don't know." Clary rubbed the back of her hand across her eyes. "Are you still going to the poetry reading?"

"I promised I would."

Clary stood up, pushing her chair back. "Then I'll go with you. I'll call her when it's over." The strap of her messenger bag slid down her arm. Simon pushed it back up absently, his fingers lingering at the bare skin of her shoulder.

The air outside was spongy with moisture, the humidity frizzing Clary's hair and sticking Simon's blue T-shirt to his back. "So, what's up with the band?" she asked. "Anything new? There was a lot of yelling in the background when I talked to you earlier."

Simon's face lit up. "Things are great," he said. "Matt says he knows someone who could get us a gig at the Scrap Bar. We're talking about names again too."

"Oh, yeah?" Clary hid a smile. Simon's band never actually produced any music. Mostly they sat around in Simon's living room, fighting about potential names and band logos. She sometimes wondered if any of them could actually play an instrument. "What's on the table?"

"We're choosing between Sea Vegetable Conspiracy and Rock Solid Panda."

Clary shook her head. "Those are both terrible."

"Eric suggested Lawn Chair Crisis."

"Maybe Eric should stick to gaming."

"But then we'd have to find a new drummer."

"Oh, is *that* what Eric does? I thought he just mooched money off you and went around telling girls at school that he was in a band in order to impress them."

"Not at all," Simon said breezily. "Eric has turned over a new leaf. He has a girlfriend. They've been going out for three months."

"Practically married," Clary said, stepping around a couple pushing a toddler in a stroller: a little girl with yellow plastic clips in her hair who was clutching a pixie doll with gold-streaked sapphire wings. Out of the corner of her eye Clary thought she saw the wings flutter. She turned her head hastily.

"Which means," Simon continued, "that I am the last member of the band *not* to have a girlfriend. Which, you know, is the whole point of being in a band. To get girls."

"I thought it was all about the music." A man with a cane cut across her path, heading for Berkeley Street. She glanced away, afraid that if she looked at anyone for too long they would sprout wings, extra arms, or long forked tongues like snakes. "Who cares if you have a girlfriend, anyway?"

"I care," Simon said gloomily. "Pretty soon the only people left without a girlfriend will be me and Wendell the school janitor. And he smells like Windex."

"At least you know he's still available."

Simon glared. "Not funny, Fray."

"There's always Sheila 'The Thong' Barbarino," Clary suggested. Clary had sat behind her in math class in ninth grade. Every time Sheila had dropped her pencil—which had been often—Clary had been treated to the sight of Sheila's underwear riding up above the waistband of her super-low-rise jeans.

"That *is* who Eric's been dating for the past three months," Simon said. "His advice, meanwhile, was that I ought to just decide which girl in school had the most rockin' bod and ask her out on the first day of classes."

"Eric is a sexist pig," Clary said, suddenly not wanting to know which girl in school Simon thought had the most rockin' bod. "Maybe you should call the band The Sexist Pigs."

"It has a ring to it." Simon seemed unfazed. Clary made a face at him, her messenger bag vibrating as her phone blared. She fished it out of the zip pocket. "Is it your mom again?" he asked.

Clary nodded. She could see her mother in her mind's eye, small and alone in the doorway of their apartment. Guilt unfurled in her chest.

She glanced up at Simon, who was looking at her, his eyes dark with concern. His face was so familiar she could have traced its lines in her sleep. She thought of the lonely weeks that stretched ahead without him, and shoved the phone back into her bag. "Come on," she said. "We're going to be late for the show."

3
Shadowhunter

By the time they got to Java Jones, Eric was already onstage, swaying back and forth in front of the microphone with his eyes squinched shut. He'd dyed the tips of his hair pink for the occasion. Behind him, Matt, looking stoned, was beating irregularly on a djembe.

"This is going to suck so hard," Clary predicted. She grabbed Simon's sleeve and tugged him toward the doorway. "If we make a run for it, we can still get away."

He shook his head determinedly. "I'm nothing if not a man of my word." He squared his shoulders. "I'll get the coffee if you find us a seat. What do you want?"

"Just coffee. Black—*like my soul*."

Simon headed off toward the coffee bar, muttering under his breath something to the effect that it was a far, far better thing he did now than he had ever done before. Clary went to find them a seat.

The coffee shop was crowded for a Monday; most of

the threadbare-looking couches and armchairs were taken up with teenagers enjoying a free weeknight. The smell of coffee and clove cigarettes was overwhelming. Finally Clary found an unoccupied love seat in a darkened corner toward the back. The only other person nearby was a blond girl in an orange tank top, absorbed in playing with her iPod. *Good,* Clary thought, *Eric won't be able to find us back here after the show to ask how his poetry was.*

The blond girl leaned over the side of her chair and tapped Clary on the shoulder. "Excuse me." Clary looked up in surprise. "Is that your boyfriend?" the girl asked.

Clary followed the line of the girl's gaze, already prepared to say, *No, I don't know him*, when she realized the girl meant Simon. He was headed toward them, face scrunched up in concentration as he tried not to drop either of his Styrofoam cups. "Uh, no," Clary said. "He's a friend of mine."

The girl beamed. "He's *cute*. Does he have a girlfriend?"

Clary hesitated a second too long before replying. "No."

The girl looked suspicious. "Is he gay?"

Clary was spared responding to this by Simon's return. The blond girl sat back hastily as he set the cups on the table and threw himself down next to Clary. "I hate it when they run out of mugs. Those things are hot." He blew on his fingers and scowled. Clary tried to hide a smile as she watched him. Normally she never thought about whether Simon was good-looking or not. He had pretty dark eyes, she supposed, and he'd filled out well over the past year or so. With the right haircut—

"You're staring at me," Simon said. "Why are you staring at me? Have I got something on my face?"

I should tell him, she thought, though some part of her was strangely reluctant. *I'd be a bad friend if I didn't.* "Don't look now, but that blond girl over there thinks you're cute," she whispered.

Simon's eyes flicked sideways to stare at the girl, who was industriously studying an issue of *Shonen Jump*. "The girl in the orange top?" Clary nodded. Simon looked dubious. "What makes you think so?"

Tell him. Go on, tell him. Clary opened her mouth to reply, and was interrupted by a burst of feedback. She winced and covered her ears as Eric, onstage, wrestled with his microphone.

"Sorry about that, guys!" he yelled. "All right. I'm Eric, and this is my homeboy Matt on the drums. My first poem is called 'Untitled.'" He screwed up his face as if in pain, and wailed into the mike. "*Come, my faux juggernaut, my nefarious loins! Slather every protuberance with arid zeal!*"

Simon slid down in his seat. "Please don't tell anyone I know him."

Clary giggled. "Who uses the word 'loins'?"

"Eric," Simon said grimly. "All his poems have loins in them."

"*Turgid is my torment!*" Eric wailed. "*Agony swells within!*"

"You bet it does," Clary said. She slid down in the seat next to Simon. "Anyway, about that girl who thinks you're cute—"

"Never mind that for a second," Simon said. Clary blinked at him in surprise. "There's something I wanted to talk to you about."

"Furious Mole is not a good name for a band," Clary said immediately.

"Not that," Simon said. "It's about what we were talking about before. About me not having a girlfriend."

"Oh." Clary lifted one shoulder in a shrug. "Oh, I don't know. Ask Jaida Jones out," she suggested, naming one of the few girls at St. Xavier's she actually liked. "She's nice, and she likes you."

"I don't want to ask Jaida Jones out."

"Why not?" Clary found herself seized with a sudden, unspecific resentment. "You don't like smart girls? Still seeking a *rockin' bod?*"

"Neither," said Simon, who seemed agitated. "I don't want to ask her out because it wouldn't really be fair to her if I did..."

He trailed off. Clary leaned forward. From the corner of her eye she could see the blond girl leaning forward too, plainly eavesdropping. "Why not?"

"Because I like someone else," Simon said.

"Okay." Simon looked faintly greenish, the way he had once when he'd broken his ankle playing soccer in the park and had had to limp home on it. She wondered what on earth about liking someone could possibly have him wound up to such a pitch of anxiety. "You're not gay, are you?"

Simon's greenish color deepened. "If I were, I would dress better."

"So, who is it, then?" Clary asked. She was about to add that if he were in love with Sheila Barbarino, Eric would kick his ass, when she heard someone cough loudly behind her. It was a derisive sort of cough, the kind of noise someone might make who was trying not to laugh out loud.

She turned around.

Sitting on a faded green sofa a few feet away from her was Jace. He was wearing the same dark clothes he'd had on the night before in the club. His arms were bare and covered with faint white lines like old scars. His wrists bore wide metal cuffs; she could see the bone handle of a knife protruding from the left one. He was looking right at her, the side of his narrow mouth quirked in amusement. Worse than the feeling of being laughed at was Clary's absolute conviction that he hadn't been sitting there five minutes ago.

"What is it?" Simon had followed her gaze, but it was obvious from the blank expression on his face that he couldn't see Jace.

But I see you. She stared at Jace as she thought it, and he raised his left hand to wave at her. He got to his feet and began walking, unhurriedly, toward the door. Clary's lips parted in surprise. He was leaving, just like that.

She felt Simon's hand on her arm. He was saying her name, asking her if something was wrong. She barely heard him. "I'll be right back," she heard herself say, as she sprang off the couch, almost forgetting to set her coffee cup down. She raced toward the door, leaving Simon staring after her.

Clary burst through the doors, terrified that Jace would have vanished into the alley shadows like a ghost. But he was there, slouched against the wall. He had just taken something out of his pocket and was punching buttons on it. He looked up in surprise as the door of the coffee shop fell shut behind her.

In the rapidly falling twilight, his hair looked coppery gold. "Your friend's poetry is terrible," he said.

Clary blinked, caught momentarily off guard. "What?"

"I said his poetry was terrible. It sounds like he ate a dictionary and started vomiting up words at random."

"I don't care about Eric's poetry." Clary was furious. "I want to know why you're following me."

"Who said I was following you?"

"*Nice* try. And you were eavesdropping, too. Do you want to tell me what this is about, or should I just call the police?"

"And tell them what?" Jace said witheringly. "That invisible people are bothering you? Trust me, little girl, the police aren't going to arrest someone they can't see."

"I told you before, my name is not 'little girl,'" she said through her teeth. "It's Clary."

"I know," he said. "Pretty name. Like the herb, clary sage. In the old days people thought eating the seeds would let you see the Fair Folk. Did you know that?"

"I have no idea what you're talking about."

"You don't know much, do you?" he said. There was a lazy contempt in his gold eyes. "You seem to be a mundane like any other mundane, yet you can see me. It's a conundrum."

"What's a mundane?"

"Someone of the human world. Someone like you."

"But *you're* human," Clary said.

"I am," he said. "But I'm not like you." There was no defensiveness in his tone. He sounded like he didn't care if she believed him or not.

"You think you're better. That's why you were laughing at us."

"I was laughing at you because declarations of love amuse me, especially when unrequited," he said. "And because your Simon is one of the most mundane mundanes I've ever encountered. And because Hodge thought you might be dangerous, but if you are, you certainly don't know it."

"*I'm* dangerous?" Clary echoed in astonishment. "I saw you kill someone last night. I saw you drive a knife up under his ribs, and—" *And I saw him slash at you with fingers like razor blades. I saw you cut and bleeding, and now you look as if nothing ever touched you.*

"I may be a killer," Jace said, "but I know what I am. Can you say the same?"

"I'm an ordinary human being, just like you said. Who's Hodge?"

"My tutor. And I wouldn't be so quick to brand myself as ordinary, if I were you." He leaned forward. "Let me see your right hand."

"My right hand?" Clary echoed. He nodded. "If I show you my hand, will you leave me alone?"

"Certainly." His voice was edged with amusement.

She held out her right hand grudgingly. It looked pale in the half-light spilling from the windows, the knuckles dotted with a light dusting of freckles. Somehow she felt as exposed as if she were pulling up her shirt and showing him her naked chest. He took her hand in his and turned it over. "Nothing." He sounded almost disappointed. "You're not left-handed, are you?"

"No. Why?"

He released her hand with a shrug. "All Shadowhunter children get Marked with the Voyance rune on their right hands—or left, if they're left-handed like I am—when they're still young. It's a permanent rune that helps us see the magical world." He showed her the back of his left hand;

it looked perfectly normal to her.

"I don't see anything," she said.

"Let your mind relax," he suggested. "Wait for it to come to you. Like waiting for something to rise to the surface of water."

"You're crazy." But she relaxed, gazing at his hand, seeing the tiny lines across the knuckles, the long joints of the fingers—

It jumped out at her suddenly, flashing like a DON'T WALK sign. A black design like an eye across the back of his hand. She blinked, and it vanished. "A tattoo?"

He smiled smugly and lowered his hand. "I thought you could do it. And it's not a tattoo—it's a Mark. They're runes, burned into our skin. Different Marks do different things. Some are permanent but the majority vanish when they've been used."

"That's why your arms aren't all inked up today?" she asked. "Even when I concentrate?"

"That's exactly why." He sounded pleased with himself. "I knew you had the Sight, at least." He glanced up at the sky. "It's nearly full dark. We should go."

"*We?* I thought you were going to leave me alone."

"I lied," Jace said without a shred of embarrassment. "Hodge said I have to bring you to the Institute with me. He wants to talk to you."

"Why would he want to talk to me?"

"Because you know about us now."

"About *us?*" she echoed. "You mean people like you. People who believe in demons."

"People who kill them," said Jace. "We're called Shadowhunters. At least, that's what we call ourselves. The

Downworlders have less complimentary names for us."

"Downworlders?"

"The Night Children—vampires. Warlocks. The fey. The magical folk of this world."

Clary shook her head. "Don't stop there. I suppose there are also, what, mermaids and werewolves and zombies?"

"Of course there are," Jace informed her. "There are reasons those stories exist. They're based in fact, even if mundanes think they're myth. Shadowhunters have a saying: *all the stories are true.* Although," he added, "to be fair, you mostly find zombies farther south, where the *voudun* priests are."

"What about mummies? Do they only hang around Egypt?"

"Don't be ridiculous. No one believes in mummies."

"They don't?"

"Of course not," Jace said. "Look, Hodge will explain all this to you when you see him."

Clary crossed her arms over her chest. "What if I don't want to see him?"

"That's your problem. You can come either willingly or unwillingly."

Clary couldn't believe her ears. "Are you threatening to *kidnap* me?"

"If you want to look at it that way," Jace said, "yes."

Clary opened her mouth to protest angrily, but was interrupted by a strident buzzing noise. Her phone was ringing again.

"Go ahead and answer that if you like," Jace said generously.

The phone stopped ringing, then started up again, loud and insistent. Clary frowned—her mom must really be freaking out. She half-turned away from Jace and began digging in her bag. By the time she unearthed the phone, it was on its third set of rings. She raised it to her ear. "Mom?"

"Oh, Clary. Oh, thank God." A sharp prickle of alarm ran up Clary's spine. Her mother sounded panicked. "Listen to me—"

"It's all right, Mom. I'm fine. I'm on my way home—"

"*No!*" Terror scraped Jocelyn's voice raw. "Don't come home! Do you understand me, Clary? Don't you dare come home. Go to Simon's. Go straight to Simon's house and stay there until I can—" A noise in the background interrupted her: the sound of something falling, shattering, something heavy striking the floor—

"Mom!" Clary shouted into the phone. "Mom, are you all right?"

A loud buzzing noise came from the phone. Clary's mother's voice cut through the static: "Just promise me you won't come home. Go to Simon's and call Luke—tell him that he's found me—" Her words were drowned out by a heavy crash like splintering wood.

"*Who's* found you? Mom, did you call the police? Did you—"

Her frantic question was cut off by a noise Clary would never forget—a harsh, slithering noise, followed by a thump. Clary heard her mother draw in a sharp breath before speaking, her voice eerily calm: "I love you, Clary."

The phone went dead.

"*Mom!*" Clary shrieked into the phone. "Mom, are you there?"

CALL ENDED, the screen said. But why would her mother have hung up like that?

"Clary," Jace said. It was the first time she'd ever heard

him say her name. "What's going on?"

Clary ignored him. Feverishly she hit the button that dialed her home number. There was no answer except a double-tone busy signal.

Clary's hands had begun to shake uncontrollably. When she tried to redial, the phone slipped out of her shaking grasp and hit the pavement hard. She dropped to her knees to retrieve it, but it was dead, a long crack visible across the front. "Dammit!" Almost in tears, she threw the phone down.

"Stop that." Jace hauled her to her feet, his hand gripping her wrist. "Has something happened?"

"Give me your phone," Clary said, grabbing the black metal oblong out of his shirt pocket. "I have to—"

"It's not a phone," Jace said, making no move to get it back. "It's a Sensor. You won't be able to use it."

"But I need to call the police!"

"Tell me what happened first." She tried to yank her wrist back, but his grip was incredibly strong. "I can *help* you."

Rage flooded through Clary, a hot tide through her veins. Without even thinking about it, she struck out at his face, her nails raking his cheek. He jerked back in surprise. Tearing herself free, Clary ran toward the lights of Seventh Avenue.

When she reached the street, she spun around, half-expecting to see Jace at her heels. But the alley was empty. For a moment she stared uncertainly into the shadows. Nothing moved inside them. She spun on her heel and ran for home.

4

RAVENER

The night had gotten even hotter, and running home felt like swimming as fast as she could through boiling soup. At the corner of her block Clary got trapped at a DON'T WALK sign. She jittered up and down impatiently on the balls of her feet while traffic whizzed by in a blur of headlights. She tried to call home again, but Jace hadn't been lying; his phone *wasn't* a phone. At least, it didn't look like any phone Clary had ever seen before. The Sensor's buttons didn't have numbers on them, just more of those bizarre symbols, and there was no screen.

Jogging up the street toward her house, she saw that the second-floor windows were lit, the usual sign that her mother was home. *Okay*, she told herself. *Everything's fine*. But her stomach tightened the moment she stepped into the entryway. The overhead light had burned out, and the foyer was in darkness. The shadows seemed full of secret movement. Shivering, she started upstairs.

"And just where do you think you're going?" said a voice.

Clary whirled. "What—"

She broke off. Her eyes were adjusting to the dimness, and she could see the shape of a large armchair, drawn up in front of Madame Dorothea's closed door. The old woman was wedged into it like an overstuffed cushion. In the dimness Clary could see only the round shape of her powdered face, the white lace fan in her hand, the dark, yawning gap of her mouth when she spoke. "Your mother," Dorothea said, "has been making a godawful racket up there. What's she doing? Moving furniture?"

"I don't think—"

"And the stairwell light's burned out, did you notice?" Dorothea rapped her fan against the arm of the chair. "Can't your mother get her boyfriend in to change it?"

"Luke isn't—"

"The skylight needs washing too. It's filthy. No wonder it's nearly pitch-black in here."

Luke is NOT the landlord, Clary wanted to say, but didn't. This was typical of her elderly neighbor. Once she got Luke to come around and change the lightbulb, she'd ask him to do a hundred other things—pick up her groceries, grout her shower. Once she'd made him chop up an old sofa with an axe so she could get it out of the apartment without taking the door off the hinges.

Clary sighed. "I'll ask."

"You'd better." Dorothea snapped her fan shut with a flick of her wrist.

Clary's sense that something was wrong only increased when she reached the apartment door. It was unlocked, hanging slightly open, spilling a wedge-shaped shaft of light onto the landing. With a feeling of increasing panic, she pushed the door open.

Inside the apartment, the lights were on, all the lamps, everything turned up to full brightness. The glow stabbed into her eyes.

Her mother's keys and pink handbag were on the small wrought iron shelf by the door, where she always left them. "Mom?" Clary called out. "Mom, I'm home."

There was no reply. She went into the living room. Both windows were open, yards of gauzy white curtains blowing in the breeze like restless ghosts. Only when the wind dropped and the curtains settled did Clary see that the cushions had been ripped from the sofa and scattered around the room. Some were torn lengthwise, cotton innards spilling onto the floor. The bookshelves had been tipped over, their contents scattered. The piano bench lay on its side, gaping open like a wound, Jocelyn's beloved music books spewing out.

Most terrifying were the paintings. Every single one had been cut from its frame and ripped into strips, which were scattered across the floor. It must have been done with a knife—canvas was almost impossible to tear with your bare hands. The empty frames looked like bones picked clean. Clary felt a scream rising up in her chest: "*Mom!*" she shrieked. "*Where are you? Mommy!*"

She hadn't called Jocelyn "Mommy" since she was eight.

Heart pumping, she raced into the kitchen. It was empty, the cabinet doors open, a smashed bottle of Tabasco sauce spilling peppery red liquid onto the linoleum. Her knees felt like bags of water. She knew she should race out of the apartment, get to a phone, call the police. But all those things seemed distant—she needed to find her mother first, needed to see that she was all right. What if robbers had come, what if her mother had put up a fight—?

What kind of robbers didn't take a wallet with them, or the TV, the DVD player, or the expensive laptops?

She was at the door to her mother's bedroom now. For a moment it looked as if this room, at least, had been left untouched. Jocelyn's handmade flowered quilt was folded carefully on the duvet. Clary's own face smiled back at her from the top of the bedside table, five years old, gap-toothed smile framed by strawberry hair. A sob rose in Clary's chest. *Mom,* she cried inside, *what happened to you?*

Silence answered her. No, not silence—a noise sounded through the apartment, raising the short hairs along the nape of her neck. Like something being knocked over—a heavy object striking the floor with a dull thud. The thud was followed by a dragging, slithering noise—and it was coming toward the bedroom. Stomach contracting in terror, Clary scrambled to her feet and turned around slowly.

For a moment she thought the doorway was empty, and she felt a wave of relief. Then she looked down.

It was crouched against the floor, a long, scaled creature with a cluster of flat black eyes set dead center in the front of its domed skull. Something like a cross between an alligator and a centipede, it had a thick, flat snout and a barbed tail that whipped menacingly from side to side. Multiple legs bunched underneath it as it readied itself to spring.

A shriek tore itself out of Clary's throat. She staggered backward, tripped, and fell, just as the creature lunged at her. She rolled to the side and it missed her by inches, sliding along the wood floor, its claws gouging deep grooves. A low growl bubbled from its throat.

She scrambled to her feet and ran toward the hallway, but the thing was too fast for her. It sprang again, landing just above the door, where it hung like a gigantic malignant spider, staring down at her with its cluster of eyes. Its jaws opened slowly, showing a row of fanged teeth spilling greenish drool. A long black tongue flickered out between its jaws as it gurgled and hissed. To her horror Clary realized that the noises it was making were words.

"Girl," it hissed. *"Flesh. Blood. To eat, oh, to eat."*

It began to slither slowly down the wall. Some part of Clary had passed beyond terror into a sort of icy stillness. The thing was on its feet now, crawling toward her. Backing away, she seized a heavy framed photo off the bureau beside her—herself and her mother and Luke at Coney Island, about to go on the bumper cars—and flung it at the monster.

The photograph hit its midsection and bounced off, striking the floor with the sound of shattering glass. The creature didn't seem to notice. It came on toward her, broken glass splintering under its feet. *"Bones, to crunch, to suck out the marrow, to drink the veins..."*

Clary's back hit the wall. She could back up no farther. She felt a movement against her hip and nearly jumped out of her skin. Her pocket. Plunging her hand inside, she drew out the plastic thing she'd taken from Jace. The Sensor was shuddering, like a cell phone set to vibrate. The hard material was almost painfully hot against her palm. She closed her hand around the Sensor just as the creature sprang.

The creature hurtled into her, knocking her to the

ground, and her head and shoulders slammed against the floor. She twisted to the side, but it was too heavy. It was on top of her, an oppressive, slimy weight that made her want to gag. *"To eat, to eat,"* it moaned. *"But it is not allowed, to swallow, to savor."*

The hot breath in her face stank of blood. She couldn't breathe. Her ribs felt like they might shatter. Her arm was pinned between her body and the monster's, the Sensor digging into her palm. She twisted, trying to work her hand free. *"Valentine will never know. He said nothing about a girl. Valentine will not be angry."* Its lipless mouth twitched as its jaws opened, slowly, a wave of stinking breath hot in her face.

Clary's hand came free. With a scream she hit out at the thing, wanting to smash it, to blind it. She had almost forgotten the Sensor. As the creature lunged for her face, jaws wide, she jammed the Sensor between its teeth and felt hot, acidic drool coat her wrist and spill in burning drops onto the bare skin of her face and throat. As if from a distance, she could hear herself screaming.

Looking almost surprised, the creature jerked back, the Sensor lodged between two teeth. It growled, a thick angry buzz, and threw its head back. Clary saw it swallow, saw the movement of its throat. *I'm next,* she thought, panicked. *I'm—*

Suddenly the thing began to twitch. Spasming uncontrollably, it rolled off Clary and onto its back, multiple legs churning the air. Black fluid poured from its mouth.

Gasping for air, Clary rolled over and started to scramble away from the thing. She'd nearly reached the door when she heard something whistle through the air next to her head. She tried to duck, but it was too late. An object slammed heavily into the back of her skull, and she collapsed forward into blackness.

Light stabbed through her eyelids, blue, white, and red. There was a high wailing noise, rising in pitch like the scream of a terrified child. Clary gagged and opened her eyes.

She was lying on cold damp grass. The night sky rippled overhead, the pewter gleam of stars washed out by city lights. Jace knelt beside her, the silver cuffs on his wrists throwing off sparks of light as he tore the piece of cloth he was holding into strips. "Don't move."

The wailing threatened to split her ears in half. Clary turned her head to the side, disobediently, and was rewarded with a razoring stab of pain that shot down her back. She was lying on a patch of grass behind Jocelyn's carefully tended rosebushes. The foliage partially hid her view of the street, where a police car, its blue-and-white light bar flashing, was pulled up to the curb, siren wailing. Already a small knot of neighbors had gathered, staring as the car door opened and two blue-uniformed officers emerged.

The *police*. She tried to sit up, and gagged again, fingers spasming into the damp earth.

"I told you not to move," Jace hissed. "That Ravener demon got you in the back of the neck. It was half-dead so it wasn't much of a sting, but we have to get you to the Institute. Hold still."

"That thing—the monster—it *talked*." Clary was shuddering uncontrollably.

"You've heard a demon talk before." Jace's hands were gentle as he slipped the strip of knotted cloth under her neck, and tied it. It was smeared with something waxy, like the gardener's salve her mother used to keep her paint- and turpentine-abused hands soft.

"The demon in Pandemonium—it looked like a person."

"It was an Eidolon demon. A shape-changer. Raveners look like they look. Not very attractive, but they're too stupid to care."

"It said it was going to eat me."

"But it didn't. You killed it." Jace finished the knot and sat back.

To Clary's relief the pain in the back of her neck had faded. She hauled herself into a sitting position. "The police are here." Her voice came out like a frog's croak. "We should—"

"There's nothing they can do. Somebody probably heard you screaming and reported it. Ten to one those aren't real police officers. Demons have a way of hiding their tracks."

"My mom," Clary said, forcing the words through her swollen throat.

"There's Ravener poison coursing through your veins *right now*. You'll be dead in an hour if you don't come with me." He got to his feet and held out a hand to her. She took it and he pulled her upright. "Come on."

The world tilted. Jace slid a hand across her back, holding her steady. He smelled of dirt, blood, and metal. "Can you walk?"

"I think so." She glanced through the densely blooming bushes. She could see the police coming up the path. One of them, a slim blond woman, held a flashlight in one hand. As she raised it, Clary saw the hand was fleshless, a skeleton hand sharpened to bone points at the fingertips. "Her hand—"

"I told you they might be demons." Jace glanced at the

back of the house. "We have to get out of here. Can we go through the alley?"

Clary shook her head. "It's bricked up. There's no way—" Her words dissolved into a fit of coughing. She raised her hand to cover her mouth. It came away red. She whimpered.

He grabbed her wrist, turned it over so the white, vulnerable flesh of her inner arm lay bare under the moonlight. Traceries of blue vein mapped the inside of her skin, carrying poisoned blood to her heart, her brain. Clary felt her knees buckle. There was something in Jace's hand, something sharp and silver. She tried to pull her hand back, but his grip was too hard: She felt a stinging kiss against her skin. When he let go, she saw an inked black symbol like the ones that covered his skin, just below the fold of her wrist. This one looked like a set of overlapping circles.

"What's that supposed to do?"

"It'll hide you," he said. "Temporarily." He slid the thing Clary had thought was a knife back into his belt. It was a long, luminous cylinder, as thick around as an index finger and tapering to a point. "My stele," he said.

Clary didn't ask what that was. She was busy trying not to fall over. The ground was heaving up and down under her feet. "Jace," she said, and she crumpled into him. He caught her as if he were used to catching fainting girls, as if he did it every day. Maybe he did. He swung her up into his arms, saying something in her ear that sounded like *Covenant*. Clary tipped her head back to look at him but saw only the stars cartwheeling across the dark sky overhead. Then the bottom dropped out of everything, and even Jace's arms around her were not enough to keep her from falling.

5

Clave and Covenant

"Do you think she'll ever wake up? It's been three days already."

"You have to give her time. Demon poison is strong stuff, and she's a mundane. She hasn't got runes to keep her strong like we do."

"Mundies die awfully easily, don't they?"

"Isabelle, you know it's bad luck to talk about death in a sickroom."

Three days, Clary thought slowly. All her thoughts ran as thickly and slowly as blood or honey. *I have to wake up.*

But she couldn't.

The dreams held her, one after the other, a river of images that bore her along like a leaf tossed in a current. She saw her mother lying in a hospital bed, eyes like bruises in her white face. She saw Luke, standing atop a pile of bones. Jace with white feathered wings sprouting out of his back, Isabelle sitting naked with her whip curled around her like a net of gold rings, Simon with crosses burned into the palms of his hands. Angels, falling and burning. Falling out of the sky.

"I told you it was the same girl."

"I know. Little thing, isn't she? Jace said she killed a Ravener."

"Yeah. I thought she was a pixie the first time we saw her. She's not pretty enough to be a pixie, though."

"Well, nobody looks their best with demon poison in their veins. Is Hodge going to call on the Brothers?"

"I hope not. They give me the creeps. Anyone who mutilates themselves like that—"

"We mutilate ourselves."

"I know, Alec, but when we do it, it isn't permanent. And it doesn't always hurt…"

"If you're old enough. Speaking of which, where is Jace? He saved her, didn't he? I would have thought he'd take some interest in her recovery."

"Hodge said he hasn't been to see her since he brought her here. I guess he doesn't care."

"Sometimes I wonder if he—Look! She moved!"

"I guess she's alive after all." A sigh. "I'll tell Hodge."

Clary's eyelids felt as if they had been sewed shut. She imagined she could feel tearing skin as she peeled them slowly open and blinked for the first time in three days.

She saw clear blue sky above her, white puffy clouds and chubby angels with gilded ribbons trailing from their wrists. *Am I dead?* she wondered. *Could heaven actually look like this?* She squeezed her eyes shut and opened them again: This time she realized that what she was staring at was an arched wooden ceiling, painted with a rococo motif of clouds and cherubs.

Painfully she hauled herself into a sitting position. Every part of her ached, especially the back of her neck. She glanced around. She was tucked into a linen-sheeted bed, one of a long row of similar beds with metal headboards. Her bed had a small nightstand beside it with a white pitcher and cup on it. Lace curtains were pulled across the windows, blocking the light, although she could hear the faint, ever-present New York sounds of traffic coming from outside.

"So, you're finally awake," said a dry voice. "Hodge will be pleased. *We* all thought you'd probably die in your sleep."

Clary turned. Isabelle was perched on the next bed, her long jet-black hair wound into two thick braids that fell past her waist. Her white dress had been replaced by jeans and a tight blue tank top, though the red pendant still winked at her throat. Her dark spiraling tattoos were gone, save the dark Voyance rune on the back of her right hand.

"Sorry to disappoint you." Clary's voice rasped like sandpaper. "Is this the Institute?"

Isabelle rolled her eyes. "Is there anything Jace *didn't* tell you?"

Clary coughed. "This is the Institute, right?"

"Yes. You're in the infirmary, not that you haven't figured that out already."

A sudden, stabbing pain made Clary clutch at her stomach. She gasped.

Isabelle looked at her in alarm. "Are you okay?"

The pain was fading, but Clary was aware of an acid feeling in the back of her throat and a strange light-headedness. "My stomach."

"Oh, right. I almost forgot. Hodge said to give you this when you woke up." Isabelle grabbed for the ceramic pitcher and poured some of the contents into the matching cup, which she handed to Clary. It was full of a cloudy liquid that steamed slightly. It smelled like herbs and something else, something rich and dark. "You haven't eaten anything in three days," Isabelle pointed out. "That's probably why you feel sick."

Clary gingerly took a sip. It was delicious, rich and satisfying with a buttery aftertaste. "What is this?"

Isabelle shrugged. "One of Hodge's tisanes. They always work." She slid off the bed, landing on the floor with a catlike arch of her back. "I'm Isabelle Lightwood, by the way. I live here."

"I know your name. I'm Clary. Clary Fray. Did Jace bring me here?"

Isabelle nodded. "Did he ever. You got ichor and blood all over the carpet in the entryway. If he'd done it while my parents were here, he'd have gotten grounded for sure." She looked at Clary more narrowly. "Jace said you killed that Ravener demon all by yourself."

A quick image of the scorpion thing with its crabbed, evil face flashed through Clary's mind; she shuddered and clutched the cup more tightly. "I guess I did."

"But you're a mundie."

"Amazing, isn't it?" Clary said, savoring the look of thinly disguised amazement on Isabelle's face. "Where is Jace? Is he around?"

Isabelle shrugged. "Somewhere," she said. "I should go tell everyone you're up. Hodge'll want to talk to you."

"Hodge is Jace's tutor, right?"

"Hodge tutors us all." She pointed. "The bathroom's through there, and I hung some of my old clothes on the towel rack in case you want to change."

Clary went to take another sip from the cup and found that it was empty. She no longer felt hungry or light-headed either, which was a relief. She set the cup down and hugged the sheet around herself. "What happened to *my* clothes?"

"They were covered in blood and poison. Jace burned them."

"Did he?" asked Clary. "Tell me, is he always really rude, or does he save that for mundanes?"

"Oh, he's rude to everyone," said Isabelle airily. "It's what makes him so damn sexy. That, and he's killed more demons than anyone else his age."

Clary looked at her, perplexed. "Isn't he your brother?"

That got Isabelle's attention. She laughed out loud. "Jace? My brother? No. Whatever gave you that idea?"

"Well, he lives here with you," Clary pointed out. "Doesn't he?"

Isabelle nodded. "Well, yes, but..."

"Why doesn't he live with his own parents?"

For a fleeting moment Isabelle looked uncomfortable. "Because they're dead."

Clary's mouth opened in surprise. "Did they die in an accident?"

"No." Isabelle fidgeted, pushing a dark lock of hair behind her left ear. "His mother died when he was born. His father was murdered when he was ten. Jace saw the whole thing."

"Oh," Clary said, her voice small. "Was it ... demons?"

Isabelle got to her feet. "Look, I'd better let everyone know you've woken up. They've been waiting for you to open your eyes for three days. Oh, and there's soap in the bathroom," she added. "You might want to clean up a little. You smell."

Clary glared at her. "Thanks a lot."

"Any time."

Isabelle's clothes looked ridiculous. Clary had to roll the legs on the jeans up several times before she stopped tripping on them, and the plunging neckline of the red tank top only emphasized her lack of what Eric would have called a "rack."

She cleaned up in the small bathroom, using a bar of hard lavender soap. Drying herself with a white hand towel left damp hair straggling around her face in fragrant tangles. She squinted at her reflection in the mirror. There was a purpling bruise high up on her left cheek, and her lips were dry and swollen.

I have to call Luke, she thought. Surely there was a phone around here somewhere. Maybe they'd let her use it after she talked to Hodge.

She found her Skechers placed neatly at the foot of her infirmary bed, her keys tied into the laces. Sliding her feet into them, she took a deep breath and left to find Isabelle.

The corridor outside the infirmary was empty. Clary glanced down it, perplexed. It looked like the sort of hallway she sometimes found herself racing down in nightmares, shadowy and infinite. Glass lamps blown into the shapes of roses hung at intervals on the walls, and the air smelled like dust and candle wax.

In the distance she could hear a faint and delicate noise, like wind chimes shaken by a storm. She set off down the corridor slowly, trailing a hand along the wall. The Victorian-looking wallpaper was faded with age, burgundy and pale gray. Each side of the corridor was lined with closed doors.

The sound she was following grew louder. Now she could identify it as the sound of a piano being played with desultory but undeniable skill, though she couldn't identify the tune.

Turning the corner, she came to a doorway, the door propped fully open. Peering in, she saw what was clearly a music room. A grand piano stood in one corner, and rows of chairs were arranged against the far wall. A covered harp occupied the center of the room.

Jace was seated at the grand piano, his slender hands moving rapidly over the keys. He was barefoot, dressed in jeans and a gray T-shirt, his tawny hair ruffled up around his head as if he'd just woken up. Watching the quick, sure movements of his hands across the keys, Clary remembered how it had felt to be lifted up by those hands, his arms holding her up and the stars hurtling down around her head like a rain of silver tinsel.

She must have made some noise, because he twisted around on the stool, blinking into the shadows. "Alec?" he said. "Is that you?"

"It's not Alec. It's me." She stepped farther into the room. "Clary."

Piano keys jangled as he got to his feet. "Our own Sleeping Beauty. Who finally kissed you awake?"

"Nobody. I woke up on my own."

"Was there anyone with you?"

"Isabelle, but she went off to get someone—Hodge,

I think. She told me to wait, but—"

"I should have warned her about your habit of never doing what you're told." Jace squinted at her. "Are those Isabelle's clothes? They look ridiculous on you."

"I could point out that you burned *my* clothes."

"It was purely precautionary." He slid the gleaming black piano cover closed. "Come on, I'll take you to Hodge."

The Institute was huge, a vast cavernous space that looked less like it had been designed according to a floor plan and more like it had been naturally hollowed out of rock by the passage of water and years. Through half-open doors Clary glimpsed countless identical small rooms, each with a stripped bed, a nightstand, and a large wooden wardrobe standing open. Pale arches of stone held up the high ceilings, many of the arches intricately carved with small figures. She noticed certain repeating motifs: angels and swords, suns and roses.

"Why does this place have so many bedrooms?" Clary asked. "I thought it was a research institute."

"This is the residential wing. We're pledged to offer safety and lodging to any Shadowhunter who requests it. We can house up to two hundred people here."

"But most of these rooms are empty."

"People come and go. Nobody stays for long. Usually it's just us—Alec, Isabelle, Max, their parents—and me and Hodge."

"Max?"

"You met the beauteous Isabelle? Alec is her elder brother. Max is the youngest, but he's overseas with his parents."

"On vacation?"

"Not exactly." Jace hesitated. "You can think of them as—

as foreign diplomats, and of this as an embassy, of sorts. Right now they're in the Shadowhunter home country, working out some very delicate peace negotiations. They brought Max with them because he's so young."

"Shadowhunter home country?" Clary's head was spinning. "What's it called?"

"Idris."

"I've never heard of it."

"You wouldn't have." That irritating superiority was back in his voice. "Mundanes don't know about it. There are wardings— protective spells—up all over the borders. If you tried to cross into Idris, you'd simply find yourself transported instantly from one border to the next. You'd never know what happened."

"So it's not on any maps?"

"Not mundie ones. For our purposes you can consider it a small country between Germany and France."

"But there isn't anything between Germany and France. Except Switzerland."

"Precisely," said Jace.

"I take it you've been there. To Idris, I mean."

"I grew up there." Jace's voice was neutral, but something in his tone let her know that more questions in that direction would not be welcome. "Most of us do. There are, of course, Shadowhunters all over the world. We have to be everywhere, because demonic activity is everywhere. But to a Shadowhunter, Idris is always 'home.'"

"Like Mecca or Jerusalem," said Clary, thoughtfully. "So most of you are brought up there, and then when you grow up—"

"We're sent where we're needed," said Jace shortly. "And there are a few, like Isabelle and Alec, who grow up away from the home country because that's where their parents are. With all the resources of the Institute here, with Hodge's training—" He broke off. "This is the library."

They had reached an arch-shaped set of wooden doors. A blue Persian cat with yellow eyes lay curled in front of them. It raised its head as they approached and yowled. "Hey, Church," Jace said, stroking the cat's back with a bare foot. The cat slit its eyes in pleasure.

"Wait," said Clary. "Alec and Isabelle and Max—they're the only Shadowhunters your age that you know, that you spend time with?"

Jace stopped stroking the cat. "Yes."

"That must get kind of lonely."

"I have everything I need." He pushed the doors open. After a moment's hesitation she followed him inside.

The library was circular, with a ceiling that tapered to a point, as if it had been built inside a tower. The walls were lined with books, the shelves so high that tall ladders set on casters were placed along them at intervals. These were no ordinary books either—these were books bound in leather and velvet, clasped with sturdy-looking locks and hinges made of brass and silver. Their spines were studded with dully glowing jewels and illuminated with gold script. They looked worn in a way that made it clear that these books were not just old but were well-used, and had been loved.

The floor was polished wood, inlaid with chips of glass and marble and bits of semiprecious stone. The inlay formed a pattern that Clary couldn't quite decipher—it might have been the constellations, or even a map of the world; she suspected she'd have to climb up into the tower and look down in order to see it properly.

In the center of the room sat a magnificent desk. It was carved from a single slab of wood, a great, heavy piece of oak that gleamed with the dull shine of years. The slab rested upon the backs of two angels, carved from marble, their wings gilded and their faces engraved with a look of suffering, as if the weight of the slab were breaking their backs. Behind the desk sat a thin man with gray-streaked hair and a long beaky nose.

"A book lover, I see," he said, smiling at Clary. "You didn't tell me that, Jace."

Jace chuckled. Clary could tell that he had come up behind her and was standing there with his hands in his pockets, grinning that infuriating grin of his. "We haven't done much talking during our short acquaintance," he said. "I'm afraid our reading habits didn't come up."

Clary turned around and shot him a glare.

"How can you tell?" she asked the man behind the desk. "That I like books, I mean."

"The look on your face when you walked in," he said, standing up and coming around from behind the desk. "Somehow I doubted you were that impressed by *me*."

Clary stifled a gasp as he rose. For a moment it seemed to her that he was strangely misshapen, his left shoulder humped and higher than the other. As he approached, she saw that the hunch was actually a bird, perched neatly on his shoulder—a glossy feathered creature with bright black eyes.

"This is Hugo," the man said, touching the bird on his shoulder. "Hugo is a raven, and, as such, he knows many things. I, meanwhile, am Hodge Starkweather, a professor of history, and, as such, I do not know nearly enough."

Clary laughed a little, despite herself, and shook his outstretched hand. "Clary Fray."

"Honored to make your acquaintance," he said. "I would be honored to make the acquaintance of anyone who could kill a Ravener with her bare hands."

"It wasn't my bare hands." It still felt odd to be congratulated for killing something. "It was Jace's—well, I don't remember what it was called, but—"

"She means my Sensor," Jace said. "She shoved it down the thing's throat. The runes must have choked it. I guess I'll need another one," he added, almost as an afterthought. "I should have mentioned that."

"There are several extra in the weapons room," said Hodge. When he smiled at Clary, a thousand small lines rayed out from around his eyes, like the cracks in an old painting. "That was quick thinking. What gave you the idea of using the Sensor as a weapon?"

Before she could reply, a sharp laugh sounded through the room. Clary had been so enraptured by the books and distracted by Hodge that she hadn't seen Alec sprawled in an overstuffed red armchair by the empty fireplace. "I can't believe you buy that story, Hodge," he said.

At first Clary didn't even register his words. She was too busy staring at him. Like many only children, she was fascinated by the resemblance between siblings, and now, in the full light of day, she could see exactly how much Alec looked like his sister. They had the same jet-black hair, the same slender eyebrows winging up at the corners, the same pale, high-colored skin. But where Isabelle was all arrogance, Alec slumped down in the chair as if he hoped nobody would notice him. His lashes were long and dark like Isabelle's, but where her eyes were black, his were the dark blue of bottle glass. They gazed at Clary with a hostility as pure and concentrated as acid.

"I'm not quite sure what you mean, Alec." Hodge raised an eyebrow. Clary wondered how old he was; there was a sort of agelessness to him, despite the gray in his hair. He wore a neat gray tweed suit, perfectly pressed. He would have looked like a kindly college professor if it hadn't been for the thick scar that drew up the right side of his face. She wondered how he had gotten it. "Are you suggesting that she didn't kill that demon after all?"

"Of course she didn't. Look at her—she's a mundie, Hodge, and a little kid, at that. There's no way she took on a Ravener."

"I'm not a little kid," Clary interrupted. "I'm sixteen years old—well, I will be on Sunday."

"The same age as Isabelle," Hodge said. "Would you call *her* a child?"

"Isabelle hails from one of the greatest Shadowhunter dynasties in history," Alec said dryly. "This girl, on the other hand, hails from New Jersey."

"I'm from Brooklyn!" Clary was outraged. "And so what? I just killed a demon in my own house, and you're going to be a dickhead about it because I'm not some spoiled-rotten rich brat like you and your sister?"

Alec looked astonished. "*What* did you call me?"

Jace laughed. "She has a point, Alec," Jace said. "It's those bridge-and-tunnel demons you really have to watch out for—"

"It's not *funny*, Jace," Alec interrupted, starting to his feet. "Are you just going to let her stand there and call me names?"

"Yes," Jace said kindly. "It'll do you good—try to think of it as endurance training."

"We may be *parabatai*," Alec said tightly. "But your flippancy is wearing on my patience."

"And your obstinacy is wearing on mine. When I found her, she was lying on the floor in a pool of blood with a dying demon practically on top of her. I watched as it vanished. If she didn't kill it, who did?"

"Raveners are stupid. Maybe it got itself in the neck with its stinger. It's happened before—"

"Now you're suggesting it committed suicide?"

Alec's mouth tightened. "It isn't right for her to be here. Mundies aren't allowed in the Institute, and there are good reasons for that. If anyone knew about this, we could be reported to the Clave."

"That's not entirely true," Hodge said. "The Law does allow us to offer sanctuary to mundanes in certain circumstances. A Ravener has already attacked Clary's mother—she could well have been next."

Attacked. Clary wondered if this was a euphemism for "murdered." The raven on Hodge's shoulder cawed softly.

"Raveners are search-and-destroy machines," Alec said. "They act under orders from warlocks or powerful demon lords. Now, what interest would a warlock or demon lord have in an ordinary mundane household?" His eyes when he looked at Clary were bright with dislike. "Any thoughts?"

Clary said, "It must have been a mistake."

"Demons don't make those kind of mistakes. If they went

after your mother, there must have been a reason. If she were innocent—"

"What do you mean, 'innocent'?" Clary's voice was quiet.

Alec looked taken aback. "I—"

"What he means," said Hodge, "is that it is extremely unusual for a powerful demon, the kind who might command a host of lesser demons, to interest himself in the affairs of human beings. No mundane may safely summon a demon—they lack that power—but there have been some, desperate and foolish, who have found a warlock to do it for them."

"My mother doesn't know any warlocks. She doesn't believe in magic." A thought occurred to Clary. "Madame Dorothea—she lives downstairs—she's a witch. Maybe the demons were after her and got my mom by mistake?"

Hodge's eyebrows shot up into his hair. "A witch lives downstairs from you?"

"She's like most witches—a fake," Jace said. "I already looked into it. There's no reason for any warlock to be interested in her unless he's in the market for nonfunctional crystal balls." He turned to Clary. "Warlocks are born magic users. Witches are humans who've taught themselves a little magic. But very few are the real thing."

"And we're back where we began." Hodge reached up to stroke the bird on his shoulder. "It seems the time has come to notify the Clave."

"No!" Jace said. "We can't—"

"It made sense to keep Clary's presence here a secret while we were not sure she would recover," Hodge said. "But now she has, and she is the first mundane to pass through the doors of the Institute in over a hundred years. You know the rules about mundane knowledge of Shadowhunters, Jace. The Clave must be informed."

"Absolutely," Alec agreed. "I could get a message to my father—"

"She's not a mundane," Jace said quietly.

Hodge's eyebrows shot back up to his hairline and stayed there. Alec, caught in the middle of a sentence, choked with surprise. In the sudden silence Clary could hear the sound of Hugo's wings rustling. "But I am," she said.

"No," said Jace. "You aren't." He turned to Hodge, and Clary saw the slight movement of his throat as he swallowed. She found this glimpse of his nervousness oddly reassuring. "That night—there were Du'sien demons, dressed like police officers. We had to get past them. Clary was too weak to run, and there wasn't time to hide—she would have died. So I used my stele—put a *mendelin* rune on the inside of her arm. I thought—"

"Are you out of your *mind?*" Hodge slammed his hand down on top of the desk so hard that Clary thought the wood might crack. "You know what the Law says about placing Marks on mundanes! You—you of all people ought to know better!"

"But it worked," said Jace. "Clary, show them your arm."

With a baffled glance in Jace's direction, she held out her bare arm. She remembered looking down at it that night in the alley, thinking how vulnerable it seemed. Now, just below the crease of her wrist, she could see three faint overlapping circles, the lines as faint as the memory of a scar that had faded with the passage of years. "See, it's almost gone," Jace said. "It didn't hurt her at all."

"That's not the point." Hodge could barely control his anger. "You could have turned her into a Forsaken."

Two bright spots of color burned high up on Alec's cheekbones. "I can't believe you, Jace. Only Shadowhunters can receive Marks from the Gray Book—they *kill* mundanes—"

"She's not a mundane. Haven't you been listening? It explains why she could see us. She must have Clave blood."

Clary lowered her arm, feeling suddenly cold. "But I don't. I couldn't."

"You must," Jace said, without looking at her. "If you didn't, that Mark I made on your arm..."

"That's enough, Jace," said Hodge, the displeasure clear in his voice. "There's no need to frighten her further."

"But I was right, wasn't I? It explains what happened to her mother, too. If she was a Shadowhunter in exile, she might well have Downworld enemies."

"My mother wasn't a Shadowhunter!"

"Your father, then," Jace said. "What about him?"

Clary returned his gaze with a flat stare. "He died. Before I was born."

Jace flinched, almost imperceptibly. It was Alec who spoke. "It's possible," he said uncertainly. "If her father were a Shadowhunter, and her mother a mundane—well, we all know it's against the Law to marry a mundie. Maybe they were in hiding."

"My mother would have told me," Clary said, although she thought of the lack of more than one photo of her father, the way her mother never spoke of him, and knew that it wasn't true.

"Not necessarily," said Jace. "We all have secrets."

"Luke," Clary said. "Our friend. He would know." With the thought of Luke came a flash of guilt and horror. "It's been three days—he must be frantic. Can I call him? Is there a phone?" She turned to Jace. "Please."

Jace hesitated, looking at Hodge, who nodded and moved aside from the desk. Behind him was a globe, made of beaten brass, that didn't look quite like other globes she had seen; there was something subtly strange about the shape of the countries and continents. Next to the globe was an old-fashioned black telephone with a silver rotary dial. Clary lifted it to her ear, the familiar dial tone washing over her like soothing water.

Luke picked up on the third ring. "Hello?"

"Luke!" She sagged against the desk. "It's me. It's Clary."

"Clary." She could hear the relief in his voice, along with something else she couldn't quite identify. "You're all right?"

"I'm fine," she said. "I'm sorry I didn't call you before. Luke, my mom—"

"I know. The police were here."

"Then you haven't heard from her." Any vestigial hope that her mother had fled the house and hidden somewhere disappeared. There was no way she wouldn't have contacted Luke. "What did the police say?"

"Just that she was missing." Clary thought of the policewoman with her skeletal hand, and shivered. "Where are you?"

"I'm in the city," Clary said. "I don't know where exactly. With some friends. My wallet's gone, though. If you've got some cash, I could take a cab to your place—"

"No," he said shortly.

The phone slipped in her sweaty hand. She caught it. "What?"

"No," he said. "It's too dangerous. You can't come here."

"We could call—"

"Look." His voice was hard. "Whatever your mother's gotten herself mixed up in, it's nothing to do with me. You're better off where you are."

"But I don't want to stay here." She heard the whine in her voice, like a child's. "I don't know these people. You—"

"I'm *not* your father, Clary. I've told you that before."

Tears burned the backs of her eyes. "I'm sorry. It's just—"

"Don't call me for favors again," he said. "I've got my own problems, I don't need to be bothered with yours," he added, and hung up the phone.

She stood and stared at the receiver, the dial tone buzzing in her ear like a big ugly wasp. She dialed Luke's number again, waited. This time it went to voice mail. She banged the phone down, her hands trembling.

Jace was leaning against the armrest of Alec's chair, watching her. "I take it he wasn't happy to hear from you?"

Clary's heart felt as if it had shrunk down to the size of a walnut: a tiny, hard stone in her chest. *I will not cry*, she thought, *Not in front of these people.*

"I think I'd like to have a talk with Clary," said Hodge. "Alone," he added firmly, seeing Jace's expression.

Alec stood up. "Fine. We'll leave you to it."

"That's hardly fair," Jace objected. "I'm the one who found her. I'm the one who saved her life! You want me here, don't you?" he appealed, turning to Clary.

Clary looked away, knowing that if she opened her mouth, she'd start to cry. As if from a distance, she heard Alec laugh.

"Not everyone wants you all the time, Jace," he said.

"Don't be ridiculous," she heard Jace say, but he sounded disappointed. "Fine, then. We'll be in the weapons room."

The door closed behind them with a definitive click. Clary's eyes were stinging the way they did when she tried to hold tears back for too long. Hodge loomed up in front of her, a fussing gray blur. "Sit down," he said. "Here, on the couch."

She sank gratefully onto the soft cushions. Her cheeks were wet. She reached up to brush the tears away, blinking. "I don't cry much usually," she found herself saying. "It doesn't mean anything. I'll be all right in a minute."

"Most people don't cry when they're upset or frightened, but rather when they're frustrated. Your frustration is understandable. You've been through a most trying time."

"Trying?" Clary wiped her eyes on the hem of Isabelle's shirt. "You could say that."

Hodge pulled the chair out from behind the desk, dragging it over so that he could sit facing her. His eyes, she saw, were gray, like his hair and tweed coat, but there was kindness in them. "Is there anything I could get for you?" he asked. "Something to drink? Some tea?"

"I don't want tea," said Clary, with muffled force. "I want to find my mother. And then I want to find out who took her in the first place, and I want to kill them."

"Unfortunately," said Hodge, "we're all out of bitter revenge at the moment, so it's either tea or nothing."

Clary dropped the hem of the shirt—now spotted all over

with wet blotches—and said, "What am I supposed to do, then?"

"You could start by telling me a little about what happened," Hodge said, rummaging in his pocket. He produced a handkerchief—crisply folded—and handed it to her. She took it with silent astonishment. She'd never before known anyone who carried a handkerchief. "The demon you saw in your apartment—was that the first such creature you'd ever seen? You had no inkling such creatures existed before?"

Clary shook her head, then paused. "One before, but I didn't realize what it was. The first time I saw Jace—"

"Right, of course, how foolish of me to forget." Hodge nodded. "In Pandemonium. That was the first time?"

"Yes."

"And your mother never mentioned them to you—nothing about another world, perhaps, that most people cannot see? Did she seem particularly interested in myths, fairy tales, legends of the fantastic—"

"No. She hated all that stuff. She even hated Disney movies. She didn't like me reading manga. She said it was childish."

Hodge scratched his head. His hair didn't move. "Most peculiar," he murmured.

"Not really," said Clary. "My mother wasn't peculiar. She was the most normal person in the world."

"Normal people don't generally find their homes ransacked by demons," Hodge said, not unkindly.

"Couldn't it have been a mistake?"

"If it had been a mistake," Hodge said, "and you were an ordinary girl, you would not have seen the demon that attacked you—or if you had, your mind would have processed it as something else entirely: a vicious dog, even another human being. That you could see it, that it spoke to you—"

"How did you know it spoke to me?"

"Jace reported that you said 'It talked.'"

"It hissed." Clary shivered, remembering. "It talked about wanting to eat me, but I think it wasn't supposed to."

"Raveners are generally under the control of a stronger demon. They're not very bright or capable on their own," explained Hodge. "Did it say what its master was looking for?"

Clary thought. "It said something about a Valentine, but—"

Hodge jerked upright, so abruptly that Hugo, who had been resting comfortably on his shoulder, launched himself into the air with an irritable caw. "*Valentine?*"

"Yes," Clary said. "I heard the same name in Pandemonium from the boy—I mean, the demon—"

"It's a name we all know," Hodge said shortly. His voice was steady, but she could see a slight tremble in his hands. Hugo, back on his shoulder, ruffed his feathers uneasily.

"A demon?"

"No. Valentine is—*was*—a Shadowhunter."

"A Shadowhunter? Why do you say *was*?"

"Because he's dead," said Hodge flatly. "He's been dead for fifteen years."

Clary sank back against the couch cushions. Her head was throbbing. Maybe she should have gone for that tea after all. "Could it be someone else? Someone with the same name?"

Hodge's laugh was a humorless bark. "No. But it could have been someone using his name to send a message." He stood up and paced to his desk, hands locked behind his back. "And this would be the time to do it."

"Why now?"

"Because of the Accords."

"The peace negotiations? Jace mentioned those. Peace with who?"

"Downworlders," Hodge murmured. He looked down at Clary. His mouth was a tight line. "Forgive me," he said. "This must be confusing for you."

"You think?"

He leaned against the desk, stroking Hugo's feathers absently. "Downworlders are those who share the Shadow World with us. We have always lived in an uneasy peace with them."

"Like vampires, werewolves, and..."

"The Fair Folk," Hodge said. "Faeries. And Lilith's children, being half-demon, are warlocks."

"So what are you Shadowhunters?"

"We are sometimes called the Nephilim," said Hodge. "In the Bible they were the offspring of humans and angels. The legend of the origin of Shadowhunters is that they were created more than a thousand years ago, when humans were being overrun by demon invasions from other worlds. Jonathan Shadowhunter, the first of the Nephilim, summoned the Angel Raziel, who mixed some of his own blood with the blood of men in a cup, and gave it to those men to drink. Those who drank the Angel's blood became Shadowhunters, as did their children and their children's children. The cup thereafter was known as the Mortal Cup. Though the legend may not be fact, what is true is that through the years, when Shadowhunter ranks were depleted, it was always possible to create more Shadowhunters using the Cup."

"*Was* always possible?"

"The Cup is gone," said Hodge. "Destroyed by Valentine, just before he died. He set a great fire and burned himself to death along with his family, his wife, and his child. Scorched the land black. No one will build there still. They say the land is cursed."

"Is it?"

"Possibly. The Council—that is the voting body of the Clave, those Shadowhunters who make final decisions of policy and law—hands down curses on occasion as punishment for breaking the Law. Valentine broke the greatest Law of all—he took up arms against his fellow Shadowhunters and slew them. He and his group, the Circle, killed dozens of their brethren along with hundreds of Downworlders during the last Accords. They were only barely defeated."

"Why would he want to turn on other Shadowhunters?"

"He didn't approve of the Accords. He despised Downworlders and felt that they should be slaughtered, wholesale, to keep this world pure for human beings. Though the Downworlders are not demons, not invaders, he felt they were demonic in nature, and that that was enough. The Clave did not agree—they felt the assistance of Downworlders was necessary if we were ever to drive off demonkind for good. And who could argue, really, that the Fair Folk do not belong in this world, when they have been here longer than we have?"

"Did the Accords get signed?"

"Yes, they were signed. When the Downworlders saw the Clave turn on Valentine and his Circle in their defense, they realized Shadowhunters were not their enemies. Ironically, with his insurrection Valentine made the continuation of the Accords possible." Hodge sat down in the chair again. "I apologize, this must be a dull history lesson for you. That was Valentine. A firebrand, a visionary, a man of great personal charm and conviction. And a killer. Now someone is invoking his name..."

"But who?" Clary asked. "And what does my mother have to do with it?"

Hodge stood up again. "I don't know. But I shall do what I can to find out. I will send messages to the Clave and also to the Silent Brothers. They may wish to speak with you."

Clary didn't ask who the Silent Brothers were. She was tired of asking questions whose answers only made her more confused. She stood up. "Is there any chance I could go home?"

Hodge looked concerned. "No, I—I wouldn't think that would be wise."

"There are things I need there, even if I'm going to stay here. Clothes—"

"We can give you money to purchase new clothes."

"Please," Clary said. "I have to see if—I have to see what's left."

Hodge hesitated, then offered a short, inverted nod. "If Jace agrees to it, you may both go." He turned to the desk, rummaging among the papers. He glanced over his shoulder as if realizing she was still there. "He's in the weapons room."

"I don't know where that is."

Hodge smiled crookedly. "Church will take you."

She glanced toward the door where the fat blue Persian

was curled up like a small ottoman. He rose as she came forward, fur rippling like liquid. With an imperious meow he led her into the hall. When she looked back over her shoulder, she saw Hodge already scribbling on a piece of paper. Sending a message to the mysterious Clave, she guessed. They didn't sound like very nice people. She wondered what their response would be.

The red ink looked like blood against the white paper. Frowning, Hodge Starkweather rolled the letter, carefully and meticulously, into the shape of a tube, and whistled for Hugo. The bird, cawing softly, settled on his wrist. Hodge winced. Years ago, in the Uprising, he had sustained a wound to that shoulder, and even as light a weight as Hugo's—or the turn of a season, a change in temperature or humidity, too sudden a movement of his arm—awakened old twinges and the memories of pains better forgotten.

There were some memories, though, that never faded. Images burst like flashbulbs behind his lids when he closed his eyes. Blood and bodies, trampled earth, a white podium stained with red. The cries of the dying. The green and rolling fields of Idris and its endless blue sky, pierced by the towers of the Glass City. The pain of loss surged up inside him like a wave; he tightened his fist, and Hugo, wings fluttering, pecked angrily at his fingers, drawing blood. Opening his hand, Hodge released the bird, who circled his head as he flew up to the skylight and then vanished.

Shaking off his sense of foreboding, Hodge reached for another piece of paper, not noticing the scarlet drops that smeared the paper as he wrote.

6
Forsaken

The weapons room looked exactly the way something called "the weapons room" sounded like it would look. Brushed metal walls were hung with every manner of sword, dagger, spike, pike, featherstaff, bayonet, whip, mace, hook, and bow. Soft leather bags filled with arrows dangled from hooks, and there were stacks of boots, leg guards, and gauntlets for wrists and arms. The place smelled of metal and leather and steel polish. Alec and Jace, no longer barefoot, sat at a long table in the center of the room, their heads bent over an object between them. Jace looked up as the door shut behind Clary. "Where's Hodge?" he said.

"Writing to the Silent Brothers."

Alec repressed a shudder. "Ugh."

She approached the table slowly, conscious of Alec's gaze. "What are you doing?"

"Polishing these." Jace moved aside so she could see what lay on the table: three long slim wands of a dully glowing silver. They did not look sharp or particularly dangerous. "Made by the Iron Sisters, our weapon makers. They're seraph blades."

"Those don't look like knives. How did you make them? Magic?"

Alec looked horrified, as if she'd asked him to put on a tutu and execute a perfect pirouette. "The funny thing about mundies," Jace said, to nobody in particular, "is how obsessed with magic they are for a bunch of people who don't even know what the word means."

"I know what it means," Clary snapped.

"No, you don't, you just think you do. Magic is a dark and elemental force, not just a lot of sparkly wands and crystal balls and talking goldfish."

"I never said it was a lot of talking goldfish, you—"

Jace waved a hand, cutting her off. "Just because you call an electric eel a rubber duck doesn't make it a rubber duck, does it? And God help the poor bastard who decides they want to take a bath with the duckie."

"You're driveling," Clary observed.

"I'm not," said Jace, with great dignity.

"Yes, you are," said Alec, rather unexpectedly. "Look, we don't do magic, okay?" he added, not looking at Clary. "That's all you need to know about it."

Clary wanted to snap at him, but restrained herself. Alec already didn't seem to like her; there was no point in aggravating his hostility. She turned to Jace. "Hodge said I can go home."

Jace nearly dropped the seraph blade he was holding. "*He said what?*"

"To look through my mother's things," she amended. "If you go with me."

"Jace," Alec exhaled, but Jace ignored him.

"If you really want to prove that my mom or dad was a Shadowhunter, we should look through my mom's things. What's left of them."

"Down the rabbit hole." Jace grinned crookedly. "Good idea. If we go right now, we should have another three, four hours of daylight."

"Do you want me to come with you?" Alec asked, as Clary and Jace moved toward the door. Clary glanced back at him. He was half-out of the chair, eyes expectant.

"No." Jace didn't turn around. "That's all right. Clary and I can handle this on our own."

The look Alec shot Clary was as sour as poison. She was glad when the door shut behind her.

Jace led the way down the hall, Clary half-jogging to keep up with his long-legged stride. "Have you got your house keys?"

Clary glanced down at her shoes. "Yeah."

"Good. Not that we couldn't break in, but we'd run a greater chance of disturbing any wards that might be up if we did."

"If you say so." The hall widened out into a marble-floored foyer, a black metal gate set into one wall. It was only when Jace pushed a button next to the gate and it lit up that she realized it was an elevator. It creaked and groaned as it rose to meet them. "Jace?"

"Yeah?"

"How did you know I had Shadowhunter blood? Was there some way you could tell?"

The elevator arrived with a final groan. Jace unlatched the gate and slid it open. The inside reminded Clary of a birdcage, all black metal and decorative bits of gilt. "I guessed," he said, latching the door behind them. "It seemed like the most likely explanation."

"You guessed? You must have been pretty sure, considering you could have killed me."

He pressed a button in the wall, and the elevator lurched into action with a vibrating groan that she felt all through the bones in her feet. "I was ninety percent sure."

"I see," Clary said.

There must have been something in her voice, because he turned to look at her. Her hand cracked across his face, a slap that rocked him back on his heels. He put his hand to his cheek, more in surprise than pain. "What the hell was that for?"

"The other ten percent," she said, and they rode the rest of the way down to the street in silence.

Jace spent the train ride to Brooklyn wrapped in an angry silence. Clary stuck close to him anyway, feeling a little bit guilty, especially when she looked at the red mark her slap had left on his cheek.

She didn't really mind the silence; it gave her a chance to think. She kept reliving the conversation with Luke, over and over in her head. It hurt to think about, like biting down on a broken tooth, but she couldn't stop doing it.

Farther down the train, two teenage girls sitting on an orange bench seat were giggling together. The sort of girls Clary had never liked at St. Xavier's, sporting pink jelly mules and fake tans. Clary wondered for a moment if they were laughing at her, before she realized with a start of surprise that they were looking at Jace.

She remembered the girl in the coffee shop who had been staring at Simon. Girls always got that look on their faces when they thought someone was cute. She had nearly forgotten that Jace was cute, given everything that had happened. He didn't have Alec's delicate cameo looks, but Jace's face was more interesting. In daylight his eyes were the color of golden syrup and were ... looking right at her. He cocked an eyebrow. "Can I help you with something?"

Clary turned instant traitor against her gender. "Those girls on the other side of the car are staring at you."

Jace assumed an air of mellow gratification. "Of course they are," he said. "I am stunningly attractive."

"Haven't you ever heard that modesty is an attractive trait?"

"Only from ugly people," Jace confided. "The meek may inherit the earth, but at the moment it belongs to the conceited. Like me." He winked at the girls, who giggled and hid behind their hair.

Clary sighed. "How come they can see you?"

"Glamours are a pain to use. Sometimes we don't bother." The incident with the girls on the train did seem to put him in a better mood. When they left the station and headed up the hill to Clary's apartment, he took one of the seraph blades out of his pocket and started flipping it back and forth between his fingers and across his knuckles, humming to himself.

"Do you have to do that?" Clary asked. "It's annoying."

Jace hummed louder. It was a loud, tuneful sort of hum,

somewhere between "Happy Birthday" and "The Battle Hymn of the Republic."

"I'm sorry I smacked you," she said.

He stopped humming. "Just be glad you hit me and not Alec. He would have hit you back."

"He seems to be itching for the chance," Clary said, kicking an empty soda can out of her path. "What was it that Alec called you? Para-something?"

"*Parabatai,*" said Jace. "It means a pair of warriors who fight together—who are closer than brothers. Alec is more than just my best friend. My father and his father were *parabatai* when they were young. His father was my godfather—that's why I live with them. They're my adopted family."

"But your last name isn't Lightwood."

"No," Jace said, and she would have asked what it was, but they had arrived at her house, and her heart had started to thump so loudly that she was sure it must be audible for miles. There was a humming in her ears, and the palms of her hands were damp with sweat. She stopped in front of the box hedges, and raised her eyes slowly, expecting to see yellow police tape cordoning off the front door, smashed glass littering the lawn, the whole thing reduced to rubble.

But there were no signs of destruction. Bathed in pleasant afternoon light, the brownstone seemed to glow. Bees droned lazily around the rosebushes under Madame Dorothea's windows.

"It looks the same," Clary said.

"On the outside." Jace reached into his jeans pocket and drew out another one of the metal and plastic contraptions she'd mistaken for a cell phone.

"So that's a Sensor? What does it do?" she asked.

"It picks up frequencies, like a radio does, but these frequencies are demonic in origin."

"Demon shortwave?"

"Something like that." Jace held the Sensor out in front of him as he approached the house. It clicked faintly as they climbed the stairs, then stopped. Jace frowned. "It's picking up trace activity, but that could just be left over from that night. I'm not getting anything strong enough for there to be demons present now."

Clary let out a breath she hadn't realized she'd been holding. "Good." She bent to retrieve her keys. When she straightened up, she saw the scratches on the front door. It must have been too dark for her to have seen them last time. They looked like claw marks, long and parallel, raked deeply into the wood.

Jace touched her arm. "I'll go in first," he said. Clary wanted to tell him that she didn't need to hide behind him, but the words wouldn't come. She could taste the terror she'd felt when she'd first seen the Ravener. The taste was sharp and coppery on her tongue like old pennies.

He pushed the door open with one hand, beckoning her after him with the hand that held the Sensor. Once inside the entryway, Clary blinked, adjusting her eyes to the dimness. The bulb overhead was still out, the skylight too filthy to let in any light, and shadows lay thick across the chipped floor. Madame Dorothea's door was firmly shut. No light showed through the gap under it. Clary wondered uneasily if anything had happened to her.

Jace raised his hand and ran it along the banister. It came

away wet, streaked with something that looked blackish red in the dim light. "Blood."

"Maybe it's mine." Her voice sounded tinny. "From the other night."

"It'd be dry by now if it were," Jace said. "Come on."

He headed up the stairs, Clary close behind him. The landing was dark, and she fumbled her keys three times before she managed to slide the right one into the lock. Jace leaned over her, watching impatiently. "Don't breathe down my neck," she hissed; her hand was shaking. Finally the tumblers caught, the lock clicking open.

Jace pulled her back. "I'll go in first."

She hesitated, then stepped aside to let him pass. Her palms were sticky, and not from the heat. In fact, it was cool inside the apartment, almost cold—chilly air seeped from the entryway, stinging her skin. She felt goose bumps rising as she followed Jace down the short hallway and into the living room.

It was empty. Startlingly, entirely empty, the way it had been when they'd first moved in—the walls and floor bare, the furniture gone, even the curtains torn down from the windows. Only faint lighter squares of paint on the wall showed where her mother's paintings had hung. As if in a dream, Clary turned and walked toward the kitchen, Jace pacing her, his light eyes narrowed.

The kitchen was just as empty, even the refrigerator gone, the chairs, the table—the kitchen cabinets stood open, their bare shelves reminding her of a nursery rhyme. She cleared her throat. "What would demons," she said, "want with our microwave?"

Jace shook his head, mouth curling under at the corners. "I don't know, but I'm not sensing any demonic presence right now. I'd say they're long gone."

She glanced around one more time. Someone had cleaned up the spilled Tabasco sauce, she noticed distantly.

"Are you satisfied?" Jace asked. "There's nothing here."

She shook her head. "I want to see my room."

He looked as if he were about to say something, then thought better of it. "If that's what it takes," he said, sliding the seraph blade into his pocket.

The light in the hallway was out, but Clary didn't need much light to navigate inside her own house. With Jace just behind her, she found the door to her bedroom and reached for the knob. It was cold in her hand—so cold it nearly hurt, like touching an icicle with your bare skin. She saw Jace look at her quickly, but she was already turning the knob, or trying to. It moved slowly, almost stickily, as if the other side of it were embedded in something glutinous and syrupy—

The door blew outward, knocking her off her feet. She skidded across the hallway floor and slammed into the wall, rolling onto her stomach. There was a dull roaring in her ears as she pulled herself up to her knees.

Jace, flat against the wall, was fumbling in his pocket, his face a mask of surprise. Looming over him like a giant in a fairy tale was an enormous man, big around as an oak tree, a broadbladed axe clutched in one gigantic dead-white hand. Tattered filthy rags hung off his grimy skin, and his hair was a single matted tangle, thick with dirt. He stank of poisonous sweat and rotting flesh. Clary was glad she couldn't see his face—the back of him was bad enough.

Jace had the seraph blade in his hand. He raised it, calling out: "Sansavi!"

A blade shot from the tube. Clary thought of old movies where bayonets were hidden inside walking sticks, released at the flick of a switch. But she'd never seen a blade like this before: clear as glass, with a glowing hilt, wickedly sharp and nearly as long as Jace's forearm. He struck out, slashing at the gigantic man, who staggered back with a bellow.

Jace whirled around, racing toward her. He caught her arm, hauling her to her feet, pushing her ahead of him down the hall. She could hear the thing behind them, following; its footsteps sounded like lead weights being dropped onto the floor, but it was coming on fast.

They sped through the entryway and out onto the landing, Jace whipping around to slam the front door shut. She heard the click of the automatic lock and caught her breath. The door shook on its hinges as a tremendous blow struck against it from inside the apartment. Clary backed away to the stairs. Jace glanced at her. His eyes were glowing with manic excitement. "Get downstairs! Get out of the—"

Another blow came, and this time the hinges gave way and the door flew outward. It would have knocked Jace over if he hadn't moved so fast that Clary barely saw it; suddenly he was on the top stair, the blade burning in his hand like a fallen star. She saw Jace look at her and shout something, but she couldn't hear him over the roar of the gigantic creature that burst from the shattered door, making straight for him. She flattened herself against the wall as it passed in a wave of heat and stink—and then its axe was flying, whipping through the air, slicing toward Jace's head. He ducked, and it thunked heavily into the banister, biting deep.

Jace laughed. The laugh seemed to enrage the creature; abandoning the axe, he lurched at Jace with his enormous fists raised. Jace brought the seraph blade around in an arcing sweep, burying it to the hilt in the giant's shoulder. For a moment the giant stood swaying. Then he lurched forward, his hands outstretched and grasping. Jace stepped aside hastily, but not hastily enough: The enormous fists caught hold of him as the giant staggered and fell, dragging Jace in his wake. Jace cried out once; there was a series of heavy and cracking thumps, and then silence.

Clary scrambled to her feet and raced downstairs. Jace lay sprawled at the foot of the steps, his arm bent beneath him at an unnatural angle. Across his legs lay the giant, the hilt of Jace's blade protruding from his shoulder. He was not quite dead, but flopping weakly, a bloody froth leaking from his mouth. Clary could see his face now—it was dead-white and papery, latticed with a black network of horrible scars that almost obliterated his features. His eye sockets were red suppurating pits. Fighting the urge to gag, Clary stumbled down the last few stairs, stepped over the twitching giant, and knelt down next to Jace.

He was so still. She laid a hand on his shoulder, felt his shirt sticky with blood—his own or the giant's, she couldn't tell. "Jace?"

His eyes opened. "Is it dead?"

"Almost," Clary said grimly.

"Hell." He winced. "My legs—"

"Hold still." Crawling around to his head, Clary slipped her hands under his arms and pulled. He grunted with pain as his legs slipped out from under the creature's spasming carcass. Clary let go, and he struggled to his feet, his left arm across his chest. She stood up. "Is your arm all right?"

"No. Broken," he said. "Can you reach into my pocket?"

She hesitated, nodded. "Which one?"

"Inside jacket, right side. Take out one of the seraph blades and hand it to me." He held still as she nervously slipped her fingers into his pocket. She was standing so close that she could smell the scent of him, sweat and soap and blood. His breath tickled the back of her neck. Her fingers closed on a tube and she drew it out, not looking at him.

"Thanks," he said. His fingers traced it briefly before he named it: "Sanvi." Like its predecessor, the tube grew into a wicked-looking dagger, its glow illuminating his face. "Don't watch," he said, going to stand over the scarred thing's body. He raised the blade over his head and brought it down. Blood fountained from the giant's throat, splattering Jace's boots.

She half-expected the giant to vanish, folding in on itself the way the kid in Pandemonium had. But it didn't. The air was full of the smell of blood: heavy and metallic. Jace made a sound low in his throat. He was white-faced, whether with pain or disgust she couldn't tell. "I told you not to watch," he said.

"I thought it would disappear," she said. "Back to its own dimension—you said."

"I said that's what happens to demons when they die." Wincing, he shrugged his jacket off his shoulder, baring the upper part of his left arm. "That wasn't a demon." With his right hand he drew something out of his belt. It was the smooth wand-shaped object he'd used to carve those overlapping circles into Clary's skin. Looking at it, she felt her forearm begin to burn.

Jace saw her staring and grinned the ghost of a grin. "This," he said, "is a stele." He held it like a pencil, touching it to the skin of his arm and beginning to draw. Thick black lines swirled from the tip, creating a tattoo-like mark. "And this," he said, "is what happens when Shadowhunters are wounded."

When he lowered his hand, the Mark began to sink into his skin, like a weighted object sinking into water. It left behind a ghostly reminder: a pale, thin scar, almost invisible.

An image rose in Clary's mind. Her mother's back, not quite covered by her bathing suit top, the blades of her shoulders and curves of her spine dappled with narrow, white marks. It was like something she had seen in a dream—her mother's back didn't really look like that, she knew. But the image nagged at her.

Jace let out a sigh, the tense look of pain leaving his face. He moved the arm, slowly at first, then more easily, lifting it up and down, clenching his fist. Clearly it was no longer broken.

"That's amazing," Clary said. "How did you—?"

"That was an *iratze*—a healing rune," Jace said. "Finishing the rune with the stele activates it." He shoved the slim wand into his belt and shrugged his jacket back on. With the toe of his boot he prodded the giant's corpse. "We're going to have to report this to Hodge," he said. "He'll freak out," he added, as if the thought of Hodge's alarm gave him some satisfaction. Jace, Clary thought, was the sort of person who liked it when things were *happening*, even things that were bad.

"Why will he freak?" Clary said. "And I get that that thing isn't a demon—that's why the Sensor didn't register it, right?"

Jace nodded. "You see the scars all over its face?"

"Yes."

"Those were made with a stele. Like this one." He tapped the wand in his belt. "You asked me what happens when you carve Marks onto someone who doesn't have Shadowhunter blood. Just one Mark could burn you, even kill you, but a lot of Marks, powerful ones? Carved into the flesh of a totally ordinary human being with no trace of Shadowhunter ancestry? You get this." He jerked his chin at the corpse. "The runes are agonizingly painful. The Marked ones go insane—the pain drives them out of their minds. They become fierce, mindless killers. They don't sleep or eat unless you make them, and they die, usually quickly. Runes have great power and can be used to do great good—but they can be used for evil. The Forsaken are evil."

Clary stared at him in horror. "But why would anyone do that to themselves?"

"Nobody would. It's something that gets done to them. The Forsaken are loyal to the one who Marked them, and they're fierce killers. They can obey simple commands, too. It's like having a—a slave army." He stepped over the dead Forsaken, and glanced over his shoulder at her. "I'm going back upstairs."

"But there's nothing there."

"There might be more of them," he said, almost as if he were hoping there would be. "You should wait here." He started up the steps.

"I wouldn't do that if I were you," said a shrill and familiar voice. "There are more of them where the first one came from."

Jace, who was nearly at the top of the stairs, spun and stared. So did Clary, although she knew immediately who had spoken. That gravelly accent was unmistakable.

"Madame Dorothea?"

The old woman inclined her head regally. She stood in the doorway of her apartment, dressed in what looked like a tent made of raw purple silk. Gold chains glittered on her wrists and roped her throat. Her long badger-striped hair straggled from the bun pinned to the top of her head.

Jace was still staring. "But..."

"More *what*?" Clary said.

"More Forsaken," replied Dorothea with a cheerfulness that, Clary felt, didn't really fit the circumstances. She glanced around the entryway. "You have made a mess, haven't you? I'm sure you weren't planning on cleaning up either. Typical."

"But you're a *mundane*," Jace said, finally finishing his sentence.

"So observant," said Dorothea, her eyes gleaming. "The Clave really broke the mold with you."

The bewilderment on Jace's face was fading, replaced by a dawning anger. "You know about the Clave?" he demanded. "You knew about them, and you knew there were Forsaken in this house, and you didn't notify them? Just the existence of Forsaken is a crime against the Covenant—"

"Neither Clave nor Covenant have ever done anything for me," said Madame Dorothea, her eyes flashing angrily. "I owe them nothing." For a moment her gravelly New York accent vanished, replaced with something else, a thicker, deeper accent that Clary didn't recognize.

"Jace, stop it," Clary said. She turned to Madame Dorothea. "If you know about the Clave and the Forsaken," she said, "then maybe you know what happened to my mother?"

Dorothea shook her head, her earrings swinging. There was something like pity on her face. "My advice to you," she said, "is to forget about your mother. She's gone."

The floor under Clary seemed to tilt. "You mean she's dead?"

"No." Dorothea spoke the word almost reluctantly. "I'm sure she's still alive. For now."

"Then I have to find her," Clary said. The world had stopped tilting; Jace was standing behind her, his hand on her elbow as if to brace her, but she barely noticed. "You understand? I have to find her before—"

Madame Dorothea held up a hand. "I don't want to involve myself in Shadowhunter business."

"But you knew my mother. She was your neighbor—"

"This is an official Clave investigation." Jace cut her off. "I can always come back with the Silent Brothers."

"Oh, for the—" Dorothea glanced at her door, then at Jace and Clary. "I suppose you might as well come in," she said, finally. "I'll tell you what I can." She started toward the door, then halted on the threshold, glaring. "But if you tell anyone I helped you, Shadowhunter, you'll wake up tomorrow with snakes for hair and an extra pair of arms."

"That might be nice, an extra pair of arms," Jace said. "Handy in a fight."

"Not if they're growing out of your..." Dorothea paused and smiled at him, not without malice. "Neck."

"Yikes," said Jace mildly.

"Yikes is right, Jace Wayland." Dorothea marched into the apartment, her purple tent flying around her like a gaudy flag.

Clary looked at Jace. "Wayland?"

"It's my name." Jace looked shaken. "I can't say I like that she knows it."

Clary glanced after Dorothea. The lights were on inside the apartment; already the heavy smell of incense was flooding the entryway, mixing unpleasantly with the stench of blood.

"Still, I think we might as well try talking to her. What have we got to lose?"

"Once you've spent a bit more time in our world," Jace said, "you won't ask me that again."

7

The Five-Dimensional Door

Madame Dorothea's apartment seemed to have roughly the same layout as Clary's, though she'd made a very different use of the space. The entryway, reeking of incense, was hung with bead curtains and astrological posters. One showed the constellations of the zodiac, another a guide to Chinese magical symbols, and another showed a hand with fingers spread, each line on the palm carefully labeled. Above the hand Latinate script spelled out the words *In Manibus Fortuna*. Narrow shelves holding stacked books ran along the wall beside the door.

One of the bead curtains rattled, and Madame Dorothea poked her head through. "Interested in chiromancy?" she said, noting Clary's gaze. "Or just nosy?"

"Neither," Clary said. "Can you really tell fortunes?"

"My mother had a great talent. She could see a man's future in his hand or the leaves at the bottom of his teacup. She taught me some of her tricks." She transferred her gaze to Jace. "Speaking of tea, young man, would you like some?"

"What?" Jace said, looking flustered.

"Tea. I find it both settles the stomach and concentrates the mind. Wonderful drink, tea."

"I'll have tea," Clary said, realizing how long it had been since she had eaten or drunk anything. She felt as if she'd been running on pure adrenaline since she woke up.

Jace succumbed. "All right. As long as it isn't Earl Grey," he added, wrinkling his fine-boned nose. "I hate bergamot."

Madame Dorothea cackled loudly and disappeared back through the bead curtain, leaving it swaying gently behind her.

Clary raised an eyebrow at Jace. "You hate bergamot?"

Jace had wandered over to the narrow bookshelf and was examining its contents. "You have a problem with that?"

"You may be the only guy my age I've ever met who knows what bergamot is, much less that it's in Earl Grey tea."

"Yes, well," Jace said, with a supercilious look, "I'm not like other guys. Besides," he added, flipping a book off the shelf, "at the Institute we have to take classes in basic medicinal uses for plants. It's required."

"I figured all your classes were stuff like Slaughter 101 and Beheading for Beginners."

Jace flipped a page. "Very funny, Fray."

Clary, who had been studying the palmistry poster, whirled on him. "Don't call me that."

He glanced up, surprised. "Why not? It's your last name, isn't it?"

The image of Simon rose up behind her eyes. Simon the last time she had seen him, staring after her as she ran out of Java Jones. She turned back to the poster, blinking. "No reason."

"I see," Jace said, and she could tell from his voice that he did see, more than she wanted him to. She heard him drop the book back onto the shelf. "This must be the trash she keeps up front to impress credible mundanes," he said, sounding disgusted. "There's not one serious text here."

"Just because it's not the kind of magic you do—" Clary began crossly.

He scowled furiously, silencing her. *"I do not do magic,"* he said. "Get it through your head: Human beings are not magic users. It's part of what makes them human. Warlocks can only use magic because they have demon blood."

Clary took a moment to process this. "But I've seen you use magic. You use enchanted weapons—"

"I use tools that are magical. And just to be able to do that, I have to undergo rigorous training. The rune tattoos on my skin protect me too. If you tried to use one of the seraph blades, for instance, it'd probably burn your skin, maybe kill you."

"What if I got the tattoos?" Clary asked. "Could I use them then?"

"No," Jace said crossly. "The Marks are only part of it. There are tests, ordeals, levels of training—look, just forget it, okay? Stay away from my blades. In fact, don't touch any of my weapons without my permission."

"Well, there goes my plan for selling them all on eBay," Clary muttered.

"Selling them on *what?*"

Clary smiled blandly at him. "A mythical place of great magical power."

Jace looked confused, then shrugged. "Most myths are true, at least in part."

"I'm starting to get that."

The bead curtain rattled again, and Madame Dorothea's head appeared. "Tea's on the table," she said. "There's no need for you two to keep standing there like donkeys. Come into the parlor."

"There's a parlor?" Clary said.

"Of course there's a parlor," said Dorothea. "Where else would I entertain?"

"I'll just leave my hat with the footman," said Jace.

Madame Dorothea shot him a dark look. "If you were half as funny as you thought you were, my boy, you'd be twice as funny as you are." She disappeared back through the curtain, her loud "Hmph!" nearly drowned out by rattling beads.

Jace frowned. "I'm not quite sure what she meant by that."

"Really," said Clary. "It made perfect sense to me." She marched through the bead curtain before he could reply.

The parlor was so dimly lit that it took several blinks for Clary's eyes to adjust. Faint light outlined the black velvet curtains drawn across the entire left wall. Stuffed birds and bats dangled from the ceiling on thin cords, shiny dark beads where their eyes should have been. The floor was layered with frayed Persian rugs that spat up puffs of dust underfoot. A group of overstuffed pink armchairs were gathered around a low table: A stack of tarot cards bound with a silk ribbon occupied one end of the table, a crystal ball on a gold stand the other. In the middle of the table was a silver tea service, laid out for company: a neat plate of stacked sandwiches, a blue teapot unfurling a thin stream of white steam, and two teacups on matching saucers set carefully in front of two of the armchairs.

"Wow," Clary said weakly. "This looks great." She took a

seat in one of the armchairs. It felt good to sit down.

Dorothea smiled, her eyes glinting with a sly humor. "Have some tea," she said, hefting the pot. "Milk? Sugar?"

Clary looked sideways at Jace, who was sitting beside her and who had taken possession of the sandwich plate. He was examining it closely. "Sugar," she said.

Jace shrugged, took a sandwich, and set the plate down. Clary watched him warily as he bit into it. He shrugged again. "Cucumber," he said, in response to her stare.

"I always think cucumber sandwiches are just the thing for tea, don't you?" Madame Dorothea inquired, of no one in particular.

"I hate cucumber," Jace said, and handed the rest of his sandwich to Clary. She bit into it—it was seasoned with just the right amount of mayonnaise and pepper. Her stomach rumbled in grateful appreciation of the first food she'd tasted since the nachos she'd eaten with Simon.

"Cucumber and bergamot," Clary said. "Is there anything else you hate that I ought to know about?"

Jace looked at Dorothea over the rim of his teacup. "Liars," he said.

Calmly the old woman set her teapot down. "You can call me a liar all you like. It's true, I'm not a warlock. But my mother was."

Jace choked on his tea. "That's impossible."

"Why impossible?" Clary asked curiously. She took a sip of her tea. It was bitter, strongly flavored with a peaty smokiness.

Jace expelled a breath. "Because they're half-human, half-demon. All warlocks are crossbreeds. And because they're crossbreeds, they can't have children. They're sterile."

"Like mules," Clary said thoughtfully, remembering something from biology class. "Mules are sterile crossbreeds."

"Your knowledge of livestock is astounding," said Jace. "All Downworlders are in some part demon, but only warlocks are the children of demon parents. It's why their powers are the strongest."

"Vampires and werewolves—they're part demon too? And faeries?"

"Vampires and werewolves are the result of diseases brought by demons from their home dimensions. Most demon diseases are deadly to humans, but in these cases they worked strange changes on the infected, without actually killing them. And faeries—"

"Faeries are fallen angels," said Dorothea, "cast down out of heaven for their pride."

"That's the legend," Jace said. "It's also said that they're the offspring of demons and angels, which always seemed more likely to me. Good and evil, mixing together. Faeries are as beautiful as angels are supposed to be, but they have a lot of mischief and cruelty in them."

Clary said, "'Supposed to be'? You mean angels don't—"

"Enough about angels," said Dorothea, suddenly practical. "It's true that warlocks can't have children. My mother adopted me because she wanted to make sure there'd be someone to attend this place after she was gone. I don't have to master magic myself. I have only to watch and guard."

"Guard what?" asked Clary.

"What indeed?" With a wink the older woman reached for a sandwich from the plate, but it was empty. Clary had eaten them all. Dorothea chuckled. "It's good to see a young woman eat her fill. In my day, girls were robust, strapping creatures, not twigs like they are nowadays."

"Thanks," Clary said. She thought of Isabelle's tiny waist and felt suddenly gigantic. She set her empty teacup down with a clatter.

Instantly, Madame Dorothea pounced on the cup and stared into it intently, a line appearing between her penciled eyebrows.

"What?" Clary said nervously. "Did I crack the cup or something?"

"She's reading your tea leaves," Jace said, sounding bored, but he leaned forward along with Clary as Dorothea turned the cup around and around in her thick fingers, scowling.

"Is it bad?" Clary asked.

"It is neither bad nor good. It is confusing." Dorothea looked at Jace. "Give me *your* cup," she commanded.

Jace looked affronted. "But I'm not done with my—"

The old woman snatched the cup out of his hand and splashed the excess tea back into the pot. Frowning, she gazed at what remained. "I see violence in your future, a great deal of blood shed by you and others. You'll fall in love with the wrong person. Also, you have an enemy."

"Only one? That's good news." Jace leaned back in his chair as Dorothea put down his cup and picked up Clary's again. She shook her head.

"There is nothing for me to read here. The images are jumbled, meaningless." She glanced at Clary. "Is there a block in your mind?"

Clary was puzzled. "A what?"

"Like a spell that might conceal a memory, or might have blocked out your Sight."

Clary shook her head. "No, of course not."

Jace leaned forward alertly. "Don't be so hasty," he said. "It's true that she claims not to remember ever having had the Sight before this week. Maybe—"

"Maybe I'm just a late developer," Clary snapped. "And don't *leer* at me, just because I said that."

Jace assumed an injured air. "I wasn't going to."

"You were working up to a leer, I could tell."

"Maybe," Jace acknowledged, "but that doesn't mean I'm not right. Something's blocking your memories, I'm almost sure of it."

"Very well, let's try something else." Dorothea put the cup down, and reached for the silk-wrapped tarot cards. She fanned the cards and held them out to Clary. "Slide your hand over these until you touch one that feels hot or cold, or seems to cling to your fingers. Then draw that one and show it to me."

Obediently Clary ran her fingers over the cards. They felt cool to the touch, and slippery, but none seemed particularly warm or cold, and none stuck to her fingers. Finally she selected one at random, and held it up.

"The Ace of Cups," Dorothea said, sounding bemused. "The love card."

Clary turned it over and looked at it. The card was heavy in her hand, the image on the front thick with real paint. It showed a hand holding up a cup in front of a rayed sun painted with gilt. The cup was made of gold, engraved with a pattern of smaller suns and studded with rubies. The style of the artwork was as familiar to her as her own breath. "This is a good card, right?"

"Not necessarily. The most terrible things men do, they do in the name of love," said Madame Dorothea, her eyes gleaming. "But it is a powerful card. What does it mean to you?"

"That my mother painted it," said Clary, and dropped the card onto the table. "She did, didn't she?"

Dorothea nodded, a look of pleased satisfaction on her face. "She painted the whole pack. A gift for me."

"So you say." Jace stood up, his eyes cold. "How well did you know Clary's mother?"

Clary craned her head to look up at him. "Jace, you don't have to—"

Dorothea sat back in her chair, the cards fanned out across her wide chest. "Jocelyn knew what I was, and I knew what she was. We didn't talk about it much. Sometimes she did favors for me—like painting this pack of cards—and in return I'd tell her the occasional piece of Downworld gossip. There was a name she asked me to keep an ear out for, and I did."

Jace's expression was unreadable. "What name was that?"

"Valentine."

Clary sat straight up in her chair. "But that's—"

"And when you say you knew what Jocelyn was, what do you mean? What was she?" Jace asked.

"Jocelyn was what she was," said Dorothea. "But in her past she'd been like you. A Shadowhunter. One of the Clave."

"No," Clary whispered.

Dorothea looked at her with sad almost kindly eyes. "It's true. She chose to live in this house precisely because—"

"Because this is a sanctuary," Jace said to Dorothea. "Isn't it? Your mother was a warlock. She made this space, hidden, protected, probably surrounded by wards—it's a perfect spot for Downworlders on the run to hide out. That's what you do, isn't it? You hide criminals here."

"You *would* call them that," Dorothea said. "You're familiar with the motto of the Covenant?"

"*Sed lex dura lex,*" said Jace automatically. "'The Law is hard, but it is the Law.'"

"Sometimes the Law is too hard. I know the Clave would have taken me away from my mother if they could. You want me to let them do the same to others?"

"So you're a philanthropist." Jace's lip curled. "I suppose you expect me to believe that Downworlders don't pay you handsomely for the privilege of your sanctuary?"

Dorothea grinned, wide enough to show a flash of gold molars. "We can't all get by on our looks like you."

Jace looked unmoved by the flattery. "I should tell the Clave about you—"

"You can't!" Clary was on her feet now. "You promised."

"I never promised anything." Jace looked mutinous. He strode to the wall and tore aside one of the velvet hangings. "You want to tell me what this is?" he demanded.

"It's a door, Jace," said Clary. It *was* a door, set strangely in the wall between the two bay windows. Clearly it couldn't be a door that led anywhere, or it would have been visible from the outside of the house. It looked as if it were made of some softly glowing metal, more buttery than brass but as heavy as iron. The knob had been cast in the shape of an eye.

"Shut up," Jace said angrily. "It's a Portal. Isn't it?"

"It's a five-dimensional door," said Dorothea, laying the tarot cards back on the table. "Dimensions aren't all straight lines, you know," she added, in response to Clary's blank look. "There are dips and folds and nooks and crannies all tucked away. It's a bit hard to explain when you've never studied dimensional theory, but, in essence, that door can take you anywhere in this dimension that you want to go. It's—"

"An escape hatch," Jace said. "That's why your mother wanted to live here. So she could always flee at a moment's notice."

"Then why didn't she—" Clary began, and broke off, suddenly horrified. "Because of me," she said. "She wouldn't leave without me that night. So she stayed."

Jace was shaking his head. "You can't blame yourself."

Feeling tears gather under her eyelids, Clary pushed past Jace to the door. "I want to see where she would have gone," she said, reaching for the door. "I want to see where she was going to escape to—"

"Clary, no!" Jace reached for her, but her fingers had already closed around the knob. It spun rapidly under her hand, the door flying open as if she'd pushed it. Dorothea lumbered to her feet with a cry, but it was too late. Before she could even finish her sentence, Clary found herself flung forward and tumbling through empty space.

8

Weapon of Choice

She was too surprised to scream. The sensation of falling was the worst part; her heart flew up into her throat and her stomach turned to water. She flung her hands out, trying to catch at something, anything that might slow her descent.

Her hands closed on branches. Leaves tore off in her grip. She thumped to the ground, hard, her hip and shoulder striking packed earth. She rolled over, sucking the air back into her lungs. She was just beginning to sit up when someone landed on top of her.

She was knocked backward. A forehead banged against hers, her knees banging against someone else's. Tangled up in arms and legs, Clary coughed hair (not her own) out of her mouth and tried to struggle out from under the weight that felt like it was crushing her flat.

"Ouch," Jace said in her ear, his tone indignant. "You elbowed me."

"Well, you *landed* on me."

He levered himself up on his arms and looked down at her placidly. Clary could see blue sky above his head, a bit of tree branch, and the corner of a gray clapboard house. "Well, you didn't leave me much choice, did you?" he asked. "Not after you decided to leap merrily through that Portal like you were jumping the F train. You're just lucky it didn't dump us out in the East River."

"You didn't have to come after me."

"Yes, I did," he said. "You're far too inexperienced to protect yourself in a hostile situation without me."

"That's sweet. Maybe I'll forgive you."

"Forgive me? For what?"

"For telling me to shut up."

His eyes narrowed. "I did not... Well, I did, but you were—"

"Never mind." Her arm, pinned under her back, was beginning to cramp. Rolling to the side to free it, she saw the brown grass of a dead lawn, a chain-link fence, and more of the gray clapboard house, now distressingly familiar.

She froze. "I know where we are."

Jace stopped spluttering. "What?"

"This is Luke's house." She sat up, pitching Jace to the side. He rolled gracefully to his feet and held out a hand to help her up. She ignored him and scrambled upright, shaking out her numb arm.

They stood in front of a small gray row house, nestled among the other row houses that lined the Williamsburg waterfront. A breeze blew off the East River, setting a small sign swinging over the brick front steps. Clary watched Jace as he read the block-lettered words aloud, GARROWAY BOOKS.

FINE USED, NEW, AND OUT-OF-PRINT. CLOSED SATURDAYS. He glanced at the dark front door, its knob wound with a heavy padlock. A few days' worth of mail lay on the doormat, untouched. He glanced at Clary. "He lives in a bookstore?"

"He lives behind the store." Clary glanced up and down the empty street, which was bordered on one end by the arched span of the Williamsburg Bridge, and by a deserted sugar factory on the other. Across the sluggishly moving river the sun was setting behind the skyscrapers of lower Manhattan, outlining them in gold. "Jace, how did we get here?"

"Through the Portal," Jace said, examining the padlock. "It takes you to whatever place you're thinking of."

"But I wasn't thinking of here," Clary objected. "I wasn't thinking of anywhere."

"You must have been." He dropped the subject, seeming uninterested. "So, since we're here anyway..."

"Yeah?"

"What do you want to do?"

"Leave, I guess," Clary said bitterly. "Luke told me not to come here."

Jace shook his head. "And you just accept that?"

Clary hugged her arms around herself. Despite the fading heat of the day, she felt cold. "Do I have a choice?"

"We always have choices," Jace said. "If I were you, I'd be pretty curious about Luke right now. Do you have keys to the house?"

Clary shook her head. "No, but sometimes he leaves the back door unlocked." She pointed to the narrow alley between Luke's row house and the next. Plastic trash cans were propped in a neat row beside stacks of folded newspapers and a plastic tub of empty soda bottles. At least Luke was still a responsible recycler.

"You sure he isn't home?" Jace asked.

She glanced at the empty curb. "Well, his truck's gone, the store's closed, and all the lights are off. I'd say probably not."

"Then lead the way."

The narrow aisle between the row houses ended in a high chain-link fence. It surrounded Luke's small back garden, where the only plants flourishing seemed to be the weeds that had sprung up through the paving stones, cracking them into powdery shards.

"Up and over," Jace said, jamming the toe of a boot into a gap in the fence. He began to climb. The fence rattled so loudly that Clary glanced around nervously, but there were no lights on in the neighbors' house. Jace cleared the top of the fence and sprang down the other side, landing in the bushes to the accompaniment of an earsplitting yowl.

For a moment Clary thought he must have landed on a stray cat. She heard Jace shout in surprise as he fell backward. A dark shadow—much too big to be feline—exploded out of the shrubbery and streaked across the yard, keeping low. Rolling to his feet, Jace darted after it, looking murderous.

Clary started to climb. As she threw her leg over the top of the fence, Isabelle's jeans caught on a twist of wire and tore up the side. She dropped to the ground, shoes scuffing the soft dirt, just as Jace cried out in triumph. "Got him!" Clary turned to see Jace sitting on top of the prone intruder, whose arms were up over his head. Jace grabbed for his wrist. "Come on, let's see your face—"

"Get the hell off me, you pretentious asshole," the intruder snarled, shoving at Jace. He struggled halfway into a sitting position, his battered glasses knocked askew.

Clary stopped dead in her tracks. "*Simon?*"

"Oh, God," said Jace, sounding resigned. "And here I'd actually hoped I'd got hold of something interesting."

"But what were you doing hiding in Luke's bushes?" Clary asked, brushing leaves out of Simon's hair. He suffered her ministrations with glaring bad grace. Somehow when she'd pictured her reunion with Simon, when all this was over, he'd been in a better mood. "That's the part I don't get."

"All right, that's enough. I can fix my own hair, Fray," Simon said, jerking away from her touch. They were sitting on the steps of Luke's back porch. Jace had propped himself on the porch railing and was assiduously pretending to ignore them, while using the stele to file the edges of his fingernails. Clary wondered if the Clave would approve.

"I mean, did Luke know you were there?" she asked.

"Of course he didn't know I was there," Simon said irritably. "I've never asked him, but I'm sure he has a fairly stringent policy about random teenagers lurking in his shrubbery."

"You're not random; he knows you." She wanted to reach out and touch his cheek, still bleeding slightly where a branch had scratched it. "The main thing is that you're all right."

"That *I'm* all right?" Simon laughed, a sharp, unhappy sound. "Clary, do you have any idea what I've been through this past couple of days? The last time I saw you, you were running out of Java Jones like a bat out of hell, and then you just ... disappeared. You never picked up your cell—then your home phone was disconnected—then Luke told me you were off staying with some relatives upstate when I *know* you don't have any other relatives. I thought I'd done something to piss you off."

"What could you possibly have done?" Clary reached for his hand, but he pulled it back without looking at her.

"I don't know," he said. "Something."

Jace, still occupied with the stele, chuckled low under his breath.

"You're my best friend," Clary said. "I wasn't mad at you."

"Yeah, well, you clearly also couldn't be bothered to call me and tell me you were shacking up with some dyed-blond wanna-be goth you probably met at Pandemonium," Simon pointed out sourly. "After I spent the past three days wondering if you were *dead*."

"I was not shacking up," Clary said, glad of the darkness as the blood rushed to her face.

"And my hair is naturally blond," said Jace. "Just for the record."

"So what have you been doing these past three days, then?" Simon said, his eyes dark with suspicion. "Do you really have a great-aunt Matilda who contracted avian flu and needed to be nursed back to health?"

"Did Luke actually say that?"

"No. He just said you had gone to visit a sick relative, and that your phone probably just didn't work out in the country. Not that I believed him. After he shooed me off his front porch, I went around the side of the house and looked in the back window. Watched him packing up a green duffel bag like he was going away for the weekend. That was when I decided to stick around and keep an eye on things."

"Why? Because he was packing a bag?"

"He was packing it full of weapons," Simon said, scrubbing at the blood on his cheek with the sleeve of his T-shirt. "Knives, a couple daggers, even a sword. Funny thing is, some of the weapons looked like they were glowing." He looked from Clary to Jace, and back again. His tone was edged as sharply as one of Luke's knives. "Now, are you going to say I was imagining it?"

"No," Clary said. "I'm not going to say that." She glanced at Jace. The last light of sunset struck gold sparks from his eyes. She said, "I'm going to tell him the truth."

"I know."

"Are you going to try to stop me?"

He looked down at the stele in his hand. "My oath to the Covenant binds me," he said. "No such oath binds you."

She turned back to Simon, taking a deep breath. "All right," she said. "Here's what you have to know."

The sun had slipped entirely past the horizon, and the porch was in darkness by the time Clary stopped speaking. Simon had listened to her lengthy explanation with a nearly impassive expression, only wincing a little when she got to the part about the Ravener demon. When she was done speaking, she cleared her dry throat, suddenly dying for a glass of water. "So," she said, "any questions?"

Simon held up his hand. "Oh, I've got questions. Several."

Clary exhaled warily. "Okay, shoot."

He pointed at Jace. "Now, he's a—what do you call people like him again?"

"He's a Shadowhunter," Clary said.

"A demon hunter," Jace clarified. "I kill demons. It's not that complicated, really."

Simon looked at Clary again. "For real?" His eyes were narrowed, as if he half-expected her to tell him that none of it was true and Jace was actually a dangerous escaped lunatic she'd decided to befriend on humanitarian grounds.

"For real."

There was an intent look on Simon's face. "And there are vampires, too? Werewolves, warlocks, all that stuff ?"

Clary gnawed her lower lip. "So I hear."

"And you kill them, too?" Simon asked, directing the question to Jace, who had put the stele back in his pocket and was examining his flawless nails for defects.

"Only when they've been naughty."

For a moment Simon merely sat and stared down at his feet. Clary wondered if burdening him with this kind of information had been the wrong thing to do. He had a stronger practical streak than almost anyone else she knew; he might hate knowing something like this, something for which there was no logical explanation. She leaned forward anxiously, just as Simon lifted his head. "That is so *awesome*," he said.

Jace looked as startled as Clary felt. "Awesome?"

Simon nodded enthusiastically enough to make the dark curls bounce on his forehead. "Totally. It's like Dungeons and Dragons, but *real*."

Jace was looking at Simon as if he were some bizarre species of insect. "It's like what?"

"It's a game," Clary explained. She felt vaguely embarrassed. "People pretend to be wizards and elves, and they kill monsters and stuff."

Jace looked stupefied.

Simon grinned. "You've never heard of Dungeons and Dragons?"

"I've heard of dungeons," Jace said. "Also dragons. Although they're mostly extinct."

Simon looked disappointed. "You've never killed a dragon?"

"He's probably never met a six-foot-tall hot elf-woman in a fur bikini, either," Clary said irritably. "Lay off, Simon."

"Real elves are about eight inches tall," Jace pointed out. "Also, they bite."

"But vampires are hot, right?" Simon said. "I mean, some of the vampires are babes, aren't they?"

Clary worried for a moment that Jace might lunge across the porch and throttle Simon senseless. Instead, he considered the question. "Some of them, maybe."

"Awesome," Simon repeated. Clary decided she had preferred it when they were fighting.

Jace slid off the porch railing. "So are we going to search the house, or not?"

Simon scrambled to his feet. "I'm game. What are we looking for?"

"We?" said Jace, with a sinister delicacy. "I don't remember inviting you along."

"Jace," Clary said angrily.

The left corner of his mouth curled up. "Just joking." He stepped aside to leave her a clear path to the door. "Shall we?"

Clary fumbled for the doorknob in the dark. It opened, triggering the porch light, which illuminated the entryway. The door that led into the bookstore was closed; Clary jiggled the knob. "It's locked."

"Allow me, mundanes," said Jace, setting her gently aside. He took his stele out of his pocket and put it to the door. Simon watched him with some resentment. No amount of vampire babes, Clary suspected, was ever going to make him like Jace.

"He's a piece of work, isn't he?" Simon muttered. "How do you stand him?"

"He saved my life."

Simon glanced at her quickly. "How—"

With a click the door swung open. "Here we go," said Jace, sliding his stele back into his pocket. Clary saw the Mark on the door—just over his head—fade as they passed through it. The back door opened onto a small storage room, the bare walls peeling paint. Cardboard boxes were stacked everywhere, their contents identified with marker scrawls: FICTION, POETRY, COOKING, LOCAL INTEREST, ROMANCE.

"The apartment's through there." Clary headed toward the door she'd indicated, at the far end of the room.

Jace caught her arm. "Wait."

She looked at him nervously. "Is something wrong?"

"I don't know." He edged between two narrow stacks of boxes, and whistled. "Clary, you might want to come over here and see this."

She glanced around. It was dim in the storage room, the only illumination the porch light shining through the window. "It's so dark—"

Light flared up, bathing the room in a brilliant glow. Simon turned his head aside, blinking. "Ouch."

Jace chuckled. He was standing on top of a sealed box, his hand raised. Something glowed in his palm, the light escaping through his cupped fingers. "Witchlight," he said.

Simon muttered something under his breath. Clary was already clambering through the boxes, pushing a way to Jace. He was standing behind a teetering pile of mysteries, the witch-light casting an eerie glow over his face. "Look at that," he said, indicating a space higher up on the wall.

At first she thought he was pointing at what looked like a pair of ornamental sconces. As her eyes adjusted, she realized they were actually loops of metal attached to short chains, the ends of which were sunk into the wall. "Are those—"

"Manacles," said Simon, picking his way through the boxes. "That's, ah..."

"Don't say 'kinky.'" Clary shot him a warning look. "This is Luke we're talking about."

Jace reached up to run his hand along the inside of one of the metal loops. When he lowered it, his fingers were dusted with red-brown powder. "Blood. And look." He pointed to the wall right around where the chains were sunk in; the plaster seemed to bulge outward. "Someone tried to yank these things out of the wall. Tried pretty hard, from the looks of it."

Clary's heart had begun to beat hard inside her chest. "Do you think Luke is all right?"

Jace lowered the witchlight. "I think we'd better find out."

The door to the apartment was unlocked. It led into Luke's living room. Despite the hundreds of books in the store itself, there were hundreds more in the apartment. Bookshelves rose to the ceiling, the volumes on them "double-parked," one row blocking another. Most were poetry and fiction, with plenty of fantasy and mystery thrown in. Clary remembered plowing through the entirety of *The Chronicles of Prydain* here, curled up in Luke's window seat as the sun went down over the East River.

"I think he's still around," called Simon, standing in the doorway of Luke's small kitchenette. "The percolator's on and there's coffee here. Still hot."

Clary peered around the kitchen door. Dishes were stacked in the sink. Luke's jackets were hung neatly on hooks inside the coat closet. She walked down the hallway and opened the door of his small bedroom. It looked the same as ever, the bed with its gray coverlet and flat pillows unmade, the top of the bureau covered in loose change. She turned away. Some part of her had been absolutely certain that when they walked in they'd find the place torn to pieces, and Luke tied up, injured or worse. Now she didn't know what to think.

Numbly she crossed the hall to the little guest bedroom where she'd so often stayed when her mother was out of town on business. They'd stay up late watching old horror movies on the flickering black-and-white TV. She even kept a backpack full of extra things here so she didn't have to lug her stuff back and forth from home.

Kneeling down, she tugged it out from under the bed by its olive green strap. It was covered with buttons, most of which Simon had given her. GAMERS DO IT BETTER. OTAKU WENCH. STILL NOT KING. Inside were some folded clothes, a few spare pairs of underwear, a hairbrush, even shampoo. *Thank God,* she thought, and kicked the bedroom door closed. Quickly she changed, stripping off Isabelle's too-big—and now grass-stained and sweaty—clothes, and pulling on a pair of her own sandblasted cords, soft as worn paper, and a blue tank top with a design of Chinese characters across the front. She tossed Isabelle's clothes into her backpack, yanked the cord shut, and left the bedroom, the pack bouncing familiarly between her shoulder blades. It was nice to have something of her own again.

She found Jace in Luke's book-lined office, examining a green duffel bag that lay unzipped across the desk. It was, as Simon had said, full of weapons—sheathed knives, a coiled whip, and something that looked like a razor-edged metal disk.

"It's a *chakhram*," said Jace, looking up as Clary came into the room. "A Sikh weapon. You whirl it around your index finger before releasing it. They're rare and hard to use. Strange that Luke would have one. They used to be Hodge's weapon of choice, back in the day. Or so he tells me."

"Luke collects stuff. Art objects. You know," Clary said, indicating the shelf behind the desk, which was lined with bronze Indian and Russian idols. Her favorite was a statuette of the Indian goddess of destruction, Kali, brandishing a sword and a severed head as she danced with her head thrown back and her eyes slitted closed. To the side of the desk was an antique Chinese screen, carved out of glowing rosewood. "Pretty things."

Jace moved the *chakhram* aside gingerly. A handful of clothes spilled out of the untied end of Luke's duffel bag, as if they had been an afterthought. "Is this yours?"

He drew out a rectangular object hidden among the clothes: a wooden-framed photograph with a long vertical crack along the glass. The crack threw a network of spidery lines across the smiling faces of Clary, Luke, and her mother. "That *is* mine," Clary said, taking it out of his hand.

"It's cracked," Jace observed.

"I know. *I* did that—I smashed it. When I threw it at the Ravener demon." She looked at him, seeing the dawning realization on his face. "That means Luke's been back to the apartment since the attack. Maybe even today—"

"He must have been the last person to come through the Portal," said Jace. "That's why it took us here. You weren't thinking of anything, so it sent us to the last place it had been."

"Nice of Dorothea to tell us he was there," said Clary.

"He probably paid her off to be quiet. Either that or she trusts him more than she trusts us. Which means he might not be—"

"Guys!" It was Simon, dashing into the office in a panic. "Someone's coming."

Clary dropped the photo. "Is it Luke?"

Simon peered back down the hall, then nodded. "It is. But he's not by himself—there are two men with him."

"Men?" Jace crossed the room in a few strides, peered through the door, and spat a curse under his breath. "Warlocks."

Clary stared. "Warlocks? But—"

Shaking his head, Jace backed away from the door. "Is there some other way out of here? A back door?"

Clary shook her head. The sound of footsteps in the hallway was audible now, striking pangs of fear into her chest.

Jace looked around desperately. His eyes came to rest on the rosewood screen. "Get behind that," he said, pointing. "*Now.*"

Clary dropped the fractured photo on the desk and slipped behind the screen, pulling Simon after her. Jace was right behind them, his stele in his hand. He had barely concealed himself when Clary heard the door swing wide open, the sound of people walking into Luke's office—then voices. Three men speaking. She looked nervously at Simon, who was very pale, and then at Jace, who had raised the stele in his hand and was moving the tip lightly, in a sort of square shape, across the back of the screen. As Clary stared, the square went clear, like a pane of glass. She heard Simon suck in his breath—a tiny sound, barely audible—and Jace shook his head at them both, mouthing words: *They can't see us through it, but we can see them.*

Biting her lip, Clary moved to the edge of the square and peered through it, conscious of Simon breathing down her neck. She could see the room beyond perfectly: the bookshelves, the desk with the duffel bag thrown across it—and Luke, ragged-looking and slightly stooped, his glasses pushed up to the top of his head, standing near the door. It was frightening even though she knew he couldn't see her, that the window Jace had made was like the glass in a police station interrogation room: strictly one-way.

Luke turned, looking back through the doorway. "Yes, feel free to look around," he said, his tone heavily weighted with sarcasm. "Nice of you to show such an interest."

A low chuckle sounded from the corner of the office. With an impatient flick of the wrist, Jace tapped the frame of his "window," and it opened out wider, showing more of the room. There were two men there with Luke, both in long reddish robes, their hoods pushed back. One was thin, with an elegant gray mustache and pointed beard. When he smiled, he showed blindingly white teeth. The other was burly, thickset as a wrestler, with close-cropped reddish hair.

"Those are warlocks?" Clary whispered softly.

Jace had gone rigid all over, stiff as a bar of iron. *He's afraid I'll make a run for it, try to get to Luke,* Clary thought. She wished she could reassure him that she wouldn't. There was something about those two men, in their thick cloaks the color of arterial blood, that was terrifying. "No," he whispered. He was as white as if he'd seen a ghost. "Shadowhunters. In warlock robes."

"Consider this a friendly follow-up, *Graymark*," said the man with the gray mustache.

"There's nothing friendly about you, Pangborn." Luke sat down on the edge of his desk, angling his body so it blocked the men's view of his duffel bag and its contents. Now that he was closer, Clary could see that his face and hands were badly bruised, his fingers scraped and bloody. A long cut along his neck disappeared down into his collar. *What on earth happened to him?*

"Blackwell, don't touch that—it's valuable," Luke said sternly.

The big redheaded man, who had picked up the statue of Kali from the top of the bookcase, ran his beefy fingers over it consideringly. "Nice," he said.

"Ah," said Pangborn, taking the statue from his companion. "She who was created to battle a demon who could not be killed by any god or man. *'Oh, Kali, my mother full of bliss! Enchantress of the almighty Shiva, in thy delirious joy thou dancest, clapping thy hands together. Thou art the Mover of all that moves, and we are but thy helpless toys.'*"

"Very nice," said Luke. "I didn't know you were a student of the Indian myths."

"All the stories are true," said Pangborn, and Clary felt a small shiver go up her spine. "Or have you forgotten even that?"

"I forget nothing," said Luke. Though he looked relaxed, Clary could see tension in the lines of his shoulders and mouth. "I suppose Valentine sent you?"

"He did," said Pangborn. "He thought you might have changed your mind."

"There's nothing to change my mind about. I already told you I don't know anything. Nice cloaks, by the way."

"Thanks," said Blackwell with a sly grin. "Skinned them off a couple of dead warlocks."

"Those are official Accord robes, aren't they?" Luke asked. "Are they from the Uprising?"

Pangborn chuckled softly. "Spoils of battle."

"Aren't you afraid someone might mistake you for the real thing?"

"Not," said Blackwell, "once they got up close."

Pangborn fondled the edge of his robe. "Do you remember the Uprising, Lucian?" he said softly. "That was a great and terrible day. Do you remember how we trained together for the battle?"

Luke's face twisted. "The past is the past. I don't know what to tell you gentlemen. I can't help you now. I don't know anything."

"'Anything' is such a general word, so unspecific," said Pangborn, sounding melancholy. "Surely someone who owns so many books must know *something*."

"If you want to know where to find a jog-toed swallow in springtime, I could direct you to the correct reference title. But if you want to know where the Mortal Cup has disappeared to..."

"Disappeared might not be quite the correct word," purred Pangborn. "*Hidden*, more like. Hidden by Jocelyn."

"That may be," said Luke. "So hasn't she told you where it is yet?"

"She has not yet regained consciousness," said Pangborn, carving the air with a long-fingered hand. "Valentine is disappointed. He was looking forward to their reunion."

"I'm sure she didn't reciprocate the sentiment," muttered Luke.

Pangborn cackled. "Jealous, Graymark? Perhaps you no longer feel about her the way you *used* to."

A trembling had started in Clary's fingers, so pronounced that she knitted her hands together tightly to try to stop them from shaking. *Jocelyn? Can they be talking about my mother?*

"I never felt any way about her, particularly," said Luke. "Two Shadowhunters, exiled from their own kind, you can see why we might have banded together. But I'm not going to try to interfere with Valentine's plans for her, if that's what he's worried about."

"I wouldn't say he was worried," said Pangborn. "More curious. We all wondered if you were still alive. Still recognizably human."

Luke arched his eyebrows. "And?"

"You seem well enough," said Pangborn grudgingly. He set the Kali statuette down on the shelf. "There was a child, wasn't there? A girl."

Luke looked taken aback. "What?"

"Don't play dumb," said Blackwell in his snarl of a voice. "We know the bitch had a daughter. They found photos of her in the apartment, a bedroom—"

"I thought you were asking about children of mine," Luke interrupted smoothly. "Yes, Jocelyn had a daughter. Clarissa. I assume she's run off. Did Valentine send you to find her?"

"Not us," said Pangborn. "But he is looking."

"We could search this place," added Blackwell.

"I wouldn't advise it," said Luke, and slid off the desk. There was a certain cold menace to his look as he stared down at the two men, though his expression hadn't changed. "What makes you think she's still alive? I thought Valentine sent Raveners to scour the place. Enough Ravener poison, and most people will crumble away to ashes, leave no trace behind."

"The Ravener was killed," said Pangborn. "It made Valentine suspicious."

"Everything makes Valentine suspicious," said Luke. "Maybe Jocelyn killed it. She was certainly capable."

Blackwell grunted. "Maybe."

Luke shrugged. "Look, I've got no idea where the girl is, but for what it's worth, I'd guess she's dead. She'd have turned up by now otherwise. Anyway, she's not much of a danger. She's fifteen years old, she's never heard of Valentine, and she doesn't believe in demons."

Pangborn chuckled. "A fortunate child."

"Not anymore," said Luke.

Blackwell raised his eyebrows. "You sound angry, Lucian."

"I'm not angry, I'm exasperated. I'm not planning on interfering with Valentine's plans, do you understand that? I'm not a fool."

"Really?" said Blackwell. "It's nice to see that you've

developed a healthy respect for your own skin over the years, Lucian. You weren't always so pragmatic."

"You do know," said Pangborn, his tone conversational, "that we'd trade her, Jocelyn, for the Cup? Safely delivered, right to your door. That's a promise from Valentine himself."

"I know," said Luke. "I'm not interested. I don't know where your precious Cup is, and I don't want to get involved in your politics. I hate Valentine," he added, "but I respect him. I know he'll mow down everyone in his path. I intend to be out of his way when it happens. He's a monster—a killing machine."

"Look who's talking," snarled Blackwell.

"I take it these are your preparations for removing yourself from Valentine's path?" said Pangborn, pointing a long finger at the half-concealed duffel bag on the desk. "Getting out of town, Lucian?"

Luke nodded slowly. "Going to the country. I plan to lay low for a while."

"We could stop you," said Blackwell. "Make you stay."

Luke smiled. It transformed his face. Suddenly he was no longer the kind, scholarly man who'd pushed Clary on the swings at the park and taught her how to ride a tricycle. Suddenly there was something feral behind his eyes, something vicious and cold. "You could try."

Pangborn glanced at Blackwell, who shook his head once, slowly. Pangborn turned back to Luke. "You'll notify us if you experience any sudden memory resurgence?"

Luke was still smiling. "You'll be first on my list to call."

Pangborn nodded shortly. "I suppose we'll take our leave. The Angel guard you, Lucian."

"The Angel does not guard those like me," said Luke. He picked the duffel bag up off the desk and knotted the top. "On your way, gentlemen?"

Lifting their hoods to cover their faces again, the two men left the room, followed a moment later by Luke. He paused a moment at the door, glancing around as if he wondered if he'd forgotten something. Then he shut it carefully behind him.

Clary stayed where she was, frozen, hearing the front door swing shut and the distant jingle of chain and keys as Luke refastened the padlock. She kept seeing the look on Luke's face, over and over, as he said he wasn't interested in what happened to her mother.

She felt a hand on her shoulder. "Clary?" It was Simon, his voice hesitant, almost gentle. "Are you okay?"

She shook her head, mutely. She felt far from okay. In fact, she felt like she'd never be okay again.

"Of course she isn't." It was Jace, his voice sharp and cold as ice shards. He took hold of the screen and moved it aside sharply. "At least now we know who would send a demon after your mother. Those men think she has the Mortal Cup."

Clary felt her lips thin into a straight line. "That's totally ridiculous *and* impossible."

"Maybe," said Jace, leaning against Luke's desk. He fixed her with eyes as opaque as smoked glass. "Have you ever seen those men before?"

"No." She shook her head. "Never."

"Lucian seemed to know them. To be friendly with them."

"I wouldn't say friendly," said Simon. "I'd say they were suppressing their hostility."

"They didn't kill him outright," said Jace. "They think he knows more than he's telling."

"Maybe," said Clary, "or maybe they're just reluctant to kill another Shadowhunter."

Jace laughed, a harsh, almost vicious noise that raised the hairs up on Clary's arms. "I doubt that."

She looked at him hard. "What makes you so sure? Do you know them?"

The laughter had gone from his voice entirely when he replied. "Do I know them?" he echoed. "You might say that. Those are the men who murdered my father."

9

The Circle and the Brotherhood

Clary stepped forward to touch Jace's arm, say something, anything—what did you say to someone who'd just seen his father's killers? Her hesitation turned out not to matter; Jace shrugged her touch off as if it stung. "We should go," he said, stalking out of the office and into the living room. Clary and Simon hurried after him. "We don't know when Luke might come back."

They left through the back entrance, Jace using his stele to lock up behind them, and made their way out onto the silent street. The moon hung like a locket over the city, casting pearly reflections on the water of the East River. The distant hum of cars going by over the Williamsburg Bridge filled the humid air with a sound like beating wings. Simon said, "Does anyone want to tell me where we're going?"

"To the L train," said Jace calmly.

"You've got to be kidding me," Simon said, blinking. "Demon slayers take the subway?"

"It's faster than driving."

"I thought it'd be something cooler, like a van with DEATH TO DEMONS painted on the outside, or..."

Jace didn't even bother to interrupt. Clary shot Jace a sideways look. Sometimes, when Jocelyn was really angry about something or was in one of her upset moods, she would get what Clary called "scary-calm." It was a calm that made Clary think of the deceptive hard sheen of ice just before it cracked under your weight. Jace was scary-calm. His face was expressionless, but something burned at the backs of his tawny eyes.

"Simon," she said. "Enough."

Simon shot her a look as if to say, *Whose side are you on?* but Clary ignored him. She was still watching Jace as they turned onto Kent Avenue. The lights of the bridge behind them lit his hair to an unlikely halo. She wondered if it was wrong that she was glad in some way that the men who'd taken her mother were the same men who'd killed Jace's father all those years ago. For now, at least, he'd have to help her find Jocelyn, whether he wanted to or not. For now, at least, he couldn't leave her alone.

"You live *here?*" Simon stood staring up at the old cathedral, with its broken-in windows and doors sealed with yellow police tape. "But it's a church."

Jace reached into the neck of his shirt and pulled out a brass key on the end of a chain. It looked like the sort of key one might use to open an old chest in an attic. Clary watched him curiously—he hadn't locked the door behind him when they'd left the Institute before, just let it slam shut. "We find it useful to inhabit hallowed ground."

"I get that but, no offense, this place is a dump," Simon said, looking dubiously at the bent iron fence that surrounded the ancient building, the trash piled up beside the steps.

Clary let her mind relax. She imagined herself taking one of her mother's turpentine rags and dabbing at the view in front of her, cleaning away the glamour as if it were old paint.

There it was: the true vision, glowing through the false one like light through dark glass. She saw the soaring spires of the cathedral, the dull gleam of the leaded windows, the brass plate fixed to the stone wall beside the door, the Institute's name etched into it. She held the vision for a moment before letting it go almost with a sigh.

"It's a glamour, Simon," she said. "It doesn't really look like this."

"If this is your idea of glamour, I'm having second thoughts about letting you make me over."

Jace fitted the key into the lock, glancing over his shoulder at Simon. "I'm not sure you're quite sensible of the honor I'm doing you," he said. "You'll be one of the few mundanes who has ever been inside the Institute."

"Probably the smell keeps the rest of them away."

"Ignore him," Clary said to Jace, and elbowed Simon in the side. "He always says exactly what comes into his head. No filters."

"Filters are for cigarettes and coffee," Simon muttered under his breath as they went inside. "Two things I could use right now, incidentally."

Clary thought longingly of coffee as they made their way up a winding set of stone stairs, each one carved with a glyph. She was beginning to recognize some of them—they tantalized her sight the way half-heard words in a foreign language sometimes tantalized her hearing, as if by just concentrating harder she could force some meaning out of them.

Clary and the two boys reached the elevator and rode up in silence. She was still thinking about coffee, big mugs of coffee that were half milk the way her mother would make them in the morning. Sometimes Luke would bring them bags of sweet rolls from the Golden Carriage Bakery in Chinatown. At the thought of Luke, Clary's stomach tightened, her appetite vanishing.

The elevator came to a hissing stop, and they were again in the entryway Clary remembered. Jace shrugged off his jacket, threw it over the back of a nearby chair, and whistled through his teeth. In a few seconds Church appeared, slinking low to the ground, his yellow eyes gleaming in the dusty air. "Church," Jace said, kneeling down to stroke the cat's gray head. "Where's Alec, Church? Where's Hodge?"

Church arched his back and meowed. Jace crinkled his nose, which Clary might have found cute in other circumstances. "Are they in the library?" He stood up, and Church shook himself, trotted a little way down the corridor, and glanced back over his shoulder. Jace followed the cat as if this were the most natural thing in the world, indicating with a wave of his hand that Clary and Simon were to fall into step behind him.

"I don't like cats," Simon said, his shoulder bumping Clary's as they maneuvered the narrow hallway.

"It's unlikely," Jace said, "knowing Church, that he likes you, either."

They were passing through one of the corridors that were lined with bedrooms. Simon's eyebrows rose. "How many people live here, exactly?"

"It's an institute," Clary said. "A place where Shadowhunters can stay when they're in the city. Like a sort of combination safe haven and research facility."

"I thought it was a church."

"It's *inside* a church."

"Because *that's* not confusing." She could hear the nerves under his flippant tone. Instead of shushing him, Clary reached down and took his hand, winding her fingers through his cold ones. His hand was clammy, but he returned the pressure with a grateful squeeze.

"I know it's weird," she said quietly, "but you just have to go along with it. Trust me."

Simon's dark eyes were serious. "I trust you," he said. "I don't trust *him*." He cut his glance toward Jace, who was walking a few paces ahead of them, apparently conversing with the cat. Clary wondered what they were talking about. Politics? Opera? The high price of tuna?

"Well, try," she said. "Right now he's the best chance I'm going to have of finding my mom."

A little shudder passed over Simon. "This place feels not right to me," he whispered.

Clary remembered how she'd felt waking up here this morning—as if everything were both alien and familiar at the same time. For Simon, clearly, there was nothing of that familiarity, only the sense of the strange, the alien and inimical. "You don't have to stay with me," she said, though she'd fought Jace on the train for the right to keep Simon with her, pointing out that after his three days of watching Luke, he might well know something that would be useful to them once they had a chance to break it down in detail.

"Yes," Simon said, "I do." And he let go of her hand as they turned through a doorway and found themselves inside a kitchen. It was an enormous kitchen, and unlike the rest of the Institute, it was all modern, with steel counters and glassed-in shelves holding rows of crockery. Next to a red cast-iron stove stood Isabelle, a round spoon in her hand, her dark hair pinned up on top of her head. Steam was rising from the pot, and ingredients were strewn everywhere—tomatoes, chopped garlic and onions, strings of dark-looking herbs, grated piles of cheese, some shelled peanuts, a handful of olives, and a whole fish, its eye staring glassily upward.

"I'm making soup," Isabelle said, waving a spoon at Jace. "Are you hungry?" She glanced behind him then, her dark gaze taking in Simon as well as Clary. "Oh, my God," she said with finality. "You brought another mundie here? Hodge is going to kill you."

Simon cleared his throat. "I'm Simon," he said.

Isabelle ignored him. "JACE WAYLAND," she said. "Explain yourself."

Jace was glaring at the cat. "I told you to bring me to Alec! Backstabbing Judas."

Church rolled onto his back, purring contentedly.

"Don't blame Church," Isabelle said. "It's not his fault Hodge is going to kill you." She plunged the spoon back into the pot. Clary wondered what exactly peanut-fish-olive-tomato soup tasted like.

"I had to bring him," Jace said. "Isabelle—today I saw two of the men who killed my father."

Isabelle's shoulders tightened, but when she turned around, she looked more upset than surprised. "I don't suppose he's one of them?" she asked, pointing her spoon at Simon.

To Clary's surprise, Simon said nothing to this. He was too busy staring at Isabelle, rapt and openmouthed. Of course, Clary realized with a sharp stab of annoyance. Isabelle was exactly Simon's type—tall, glamourous, and beautiful. Come to think of it, maybe that was everyone's type. Clary stopped wondering about the peanut-fish-olive-tomato soup and started wondering what would happen if she dumped the contents of the pot on Isabelle's head.

"Of course not," Jace said. "Do you think he'd be alive now if he were?"

Isabelle cast an indifferent look at Simon. "I suppose not," she said, absently dropping a piece of fish on the floor. Church fell on it ravenously.

"No wonder he brought us here," said Jace disgustedly. "I can't believe you've been stuffing him with fish again. He's looking distinctly podgy."

"He does not look podgy. Besides, none of the rest of you ever eat anything. I got this recipe from a water sprite at the Chelsea Market. He said it was delicious—"

"If you knew how to cook, maybe I *would* eat," Jace muttered.

Isabelle froze, her spoon poised dangerously. "*What* did you say?"

Jace edged toward the fridge. "I said I'm going to look for a snack to eat."

"That's what I thought you said." Isabelle returned her attention to the soup. Simon continued to stare at Isabelle. Clary, inexplicably furious, dropped her backpack on the floor and followed Jace to the refrigerator.

"I can't believe you're eating," she hissed.

"What should I be doing instead?" he inquired with maddening calm. The inside of the fridge was filled with milk cartons whose expiration dates reached back several weeks, and plastic Tupperware containers labeled with masking tape lettered in red ink: HODGE'S. DO NOT EAT.

"Wow, he's like a crazy roommate," Clary observed, momentarily diverted.

"What, Hodge? He just likes things in order." Jace took one of the containers out of the fridge and opened it. "Hmm. Spaghetti."

"Don't ruin your appetite," Isabelle called.

"That," said Jace, kicking the fridge door shut and seizing a fork from a drawer, "is exactly what I intend to do." He looked at Clary. "Want some?"

She shook her head.

"Of course not," he said around a mouthful, "you ate all those sandwiches."

"It wasn't *that* many sandwiches." She glanced over at Simon, who appeared to have succeeded in engaging Isabelle in conversation. "Can we go find Hodge now?"

"You seem awfully eager to get out of here."

"Don't you want to tell him what we saw?"

"I haven't decided yet." Jace set the container down and thoughtfully licked spaghetti sauce off his knuckle. "But if you want to go so badly—"

"I do."

"Fine."

He seemed awfully calm, she thought, not scary-calm as he had been before, but more contained than he ought to be.

She wondered how often he let glimpses of his real self peek through the facade that was as hard and shiny as the coat of lacquer on one of her mother's Japanese boxes.

"Where are you going?" Simon looked up as they reached the door. Jagged bits of dark hair fell into his eyes; he looked stupidly dazed, Clary thought unkindly, as if someone had hit him across the back of the head with a two-by-four.

"To find Hodge," she said. "I need to tell him about what happened at Luke's."

Isabelle looked up. "Are you going to tell him that you saw those men, Jace? The ones that—"

"I don't know." He cut her off. "So keep it to yourself for now."

She shrugged. "All right. Are you going to come back? Do you want any soup?"

"No," said Jace.

"Do you think Hodge will want any soup?"

"No one wants any soup."

"I want some soup," Simon said.

"No, you don't," said Jace. "You just want to sleep with Isabelle."

Simon was appalled. "That is *not* true."

"How flattering," Isabelle murmured into the soup, but she was smirking.

"Oh, yes it is," said Jace. "Go ahead and ask her—then she can turn you down and the rest of us can get on with our lives while you fester in miserable humiliation." He snapped his fingers. "Hurry up, mundie boy, we've got work to do."

Simon looked away, flushed with embarrassment. Clary, who a moment ago would have been meanly pleased, felt a rush of anger toward Jace. "Leave him alone," she snapped. "There's no need to be sadistic just because he isn't one of *you*."

"One of *us*," said Jace, but the sharp look had gone out of his eyes. "I'm going to find Hodge. Come along or not, it's your choice." The kitchen door swung shut behind him, leaving Clary alone with Simon and Isabelle.

Isabelle ladled some of the soup into a bowl and pushed it across the counter toward Simon without looking at him. She was still smirking, though—Clary could feel it. The soup was a dark green color, studded with floating brown things.

"I'm going with Jace," Clary said. "Simon...?"

"Mmgnstayhr," he mumbled, looking at his feet.

"What?"

"I'm going to stay here." Simon parked himself on a stool. "I'm hungry."

"Fine." Clary's throat felt tight, as if she'd swallowed something either very hot or very cold. She stalked out of the kitchen, Church slinking at her feet like a cloudy gray shadow.

In the hallway Jace was twirling one of the seraph blades between his fingers. He pocketed it when he saw her. "Kind of you to leave the lovebirds to it."

Clary frowned at him. "Why are you always such an asshat?"

"An asshat?" Jace looked as if he were about to laugh.

"What you said to Simon—"

"I was trying to save him some pain. Isabelle will cut out his heart and walk all over it in high-heeled boots. That's what she does to boys like that."

"Is that what she did to you?" Clary said, but Jace only

shook his head before turning to Church.

"Hodge," he said. "And *really* Hodge this time. Bring us anywhere else, and I'll make you into a tennis racket."

The Persian snorted and slunk down the hall ahead of them. Clary, trailing a little behind Jace, could see the stress and tiredness in the line of Jace's shoulders. She wondered if the tension ever really left him. "Jace."

He looked at her. "What?"

"I'm sorry. For snapping at you."

He chuckled. "Which time?"

"You snap at me, too, you know."

"I know," he said, surprising her. "There's something about you that's so—"

"Irritating?"

"Unsettling."

She wanted to ask if he meant that in a good or a bad way, but didn't. She was too afraid he'd make a joke out of the answer. She cast about for something else to say. "Does Isabelle always make dinner for you?" she asked.

"No, thank God. Most of the time the Lightwoods are here and Maryse—that's Isabelle's mother—she cooks for us. She's an amazing cook." He looked dreamy, the way Simon had looked gazing at Isabelle over the soup.

"Then how come she never taught Isabelle?" They were passing through the music room now, where she'd found Jace playing the piano that morning. Shadows had gathered thickly in the corners.

"Isabelle never wanted to learn. She's always been first and foremost interested in being a fighter. She comes from a long line of women warriors," he said, and there was a tinge of pride in his voice. "She's one of the best Shadowhunters I've ever known."

"Better than Alec?"

Church, streaking soundlessly ahead of them through the gloom, came to a sudden halt and meowed. He was crouched at the foot of a metal spiral staircase that spun up into a hazy half-light overhead. "So he's in the greenhouse," Jace said. It took Clary a moment before she realized he was speaking to the cat. "No surprise there."

"The greenhouse?" Clary said.

Jace swung himself onto the first step. "Hodge likes it up there. He grows medicinal plants, things we can use. Most of them only grow in Idris. I think it reminds him of home."

Clary followed him. Her shoes clattered on the metal steps; Jace's didn't. "Is he better than Isabelle?" she asked again. "Alec, I mean."

He paused and looked down at her, leaning down from the steps as if he were poised to fall. She remembered her dream: *angels, falling and burning*. "Better?" he said. "At demon-slaying? No, not really. He's never killed a demon."

"Really?"

"I don't know why not. Maybe because he's always protecting Izzy and me." They had reached the top of the stairs. A set of double doors greeted them, carved with patterns of leaves and vines. Jace shouldered them open.

The smell struck Clary the moment she passed through the doors: a green, sharp smell, the smell of living and growing things, of dirt and the roots that grew in dirt. She had been expecting something much smaller, something the size of the little greenhouse out behind St. Xavier's, where the AP biology students cloned pea pods, or whatever it was they did. This was a huge glass-walled enclosure, lined with trees whose thickly leaved branches breathed out cool green-scented air. There were bushes hung with glossy berries, red and purple and black, and small trees hung with oddly-shaped fruits she'd never seen before.

Clary exhaled. "It smells like…" *Springtime,* she thought, *before the heat comes and crushes the leaves into pulp and withers the petals off the flowers.*

"Home," said Jace, "to me." He pushed aside a hanging frond and ducked past it. Clary followed.

The greenhouse was laid out in what seemed to Clary's untrained eye no particular pattern, but everywhere she looked was a riot of color: blue purple blossoms spilling down the side of a shining green hedge, a trailing vine studded with jewel toned orange buds. They emerged into a cleared space where a low granite bench rested against the bole of a drooping tree with silvery green leaves. Water glimmered in a stone-bound rock pool. Hodge sat on the bench, his black bird perched on his shoulder. He had been staring thoughtfully down at the water, but looked skyward at their approach. Clary followed his gaze upward and saw the glass roof of the greenhouse shining above them like the surface of an inverted lake.

"You look like you're waiting for something," Jace observed, breaking a leaf off a nearby bough and twirling it between his fingers. For someone who seemed so contained, he had a lot of nervous habits. Perhaps he just liked to be constantly in motion.

"I was lost in thought." Hodge rose from the bench, stretching out his arm for Hugo. The smile faded from his face as he looked at them. "What happened? You look as if—"

"We were attacked," Jace said shortly. "Forsaken."

"Forsaken warriors? Here?"

"Warrior," said Jace. "We only saw one."

"But Dorothea said there were more," Clary added.

"Dorothea?" Hodge held a hand up. "This might be easier if you took events in order."

"Right." Jace gave Clary a warning look, cutting her off before she could start talking. Then he launched into a recital of the afternoon's events, leaving out only one detail—that the men in Luke's apartment had been the same men who'd killed his father seven years ago. "Clary's mother's friend—or whatever he is, really—goes by the name Luke Garroway," Jace finished finally. "But while we were at his house, the two men who claimed they were emissaries of Valentine referred to him as Lucian Graymark."

"And their names were..."

"Pangborn," said Jace. "And Blackwell."

Hodge had gone very pale. Against his gray skin the scar along his cheek stood out like a twist of red wire. "It is as I feared," he said, half to himself. "The Circle is rising again."

Clary looked at Jace for clarification, but he seemed as puzzled as she was. "The Circle?" he said.

Hodge was shaking his head as if trying to clear cobwebs from his brain. "Come with me," he said. "It's time I showed you something."

The gas lamps were lit in the library, and the polished oak surfaces of the furniture seemed to smolder like somber jewels. Streaked with shadows, the stark faces of the angels holding up the enormous desk looked even more suffused with pain. Clary sat on the red sofa, legs drawn up, Jace leaning restlessly against the sofa arm beside her. "Hodge, if you need help looking—"

"Not at all." Hodge emerged from behind the desk, brushing dust from the knees of his trousers. "I've found it."

He was carrying a large book bound in brown leather. He paged through it with an anxious finger, blinking owl-like behind his glasses and muttering: "Where ... where ... ah, here it is!" He cleared his throat before he read aloud: "*I hereby render unconditional obedience to the Circle and its principles... I will be ready to risk my life at any time for the Circle, in order to preserve the purity of the bloodlines of Idris, and for the mortal world with whose safety we are charged.*"

Jace made a face. "What was that from?"

"It was the loyalty oath of the Circle of Raziel, twenty years ago," said Hodge, sounding strangely tired.

"It sounds creepy," said Clary. "Like a fascist organization or something."

Hodge set the book down. He looked as pained and grave as the statuary angels beneath the desk. "They were a group," he said slowly, "of Shadowhunters, led by Valentine, dedicated to wiping out all Downworlders and returning the world to a 'purer' state. Their plan was to wait for the Downworlders to arrive in Idris to sign the Accords. They must be signed again each fifteen years, to keep their magic potent," he added, for Clary's benefit. "Then, they planned to slaughter them all, unarmed and defenseless. This terrible act, they thought, would spark off a war between humans and Downworlders—one they intended to win."

"That was the Uprising," said Jace, finally recognizing in

Hodge's story one that was already familiar to him. "I didn't know Valentine and his followers had a name."

"The name isn't spoken often nowadays," said Hodge. "Their existence remains an embarrassment to the Clave. Most documents pertaining to them have been destroyed."

"Then why do you have a copy of that oath?" Jace asked.

Hodge hesitated—only for a moment, but Clary saw it, and felt a small and inexplicable shiver of apprehension run up her spine. "Because," he said, finally, "I helped write it."

Jace looked up at that. "You were in the Circle."

"I was. Many of us were." Hodge was looking straight ahead. "Clary's mother as well."

Clary jerked back as if he'd slapped her. "*What?*"

"I said—"

"I know what you said! My mother would never have belonged to something like that. Some kind of—some kind of hate group."

"It wasn't—" Jace began, but Hodge cut him off.

"I doubt," he said slowly, as if the words pained him, "that she had much choice."

Clary stared. "What are you talking about? Why wouldn't she have had a choice?"

"Because," said Hodge, "she was Valentine's wife."

Part Two

Easy is the Descent

Facilis descensus Averni:
Noctes atque dies patet atri ianua Ditis.
Sed gradium revocare superasque evadere ad auras;
Hoc opus, hic labor, est.
—Virgil, *The Aeneid*

10

City of Bones

There was a moment of astonished silence before both Clary and Jace began speaking at once.

"Valentine had a wife? He was *married?* I thought—"

"That's impossible! My mother would never—she was only ever married to my father! She didn't have an ex-husband!"

Hodge raised his hands wearily. "Children—"

"I'm not a child." Clary spun away from the desk. "And I don't want to hear any more."

"Clary," said Hodge. The kindness in his voice hurt; she turned slowly, and looked at him across the room. She thought how odd it was that, with his gray hair and scarred face, he looked so much older than her mother. And yet they had been "young people" together, had joined the Circle together, had known Valentine together. "My mother wouldn't..." she began, and trailed off. She was no longer sure how well she knew Jocelyn. Her mother had become a stranger to her, a liar, a hider of secrets. What *wouldn't* she have done?

"Your mother left the Circle," said Hodge. He didn't move toward her but watched her across the room with a bird's bright-eyed stillness. "Once we realized how extreme Valentine's views had become—once we knew what he was prepared to do—many of us left. Lucian was the first to leave. That was a blow to Valentine. They had been very close." Hodge shook his head. "Then Michael Wayland. Your father, Jace."

Jace raised his eyebrows, but said nothing.

"There were those who stayed loyal. Pangborn. Blackwell. The Lightwoods—"

"The Lightwoods? You mean Robert and Maryse?" Jace looked thunderstruck. "What about you? When did you leave?"

"I didn't," said Hodge softly. "Neither did they... We were afraid, too afraid of what he might do. After the Uprising the loyalists like Blackwell and Pangborn fled. We stayed and cooperated with the Clave. Gave them names. Helped them track down the ones who had run away. For that we received clemency."

"Clemency?" Jace's look was quick, but Hodge saw it.

He said, "You are thinking of the curse that binds me here, aren't you? You always assumed it was a vengeance spell cast by an angry demon or warlock. I let you think it. But it is not the truth. The curse that binds me was cast by the Clave."

"For being in the Circle?" Jace asked, his face a mask of astonishment.

"For not leaving it before the Uprising."

"But the Lightwoods weren't punished," Clary said. "Why not? They'd done the same thing you'd done."

"There were extenuating circumstances in their case—

they were married, they had a child. Although it is not as if they reside in this outpost, far from home, by their own choice. We were banished here, the three of us—the four of us, I should say; Alec was a squalling baby when we left the Glass City. They can return to Idris on official business only, and then only for short times. I can never return. I will never see the Glass City again."

Jace stared. It was as if he were looking at his tutor with new eyes, Clary thought, though it wasn't Jace who had changed. He said, "The Law is hard, but it is the Law."

"I taught you that," said Hodge, dry amusement in his voice. "And now you turn my lessons back at me. Rightly too." He looked as if he wanted to sink down into a nearby chair, but held himself upright nevertheless. In his rigid posture there was something of the soldier he had once been, Clary thought.

"Why didn't you tell me before?" she said. "That my mother was married to Valentine. You knew her name—"

"I knew her as Jocelyn Fairchild, not Jocelyn Fray," said Hodge. "And you were so insistent on her ignorance of the Shadow World, you convinced me it could not be the Jocelyn I knew—and perhaps I did not want to believe it. No one would wish for Valentine's return." He shook his head again. "When I sent for the Brothers of the Bone City this morning, I had no idea just what news we would have for them," he said. "When the Clave finds out Valentine may have returned, that he is seeking the Cup, there will be an uproar. I can only hope it does not disrupt the Accords."

"I bet Valentine would like that," Jace said. "But why does he want the Cup so badly?"

Hodge's face was gray. "Isn't that obvious?" he said. "So he can build himself an army."

Jace looked startled. "But that would never—"

"Dinnertime!" It was Isabelle, standing framed in the door of the library. She still had the spoon in her hand, though her hair had escaped from its bun and was straggling down her neck. "Sorry if I'm interrupting," she added, as an afterthought.

"Dear God," said Jace, "the dread hour is nigh."

Hodge looked alarmed. "I—I—I had a very filling breakfast," he stammered. "I mean lunch. A filling lunch. I couldn't possibly eat—"

"I threw out the soup," Isabelle said. "And ordered Chinese from that place downtown."

Jace unhitched himself from the desk and stretched. "Great. I'm starved."

"I might be able to eat a bite," admitted Hodge meekly.

"You two are terrible liars," said Isabelle darkly. "Look, I know you don't like my cooking—"

"So stop doing it," Jace advised her reasonably. "Did you order mu shu pork? You know I love mu shu pork."

Isabelle cast her eyes skyward. "Yes. It's in the kitchen."

"Awesome." Jace ducked by her with an affectionate ruffle of her hair. Hodge went after him, pausing only to pat Isabelle on the shoulder—then he was gone, with a funny apologetic duck of the head. Had Clary really only a few minutes before been able to see the ghost in him of his old warrior self?

Isabelle was looking after Jace and Hodge, twisting the spoon in her scarred, pale fingers. Clary said, "Is he really?"

Isabelle didn't look at her. "Is who really what?"

"Jace. Is he really a terrible liar?"

Now Isabelle did turn her eyes on Clary, and they were large and dark and unexpectedly thoughtful. "He's not a liar at all. Not about important things. He'll tell you horrible truths, but he won't lie." She paused before she added quietly: "That's why it's generally better not to ask him anything unless you know you can stand to hear the answer."

The kitchen was warm and full of light and the salt-sweet smell of takeout Chinese food. The smell reminded Clary of home; she sat and looked at her glistening plate of noodles, toyed with her fork, and tried not to look at Simon, who was staring at Isabelle with an expression more glazed than the General Tso's Duckling.

"Well, I think it's kind of romantic," said Isabelle, sucking tapioca pearls through an enormous pink straw.

"What is?" asked Simon, instantly alert.

"That whole business about Clary's mother being married to Valentine," said Isabelle. Jace and Hodge had filled her in, though Clary noted that both had left out the part about the Lightwoods having been in the Circle, and the curses the Clave had handed down. "So now he's back from the dead and he's come looking for her. Maybe he wants to get back together."

"I kind of doubt he sent a Ravener demon to her house because he wants to 'get back together,'" said Alec, who had turned up when the food was served. Nobody had asked him where he'd been, and he hadn't offered the information. He was sitting next to Jace, across from Clary, and was avoiding looking at her.

"It wouldn't be my move," Jace agreed. "First the candy and flowers, then the apology letters, *then* the ravenous demon hordes. In that order."

"He might have sent her candy and flowers," Isabelle said. "We don't know."

"Isabelle," said Hodge patiently, "this is the man who rained down destruction on Idris the like of which it had never seen, who set Shadowhunter against Downworlder and made the streets of the Glass City run with blood."

"That's sort of hot," Isabelle argued, "that evil thing."

Simon tried to look menacing, but gave it up when he saw Clary staring at him. "So why does Valentine want this Cup so bad, and why does he think Clary's mom has it?" he asked.

"You said it was so he could make an army," Clary said, turning to Hodge. "You mean because you can use the Cup to make Shadowhunters?"

"Yes."

"So Valentine could just walk up to any guy on the street and make a Shadowhunter out of him? Just with the Cup?" Simon leaned forward. "Would it work on me?"

Hodge gave him a long and measured look. "Possibly," he said. "But the reason that very few mundanes are ever chosen to Ascend and become Nephilim is that most would never survive the transition. It takes special strength and resilience. Before they can be turned, they must be extensively trained and tested—but Valentine would never bother with that. He would use the Cup on any human he could capture, and cull out the twenty percent who survived to become his army. An army he could use to attack the Clave."

Alec was looking at Hodge with the same horror Clary

felt. "How do you know he'd do that?"

"Because," Hodge said, "when he was in the Circle, that was his plan. He said it was the only way to build the kind of force that was needed to defend our world."

"But that's murder," said Isabelle, who looked a little green.

"He said that we had made the world safe for humans for a thousand years," said Hodge, "and now was their time to repay us with their own sacrifice."

"Their *lives*?" demanded Jace, his cheeks flushed. "That goes against everything we're supposed to be about. Protecting the helpless, safeguarding humanity—"

Hodge pushed his plate away. "Valentine was insane," he said. "Brilliant, but insane. He cared about nothing but killing demons and Downworlders. Nothing but making the world pure. He would have sacrificed his own son for the cause and could not understand how anyone else would not."

"He had a son?" said Alec.

"I was speaking figuratively," said Hodge, reaching for his handkerchief. He used it to mop his forehead before returning it to his pocket. His hand, Clary saw, was trembling slightly. "When his land burned, when his home was destroyed, it was assumed that he had burned himself and the Cup to ashes rather than relinquish either to the Clave. His bones were found in the ashes, along with the bones of his wife."

"But my mother lived," said Clary. "She didn't die in that fire."

"And neither, it seems now, did Valentine," said Hodge. "The Clave will not be pleased to have been fooled. But more importantly, they will want to secure the Cup. And more importantly than that, they will want to make sure Valentine does not."

"It seems to me that the first thing we'd better do is find Clary's mother," said Jace. "Find her, find the Cup, get it before Valentine does."

This sounded fine to Clary, but Hodge looked at Jace as if he'd proposed juggling nitroglycerine as a solution. "Absolutely not."

"Then what do we do?"

"Nothing," Hodge said. "All this is best left to skilled, experienced Shadowhunters."

"I am skilled," protested Jace, with a wave of his hand. A silver ring glittered on one slim finger, a ring Clary didn't recall him wearing before. "I *am* experienced."

Hodge's tone was firm, nearly parental. "I know that you are, but you're still a child, or nearly one."

Jace looked at Hodge through slitted eyes. His lashes were long, casting shadows down over his angular cheekbones. In someone else it would have been a shy look, even an apologetic one, but on Jace it looked narrow and menacing. "I am *not* a child."

"Hodge is right," said Alec. He was looking at Jace, and Clary thought that he must be one of the few people in the world who looked at Jace not as if he were afraid of him, but as if he were afraid *for* him. "Valentine is dangerous. I know you're a good Shadowhunter. You're probably the best our age. But Valentine's one of the best there ever was. It took a huge battle to bring him down."

"And he didn't exactly stay down," said Isabelle, examining her fork tines. "Apparently."

"But we're here," said Jace. "We're here and because of the

Accords, nobody else is. If we don't do something—"

"We are going to do something," said Hodge. "I'll send the Clave a message tonight. They could have a force of Nephilim here by tomorrow if they wanted. They'll take care of this. You have done more than enough."

Jace subsided, but his eyes were still glittering. "I don't like it."

"You don't have to like it," said Alec. "You just have to shut up and not do anything stupid."

"But what about my mother?" Clary demanded. "She can't wait for some representative from the Clave to show up. Valentine has her right now—Pangborn and Blackwell said so—and he could be..." She couldn't bring herself to say the word *torture*, but Clary knew she wasn't the only one thinking it. Suddenly no one at the table could meet her eyes.

Except Simon. "Hurting her," he said, finishing her sentence. "Except, Clary, they also said she was unconscious and that Valentine wasn't happy about it. He seems to be waiting for her to wake up."

"I'd stay unconscious if I were her," Isabelle muttered.

"But that could be any time," said Clary, ignoring Isabelle. "I thought the Clave was pledged to protect people. Shouldn't there be Shadowhunters here right now? Shouldn't they already be searching for her?"

"That would be easier," snapped Alec, "if we had the slightest idea where to look."

"But we do," said Jace.

"You do?" Clary looked at him, startled and eager. "Where?"

"Here." Jace leaned forward and touched his fingers to the side of her temple, so gently that a flush crept up her face.

"Everything we need to know is locked up in your head, under those pretty red curls."

Clary reached up to touch her hair protectively. "I don't think—"

"So what are you going to do?" Simon asked sharply. "Cut her head open to get at it?"

Jace's eyes sparked, but he said calmly, "Not at all. The Silent Brothers can help her retrieve her memories."

"You *hate* the Silent Brothers," protested Isabelle.

"I don't hate them," said Jace candidly. "I'm afraid of them. It's not the same thing."

"I thought you said they were librarians," said Clary.

"They are librarians."

Simon whistled. "Those must be some killer late fees."

"The Silent Brothers are archivists, but that is not all they are," interrupted Hodge, sounding as if he were running out of patience. "In order to strengthen their minds, they have chosen to take upon themselves some of the most powerful runes ever created. The power of these runes is so great that the use of them—" He broke off and Clary heard Alec's voice in her head, saying: *They mutilate themselves.* "Well, it warps and twists their physical forms. They are not warriors in the sense that other Shadowhunters are warriors. Their powers are of the mind, not the body."

"They can read minds?" Clary said in a small voice.

"Among other things. They are among the most feared of all demon hunters."

"I don't know," said Simon, "it doesn't sound so bad to me. I'd rather have someone mess around inside my head than chop it off."

"Then you're a bigger idiot than you look," said Jace, regarding him with scorn.

"Jace is right," said Isabelle, ignoring Simon. "The Silent Brothers *are* really creepy."

Hodge's hand was clenched on the table. "They are very powerful," he said. "They walk in darkness and do not speak, but they can crack open a man's mind the way you might crack open a walnut—and leave him screaming alone in the dark if that is what they desire."

Clary looked at Jace, appalled. "You want to give me to *them?*"

"I want them to *help* you." Jace leaned across the table, so close she could see the darker amber flecks in his light eyes. "Maybe we don't get to look for the Cup," he said softly. "Maybe the Clave will do that. But what's in your mind belongs to you. Someone's hidden secrets there, secrets you can't see. Don't you want to know the truth about your own life?"

"I don't want someone else inside my head," she said weakly. She knew he was right, but the idea of turning herself over to beings that even the Shadowhunters thought were creepy sent a chill through her blood.

"I'll go with you," said Jace. "I'll stay with you while they do it."

"That's enough." Simon had stood up from the table, red with anger. "Leave her alone."

Alec glanced over at Simon as if he'd just noticed him, raking tumbled black hair out of his eyes and blinking. "What are you still doing here, mundane?"

Simon ignored him. "I said, leave her alone."

Jace glanced over at him, a slow, sweetly poisonous

glance. "Alec is right," he said. "The Institute is sworn to shelter Shadowhunters, not their mundane friends. Especially when they've worn out their welcome."

Isabelle got up and took Simon's arm. "I'll show him out." For a moment it looked like he might resist her, but he caught Clary's eye across the table as she shook her head slightly. He subsided. Head up, he let Isabelle lead him from the room.

Clary stood up. "I'm tired," she said. "I want to go to sleep."

"You've hardly eaten anything—" Jace protested.

She brushed aside his reaching hand. "I'm not hungry."

It was cooler in the hallway than it had been in the kitchen. Clary leaned against the wall, pulling at her shirt, which was sticking to the cold sweat on her chest. Far down the hall she could see Isabelle's and Simon's retreating figures, swallowed up by shadows. She watched them go silently, a shivery odd feeling growing in the pit of her stomach. When had Simon become Isabelle's responsibility, instead of hers? If there was one thing she was learning from all this, it was how easy it was to lose everything you had always thought you'd have forever.

The room was all gold and white, with high walls that gleamed like enamel, and a roof, high above, clear and glittering like diamonds. Clary wore a green velvet dress and carried a gold fan in her hand. Her hair, twisted into a knot that spilled curls, made her head feel strangely heavy every time she turned to look behind her.

"You see someone more interesting than me?" asked Simon. In the dream he was mysteriously an expert dancer. He steered her through the crowd as if she were a leaf caught in a river current. He was wearing all black, like a Shadowhunter, and it showed his coloring to good advantage: dark hair, lightly browned skin, white

teeth. He's handsome, *Clary thought, with a jolt of surprise.*

"There's no one more interesting than you," Clary said. "It's just this place. I've never seen anything like it." She turned again as they passed a champagne fountain: an enormous silver dish, the centerpiece a mermaid with a jar pouring sparkling wine down her bare back. People were filling their glasses from the dish, laughing and talking. The mermaid turned her head as Clary passed, and smiled. The smile showed white teeth as sharp as a vampire's.

"Welcome to the Glass City," said a voice that wasn't Simon's. Clary found that Simon had disappeared and she was now dancing with Jace, who was wearing white, the material of his shirt a thin cotton; she could see the black Marks through it. There was a bronze chain around his throat, and his hair and eyes looked more gold than ever; she thought about how she would like to paint his portrait with the dull gold paint one sometimes saw in Russian icons.

"Where's Simon?" she asked as they spun again around the champagne fountain. Clary saw Isabelle there, with Alec, both of them in royal blue. They were holding hands like Hansel and Gretel in the dark forest.

"This place is for the living," said Jace. His hands were cool on hers, and she was aware of them in a way she had not been of Simon's.

She narrowed her eyes at him. "What do you mean?"

He leaned close. She could feel his lips against her ear. They were not cool at all. "Wake up, Clary," he whispered. "Wake up. Wake up."

She bolted upright in bed, gasping, hair plastered to her neck with cold sweat. Her wrists were held in a hard grip; she tried to pull away, then realized who was restraining her. "Jace?"

"Yeah." He was sitting on the edge of the bed—how had she gotten into a bed?—looking tousled and half-awake, with early-morning hair and sleepy eyes.

"Let go of me."

"Sorry." His fingers slipped from her wrists. "You tried to hit me the second I said your name."

"I'm a little jumpy, I guess." She glanced around. She was in a small bedroom furnished in dark wood. By the quality of the faint light coming in through the half-open window, she guessed it was dawn, or just after. Her backpack was propped against one wall. "How did I get here? I don't remember..."

"I found you asleep on the floor in the hallway." Jace sounded amused. "Hodge helped me get you into bed. Thought you'd be more comfortable in a guest room than in the infirmary."

"Wow. I don't remember anything." She ran her hands through her hair, pushing draggled curls out of her eyes. "What time is it, anyway?"

"About five."

"In the *morning*?" She glared at him. "You'd better have a good reason for waking me up."

"Why, were you having a good dream?"

She could still hear music in her ears, feel the heavy jewels brushing her cheeks. "I don't remember."

He stood up. "One of the Silent Brothers is here to see you. Hodge sent me to wake you up. Actually, he offered to wake you up himself, but since it's five a.m., I figured you'd be less cranky if you had something nice to look at."

"Meaning you?"

"What else?"

"I didn't agree to this, you know," she snapped. "This Silent Brother thing."

"Do you want to find your mother," he said, "or not?"

She stared at him.

"You just have to meet Brother Jeremiah. That's all. You might even like him. He's got a great sense of humor for a guy who never says anything."

She put her head in her hands. "Get out. Get out so I can change."

She swung her legs out of bed the moment the door shut behind him. Though it was barely dawn, humid heat was already beginning to gather in the room. She pushed the window shut and went into the bathroom to wash her face and rinse her mouth, which tasted like old paper.

Five minutes later she was sliding her feet into her green sneakers. She'd changed into cutoffs and a plain black T-shirt. If only her thin freckled legs looked more like Isabelle's lanky smooth limbs. But it couldn't be helped. She pulled her hair back into a ponytail and went to join Jace in the hallway.

Church was there with him, muttering and circling restlessly.

"What's with the cat?" Clary asked.

"The Silent Brothers make him nervous."

"Sounds like they make everyone nervous."

Jace smiled thinly. Church meowed as they set off down the hall, but didn't follow them. At least the thick stones of the cathedral walls still held some of the night's chill: The corridors were dark and cool.

When they reached the library, Clary was surprised to see that the lamps were off. The library was lit only by the milky glow that filtered down through the high windows set into the vaulted roof. Hodge sat behind the enormous desk in a suit, his gray-streaked hair silvered by the dawn light. For a moment she thought he was alone in the room: that Jace had been playing a joke on her. Then she saw a figure move out of the dimness, and she realized that what she had thought was a patch of darker shadow was a man. A tall man in a heavy robe that fell from neck to foot, covering him completely. The hood of the robe was raised, hiding his face. The robe itself was the color of parchment, and the intricate runic designs along the hem and sleeves looked as if they had been inked there in drying blood. The hair rose along Clary's arms and on the back of her neck, prickling almost painfully.

"This," said Hodge, "is Brother Jeremiah of the Silent City."

The man came toward them, his heavy cloak swirling as he moved, and Clary realized what it was about him that was strange: He made no sound at all as he walked, not the slightest footstep. Even his cloak, which should have rustled, was silent. She would almost have wondered if he were a ghost—but no, she thought as he halted in front of them, there was a strange, sweet smell about him, like incense and blood, the smell of something living.

"And this, Jeremiah," Hodge said, rising from his desk, "is the girl I wrote to you about. Clarissa Fray."

The hooded face turned slowly toward her. Clary felt cold to her fingertips. "Hello," she said.

There was no reply.

"I decided you were right, Jace," said Hodge.

"I *was* right," said Jace. "I usually am."

Hodge ignored this. "I sent a letter to the Clave about all

this last night, but Clary's memories are her own. Only she can decide how she wants to deal with the contents of her own head. If she wants the help of the Silent Brothers, she should have that choice."

Clary said nothing. Dorothea had said there was a block in her mind, hiding something. Of course she wanted to know what it was. But the shadowy figure of the Silent Brother was so—well, *silent*. Silence itself seemed to flow from him like a dark tide, black and thick as ink. It chilled her bones.

Brother Jeremiah's face was still turned toward her, nothing but darkness visible underneath his hood. *This is Jocelyn's daughter?*

Clary gave a little gasp, stepping back. The words had echoed inside her head, as if she'd thought them herself—but she hadn't.

"Yes," said Hodge, and added quickly, "but her father was a mundane."

That does not matter, said Jeremiah. *The blood of the Clave is dominant.*

"Why did you call my mother Jocelyn?" said Clary, searching in vain for some sign of a face beneath the hood. "Did you know her?"

"The Brothers keep records on all members of the Clave," explained Hodge. "Exhaustive records—"

"Not that exhaustive," said Jace, "if they didn't even know she was still alive."

It is likely that she had the assistance of a warlock in her disappearance. Most Shadowhunters cannot so easily escape the Clave. There was no emotion in Jeremiah's voice; he sounded neither approving nor disapproving of Jocelyn's actions.

"There's something I don't understand," Clary said. "Why would Valentine think my mom had the Mortal Cup? If she went through so much trouble to disappear, like you said, then why would she bring it with her?"

"To keep him from getting his hands on it," said Hodge. "She above all people would have known what would happen if Valentine had the Cup. And I imagine she didn't trust the Clave to hold on to it. Not after Valentine got it away from them in the first place."

"I guess." Clary couldn't keep the doubt from her voice. The whole thing seemed so unlikely. She tried to picture her mother fleeing under cover of darkness, with a big gold cup stashed in the pocket of her overalls, and failed.

"Jocelyn turned against her husband when she found out what he intended to do with the Cup," said Hodge. "It's not unreasonable to assume she would do everything in her power to keep the Cup from falling into his hands. The Clave themselves would have looked first to her if they'd thought she was still alive."

"It seems to me," Clary said with an edge to her voice, "that no one the Clave thinks is dead, is ever actually dead. Maybe they should invest in dental records."

"My father's dead," said Jace, the same edge in his voice. "I don't need dental records to tell me that."

Clary turned on him in some exasperation. "Look, I didn't mean—"

That is enough, interrupted Brother Jeremiah. *There is truth to be learned here, if you are patient enough to listen to it.*

With a quick gesture he raised his hands and drew the hood back from his face. Forgetting Jace, Clary fought the urge to cry out. The archivist's head was bald, smooth and white as an egg, darkly indented where his eyes had once been. They were gone now. His lips were crisscrossed with a pattern of dark lines that resembled surgical stitches. She understood now what Alec had meant by mutilation.

The Brothers of the Silent City do not lie, said Jeremiah. *If you want the truth from me, you shall have it, but I shall ask of you the same in return.*

Clary lifted her chin. "I'm not a liar either."

The mind cannot lie. Jeremiah moved toward her. *It is your memories I want.*

The smell of blood and ink was stifling. Clary felt a wave of panic. "Wait—"

"Clary." It was Hodge, his tone gentle. "It's entirely possible that there are memories you have buried or repressed, memories formed when you were too young to have a conscious recollection of them, that Brother Jeremiah can reach. It could help us a great deal."

She said nothing, biting the inside of her lip. She hated the idea of someone reaching inside her head, touching memories so private and hidden that even she couldn't reach them.

"She doesn't have to do anything she doesn't want to do," Jace said suddenly. "Does she?"

Clary interrupted Hodge before he could reply. "It's all right. I'll do it."

Brother Jeremiah nodded curtly, and moved toward her with the soundlessness that sent chills up her spine. "Will it hurt?" she whispered.

He didn't reply, but his narrow white hands came up to touch her face. The skin of his fingers was thin as parchment paper, inked all over with runes. She could feel the power in them, jumping like static electricity to sting her skin. She closed her eyes, but not before she saw the anxious expression that crossed Hodge's face.

Colors swirled up against the darkness behind her eyelids. She felt a pressure, a drawing pull in her head and hands and feet. She clenched her hands, straining against the weight, the blackness. She felt as if she were pressed up against something hard and unyielding, being slowly crushed. She heard herself gasp and went suddenly cold all over, cold as winter. In a flash she saw an icy street, gray buildings looming overhead, an explosion of whiteness stinging her face in freezing particles—

"That's *enough*." Jace's voice cut through the winter chill, and the falling snow vanished, a shower of white sparks. Clary's eyes sprang open.

Slowly the library came back into focus—the book-lined walls, the anxious faces of Hodge and Jace. Brother Jeremiah stood unmoving, a carved idol of ivory and red ink. Clary became aware of the sharp pains in her hands, and glanced down to see red lines scored across her skin where her nails had dug in.

"*Jace*," Hodge said reprovingly.

"Look at her hands." Jace gestured toward Clary, who curled her fingers in to cover her injured palms.

Hodge put a broad hand on her shoulder. "Are you all right?"

Slowly she moved her head in a nod. The crushing weight had gone, but she could feel the sweat that drenched her hair, pasted her shirt to her back like sticky tape.

There is a block in your mind, said Brother Jeremiah. *Your memories cannot be reached.*

"A block?" asked Jace. "You mean she's repressed her memories?"

No. I mean they have been blocked from her conscious mind by a spell. I cannot break it here. She will have to come to the Bone City and stand before the Brotherhood.

"A spell?" said Clary incredulously. "Who would have put a spell on me?"

Nobody answered her. Jace looked at his tutor. He was surprisingly pale, Clary thought, considering that this had been his idea. "Hodge, she shouldn't have to go if she doesn't—"

"It's all right." Clary took a deep breath. Her palms ached where her nails had cut them, and she wanted badly to lie down somewhere dark and rest. "I'll go. I want to know the truth. I want to know what's in my head."

Jace nodded once. "Fine. Then I'll go with you."

Leaving the Institute was like climbing into a wet, hot canvas bag. Humid air pressed down on the city, turning the air to grimy soup. "I don't see why we have to leave separately from Brother Jeremiah," Clary grumbled. They were standing on the corner outside the Institute. The streets were deserted except for a garbage truck trundling slowly down the block. "What, is he embarrassed to be seen with Shadowhunters or something?"

"The Brotherhood *are* Shadowhunters," Jace pointed out. Somehow he managed to look cool despite the heat. It made Clary want to smack him.

"I suppose he went to get his car?" she inquired sarcastically.

Jace grinned. "Something like that."

She shook her head. "You know, I'd feel a lot better about this if Hodge had come with us."

"What, I'm not protection enough for you?"

"It's not protection I need right now—it's someone who can help me think." Suddenly reminded, she clapped a hand over her mouth. "Oh—Simon!"

"No, I'm Jace," said Jace patiently. "Simon is the weaselly little one with the bad haircut and dismal fashion sense."

"Oh, shut up," she replied, but it was more automatic than heartfelt. "I meant to call before I went to sleep. See if he got home okay."

Shaking his head, Jace regarded the heavens as if they were about to open up and reveal the secrets of the universe. "With everything that's going on, you're worried about Weasel Face?"

"Don't call him that. He doesn't look like a weasel."

"You may be right," said Jace. "I've met an attractive weasel or two in my time. He looks more like a rat."

"He does not—"

"He's probably at home lying in a puddle of his own drool. Just wait till Isabelle gets bored with him and you have to pick up the pieces."

"Is Isabelle likely to get bored with him?" Clary asked.

Jace thought about this. "Yes," he said.

Clary wondered if perhaps Isabelle was smarter than Jace gave her credit for. Maybe she would realize what an amazing guy Simon was: how funny, how smart, how cool. Maybe they'd start dating. The idea filled her with a nameless horror.

Lost in thought, it took her several moments to realize that Jace had been saying something to her. When she blinked at him, she saw a wry grin spread across his face. "What?" she asked, ungraciously.

"I wish you'd stop desperately trying to get my attention like this," he said. "It's become embarrassing."

"Sarcasm is the last refuge of the imaginatively bankrupt," she told him.

"I can't help it. I use my rapier wit to hide my inner pain."

"Your pain will be outer soon if you don't get out of traffic. Are you *trying* to get run over by a cab?"

"Don't be ridiculous," he said. "We could never get a cab that easily in this neighborhood."

As if on cue, a narrow black car with tinted windows rumbled up to the curb and paused in front of Jace, engine purring. It was long and sleek and low to the ground like a limousine, the windows curved outward.

Jace looked at her sideways; there was amusement in his glance, but also a certain urgency. She glanced at the car again, letting her gaze relax, letting the strength of what was real pierce the veil of glamour.

Now the car looked like Cinderella's carriage, except instead of being pink and gold and blue like an Easter egg, it was black as velvet, its windows darkly tinted. The wheels were black, the leather trimmings all black. On the black metal driver's bench sat Brother Jeremiah, holding a set of reins in his gloved hands. His face was hidden beneath the cowl of his parchment-colored robe. On the other end of the reins were two horses, black as smoke, snarling and pawing at the sky.

"Get in," said Jace. When she continued to stand there gaping, he took her arm and half-pushed her in through the open door of the carriage, swinging himself up after her. The carriage began to move before he had closed the door behind them. He fell back in his seat—plush and glossily upholstered—and looked over at her. "A personal escort to the Bone City is nothing to turn your nose up at."

"I wasn't turning my nose up. I was just surprised. I wasn't expecting ... I mean, I thought it was a car."

"Just relax," said Jace. "Enjoy that new-carriage smell."

Clary rolled her eyes and turned to look out the windows. She would have thought that a horse and carriage wouldn't have stood a chance in Manhattan traffic, but they were moving downtown easily, their soundless progression unnoticed by the snarl of taxis, buses, and SUVs that choked the avenue. In front of them a yellow cab switched lanes, cutting off their forward progress. Clary tensed, worried about the horses—then the carriage lurched upward as the horses sprang lightly to the top of the cab. She choked off a gasp. The carriage, rather than dragging along the ground, sailed up behind the horses, rolling lightly and soundlessly up and over the cab's roof and down the other side. Clary glanced backward as the carriage hit the pavement again with a jolt—the cab driver was smoking and staring ahead, utterly oblivious. "I always thought cab drivers didn't pay attention to traffic, but this is ridiculous," she said weakly.

"Just because you can see through glamour now..." Jace let the end of the sentence hang delicately in the air between them.

"I can only see through it when I concentrate," she said. "It hurts my head a little."

"I bet that's because of the block in your mind. The Brothers will take care of that."

"Then what?"

"Then you'll see the world as it is—infinite," said Jace with a dry smile.

"Don't quote Blake at me."

The smile turned less dry. "I didn't think you'd recognize it. You don't strike me as someone who reads a lot of poetry."

"Everyone knows that quote because of the Doors."

Jace looked at her blankly.

"The Doors. They were a band."

"If you say so," he said.

"I suppose you don't have much time for enjoying music," Clary said, thinking of Simon, for whom music was his entire life, "in your line of work."

He shrugged. "Maybe the occasional wailing chorus of the damned."

Clary looked at him quickly, to see if he was joking, but he was expressionless.

"But you were playing the piano yesterday," she began, "at the Institute. So you must—"

The carriage lurched upward again. Clary grabbed at the edge of her seat and stared—they were rolling along the top of a downtown M1 bus. From this vantage point she could see the upper floors of the old apartment buildings that lined the avenue, elaborately carved with gargoyles and ornamental cornices.

"I was just messing around," said Jace, without looking at her. "My father insisted I learn to play an instrument."

"He sounds strict, your father."

Jace's tone was sharp. "Not at all. He indulged me. He taught me everything—weapons training, demonology, arcane lore, ancient languages. He gave me anything I wanted. Horses, weapons, books, even a hunting falcon."

But weapons and books aren't exactly what most kids want for Christmas, Clary thought as the carriage thunked back down to the pavement. "Why didn't you mention to Hodge that you knew the men that Luke was talking to? That they were the ones who killed your dad?"

Jace looked down at his hands. They were slim and careful hands, the hands of an artist, not a warrior. The ring she had noticed earlier flashed on his finger. She would have thought there would have been something feminine about a boy wearing a ring, but there wasn't. The ring itself was solid and heavy-looking, made of a dark burned-looking silver with a pattern of stars around the band. The letter W was carved into it. "Because if I did," he said, "he'd know I wanted to kill Valentine myself. And he'd never let me try."

"You mean you want to kill him for revenge?"

"For justice," said Jace. "I never knew who killed my father. Now I do. This is my chance to make it right."

Clary didn't see how killing one person could make right the death of another, but she sensed there was no point saying that. "But you knew who killed him," she said. "It was those men. You said..."

Jace wasn't looking at her, so Clary let her voice trail off. They were rolling through Astor Place now, narrowly dodging a purple New York University tram as it cut through traffic. Passing pedestrians looked crushed by the heavy air, like insects pinned under glass. Some groups of homeless kids were crowded around the base of a big brass statue, folded cardboard signs asking for money propped up in front of them. Clary saw a girl about her own age with a smoothly shaved bald head leaning against a brown-skinned boy with dreadlocks, his face adorned with a dozen piercings. He turned his head as the carriage rolled by as if he could see it, and she caught the gleam of his eyes. One of them was clouded, as though it had no pupil.

"I was ten," Jace said. She turned to look at him. He was without expression. It always seemed like some color drained out of him when he talked about his father. "We lived in a manor house, out in the country. My father always said it was safer away from people. I heard them coming up the drive and went to tell him. He told me to hide, so I hid. Under the stairs. I saw those men come in. They had others with them. Not men. Forsaken. They overpowered my father and cut his throat. The blood ran across the floor. It soaked my shoes. I didn't move."

It took a moment for Clary to realize he was done speaking, and another to find her voice. "I'm so sorry, Jace."

His eyes gleamed in the darkness. "I don't understand why mundanes always apologize for things that aren't their fault."

"I'm not apologizing. It's a way of—empathizing. Of saying that I'm sorry you're unhappy."

"I'm not unhappy," he said. "Only people with no purpose are unhappy. I've got a purpose."

"Do you mean killing demons, or getting revenge for your father's death?"

"Both."

"Would your father really want you to kill those men? Just for revenge?"

"A Shadowhunter who kills another of his brothers is worse

than a demon and should be put down like one," Jace said, sounding as if he were reciting the words from a textbook.

"But are all demons evil?" she said. "I mean, if all vampires aren't evil, and all werewolves aren't evil, maybe—"

Jace turned on her, looking exasperated. "It's not the same thing at all. Vampires, werewolves, even warlocks, they're part-human. Part of this world, born in it. They belong here. But demons come from other worlds. They're interdimensional parasites. They come to a world and use it up. They can't build, just destroy—they can't make, only use. They drain a place to ashes and when it's dead, they move on to the next one. It's life they want—not just your life or mine, but all the life of this world, its rivers and cities, its oceans, its everything. And the only thing that stands between them and the destruction of all *this*"—he pointed outside the window of the carriage, waving his hand as if he meant to indicate everything in the city from the skyscrapers uptown to the clog of traffic on Houston Street—"is the Nephilim."

"Oh," Clary said. There didn't seem to be much else *to* say. "How many other worlds are there?"

"No one knows. Hundreds? Millions, maybe."

"And they're all—dead worlds? Used up?" Clary felt her stomach drop, though it might have been only the jolt as they rolled up and over a purple Mini. "That seems so sad."

"I didn't say that." The dark orangey light of city haze spilled in through the window, outlining his sharp profile. "There are probably other living worlds like ours. But only demons can travel between them. Because they're mostly noncorporeal, partly, but nobody knows exactly why. Plenty of warlocks have tried it, and it's never worked. Nothing from

Earth can pass through the wardings between the worlds. If we could," he added, "we might be able to block them from coming here, but nobody's even been able to figure out how to do that. In fact, more and more of them are coming through. There used to be only small demon invasions into this world, easily contained. But even in my lifetime more and more of them have spilled in through the wardings. The Clave is always having to dispatch Shadowhunters, and a lot of times they don't come back."

"But if you had the Mortal Cup, you could make more, right? More demon hunters?" Clary asked tentatively.

"Sure," Jace said. "But we haven't had the Cup for years now, and a lot of us die young. So our numbers slowly dwindle."

"Aren't you, uh..." Clary searched for the right word. "Reproducing?"

Jace burst out laughing just as the carriage made a sudden, sharp left turn. He braced himself, but Clary was thrown against him. He caught her, hands holding her lightly but firmly away from him. She felt the cool impress of his ring like a sliver of ice against her sweaty skin. "Sure," he said. "We love reproducing. It's one of our favorite things."

Clary pulled away from him, her face burning in the darkness, and turned to look out the window. They were rolling toward a heavy wrought iron gate, trellised with dark vines.

"We're here," announced Jace as the smooth roll of wheels over pavement turned to the jounce of cobblestones. Clary glimpsed words across the arch as they rolled under it: NEW YORK CITY MARBLE CEMETERY.

"But they stopped burying people in Manhattan a century ago because they ran out of room—didn't they?" she said.

They were moving down a narrow alley with high stone walls on either side.

"The Bone City has been here longer than that." The carriage came to a shuddering halt. Clary jumped as Jace stretched his arm out, but he was only reaching past her to open the door on her side. His arm was lightly muscled and downed with golden hairs fine as pollen.

"You don't get a choice, do you?" she asked. "About being a Shadowhunter. You can't just opt out."

"Not easily, or without risk," he said. The door swung open, letting in a blast of muggy air. The carriage had drawn to a stop on a wide square of green grass surrounded by mossy marble walls. "But if I had a choice, this is still what I'd choose."

"Why?" she asked.

He raised an eyebrow, which made Clary instantly jealous. She'd always wanted to be able to do that. "Because," he said. "It's what I'm good at."

He jumped down from the carriage. Clary slid to the edge of her seat, dangling her legs. It was a long drop to the cobblestones. She jumped. The impact stung her feet, but she didn't fall. She swung around in triumph to find Jace watching her. "I would have helped you down," he said.

She blinked. "It's okay. You didn't have to."

He glanced behind him. Brother Jeremiah was descending from his perch behind the horses in a silent fall of robes. He cast no shadow on the sun-baked grass.

Come, he said. He glided away from the carriage and the comforting lights of Second Avenue, moving toward the dark center of the garden. It was clear that he expected them to follow.

The grass was dry and crackling underfoot, the marble walls to either side smooth and pearly. There were names carved into the stone of the walls, names and dates. It took Clary a moment to realize that they were grave markers. A chill scraped up her spine. Where were the bodies? In the walls, buried upright as if they'd been walled in alive...?

She had forgotten to look where she was going. When she collided with something unmistakably alive, she yelped out loud.

It was Jace. "Don't screech like that. You'll wake the dead."

She frowned at him. "Why are we stopping?"

He pointed at Brother Jeremiah, who had come to a halt in front of a statue just slightly taller than he was, its base overgrown with moss. The statue was of an angel. The marble of the statue was so smooth it was almost translucent. The face of the angel was fierce and beautiful and sad. In long white hands the angel held a cup, its rim studded with marble jewels. Something about the statue tickled Clary's memory with an uneasy familiarity. There was a date inscribed on the base, 1234, and words inscribed around it: NEPHILIM: FACILIS DESCENSUS AVERNI.

"Is that meant to be the Mortal Cup?" she asked.

Jace nodded. "And that's the motto of the Nephilim—the Shadowhunters—there on the base."

"What does it mean?"

Jace's grin was a white flash in the darkness. "It means 'Shadowhunters: Looking Better in Black Than the Widows of our Enemies Since 1234.'"

"Jace—"

It means, said Jeremiah, *"The descent into Hell is easy."*

"Nice and cheery," said Clary, but a shiver passed over her skin despite the heat.

"It's the Brothers' little joke, having that here," said Jace. "You'll see."

She looked at Brother Jeremiah. He had drawn a stele, faintly glowing, from some inner pocket of his robe, and with the tip he traced the pattern of a rune on the statue's base. The mouth of the stone angel suddenly gaped wide in a silent scream, and a yawning black hole opened in the grassy turf at Jeremiah's feet. It looked like an open grave.

Slowly Clary approached the edge of it and peered inside. A set of granite steps led down into the hole, their edges worn soft by years of use. Torches were set along the steps at intervals, flaring hot green and icy blue. The bottom of the stairs was lost in darkness.

Jace took the stairs with the ease of someone who finds a situation familiar if not exactly comfortable. Halfway to the first torch, he paused and looked up at her. "Come *on*," he said impatiently.

Clary had barely set her foot on the first step when she felt her arm caught in a cold grip. She looked up in astonishment. Brother Jeremiah was holding her wrist, his icy white fingers digging into the skin. She could see the bony gleam of his scarred face beneath the edge of his cowl.

Do not fear, said his voice inside her head. *It would take more than a single human cry to wake these dead.*

When he released her arm, she skittered down the stairs after Jace, her heart pounding against her ribs. He was waiting for her at the foot of the steps. He'd taken one of the green burning torches out of its bracket and was holding it at eye level. It lent a pale green cast to his skin. "You all right?"

She nodded, not trusting herself to speak. The stairs ended in a shallow landing; ahead of them stretched a tunnel, long and black, ridged with the curling roots of trees. A faint bluish light was visible at the tunnel's end. "It's so ... dark," she said lamely.

"You want me to hold your hand?"

Clary put both her hands behind her back like a small child. "Don't talk down to me."

"Well, I could hardly talk *up* to you. You're too short." Jace glanced past her, the torch showering sparks as he moved. "No need to stand on ceremony, Brother Jeremiah," he drawled. "Lead on. We'll be right behind you."

Clary jumped. She still wasn't used to the archivist's silent comings and goings. He moved noiselessly from where he had been standing behind her and headed into the tunnel. After a moment she followed, knocking Jace's outstretched hand aside as she went.

Clary's first sight of the Silent City was of row upon row of tall marble arches that rose overhead, disappearing into the distance like the orderly rows of trees in an orchard. The marble itself was a pure, ashy ivory, hard and polished-looking, inset in places with narrow strips of onyx, jasper, and jade. As they moved away from the tunnel and toward the forest of arches, Clary saw that the floor was inscribed with the same runes that sometimes decorated Jace's skin with lines and whorls and swirling patterns.

As the three of them passed through the first arch, something large and white loomed up on her left side, like an iceberg off the bow of the *Titanic*. It was a block of white stone, smooth and square, with a sort of door inset into the front. It reminded her of a child-size playhouse, almost but not quite big enough for her to stand up inside.

"It's a mausoleum," said Jace, directing a flash of torchlight at it. Clary could see that a rune was carved into the door, which was sealed shut with bolts of iron. "A tomb. We bury our dead here."

"All your dead?" she said, half-wanting to ask him if his father was buried here, but he had already moved ahead, out of earshot. She hurried after him, not wanting to be alone with Brother Jeremiah in this spooky place. "I thought you said this was a library."

There are many levels to the Silent City, interjected Jeremiah. *And not all the dead are buried here. There is another ossuary in Idris, of course, much larger. But on this level are the mausoleums and the place of burning.*

"The place of burning?"

Those who die in battle are burned, their ashes used to make the marble arches that you see here. The blood and bone of demon slayers is itself a powerful protection against evil. Even in death, the Clave serves the cause.

How exhausting, Clary thought, *to fight all your life and then be expected to continue that fight even when your life was over.* At the edges of her vision she could see the square white vaults rising on either side of her in orderly rows of tombs, each door locked from the outside. She understood now why this was called the Silent City: Its only inhabitants were the mute Brothers and the dead they so zealously guarded.

They had reached another staircase leading down into

more twilight; Jace thrust the torch ahead of him, streaking the walls with shadows. "We're going to the second level, where the archives and the council rooms are," he said, as if to reassure her.

"Where are the living quarters?" Clary asked, partly to be polite, partly out of a real curiosity. "Where do the Brothers sleep?

Sleep?

The silent word hung in the darkness between them. Jace laughed, and the flame of the torch he held flickered. "You had to ask."

At the foot of the stairs was another tunnel, which widened out at the end into a square pavilion, each corner of which was marked by a spire of carved bone. Torches burned in long onyx holders along the sides of the square, and the air smelled of ashes and smoke. In the center of the pavilion was a long table of black basalt veined in white. Behind the table, against the dark wall, hung an enormous silver sword, point down, its hilt carved in the shape of outspread wings. Seated at the table was a row of Silent Brothers, each wrapped and cowled in the same parchment-colored robes as Jeremiah.

Jeremiah wasted no time. *We have arrived. Clarissa, stand before the Council.*

Clary glanced at Jace, but he was blinking, clearly confused. Brother Jeremiah must have spoken only inside *her* head. She looked at the table, at the long row of silent figures muffled in their heavy robes. Alternating squares made up the pavilion floor: golden bronze and a darker red. Just in front of the table was a larger square, made of white marble and embossed with a parabolic design of silver stars.

Clary stepped into the center of the black square as if she were stepping in front of a firing squad. She raised her head. "All right," she said. "Now what?"

The Brothers made a sound then, a sound that raised the hairs up all along Clary's neck and the backs of her arms. It was a sound like a sigh or a groan. In unison they raised their hands and pushed their cowls back, baring their scarred faces and the pits of their empty eyes.

Though she had seen Brother Jeremiah's uncovered face already, Clary's stomach knotted. It was like looking at a row of skeletons, like one of those medieval woodcuts where the dead walked and talked and danced on the piled bodies of the living. Their stitched mouths seemed to grin at her.

The Council greets you, Clarissa Fray, she heard, and it was not just one silent voice inside her head but a dozen, some low and rough, some smooth and monotone, but all were demanding, insistent, pushing at the fragile barriers around her mind.

"Stop," she said, and to her astonishment her voice came out firm and strong. The din inside her mind ceased as suddenly as a record that had stopped spinning. "You can go inside my head," she said, "but only when I'm ready."

If you do not want our help, there is no need for this. You are the one who asked for our assistance, after all.

"You want to know what's in my mind, just like I do," she said. "That doesn't mean you can't be careful about it."

The Brother who sat in the center seat templed his thin white fingers beneath his chin. *It is an interesting puzzle, admittedly,* he said, and the voice inside her mind was dry and neutral. *But there is no need for the use of force, if you do not resist.*

She gritted her teeth. She wanted to resist them, wanted to pry those intrusive voices out of her head. To stand by and allow such a violation of her most intimate, personal self—

But there was every chance that had already happened, she reminded herself. This was nothing more than the excavation of a past crime, the theft of her memory. If it worked, what had been taken from her would be restored. She closed her eyes.

"Go ahead," she said.

The first contact came as a whisper inside her head, delicate as the brush of a falling leaf. *State your name for the Council.*

Clarissa Fray.

The first voice was joined by others. *Who are you?*

I'm Clary. My mother is Jocelyn Fray. I live at 807 Berkeley Place in Brooklyn. I am fifteen years old. My father's name was—

Her mind seemed to snap in on itself, like a rubber band, and she reeled soundlessly into a whirlwind of images cast against the insides of her closed eyelids. Her mother was hurrying her down a night-black street between piles of heaped and dirty snow. Then a lowering sky, gray and leaden, rows of black trees stripped bare. An empty square cut into the earth, a plain coffin lowered into it. *Ashes to ashes.* Jocelyn wrapped in her patchwork quilt, tears spilling down her cheeks, quickly closing a box and shoving it under a cushion as Clary came into the room. She saw the initials on the box again: J. C.

The images came faster now, like the pages of one of those books where the drawings seemed to move when you flipped them. Clary stood on top of a flight of stairs, looking down a narrow corridor, and there was Luke again, his green duffel bag at his feet. Jocelyn stood in front of him, shaking her head. "Why now, Lucian? I thought that you were dead..." Clary blinked; Luke looked different, almost a stranger, bearded, his hair long and tangled—and branches came down to block her view; she was in the park again, and green faeries, tiny as toothpicks, buzzed among the red flowers. She reached for one in delight, and her mother swung her up into her arms with a cry of terror. Then it was winter on the black street again, and they were hurrying, huddled under an umbrella, Jocelyn half-pushing and half-dragging Clary between the looming banks of snow. A granite doorway loomed up out of the falling whiteness; there were words carved above the door. THE MAGNIFICENT. Then she was standing inside an entryway that smelled of iron and melting snow. Her fingers were numb with cold. A hand under her chin directed her to look up, and she saw a row of words scrawled along the wall. Two words leaped out at her, burning into her eyes: MAGNUS BANE.

A sudden pain lanced through her right arm. She shrieked as the images fell away and she spun upward, breaking the surface of consciousness like a diver breaking up through a wave. There was something cold pressed against her cheek. She pried her eyes open and saw silver stars. She blinked twice before she realized that she was lying on the marble floor, her knees curled up to her chest. When she moved, hot pain shot up her arm.

She sat up gingerly. The skin over her left elbow was split and bleeding. She must have landed on it when she fell. There was blood on her shirt. She looked around, disoriented, and saw Jace looking at her, unmoving but very tense around the mouth.

Magnus Bane. The words meant something, but what? Before she could ask the question aloud, Brother Jeremiah interrupted her.

The block inside your mind is stronger than we had anticipated, he said. *It can be safely undone only by the one who put it there. For us to remove it would be to kill you.*

She scrambled to her feet, cradling her injured arm. "But I don't know who put it there. If I knew that, I wouldn't have come here."

The answer to that is woven into the thread of your thoughts, said Brother Jeremiah. *In your waking dream you saw it written.*

"Magnus Bane? But—that's not even a name!"

It is enough. Brother Jeremiah got to his feet. As if this were a signal, the rest of the Brothers rose alongside him. They inclined their heads toward Jace, a gesture of silent acknowledgment, before they filed away among the pillars and were gone. Only Brother Jeremiah remained. He watched impassively as Jace hurried over to Clary.

"Is your arm all right? Let me see," he demanded, seizing her wrist.

"Ouch! It's fine. Don't do that, you're making it worse," Clary said, trying to pull away.

"You bled on the Speaking Stars," he said. Clary looked and saw that he was right: There was a smear of her blood on the white and silver marble. "I bet there's a law somewhere about that." He turned her arm over, more gently than she would have thought he was capable of. He caught his lower lip between his teeth and whistled; she glanced down and saw that a glove of blood covered her lower arm from the elbow to the wrist. The arm was throbbing, stiff, and painful.

"Is this when you start tearing strips off your T-shirt to bind up my wound?" she joked. She hated the sight of blood, especially her own.

"If you wanted me to rip my clothes off, you should have just asked." He dug into his pocket and brought out his stele. "It would have been a lot less painful."

Remembering the stinging sensation when the stele had touched her wrist, she braced herself, but all she felt as the glowing instrument glided lightly over her injury was a faint warmth. "There," he said, straightening up. Clary flexed her arm in wonder—though the blood was still there, the wound was gone, as were the pain and stiffness. "And next time you're planning to injure yourself to get my attention, just remember that a little sweet talk works wonders."

Clary felt her mouth twitch into a smile. "I'll keep that in mind," she said, and as he turned away, she added, "And thanks."

He slid the stele into his back pocket without turning to look at her, but she thought she saw a certain gratification in the set of his shoulders. "Brother Jeremiah," he said, rubbing his hands together, "you've been very quiet all this time. Surely you have some thoughts you'd like to share?"

I am charged with leading you from the Silent City, and that is all, said the archivist. Clary wondered if she were imagining it, or if there was actually a faintly affronted tone to his "voice."

"We could always show ourselves out," Jace suggested hopefully. "I'm sure I remember the way—"

The marvels of the Silent City are not for the eyes of the uninitiated, said Jeremiah, and he turned his back on them with a soundless swish of robes. *This way*.

When they emerged into the open, Clary took deep breaths of the thick morning air, relishing the city stench of smog, dirt, and humanity. Jace looked around thoughtfully. "It's going to rain," he said.

He was right, Clary thought, looking up at the iron-gray sky. "Are we taking a carriage back to the Institute?"

Jace looked from Brother Jeremiah, still as a statue, to the carriage, looming like a black shadow in the archway that led to the street. Then he broke into a grin.

"No way," he said. "I hate those things. Let's hail a cab."

11

Magnus Bane

Jace leaned forward and banged his hand against the partition separating them from the cab driver. "Turn left! Left! I said to take Broadway, you brain-dead moron!"

The taxi driver responded by jerking the wheel so hard to the left that Clary was thrown against Jace. She let out a yelp of resentment. "Why are we taking Broadway, anyway?"

"I'm starving," Jace said. "And there's nothing at home except leftover Chinese." He took his phone out of his pocket and started dialing. "Alec! Wake up!" he shouted. Clary could hear an irritated buzzing on the other end. "Meet us at Taki's. Breakfast. Yeah, you heard me. Breakfast. What? It's only a few blocks away. Get going."

He clicked off and shoved the phone into one of his many pockets as they pulled up to a curb. Handing the driver a wad of bills, Jace elbowed Clary out of the car. When he landed on the pavement behind her, he stretched like a cat and spread his arms wide. "Welcome to the greatest restaurant in New York."

It didn't look like much—a low brick building that sagged in the middle like a collapsed soufflé. A battered neon sign proclaiming the restaurant's name hung sideways and was sputtering. Two men in long coats and tipped-forward felt hats slouched in front of the narrow doorway. There were no windows.

"It looks like a prison," said Clary.

He pointed at her. "But in prison could you order a spaghetti *fra diavolo* that makes you want to kiss your fingers? I don't *think* so."

"I don't want spaghetti. I want to know what a Magnus Bane is."

"It's not a what. It's a who," said Jace. "It's a name."

"Do you know who he *is*?"

"He's a warlock," said Jace in his most reasonable voice. "Only a warlock could have put a block in your mind like that. Or maybe one of the Silent Brothers, but clearly it wasn't them."

"Is he a warlock you've *heard of*?" demanded Clary, who was rapidly tiring of Jace's reasonable voice.

"The name does sound familiar—"

"Hey!" It was Alec, looking like he'd rolled out of bed and pulled jeans on over his pajamas. His hair, unbrushed, stuck out wildly around his head. He loped toward them, eyes on Jace, ignoring Clary as usual. "Izzy's on her way," he said. "She's bringing the mundane."

"Simon? Where did he come from?" Jace asked.

"He showed up first thing this morning. Couldn't stay away from Izzy, I guess. Pathetic." Alec sounded amused. Clary wanted to kick him. "Anyway, are we going in or what? I'm starving."

"Me too," said Jace. "I could really go for some fried mouse tails."

"Some what?" asked Clary, sure that she'd heard wrong.

Jace grinned at her. "Relax," he said. "It's just a diner."

They were stopped at the front door by one of the slouching men. As he straightened, Clary caught a glimpse of his face under the hat. His skin was dark red, his squared-off hands ending in blue-black nails. Clary felt herself stiffen, but Jace and Alec seemed unconcerned. They said something to the man, who nodded and stepped back, allowing them to pass.

"*Jace,*" Clary hissed as the door shut behind them. "Who was that?"

"You mean Clancy?" Jace asked, glancing around the brightly lit restaurant. It was pleasant inside, despite the lack of windows. Cozy wooden booths nestled up against each other, each one lined with brightly colored cushions. Endearingly mismatched crockery lined the counter, behind which stood a blond girl in a waitress's pink-and-white apron, nimbly counting out change to a stocky man in a flannel shirt. She saw Jace, waved, and gestured that they should sit wherever they wanted. "Clancy keeps out undesirables," said Jace, herding her to one of the booths.

"He's a *demon,*" she hissed. Several customers turned to look at her—a boy with spiky blue dreads was sitting next to a beautiful Indian girl with long black hair and gauzelike golden wings sprouting from her back. The boy frowned darkly. Clary was glad the restaurant was almost empty.

"No, he isn't," said Jace, sliding into a booth. Clary moved to sit beside him, but Alec was already there. She settled gingerly onto the booth seat opposite them, her arm still stiff despite Jace's ministrations. She felt hollow inside, as if the Silent Brothers had reached into her and scooped out her insides, leaving her light and dizzy. "He's an ifrit," Jace explained. "They're warlocks with no magic. Half demons who can't cast spells for whatever reason."

"Poor bastards," said Alec, picking up his menu. Clary picked hers up too, and stared. Locusts and honey were featured as a special, as were plates of raw meat, whole raw fish, and something called a toasted bat sandwich. A page of the beverage section was devoted to the different types of blood they had on tap—to Clary's relief, they were different kinds of animal blood, rather than type A, type O, or type B-negative.

"Who eats whole raw fish?" she inquired aloud.

"Kelpies," said Alec. "Selkies. Maybe the occasional nixie."

"Don't order any of the faerie food," said Jace, looking at her over the top of his menu. "It tends to make humans a little crazy. One minute you're munching a faerie plum, the next minute you're running naked down Madison Avenue with antlers on your head. Not," he added hastily, "that this has ever happened to me."

Alec laughed. "Do you remember—" he began, and launched into a story that contained so many mysterious names and proper nouns that Clary didn't even bother trying to follow it. She was looking at Alec instead, watching him as he talked to Jace. There was a kinetic, almost feverish energy to him that hadn't been there before. Something about Jace sharpened him, brought him into focus. If she were going to draw them together, she thought, she would make Jace a little blurry, while Alec stood out, all sharp, clear planes and angles.

Jace was looking down as Alec spoke, smiling a little and tapping his water glass with a fingernail. She sensed he was thinking of other things. She felt a sudden flash of sympathy for Alec. Jace couldn't be an easy person to care about. *I was laughing at you because declarations of love amuse me, especially when unrequited.*

Jace looked up as the waitress passed. "Are we ever going to get any coffee?" he said aloud, interrupting Alec midsentence.

Alec subsided, his energy fading. "I..."

Clary spoke up hastily. "What's all the raw meat for?" she asked, indicating the third page of her menu.

"Werewolves," said Jace. "Though I don't mind a bloody steak myself every once in a while." He reached across the table and flipped Clary's menu over. "Human food is on the back."

She perused the perfectly ordinary menu selections with a feeling of stupefaction. It was all too much. "They have *smoothies* here?"

"There's this apricot-plum smoothie with wildflower honey that's simply divine," said Isabelle, who had appeared with Simon at her side. "Shove over," she said to Clary, who scooted so close to the wall that she could feel the cold bricks pressing into her arm. Simon, sliding in next to Isabelle, offered her a half-embarrassed smile that she didn't return. "You should have one."

Clary wasn't sure if Isabelle was talking to her or to Simon, so she said nothing. Isabelle's hair tickled her face, smelling of some kind of vanilla perfume. Clary fought the urge to sneeze. She hated vanilla perfume. She'd never understood why some girls felt the need to smell like dessert.

"So how did it go at the Bone City?" Isabelle asked, flipping her menu open. "Did you find out what's in Clary's head?"

"We got a name," said Jace. "Magnus—"

"Shut *up*," Alec hissed, thwacking Jace with his closed menu.

Jace looked injured. "Jesus." He rubbed his arm. "What's your problem?"

"This place is full of Downworlders. You know that. I think you should try to keep the details of our investigation secret."

"*Investigation?*" Isabelle laughed. "Now we're detectives? Maybe we should all have code names."

"Good idea," said Jace. "I shall be Baron Hotschaft Von Hugenstein."

Alec spit his water back into his glass. At that moment the waitress arrived to take their order. Up close she was still a pretty blond girl, but her eyes were unnerving—entirely blue, with no white or pupil at all. She smiled with sharp little teeth. "Know what you're having?"

Jace grinned. "The usual," he said, and got a smile from the waitress in return.

"Me too," Alec chimed in, though he didn't get the smile. Isabelle fastidiously ordered a fruit smoothie, Simon asked for coffee, and Clary, after a moment's hesitation, chose a large coffee and coconut pancakes. The waitress winked a blue eye at her and flounced off.

"Is she an ifrit too?" Clary asked, watching her go.

"Kaelie? No. Part-fey, I think," said Jace.

"She's got nixie eyes," said Isabelle thoughtfully.

"You really don't know what she is?" asked Simon.

Jace shook his head. "I respect her privacy." He nudged

Alec. "Hey, let me out for a second."

Scowling, Alec moved aside. Clary watched Jace as he strode over to Kaelie, who was leaning against the bar, talking to the cook through the pass-through to the kitchen. All Clary could see of the cook was a bent head in a white chef's hat. Tall furry ears poked through holes cut into either side of the hat.

Kaelie turned to smile at Jace, who put an arm around her. She snuggled in. Clary wondered if this was what Jace meant by respecting her privacy.

Isabelle rolled her eyes. "He really shouldn't tease the waitstaff like that."

Alec looked at her. "You don't think he means it? That he likes her, I mean."

Isabelle shrugged. "She's a Downworlder," she said, as if that explained everything.

"I don't get it," said Clary.

Isabelle glanced at her without interest. "Get what?"

"This whole Downworlder thing. You don't hunt them, because they aren't exactly demons, but they're not exactly people, either. Vampires kill, they drink blood—"

"Only rogue vampires drink human blood from living people," interjected Alec. "And those, we're allowed to kill."

"And werewolves are what? Just overgrown puppies?"

"They kill demons," said Isabelle. "So if they don't bother us, we don't bother them."

Like letting spiders live because they eat mosquitoes, Clary thought. "So they're good enough to let live, good enough to make your food for you, good enough to flirt with—but not *really* good enough? I mean, not as good as people."

Isabelle and Alec looked at her as if she were speaking

Urdu. "Different from people," said Alec finally.

"Better than mundanes?" said Simon.

"No," Isabelle said decidedly. "You could turn a mundane into a Shadowhunter. I mean, we came from mundanes. But you could never turn a Downworlder into one of the Clave. They can't withstand the runes."

"So they're weak?" asked Clary.

"I wouldn't say that," said Jace, sliding back into his seat next to Alec. His hair was mussed and there was a lipstick mark on his cheek. "At least not with a peri, a djinn, an ifrit, and God knows what else listening in." He grinned as Kaelie appeared and distributed their food. Clary regarded her pancakes consideringly. They looked fantastic: golden brown, drenched with honey. She took a bite as Kaelie wobbled off on her high heels.

They were delicious.

"I told you it was the greatest restaurant in Manhattan," said Jace, eating fries with his fingers.

She glanced at Simon, who was stirring his coffee, head down.

"Mmmf," said Alec, whose mouth was full.

"Right," said Jace. He looked at Clary. "It's not one-way," he said. "We may not always like Downworlders, but they don't always like us, either. A few hundred years of the Accords can't wipe out a thousand years of hostility."

"I'm sure she doesn't know what the Accords are, Jace," said Isabelle around her spoon.

"I do, actually," said Clary.

"I don't," said Simon.

"Yes, but nobody cares what you know." Jace examined

a fry before biting into it. "I enjoy the company of certain Downworlders at certain times and places. But we don't really get invited to the same parties."

"Wait." Isabelle suddenly sat up straight. "What did you say that name was?" she demanded, turning to Jace. "The name in Clary's head."

"I didn't," said Jace. "At least, I didn't finish it. It's Magnus Bane." He grinned at Alec mockingly. "Rhymes with 'over-careful pain in the ass.'"

Alec muttered a retort into his coffee. It rhymed with something that sounded a lot more like "ducking glass mole." Clary smiled inwardly.

"It can't be—but I'm almost totally sure—" Isabelle dug into her purse and pulled out a folded piece of blue paper. She wiggled it between her fingers. "Look at *this*."

Alec held out his hand for the paper, glanced at it with a shrug, and handed it to Jace. "It's a party invitation. For somewhere in Brooklyn," he said. "I hate Brooklyn."

"Don't be such a snob," said Jace. Then, just as Isabelle had, he sat up straight and stared. "Where did you get this, Izzy?"

She fluttered her hand airily. "From that kelpie in Pandemonium. He said it would be awesome. He had a whole stack of them."

"What is it?" Clary demanded impatiently. "Are you going to show the rest of us, or not?"

Jace turned it around so they could all read it. It was printed on thin paper, nearly parchment, in a thin, elegant, spidery hand. It announced a gathering at the humble home of Magnus the Magnificent Warlock, and promised attendees "*a rapturous evening of delights beyond your wildest imaginings.*"

"Magnus," said Simon. "Magnus like Magnus Bane?"

"I doubt there are that many warlocks named Magnus in the Tristate Area," said Jace.

Alec blinked at it. "Does that mean we have to go to the party?" he inquired of no one in particular.

"We don't *have* to do anything," said Jace, who was reading the fine print on the invitation. "But according to this, Magnus Bane is the High Warlock of Brooklyn." He looked at Clary. "I, for one, am a little curious as to what the High Warlock of Brooklyn's name is doing inside your head."

The party didn't start until midnight, so with a whole day to kill, Jace and Alec disappeared to the weapons room and Isabelle and Simon announced their intention of going for a walk in Central Park so that she could show him the faerie circles. Simon asked Clary if she wanted to come along. Stifling a murderous rage, she refused on the grounds of exhaustion.

It wasn't exactly a lie—she *was* exhausted, her body still weakened from the aftereffects of the poison and the too-early rising. She lay on her bed in the Institute, shoes kicked off, willing herself to sleep, but sleep wouldn't come. The caffeine in her veins fizzed like carbonated water, and her mind was full of darting images. She kept seeing her mother's face looking down at her, her expression panicked. Kept seeing the Speaking Stars, hearing the voices of the Silent Brothers in her head. *Why* would there be a block in her mind? Why would a powerful warlock have put it there, and to what purpose? She wondered what memories she might have lost, what experiences she'd had that she couldn't now recall. Or maybe everything she thought she *did* remember was a lie...

She sat up, no longer able to bear where her thoughts were taking her. Barefoot, she padded out into the corridor and toward the library. Maybe Hodge could help her.

But the library was empty. Afternoon light slanted in through the parted curtains, laying bars of gold across the floor. On the desk lay the book Hodge had read out of earlier, its worn leather cover gleaming. Beside it Hugo slept on his perch, beak tucked under wing.

My mother knew that book, Clary thought. *She touched it, read out of it*. The ache to hold something that was a part of her mother's life felt like a gnawing at the pit of her stomach. She crossed the room hastily and laid her hands on the book. It felt warm, the leather heated by sunlight. She raised the cover.

Something folded slid out from between the pages and fluttered to the floor at her feet. She bent to retrieve it, smoothing it open reflexively.

It was the photograph of a group of young people, none much older than Clary herself. She knew it had been taken at least twenty years ago, not because of the clothes they were wearing—which, like most Shadowhunter gear, were nondescript and black—but because she recognized her mother instantly: Jocelyn, no more than seventeen or eighteen, her hair halfway down her back and her face a little rounder, the chin and mouth less defined. *She looks like me*, Clary thought dazedly.

Jocelyn's arm was around a boy Clary didn't recognize. It gave her a jolt. She'd never thought of her mother being involved with anyone other than her father, since Jocelyn had never dated or seemed interested in romance. She wasn't like most single mothers, who trolled PTA meetings for likely-looking dads, or Simon's mom, who was always checking her profile on JDate. The boy was good-looking, with hair so fair it was nearly white, and black eyes.

"That's Valentine," said a voice at her elbow. "When he was seventeen."

She leaped back, almost dropping the photo. Hugo gave a startled and unhappy caw before settling back down on his perch, feathers ruffled.

It was Hodge, looking at her with curious eyes.

"I'm so sorry," she said, setting the photograph down on the desk and backing hastily away. "I didn't mean to pry into your things."

"It's all right." He touched the photograph with a scarred and weathered hand—a strange contrast to the neat spotlessness of his tweed cuffs. "It's a piece of your past, after all."

Clary drifted back toward the desk as if the photo exerted a magnetic pull. The white-haired boy in the photo was smiling at Jocelyn, his eyes crinkled in that way that boys' eyes crinkled when they really liked you. Nobody, Clary thought, had ever looked at *her* that way. Valentine, with his cold, fine-featured face, looked absolutely unlike her own father, with his open smile and the bright hair she'd inherited. "Valentine looks ... sort of nice."

"Nice he wasn't," said Hodge, with a twisted smile, "but he was charming and clever and very persuasive. Do you recognize anyone else?"

She looked again. Standing behind Valentine, a little to the left, was a thin boy with a shock of light brown hair. He had the big shoulders and gawky wrists of someone who hadn't grown into his height yet. "Is that you?"

Hodge nodded. "And...?"

She had to look twice before she identified someone else she knew: so young as to be nearly unrecognizable. In the end his glasses gave him away, and the eyes behind them, light blue as seawater. "Luke," she said.

"Lucian. And here." Leaning over the photo, Hodge indicated an elegant-looking teenage couple, both dark-haired, the girl half a head taller than the boy. Her features were narrow and predatory, almost cruel. "The Lightwoods," he said. "And there"—he indicated a very handsome boy with curling dark hair, high color in his square-jawed face—"is Michael Wayland."

"He doesn't look anything like Jace."

"Jace resembles his mother."

"Is this, like, a class photo?" Clary asked.

"Not quite. This is a picture of the Circle, taken in the year it was formed. That's why Valentine, the leader, is in the front, and Luke is on his right side—he was Valentine's second in command."

Clary turned her gaze away. "I still don't understand why my mother would join something like that."

"You must understand—"

"You keep saying that," Clary said crossly. "I don't see why I must understand anything. You tell me the truth, and I'll either understand it or I won't."

The corner of Hodge's mouth twitched. "As you say." He paused to reach out a hand and stroke Hugo, who was strutting along the edge of the desk importantly. "The Accords have never had the support of the whole Clave. The more venerable families, especially, cling to the old times, when

Downworlders were for killing. Not just out of hatred but because it made them feel safer. It is easier to confront a threat as a mass, a group, not individuals who must be evaluated one by one ... and most of us knew someone who had been injured or killed by a Downworlder. There is nothing," he added, "quite like the moral absolutism of the young. It's easy, as a child, to believe in good and evil, in light and dark. Valentine never lost that—neither his destructive idealism nor his passionate loathing of anything he considered 'nonhuman.'"

"But he loved my mother," said Clary.

"Yes," said Hodge. "He loved your mother. And he loved Idris..."

"What was so great about Idris?" Clary asked, hearing the grumpiness in her own voice.

"It was," Hodge began, and corrected himself, "it *is*, home—for the Nephilim, where they can be their true selves, a place where there is no need for hiding or glamour. A place blessed by the Angel. You have never seen a city until you have seen Alicante of the glass towers. It is more beautiful than you can imagine." There was raw pain in his voice.

Clary thought suddenly of her dream. "Were there ever ... dances in the Glass City?"

Hodge blinked at her as if waking up from a dream. "Every week. I never attended, but your mother did. And Valentine." He chuckled softly. "I was more of a scholar. I spent my days in the library in Alicante. The books you see here are only a fraction of the treasures it holds. I thought perhaps I might join the Brotherhood someday, but after what I did, of course, they would not have me."

"I'm sorry," Clary said awkwardly. Her mind was still full of the memory of her dream. *Was there a mermaid fountain where they danced? Did Valentine wear white, so that my mother could see the Marks on his skin even through his shirt?*

"Can I keep this?" she asked, indicating the photograph.

A flicker of hesitation passed over Hodge's face. "I would prefer you not show it to Jace," he said. "He has enough to contend with, without photos of his dead father turning up."

"Of course." She hugged it to her chest. "Thank you."

"It's nothing." He looked at her quizzically. "Did you come to the library to see me, or for some other purpose?"

"I was wondering if you'd heard from the Clave. About the Cup. And—my mom."

"I got a short reply this morning."

She could hear the eagerness in her own voice. "Have they sent people? Shadowhunters?"

Hodge looked away from her. "Yes, they have."

"Why aren't they staying here?" she asked.

"There is some concern that the Institute is being watched by Valentine. The less he knows, the better." He saw her miserable expression, and sighed. "I'm sorry I can't tell you more, Clarissa. I am not much trusted by the Clave, even now. They told me very little. I wish I could help you."

There was something about the sadness in his voice that made her reluctant to push him for more information. "You can," she said. "I can't sleep. I keep thinking too much. Could you..."

"Ah, the unquiet mind." His voice was full of sympathy. "I can give you something for that. Wait here."

***

The potion Hodge gave her smelled pleasantly of juniper and leaves. Clary kept opening the vial and smelling it on her way back down the corridor. It was unfortunately still open when she entered her bedroom and found Jace sprawled out on the bed, looking at her sketchbook. With a little shriek of astonishment, she dropped the vial; it bounced across the floor, spilling pale-green liquid onto the hardwood.

"Oh, dear," said Jace, sitting up, the sketchbook abandoned. "I hope that wasn't anything important."

"It was a sleeping potion," she said angrily, toeing the vial with the tip of a sneaker. "And now it's gone."

"If only Simon were here. He could probably bore you to sleep."

Clary was in no mood to defend Simon. Instead she sat down on the bed, picking up the sketchbook. "I don't usually let people look at this."

"Why not?" Jace looked tousled, as if he'd been asleep himself. "You're a pretty good artist. Sometimes even excellent."

"Well, because—it's like a diary. Except I don't think in words, I think in pictures, so it's all drawings. But it's still private." She wondered if she sounded as crazy as she suspected.

Jace looked wounded. "A diary with no drawings of me in it? Where are the torrid fantasies? The romance novel covers? The—"

"Do *all* the girls you meet fall in love with you?" Clary asked quietly.

The question seemed to deflate him, like a pin popping a balloon. "It's not *love*," he said, after a pause. "At least—"

"You could try not being charming all the time," Clary said. "It might be a relief for everyone."

He looked down at his hands. They were like Hodge's hands already, snowflaked with tiny white scars, though the skin was young and unlined. "If you're really tired, I could put you to sleep," he said. "Tell you a bedtime story."

She looked at him. "Are you serious?"

"I'm always serious."

She wondered if being tired had made them both a little crazy. But Jace didn't look tired. He looked almost sad. She set the sketchbook down on the night table, and lay down, curling sideways on the pillow. "Okay."

"Close your eyes."

She closed them. She could see the afterimage of lamplight reflected against her inner lids, like tiny starbursts.

"Once there was a boy," said Jace.

Clary interrupted immediately. "A Shadowhunter boy?"

"Of course." For a moment a bleak amusement colored his voice. Then it was gone. "When the boy was six years old, his father gave him a falcon to train. Falcons are raptors—killing birds, his father told him, the Shadowhunters of the sky.

"The falcon didn't like the boy, and the boy didn't like it, either. Its sharp beak made him nervous, and its bright eyes always seemed to be watching him. It would slash at him with beak and talons when he came near: For weeks his wrists and hands were always bleeding. He didn't know it, but his father had selected a falcon that had lived in the wild for over a year, and thus was nearly impossible to tame. But the boy tried, because his father had told him to make the falcon obedient, and he wanted to please his father.

"He stayed with the falcon constantly, keeping it awake

by talking to it and even playing music to it, because a tired bird was meant to be easier to tame. He learned the equipment: the jesses, the hood, the brail, the leash that bound the bird to his wrist. He was meant to keep the falcon blind, but he couldn't bring himself to do it—instead he tried to sit where the bird could see him as he touched and stroked its wings, willing it to trust him. He fed it from his hand, and at first it would not eat. Later it ate so savagely that its beak cut the skin of his palm. But the boy was glad, because it was progress, and because he wanted the bird to know him, even if the bird had to consume his blood to make that happen.

"He began to see that the falcon was beautiful, that its slim wings were built for the speed of flight, that it was strong and swift, fierce and gentle. When it dived to the ground, it moved like light. When it learned to circle and come to his wrist, he nearly shouted with delight. Sometimes the bird would hop to his shoulder and put its beak in his hair. He knew his falcon loved him, and when he was certain it was not just tamed but perfectly tamed, he went to his father and showed him what he had done, expecting him to be proud.

"Instead his father took the bird, now tame and trusting, in his hands and broke its neck. 'I told you to make it obedient,' his father said, and dropped the falcon's lifeless body to the ground. 'Instead, you taught it to love you. Falcons are not meant to be loving pets: They are fierce and wild, savage and cruel. This bird was not tamed; it was broken.'

"Later, when his father left him, the boy cried over his pet, until eventually his father sent a servant to take the body of the bird away and bury it. The boy never cried again, and he never forgot what he'd learned: that to love is to destroy, and that to be loved is to be the one destroyed."

Clary, who had been lying still, hardly breathing, rolled onto her back and opened her eyes. "That's an *awful* story," she said indignantly.

Jace had his legs pulled up, his chin on his knees. "Is it?" he said ruminatively.

"The boy's father is horrible. It's a story about child abuse. I should have known that's what Shadowhunters think a bedtime story is like. Anything that gives you screaming nightmares—"

"Sometimes the Marks can give you screaming nightmares," said Jace. "If you get them when you're too young." He looked at her thoughtfully. The late afternoon light came in through the curtains and made his face a study in contrasts. *Chiaroscuro*, she thought. The art of shadows and light. "It's a good story if you think about it," he said. "The boy's father is just trying to make him stronger. Inflexible."

"But you have to learn to bend a little," said Clary with a yawn. Despite the story's content, the rhythm of Jace's voice had made her sleepy. "Or you'll break."

"Not if you're strong enough," said Jace firmly. He reached out, and she felt the back of his hand brush her cheek; she realized her eyes were slipping shut. Exhaustion made her bones liquid; she felt as if she might wash away and vanish. As she fell into sleep, she heard the echo of words in her mind. *He gave me everything I wanted. Horses, weapons, books, even a hunting falcon.*

"Jace," she tried to say. But sleep had her in its claws; it drew her down, and she was silent.

* * *

She was woken by an urgent voice. "Get *up*!"

Clary opened her eyes slowly. They felt gluey, stuck together. Something was tickling her face. It was someone's hair. She sat up quickly, and her head struck something hard.

"Ow! You hit me in the head!" It was a girl's voice. Isabelle. She flicked on the light next to the bed and regarded Clary resentfully, rubbing at her scalp. She seemed to shimmer in the lamplight—she was wearing a long silvery skirt and a sequined top, and her nails were painted like glittering coins. Strands of silver beads were caught in her dark hair. She looked like a moon goddess. Clary hated her.

"Well, nobody told you to lean over me like that. You practically scared me to death." Clary rubbed at her own head. There was a sore spot just above her eyebrow. "What do you want, anyway?"

Isabelle indicated the dark night sky outside. "It's almost midnight. We've got to leave for the party, and *you're* still not dressed."

"I was just going to wear this," Clary said, indicating her jeans and T-shirt ensemble. "Is that a problem?"

"Is that a problem?" Isabelle looked like she might faint. "Of course it's a problem! No Downworlder would wear those clothes. And it's a party. You'll stick out like a sore thumb if you dress that ... casually," she finished, looking as if the word she'd wanted to use was a lot worse than "casually."

"I didn't know we were dressing up," Clary said sourly. "I don't have any party clothes with me."

"You'll just have to borrow mine."

"Oh *no*." Clary thought of the too-big T-shirt and jeans. "I mean, I couldn't. Really."

Isabelle's smile was as glittering as her nails. "I insist."

"I'd really rather wear my own clothes," Clary protested, squirming uncomfortably as Isabelle positioned her in front of the floor-length mirror in her bedroom.

"Well, you can't," Isabelle said. "You look about eight years old, and worse, you look like a mundane."

Clary set her jaw rebelliously. "None of your clothes are going to fit me."

"We'll see about that."

Clary watched Isabelle in the mirror as she rifled through her closet. Her room looked as if a disco ball had exploded inside it. The walls were black and shimmered with swirls of sponged-on golden paint. Clothes were strewn everywhere: on the rumpled black bed, hung over the backs of the wooden chairs, spilling out of the closet and the tall wardrobe propped against one wall. Her vanity table, its mirror rimmed with spangled pink fur, was covered in glitter, sequins, and pots of blush and powder.

"Nice room," Clary said, thinking longingly of her orange walls at home.

"Thanks. I painted it myself." Isabelle emerged from the closet, holding something black and slinky. She tossed it at Clary.

Clary held the cloth up, letting it unfold. "It looks awfully small."

"It's stretchy," said Isabelle. "Now go put it on."

Hastily, Clary retreated to the small bathroom, which

was painted bright blue. She wriggled the dress on over her head— it was tight, with tiny spaghetti straps. Trying not to inhale too deeply, she returned to the bedroom, where Isabelle was sitting on the bed, sliding a set of jeweled toe rings onto her sandaled feet. "You're so lucky to have such a flat chest," Isabelle said. "I could never wear that without a bra."

Clary scowled. "It's too short."

"It's not short. It's fine," Isabelle said, toeing around under the bed. She kicked out a pair of boots and some black fishnet tights. "Here, you can wear these with it. They'll make you look taller."

"Right, because I'm flat-chested *and* a midget." Clary tugged the hem of the dress down. It just brushed the tops of her thighs. She hardly ever wore skirts, much less short ones, so seeing this much of her own legs was alarming. "If it's this short on me, how short must it be on you?" she mused aloud to Isabelle.

Isabelle grinned. "On me it's a shirt."

Clary flopped down on the bed and pulled the tights and boots on. The shoes were a little loose around the calves, but didn't slide around on her feet. She laced them to the top and stood up, looking at herself in the mirror. She had to admit that the combination of short black dress, fishnets, and high boots was fairly badass. The only thing that spoiled it was—

"Your hair," Isabelle said. "It needs fixing. Desperately. Sit." She pointed imperiously toward the vanity table. Clary sat, and squinched her eyes shut as Isabelle yanked her hair out of its braids—none too kindly—brushed it out, and shoved what felt like bobby pins into it. She opened her eyes just as a powder puff smacked her in the face, releasing a dense cloud of glitter. Clary coughed and glared at Isabelle accusingly.

The other girl laughed. "Don't look at me. Look at yourself."

Glancing in the mirror, Clary saw that Isabelle had pulled her hair up into an elegant swirl on the top of her head, held in place with sparkling pins. Clary was reminded suddenly of her dream, the heavy hair weighing her head down, dancing with Simon... She stirred restlessly.

"Don't get up yet," Isabelle said. "We're not done." She seized an eyeliner pen. "Open your eyes."

Clary widened her eyes, which was good for keeping herself from crying. "Isabelle, can I ask you something?'

"Sure," said Isabelle, wielding the eyeliner expertly.

"Is Alec gay?"

Isabelle's wrist jerked. The eyeliner skidded, inking a long line of black from the corner of Clary's eye to her hairline. "Oh, hell," Isabelle said, putting the pen down.

"It's all right," Clary began, putting her hand up to her eye.

"No, it isn't." Isabelle sounded near tears as she scrabbled around among the piles of junk on top of the vanity. Eventually she came up with a cotton ball, which she handed to Clary. "Here. Use this." She sat down on the edge of the bed, ankle bracelets jingling, and looked at Clary through her hair. "How did you guess?" she said finally.

"I—"

"You absolutely can't tell anyone," said Isabelle.

"Not even Jace?"

"Especially not Jace!"

"All right." Clary heard the stiffness in her own voice. "I

guess I didn't realize it was such a big deal."

"It would be to my parents," said Isabelle quietly. "They would disown him and throw him out of the Clave—"

"What, you can't be gay and a Shadowhunter?"

"There's no official rule about it. But people don't like it. I mean, less with people our age—I think," she added, uncertainly, and Clary remembered how few other people her age Isabelle had ever really met. "But the older generation, no. If it happens, you don't talk about it."

"Oh," said Clary, wishing she'd never mentioned it.

"I love my brother," said Isabelle. "I'd do anything for him. But there's nothing I can do."

"At least he has you," said Clary awkwardly, and she thought for a moment of Jace, who thought of love as something that broke you into pieces. "Do you really think that Jace would ... mind?"

"I don't know," said Isabelle, in a tone that indicated she'd had enough of the topic. "But it's not my choice to make."

"I guess not," Clary said. She leaned in to the mirror, using the cotton Isabelle had given her to dab away the excess eye makeup. When she sat back, she nearly dropped the cotton ball in surprise: What had Isabelle *done* to her? Her cheekbones looked sharp and angular, her eyes deep-set, mysterious, and a luminous green.

"I look like my mom," she said in surprise.

Isabelle raised her eyebrows. "What? Too middle-aged? Maybe some more glitter—"

"No more glitter," Clary said hastily. "No, it's good. I like it."

"Great." Isabelle bounced up off the bed, her anklets chiming. "Let's go."

"I need to stop by my room and grab something," Clary said, standing up. "Also—do I need any weapons? Do you?"

"I've got plenty." Isabelle smiled, kicking her feet up so that her anklets jingled like Christmas bells. "These, for instance. The left one is electrum, which is poisonous to demons, and the right one is blessed iron, in case I run across any unfriendly vampires or even faeries—faeries hate iron. They both have strength runes carved into them, so I can pack a hell of a kick."

"Demon hunting and fashion," Clary said. "I never would have thought they went together."

Isabelle laughed out loud. "You'd be surprised."

The boys were waiting for them in the entryway. They were wearing black, even Simon, in a slightly too-big pair of black pants and his own shirt turned inside out to hide the band logo. He was standing uncomfortably to the side while Jace and Alec slouched together against the wall, looking bored. Simon glanced up as Isabelle strode into the entryway, her gold whip coiled around her wrist, her metal ankle chains chiming like bells. Clary expected him to look stunned—Isabelle did look amazing—but his eyes slid past her to Clary, where they rested with a look of astonishment.

"What *is* that?" he demanded, straightening up. "That you're wearing, I mean."

Clary looked down at herself. She'd thrown a light jacket on to make her feel less naked and grabbed her backpack from her room. It was slung over her shoulder, bumping familiarly between her shoulder blades. But Simon wasn't looking at her backpack; he was looking at her legs as if he'd never seen them before.

"It's a dress, Simon," Clary said dryly. "I know I don't wear them that much, but really."

"It's so *short*," he said in confusion. Even half in demon hunter clothes, Clary thought, he looked like the sort of boy who'd come over to your house to pick you up for a date and be polite to your parents and nice to your pets.

Jace, on the other hand, looked like the sort of boy who'd come over to your house and burn it down for kicks. "I like the dress," he said, unhitching himself from the wall. His eyes ran up and down her lazily, like the stroking paws of a cat. "It needs a little something extra, though."

"So now you're a fashion expert?" Her voice came out unevenly—he was standing very close to her, close enough that she could feel the warmth of him, smell the faint burned scent of newly applied Marks.

He took something out of his jacket and handed it to her. It was a long thin dagger in a leather sheath. The hilt of the dagger was set with a single red stone carved in the shape of a rose.

She shook her head. "I wouldn't even know how to use that—"

He pressed it into her hand, curling her fingers around it. "You'd learn." He dropped his voice. "It's in your blood."

She drew her hand back slowly. "All right."

"I could give you a thigh sheath to put that in," Isabelle offered. "I've got tons."

"CERTAINLY NOT," said Simon.

Clary shot him an irritated look. "Thanks, but I'm not

really a thigh sheath kind of girl." She slid the dagger into the outside pocket on her backpack.

She looked up from closing it to find Jace watching her through hooded eyes. "And one last thing," he said. He reached over and pulled the sparkling pins out of her hair, so that it fell in warm and heavy curls down her neck. The sensation of hair tickling her bare skin was unfamiliar and oddly pleasant.

"Much better," he said, and she thought this time that maybe his voice was slightly uneven too.

12

Dead Man's Party

The directions on the invitation took them to a largely industrial neighborhood in Brooklyn whose streets were lined with factories and warehouses. Some, Clary could see, had been converted into lofts and galleries, but there was still something forbidding about their looming square shapes, boasting only a few windows covered in iron grilles.

They made their way from the subway station, Isabelle navigating with the Sensor, which seemed to have a sort of mapping system built in. Simon, who loved gadgets, was fascinated—or at least he was pretending it was the Sensor he was fascinated with. Hoping to avoid them, Clary lagged behind as they crossed through a scrubby park, its badly kept grass burned brown by the summer heat. To her right the spires of a church gleamed gray and black against the starless night sky.

"Keep up," said an irritable voice in her ear. It was Jace, who had dropped back to walk beside her. "I don't want to have to keep looking behind me to make sure nothing's happened to you."

"So don't bother."

"Last time I left you alone, a demon attacked you," he pointed out.

"Well, I'd certainly hate to interrupt your pleasant night stroll with my sudden death."

He blinked. "There is a fine line between sarcasm and outright hostility, and you seem to have crossed it. What's up?"

She bit her lip. "This morning, weird creepy guys dug around in my brain. Now I'm going to meet the weird creepy guy who originally dug around in my brain. What if I don't like what he finds?"

"What makes you think you won't?"

Clary pulled her hair away from her sticky skin. "I hate it when you answer a question with a question."

"No you don't, you think it's charming. Anyway, wouldn't you rather know the truth?"

"No. I mean, maybe. I don't know." She sighed. "Would you?"

"This is the right street!" called Isabelle, a quarter of a block ahead. They were on a narrow avenue lined with old warehouses, though most now bore the signs of human residence: window boxes filled with flowers, lace curtains blowing in the clammy night breeze, numbered plastic trash cans stacked on the sidewalk. Clary squinted hard, but there was no way to tell if this was the street she'd seen at the Bone City—in her vision it had been nearly obliterated with snow.

She felt Jace's fingers brush her shoulder. "Absolutely. Always," he murmured.

She looked sideways at him, not understanding. "What?"

"The truth," he said. "I would—"

"Jace!" It was Alec. He was standing on the pavement, not far away; Clary wondered why his voice had sounded so loud.

Jace turned, his hand falling away from her shoulder. "Yes?"

"Think we're in the right place?" Alec was pointing at something Clary couldn't see; it was hidden behind the bulk of a large black car.

"What's that?" Jace joined Alec; Clary heard him laugh. Coming around the car, she saw what they were looking at: several motorcycles, sleek and silvery, with low-slung black chassis. Oily-looking tubes and pipes slithered up and around them, ropy as veins. There was a queasy sense of something organic about the bikes, like the bio-creatures in a Giger painting.

"Vampires," Jace said.

"They look like motorcycles to me," said Simon, joining them with Isabelle at his side. She frowned at the bikes.

"They are, but they've been altered to run on demon energies," she explained. "Vampires use them—it lets them get around fast at night. It's not strictly Covenant, but..."

"I've heard some of the bikes can fly," said Alec eagerly. He sounded like Simon with a new video game. "Or go invisible at the flick of a switch. Or operate under water."

Jace had jumped down off the curb and was circling the bikes, examining them. He reached out a hand and stroked one of the bikes along the sleek chassis. It had words painted along the side, in silver: NOX INVICTUS. "Victorious night," he translated.

Alec was looking at him strangely. "What are you doing?"

Clary thought she saw Jace slide his hand back inside his jacket. "Nothing."

"Well, hurry up," said Isabelle. "I didn't get this dressed up to watch you mess around in the gutter with a bunch of motorcycles."

"They are pretty to look at," said Jace, hopping back up on the pavement. "You have to admit that."

"So am I," said Isabelle, who didn't look inclined to admit anything. "Now hurry up."

Jace was looking at Clary. "This building," he said, pointing at the red brick warehouse. "Is this the one?"

Clary exhaled. "I think so," she said uncertainly. "They all look the same."

"One way to find out," said Isabelle, mounting the steps with a determined stride. The rest of them followed, crowding close to one another in the foul-smelling entryway. A naked bulb hung from a cord overhead, illuminating a large metalbound door and a row of apartment buzzers along the left wall. Only one had a name written over it: BANE.

Isabelle pressed the buzzer. Nothing happened. She pressed it again. She was about to press it a third time when Alec caught her wrist. "Don't be rude," he said.

She glared at him. "Alec—"

The door flew open.

A slender man standing in the doorway regarded them curiously. It was Isabelle who recovered herself first, flashing a brilliant smile. "Magnus? Magnus Bane?"

"That would be me." The young man blocking the doorway was as tall and thin as a rail, his hair a crown of dense black spikes. He was Asian, with an elegantly high-cheekboned, handsome face, broad-shouldered despite his slim frame. He was certainly dressed for a party, in tight jeans and a black shirt covered with dozens of metal buckles. His eyes were crusted with a raccoon mask of charcoal glitter, his lips painted a dark shade of blue. He raked a ring-laden hand through his spiked hair and regarded them thoughtfully. "Children of the Nephilim," he said. "Well, well. I don't recall inviting you."

Isabelle took out her invitation and waved it like a white flag. "I have an invitation. These"—she indicated the rest of the group with a grand wave of her arm—"are my friends."

Magnus plucked the invitation out of her hand and looked at it with fastidious distaste. "I must have been drunk," he said. He threw the door open. "Come in. And try not to murder any of my guests."

Jace edged into the doorway, sizing up Magnus with his eyes. "Even if one of them spills a drink on my new shoes?"

"Even then." Magnus's hand shot out, so fast it was barely a blur. He plucked the stele out of Jace's hand—Clary hadn't even realized he was holding it—and held it up. Jace looked faintly abashed. "As for this," Magnus said, sliding it into Jace's jeans pocket, "keep it in your pants, Shadowhunter."

Magnus grinned and started up the stairs, leaving a surprised-looking Jace holding the door. "Come on," he said, waving the rest of them inside. "Before anyone thinks it's *my* party."

They pushed past Jace, laughing nervously. Only Isabelle stopped to shake her head. "Try not to piss him off, please. Then he won't help us."

Jace looked bored. "I know what I'm doing."

"I hope so." Isabelle flounced past him in a swirl of skirts.

Magnus's apartment was at the top of a long flight of rickety stairs. Simon hurried to catch up with Clary, who was regretting having put her hand on the banister to steady herself. It was sticky with something that glowed a faint and sickly green.

"Yech," said Simon, and offered her a corner of his T-shirt to wipe her hand on. She did. "Is everything all right? You seem—distracted."

"He just looks so familiar. Magnus, I mean."

"You think he goes to St. Xavier's?"

"Very funny." She looked at him sourly.

"You're right. He's too old to be a student. I think I had him for chem last year."

Clary laughed out loud. Immediately Isabelle was beside her, breathing down her neck. "Am I missing something funny? Simon?"

Simon had the grace to look embarrassed, but said nothing. Clary muttered, "You're not missing anything," and dropped behind them. Isabelle's lug-soled boots were starting to hurt her feet. By the time she reached the top of the stairs she was limping, but she forgot the pain as soon as she walked through Magnus's front door.

The loft was huge and almost totally empty of furniture. Floor-to-ceiling windows were smeared with a thick film of dirt and paint, blocking out most of the ambient light from the street. Big metal pillars wound with colored lights held up an arched, sooty ceiling. Doors torn off their hinges and laid across dented metal garbage cans made a makeshift bar at one end of the room. A lilac-skinned woman in a metallic bustier was ranging drinks along the bar in tall, harshly colored glasses that tinted the fluid inside them: blood red, cyanosis blue, poison green. Even for a New York bartender she worked with an amazingly speedy efficiency—probably helped along by the fact that she had a second set of long, graceful arms to go with the first. Clary was reminded of Luke's Indian goddess statue.

The rest of the crowd was just as strange. A good-looking boy with wet green-black hair grinned at her over a platter of what looked like raw fish. His teeth were sharp and serrated, like a shark's. Beside him stood a girl with long dirty-blond hair, braided with flowers. Under the skirt of her short green dress, her feet were webbed like a frog's. A group of young women so pale Clary wondered if they were wearing white stage makeup sipped scarlet liquid too thick to be wine from fluted crystal glasses. The center of the room was packed with bodies dancing to the pounding beat that bounced off the walls, though Clary couldn't see a band anywhere.

"You like the party?"

She turned to see Magnus lounging against one of the pillars. His eyes shone in the darkness. Glancing around, she saw that Jace and the others were gone, swallowed up by the crowd.

She tried to smile. "Is it in honor of anything?"

"My cat's birthday."

"Oh." She glanced around. "Where's your cat?"

He unhitched himself from the pillar, looking solemn. "I don't know. He ran away."

Clary was spared responding to this by the reappearance

of Jace and Alec. Alec looked sullen as usual. Jace was wearing a strand of tiny glowing flowers around his neck and seemed pleased with himself. "Where are Simon and Isabelle?" Clary said.

"On the dance floor." He pointed. She could just see them on the edge of the packed square of bodies. Simon was doing what he usually did in lieu of dancing, which was to bounce up and down on the balls of his feet, looking uncomfortable. Isabelle was slinking in a circle around him, sinuous as a snake, trailing her fingers across his chest. She was looking at him as if she were planning to drag him off into a corner to have sex. Clary hugged her arms around herself, her bracelets clanking together. *If they dance any closer together, they won't have to go off in a corner to have sex.*

"Look," Jace said, turning to Magnus, "we really need to talk to—"

"MAGNUS BANE!" The deep, booming voice belonged to a surprisingly short man who looked to be in his early thirties. He was compactly muscular, with a bald head shaved smooth and a pointed goatee. He leveled a trembling finger at Magnus. "*Someone* just poured holy water into the gas tank on my bike. It's ruined. Destroyed. All the pipes are melted."

"Melted?" murmured Magnus. "How dreadful."

"I want to know who did it." The man bared his teeth, showing long pointed canines. Clary stared in fascination. They didn't look at all the way she'd imagined vampire fangs: These were as thin and sharp as needles. "I thought you swore there'd be no wolf-men here tonight, *Bane*."

"I invited none of the Moon's Children," Magnus said, examining his glittery nails. "Precisely because of your stupid little feud. If any of them decided to sabotage your bike, they weren't a guest of mine, and are therefore..." He offered a winsome smile. "Not my responsibility."

The vampire roared with rage, jabbing his finger toward Magnus. "Are you trying to tell me that—"

Magnus's glitter-coated index finger twitched just a fraction, so slightly that Clary almost thought he hadn't moved at all. Mid-roar the vampire gagged and clutched at his throat. His mouth worked, but no sound came out.

"You've worn out your welcome," Magnus said lazily, opening his eyes very wide. Clary saw, with a jolt of surprise, that they had vertical slit pupils, like a cat's. "Now go." He splayed the fingers of his hand, and the vampire turned as smartly as if someone had grabbed his shoulders and spun him around. He marched back into the crowd, heading toward the door.

Jace whistled under his breath. "That was impressive."

"You mean that little hissy fit?" Magnus cast his eyes toward the ceiling. "I know."

Alec made a choking noise. After a moment Clary recognized it as laughter. *He ought to do that more often.*

"We put the holy water in his gas tank, you know," he said.

"ALEC," said Jace. "Shut up."

"I assumed that," said Magnus, looking amused. "Vindictive little bastards, aren't you? You know their bikes run on demon energies. I doubt he'll be able to repair it."

"One less leech with a fancy ride," said Jace. "My heart bleeds."

"I heard some of them can make their bikes fly," put in Alec, who looked animated for once. He was almost smiling.

"Merely an old warlocks' tale," said Magnus, his cat's eyes glittering. "So is that why you wanted to crash my party? Just to wreck some bloodsucker bikes?"

"No." Jace was all business again. "We need to talk to you. Preferably somewhere private."

Magnus raised an eyebrow. *Damn*, Clary thought, *another one*. "Am I in trouble with the Clave?"

"No," said Jace.

"Probably not," said Alec. "Ow!" He glared at Jace, who had kicked him sharply in the ankle.

"No," Jace repeated. "We can talk to you under the seal of the Covenant. If you help us, anything you say will be confidential."

"And if I don't help you?"

Jace spread his hands wide. The rune tattoos on his palms stood out stark and black. "Maybe nothing. Maybe a visit from the Silent City."

Magnus's voice was honey poured over shards of ice. "That's quite a choice you're offering me, little Shadowhunter."

"It's no choice at all," said Jace.

"Yes," said the warlock. "That's exactly what I meant."

Magnus's bedroom was a riot of color: canary-yellow sheets and bedspread draped over a mattress on the floor, electric-blue vanity table strewn with more pots of paint and makeup than Isabelle's. Rainbow velvet curtains hid the floor-to-ceiling windows, and a tangled wool rug covered the floor.

"Nice place," said Jace, drawing aside a heavy swag of curtain. "Guess it pays well, being the High Warlock of Brooklyn?"

"It pays," Magnus said. "Not much of a benefit package, though. No dental." He shut the door behind him and leaned against it. When he crossed his arms, his T-shirt rode up, showing a strip of flat golden stomach unmarked by a navel. "So," he said. "What's on your devious little minds?"

"It's not them, actually," Clary said, finding her voice before Jace could reply. "I'm the one who wanted to talk to you."

Magnus turned his inhuman eyes on her. "You are not one of them," he said. "Not of the Clave. But you can see the Invisible World."

"My mother was one of the Clave," Clary said. It was the first time she had said it out loud and known it to be true. "But she never told me. She kept it a secret. I don't know why."

"So ask her."

"I can't. She's..." Clary hesitated. "She's gone."

"And your father?"

"He died before I was born."

Magnus exhaled irritably. "As Oscar Wilde once said, 'To lose one parent may be regarded as a misfortune. To lose both seems like carelessness.'"

Clary heard Jace make a small hissing sound, like air being sucked through his teeth. She said, "I didn't lose my mother. She was taken from me. By Valentine."

"I don't know any Valentine," said Magnus, but his eyes flickered like wavering candle flames, and Clary knew he was lying. "I'm sorry for your tragic circumstances, but I fail to see what any of this has to do with me. If you could tell me—"

"She can't tell you, because she doesn't remember," Jace said sharply. "Someone erased her memories. So we went to the Silent City to see what the Brothers could pull out of her head. They got two words. I think you can guess what they were."

There was a short silence. Finally, Magnus let his mouth turn up at the corner. His smile was bitter. "My signature," he said. "I knew it was folly when I did it. An act of hubris..."

"You *signed* my mind?" Clary said in disbelief.

Magnus raised his hand, tracing the fiery outlines of letters against the air. When he dropped his hand, they hung there, hot and golden, making the painted lines of his eyes and mouth burn with reflected light. MAGNUS BANE.

"I was proud of my work on you," he said slowly, looking at Clary. "So clean. So perfect. What you saw you would forget, even as you saw it. No image of pixie or goblin or long-legged beastie would remain to trouble your blameless mortal sleep. It was the way she wanted it."

Clary's voice was thin with tension. "The way who wanted it?"

Magnus sighed, and at the touch of his breath, the fire-letters sifted away to glowing ash. Finally he spoke—and though she was not surprised, though she had known exactly what he was going to say, still she felt the words like a blow against her heart.

"Your mother," he said.

13
The Memory of Whiteness

"My mother did this to me?" Clary demanded, but her surprised outrage didn't sound convincing, even to her own ears. Looking around, she saw pity in Jace's eyes, in Alec's—even Alec had guessed and felt sorry for her. "Why?"

"I don't know." Magnus spread his long white hands. "It's not my job to ask questions. I do what I get paid to do."

"Within the bounds of the Covenant," Jace reminded him, his voice soft as cat's fur.

Magnus inclined his head. "Within the bounds of the Covenant, of course."

"So the Covenant's all right with this—this mind-rape?" Clary asked bitterly. When no one answered, she sank down on the edge of Magnus's bed. "Was it only once? Was there something specific she wanted me to forget? Do you know what it was?"

Magnus paced restlessly to the window. "I don't think you understand. The first time I ever saw you, you must have been about two years old. I was watching out this window"—he tapped the glass, freeing a shower of dust and paint chips—"and I saw her hurrying up the street, holding something wrapped in a blanket. I was surprised when she stopped at my door. She looked so ordinary, so young."

The moonlight touched his hawkish profile with silver. "She unwrapped the blanket when she came in my door. You were inside it. She set you down on the floor and you started ranging around, picking things up, pulling my cat's tail—you screamed like a banshee when the cat scratched you, so I asked your mother if you *were* part banshee. She didn't laugh." He paused. They were all watching him intently now, even Alec. "She told me she was a Shadowhunter. There was no point in her lying about it; Marks show up, even when they've faded with time, like faint silver scars against the skin. They flickered when she moved." He rubbed at the glitter makeup around his eyes. "She told me she'd hoped you'd been born with a blind Inner Eye—some Shadowhunters have to be taught to see the Shadow World. But she'd caught you that afternoon, teasing a pixie trapped in a hedge. She knew you could see. So she asked me if it was possible to blind you of the Sight."

Clary made a little noise, a pained exhalation of breath, but Magnus went on remorselessly.

"I told her that crippling that part of your mind might leave you damaged, possibly insane. She didn't cry. She wasn't the sort of woman who weeps easily, your mother. She asked me if there was another way, and I told her you could be made to forget those parts of the Shadow World that you could see, even as you saw them. The only caveat was that she'd have to come to me every two years as the results of the spell began to fade."

"And did she?" asked Clary.

Magnus nodded. "I've seen you every two years since that first time—I've watched you grow up. You're the only child I have ever watched grow up that way, you know. In my business one isn't generally that welcome around human children."

"So you recognized Clary when we walked in," Jace said. "You must have."

"Of course I did." Magnus sounded exasperated. "And it was a shock, too. But what would you have done? She didn't know me. She wasn't supposed to know me. Just the fact that she was here meant the spell had started to fade—and in fact, we were due for another visit about a month ago. I even came by your house when I got back from Tanzania, but Jocelyn said that you two had had a fight and you'd run off. She said she'd call on me when you came back, but"—an elegant shrug—"she never did."

A cold wash of memory prickled Clary's skin. She remembered standing in the foyer next to Simon, straining to remember something that danced just at the edge of her vision... *I thought I saw Dorothea's cat, but it was just a trick of the light.*

But Dorothea didn't have a cat. "You were there, that day," Clary said. "I saw you coming out of Dorothea's apartment. I remember your eyes."

Magnus looked as if he might purr. "I'm memorable, it's true," he gloated. Then he shook his head. "You shouldn't remember me," he said. "I threw up a glamour as hard as a wall as soon as I saw you. You should have run right into it face-first—psychically speaking."

If you run into a psychic wall face-first, do you wind up with psychic bruises? Clary said, "If you take the spell off me, will I be able to remember all the things I've forgotten? All the memories you stole?"

"I can't take it off you." Magnus looked uncomfortable.

"What?" Jace sounded furious. "Why not? The Clave requires you—"

Magnus looked at him coldly. "I don't like being told what to do, little Shadowhunter."

Clary could see how much Jace disliked being referred to as "little," but before he could snap out a reply, Alec spoke. His voice was soft, thoughtful. "Don't you know how to reverse it?" he asked. "The spell, I mean."

Magnus sighed. "Undoing a spell is a great deal more difficult than creating it in the first place. The intricacy of this one, the care I put into weaving it—if I made even the smallest mistake in unraveling it, her mind could be damaged forever. Besides," he added, "it's already begun to fade. The effects will vanish over time on their own."

Clary looked at him sharply. "Will I get all my memories back then? Whatever was taken out of my head?"

"I don't know. They might come back all at once, or in stages. Or you might never remember what you've forgotten over the years. What your mother asked me to do was unique, in my experience. I've no idea what will happen."

"But I don't want to wait." Clary folded her hands tightly in her lap, her fingers clamped together so hard that the tips turned white. "All my life I've felt like there was something wrong with me. Something missing or damaged. Now I know—"

"I didn't damage you." It was Magnus's turn to interrupt, his lips curled back angrily to show sharp white teeth. "Every teenager in the world feels like that, feels broken or out of place, different somehow, royalty mistakenly born into a family of peasants. The difference in your case is that it's true. You *are* different. Maybe not better—but different. And it's no picnic being different. You want to know what it's like when you happen to be born with the devil's mark?" He pointed at his eyes, fingers splayed. "When your 'father' flinches at the sight of you and your mother hangs herself in the barn, driven mad by what she's done—or what's been down to her? When I was ten, the man who raised me tried to drown me in the creek. He knew I was no son of his; that my real father was a demon. I lashed out at him with everything I had—burned him where he stood. I went to the Silent Brothers eventually, for sanctuary. They hid me. They say that pity's a bitter thing, but it's better than hate. When I found out what I was really, only half a human being, I hated myself. Anything's better than that."

There was silence when Magnus was done speaking. To Clary's surprise, it was Alec who broke it. "It wasn't your fault," he said. "You can't help how you're born."

Magnus's expression was closed. "I'm over it," he said. "I think you get my point. Different isn't better, Clarissa. Your mother was trying to protect you. Don't throw it back in her face."

Clary's hands relaxed their grip on each other. "I don't care if I'm different," she said. "I just want to be who I really am."

Magnus swore, in a language she didn't know. It

sounded like crackling flames. "All right. Listen. I can't undo what I've done, but I can give you something else. A piece of what would have been yours if you'd been raised a true child of the Nephilim." He stalked across the room to the bookcase and dragged down a heavy volume bound in rotting green velvet. He flipped through the pages, shedding dust and bits of blackened cloth. The pages were thin, almost translucent eggshell parchment, each marked with a stark black rune.

Jace's eyebrows went up. "Is that a copy of the Gray Book?"

Magnus, feverishly flipping pages, said nothing.

"Hodge has one," Alec observed. "He showed it to me once."

"It's not gray," Clary felt compelled to point out. "It's green."

"If there was such a thing as terminal literalism, you'd have died in childhood," said Jace, brushing dust off the windowsill and eyeing it as if considering whether it was clean enough to sit on. "Gray is short for 'Gramarye.' It means 'magic, hidden wisdom.' In it is copied every rune the Angel Raziel wrote in the original Book of the Covenant. There aren't many copies because each one has to be specially made. Some of the runes are so powerful they'd burn through regular pages."

Alec looked impressed. "I didn't know all that."

Jace hopped up on the windowsill and swung his legs. "Not all of us sleep through history lessons."

"I do not—"

"Oh, yes you do, and drool on the desk besides."

"Shut up," said Magnus, but he said it quite mildly. He hooked his finger between two pages of the book and came over to Clary, setting it carefully in her lap. "Now, when I open the book, I want you to study the page. Look at it until you feel something change inside your mind."

"Will it hurt?" Clary asked nervously.

"All knowledge hurts," he replied, and stood up, letting the book fall open in her lap. Clary stared down at the clean white page with the black rune Mark spilled across it. It looked something like a winged spiral, until she tilted her head, and then it seemed like a staff wound around with vines. The mutable corners of the pattern tickled her mind like feathers brushed against sensitive skin. She felt the shivery flicker of reaction, making her want to close her eyes, but she held them open until they stung and blurred. She was about to blink when she felt it: a click inside her head, like a key turning in a lock.

The rune on the page seemed to spring into sharp focus, and she thought, involuntarily, *Remember*. If the rune were a word, it would have been that one, but there was more meaning to it than any word she could imagine. It was a child's first memory of light falling through crib bars, the recollected scent of rain and city streets, the pain of unforgotten loss, the sting of remembered humiliation, and the cruel forgetfulness of old age, when the most ancient of memories stand out with agonizingly clear precision and the nearest of incidents are lost beyond recall.

With a little sigh she turned to the next page, and the next, letting the images and sensations flow over her. *Sorrow. Thought. Strength. Protection. Grace*—and then cried out in reproachful surprise as Magnus snatched the book off her lap.

"That's enough," he said, sliding it back onto its shelf.

He dusted his hands off on his jeans, leaving streaks of gray. "If you read all the runes at once, you'll give yourself a headache."

"But—"

"Most Shadowhunter children grow up learning one rune at a time over a period of years," said Jace. "The Gray Book contains runes even I don't know."

"Imagine that," said Magnus.

Jace ignored him. "Magnus showed you the rune for understanding and remembrance. It opens your mind up to reading and recognizing the rest of the Marks."

"It also may serve as a trigger to activate dormant memories," said Magnus. "They could return to you more quickly than they would otherwise. It's the best I can do."

Clary looked down at her lap. "I still don't remember anything about the Mortal Cup."

"Is *that* what this is about?" Magnus sounded actually astonished. "You're after the Angel's Cup? Look, I've been through your memories. There was nothing in them about the Mortal Instruments."

"Mortal Instruments? " Clary echoed, bewildered. "I thought—"

"The Angel gave three items to the first Shadowhunters. A cup, a sword, and a mirror. The Silent Brothers have the sword; the cup and the mirror were in Idris, at least until Valentine came along."

"Nobody knows where the mirror is," said Alec. "Nobody's known for ages."

"It's the Cup that concerns us," said Jace. "Valentine's looking for it."

"And you want to get to it before he does?" Magnus asked, his eyebrows winging upward.

"I thought you said you didn't know who Valentine was?" Clary pointed out.

"I lied," Magnus admitted candidly. "I'm not one of the fey, you know. I'm not required to be truthful. And only a fool would get between Valentine and his revenge."

"Is that what you think he's after? Revenge?" said Jace.

"I would guess so. He suffered a grave defeat, and he hardly seemed—seems—the type of man to suffer defeat gracefully."

Alec looked harder at Magnus. "Were you at the Uprising?"

Magnus's eyes locked with Alec's. "I was. I killed a number of your folk."

"Circle members," said Jace quickly. "Not ours—"

"If you insist on disavowing that which is ugly about what you do," said Magnus, still looking at Alec, "you will never learn from your mistakes."

Alec, plucking at the coverlet with one hand, flushed an unhappy red. "You don't seem surprised to hear that Valentine's still alive," he said, avoiding Magnus's gaze.

Magnus spread his hands wide. "Are you?"

Jace opened his mouth, then closed it again. He looked actually baffled. Eventually, he said, "So you won't help us find the Mortal Cup?"

"I wouldn't if I could," said Magnus, "which, by the way, I can't. I've no idea where it is, and I don't care to know. Only a fool, as I said."

Alec sat up straighter. "But without the Cup, we can't—"

"Make more of you. I know," said Magnus. "Perhaps

not everyone regards that as quite the disaster that you do. Mind you," he added, "if I had to choose between the Clave and Valentine, I would choose the Clave. At least they're not actually sworn to wipe out my kind. But nothing the Clave has done has earned my unswerving loyalty either. So no, I'll sit this one out. Now if we're done here, I'd like to get back to my party before any of the guests eat each other."

Jace, who was clenching and unclenching his hands, looked like he was about to say something furious, but Alec, standing up, put a hand on his shoulder. Clary couldn't quite tell in the dimness, but it looked as if Alec was squeezing rather hard. "Is that likely?" he asked.

Magnus was looking at him with some amusement. "It's happened before."

Jace muttered something to Alec, who let go. Detaching himself, he came over to Clary. "Are you all right?" he asked in a low voice.

"I think so. I don't feel any different..."

Magnus, standing by the door, snapped his fingers impatiently. "Move it along, teenagers. The only person who gets to canoodle in my bedroom is my magnificent self."

"Canoodle?" repeated Clary, never having heard the word before.

"Magnificent?" repeated Jace, who was just being nasty. Magnus growled. The growl sounded like "Get out."

They got, Magnus trailing behind them as he paused to lock the bedroom door. The tenor of the party seemed subtly different to Clary. Perhaps it was just her slightly altered vision: Everything seemed clearer, crystalline edges sharply defined. She watched a group of musicians take the small stage at the center of the room. They wore flowing garments in deep colors of gold, purple, and green, and their high voices were sharp and ethereal.

"I hate faerie bands," Magnus muttered as the musicians segued into another haunting song, the melody as delicate and translucent as rock crystal. "All they ever play is mopey ballads."

Jace, glancing around the room, laughed. "Where's Isabelle?"

A rush of guilty concern hit Clary. She'd forgotten about Simon. She spun around, looking for the familiar skinny shoulders and shock of dark hair. "I don't see him. Them, I mean."

"There she is." Alec spotted his sister and waved her over, looking relieved. "Over here. And watch out for the phouka."

"Watch out for the phouka?" Jace repeated, glancing toward a thin brown-skinned man in a green paisley vest who eyed Isabelle thoughtfully as she walked by.

"He pinched me when I passed him earlier," Alec said stiffly. "In a highly personal area."

"I hate to break it to you, but if he's interested in your highly personal areas, he probably isn't interested in your sister's."

"Not necessarily," said Magnus. "Faeries aren't particular."

Jace curled his lip scornfully in the warlock's direction. "You still here?"

Before Magnus could reply, Isabelle was on top of them, looking pink-faced and blotchy and smelling strongly of alcohol. "Jace! Alec! Where have you been? I've been looking all over—"

"Where's Simon?" Clary interrupted.

Isabelle wobbled. "He's a rat," she said darkly.

"Did he do something to you?" Alec was full of brotherly concern. "Did he touch you? If he tried anything—"

"No, Alec," Isabelle said irritably. "Not like that. He's a *rat*."

"She's drunk," said Jace, beginning to turn away in disgust.

"I'm not," Isabelle said indignantly. "Well, maybe a little, but that's not the point. The point is, Simon drank one of those blue drinks—I told him not to, but he didn't listen—and he *turned into a rat*."

"A *rat*?" Clary repeated incredulously. "You don't mean..."

"I mean a rat," Isabelle said. "Little. Brown. Scaly tail."

"The Clave isn't going to like this," said Alec dubiously. "I'm pretty sure turning mundanes into rats is against the Law."

"Technically she didn't turn him into a rat," Jace pointed out. "The worst she could be accused of is negligence."

"Who *cares* about the stupid Law?" Clary screamed, grabbing hold of Isabelle's wrist. "My best friend is a rat!"

"Ouch!" Isabelle tried to pull her wrist back. "Let go of me!"

"Not until you tell me where he is." She'd never wanted to smack anyone as much as she wanted to smack Isabelle right at that moment. "I can't believe you just left him—he's probably terrified—"

"If he hasn't been stepped on," Jace pointed out unhelpfully.

"I didn't leave him. He ran under the bar," Isabelle protested, pointing. "Let go! You're denting my bracelet."

"Bitch," Clary said savagely, and flung a surprised-looking Isabelle's hand back at her, hard. She didn't stop for a reaction; she was running toward the bar. Dropping to her knees, she peered into the dark space under it. In the moldy-smelling gloom, she thought she could just detect a pair of glinting, beady eyes.

"Simon?" she said, her voice choked. "Is that you?"

Simon-the-rat crept forward slightly, his whiskers trembling. She could see the shape of his small rounded ears, flat against his head, and the sharp point of his nose. She fought down a feeling of revulsion—she'd never liked rats, with their yellowy squared-off teeth all ready to bite. She wished he'd been turned into a hamster.

"It's me, Clary," she said slowly. "Are you okay?"

Jace and the others arrived behind her, Isabelle looking more annoyed now than tearful. "Is he under there?" Jace asked curiously.

Clary, still on her hands and knees, nodded. "Shh. You'll frighten him off." She pushed her fingers gingerly under the edge of the bar, and wiggled them. "Please come out, Simon. We'll get Magnus to reverse the spell. It'll be okay."

She heard a squeak, and the rat's pink nose poked out from beneath the bar. With an exclamation of relief, Clary seized the rat in her hands. "Simon! You understood me!"

The rat, huddled in the hollow of her palms, squeaked glumly. Delighted, she hugged him to her chest. "Oh, poor baby," she crooned, almost as if he really were a pet. "Poor Simon, it'll be fine, I promise—"

"I wouldn't feel too sorry for him," Jace said. "That's probably the closest he's ever gotten to second base."

"Shut *up*!" Clary glared at Jace furiously, but she did loosen her grip on the rat. His whiskers were trembling, whether in anger or agitation or simple terror, she couldn't tell. "Get

Magnus," she said sharply. "We have to turn him back."

"Let's not be hasty." Jace was actually grinning, the bastard. He reached toward Simon as if he meant to pet him. "He's cute like that. Look at his little pink nose."

Simon bared long yellow teeth at Jace and made a snapping motion. Jace pulled his outstretched hand back. "Izzy, go fetch our magnificent host."

"Why me?" Isabelle looked petulant.

"Because it's your fault the mundane's a rat, idiot," he said, and Clary was struck by how rarely any of them, other than Isabelle, ever said Simon's actual name. "And we can't leave him here."

"You'd be happy to leave him if it weren't for *her*," Isabelle said, managing to inject the single syllable word with enough venom to poison an elephant. She stalked off, her skirt flouncing around her hips.

"I can't believe she let you drink that blue drink," Clary said to rat-Simon. "Now you see what you get for being so shallow."

Simon squeaked irritably. Clary heard someone chuckle and glanced up to see Magnus leaning over her. Isabelle stood behind him, her expression furious. "*Rattus norvegicus,*" said Magnus, peering at Simon. "A common brown rat, nothing exotic."

"I don't care what kind of rat he is," Clary said crossly. "I want him turned back."

Magnus scratched his head thoughtfully, shedding glitter. "No point," he said.

"That's what I said." Jace looked pleased.

"NO POINT?" Clary shouted, so loudly that Simon hid

his head under her thumb. "HOW CAN YOU SAY THERE'S NO POINT?"

"Because he'll turn back on his own in a few hours," said Magnus. "The effect of the cocktails is temporary. No point working up a transformation spell; it'll just traumatize him. Too much magic is hard on mundanes, their systems aren't used to it."

"I doubt his system is used to being a rat, either," Clary pointed out. "You're a warlock, can't you just reverse the spell?"

Magnus considered. "No," he said.

"You mean you won't."

"Not for free, darling, and you can't afford me."

"I can't take a rat home on the subway either," Clary said plaintively. "I'll drop him, or one of the MTA police will arrest me for transporting pests on the transit system." Simon chirped his annoyance. "Not that you're a pest, of course."

A girl who had been shouting by the door was now joined by six or seven others. The sound of angry voices rose above the hum of the party and the strains of the music. Magnus rolled his eyes. "Excuse me," he said, backing into the crowd, which closed behind him instantly.

Isabelle, wobbling on her sandals, expelled a gusty sigh. "So much for *his* help."

"You know," Alec said, "you could always put the rat in your backpack."

Clary looked at him hard, but couldn't find anything wrong with the idea. It wasn't as if she had a pocket she could have tucked him in. Isabelle's clothes didn't allow for pockets; they were too tight. Clary was amazed they allowed for Isabelle.

Shrugging off her pack, she found a hiding place for the

small brown rat that had once been Simon, nestled between her rolled-up sweater and her sketchpad. He curled up atop her wallet, looking reproachful. "I'm sorry," she said miserably.

"Don't bother," Jace said. "Why mundanes always insist on taking responsibility for things that aren't their fault is a mystery to me. You didn't force that cocktail down his idiotic throat."

"If it weren't for me, he wouldn't have been here at all," Clary said in a small voice.

"Don't flatter yourself. He came because of Isabelle."

Angrily Clary jerked the top of the bag closed and stood up. "Let's get out of here. I'm sick of this place."

The tight knot of shouting people by the door turned out to be more vampires, easily recognizable by the pallor of their skin and the dead blackness of their hair. *They must dye it*, Clary thought, they couldn't possibly all be naturally dark-haired, and besides, some of them had blond eyebrows. They were loudly complaining about their vandalized motorbikes and the fact that some of their friends were missing and unaccounted for.

"They're probably drunk and passed out somewhere," Magnus said, waving long white fingers in a bored manner. "You know how you lot tend to turn into bats and piles of dust when you've downed a few too many Bloody Marys."

"They mix their vodka with real blood," Jace said in Clary's ear.

The pressure of his breath made her shiver. "Yes, I got that, thanks."

"We can't go around picking up every pile of dust in the place just in case it turns out to be Gregor in the morning," said a girl with a sulky mouth and painted-on eyebrows.

"Gregor will be fine. I rarely sweep," soothed Magnus. "I'm happy to send any stragglers back to the hotel come tomorrow—in a car with blacked-out windows, of course."

"But what about our motorbikes?" said a thin boy whose blond roots showed under his bad dye job. A gold earring in the shape of a stake hung from his left earlobe. "It'll take hours to fix them."

"You've got until sunrise," said Magnus, temper visibly fraying. "I suggest you get started." He raised his voice. "All right, that's IT! Party's over! Everybody out!" He waved his arms, shedding glitter.

With a single loud twang the band ceased playing. A drone of loud complaint rose from the partygoers, but they moved obediently toward the doorway. None of them stopped to thank Magnus for the party.

"Come on." Jace pushed Clary toward the exit. The crowd was dense. She held her backpack in front of her, hands wrapped protectively around it. Someone bumped her shoulder, hard, and she yelped and moved sideways, away from Jace. A hand brushed her backpack. She looked up and saw the vampire with the stake earring grinning at her. "Hey, pretty thing," he said. "What's in the bag?"

"Holy water," said Jace, reappearing beside her as if he'd been conjured up like a genie. A sarcastic blond genie with a bad attitude.

"Oooh, a *Shadowhunter*," said the vampire. "Scary." With a wink he melted back into the crowd.

"Vampires are *such* prima donnas," Magnus sighed from the doorway. "Honestly, I don't know why I have these parties."

"Because of your cat," Clary reminded him.

Magnus perked up. "That's true. Chairman Meow deserves my every effort." He glanced at her and the tight knot of Shadowhunters just behind her. "You on your way out?"

Jace nodded. "Don't want to overstay our welcome."

"What welcome?" Magnus asked. "I'd say it was a pleasure to meet you, but it wasn't. Not that you aren't all fairly charming, and as for you—" He dropped a glittery wink at Alec, who looked astounded. "Call me?"

Alec blushed and stuttered and probably would have stood there all night if Jace hadn't grasped his elbow and hauled him toward the door, Isabelle at their heels. Clary was about to follow when she felt a light tap on her arm; it was Magnus. "I have a message for you," he said. "From your mother."

Clary was so surprised she nearly dropped the pack. "From my mother? You mean, she asked you to tell me something?"

"Not exactly," Magnus said. His feline eyes, slit by their single vertical pupils like fissures in a green-gold wall, were serious for once. "But I knew her in a way that you didn't. She did what she did to keep you out of a world that she hated. Her whole existence, the running, the hiding—the lies, as you called them—were to keep you safe. Don't waste her sacrifices by risking your life. She wouldn't want that."

"She wouldn't want me to save her?"

"Not if it meant putting yourself in danger."

"But I'm the only person who cares what happens to her—"

"No," Magnus said. "You aren't."

Clary blinked. "I don't understand. Is there—Magnus, if you know something—"

He cut her off with brutal precision. "And one last thing." His eyes flicked toward the door, through which Jace, Alec, and Isabelle had disappeared. "Keep in mind that when your mother fled from the Shadow World, it wasn't the monsters she was hiding from. Not the warlocks, the wolf-men, the Fair Folk, not even the demons themselves. It was *them*. It was the Shadowhunters."

They were waiting for her outside the warehouse. Jace, hands in pockets, was leaning against the stairway railing and watching as the vampires stalked around their broken motorcycles, cursing and swearing. He had a faint smile on his face. Alec and Isabelle stood a little way off. Isabelle was wiping at her eyes, and Clary felt a wave of irrational anger—Isabelle barely knew Simon. This wasn't *her* disaster. Clary was the one who had the right to be carrying on, not the Shadowhunter girl.

Jace unhitched himself from the railing as Clary emerged. He fell into step beside her, not speaking. He seemed lost in thought. Isabelle and Alec, hurrying ahead, sounded like they were arguing with each other. Clary stepped up her pace a little, craning her neck to hear them better.

"It's not your fault," Alec was saying. He sounded weary, as if he'd been through this sort of thing with his sister before. Clary wondered how many boyfriends she'd turned into rats by accident. "But it ought to teach you not to go to so many Downworld parties," he added. "They're always more trouble than they're worth."

Isabelle sniffed loudly. "If anything had happened to him, I—I don't know what I would have done."

"Probably whatever it is you did before," said Alec in a

bored voice. "It's not like you knew him all that well."

"That doesn't mean that I don't—"

"What? Love him?" Alec scoffed, raising his voice. "You need to *know* someone to love them."

"But that's not all it is." Isabelle sounded almost sad. "Didn't you have any fun at the party, Alec?"

"No."

"I thought you might like Magnus. He's nice, isn't he?"

"Nice?" Alec looked at her as if she were insane. "Kittens are nice. Warlocks are—" He hesitated. "Not," he finished, lamely.

"I thought you might hit it off." Isabelle's eye makeup glittered as bright as tears as she glanced over at her brother. "Get to be friends."

"I have friends," Alec said, and looked over his shoulder, almost as if he couldn't help it, at Jace.

But Jace, his golden head down, lost in thought, didn't notice.

On impulse Clary reached to open the pack and glance into it—and frowned. The pack was open. She flashed back to the party—she'd lifted the pack, pulled the zipper closed. She was sure of it. She yanked the bag open, her heart pounding.

She remembered the time she'd had her wallet stolen on the subway. She remembered opening her bag, not seeing it there, her mouth drying up in surprise—*Did I drop it? Have I lost it?* And realizing: *It's gone*. This was like that, only a thousand times worse. Mouth dry as bone, Clary pawed through the pack, shoving aside clothes and sketchpad, her fingernails scraping the bottom. Nothing.

She'd stopped walking. Jace was hovering just ahead

of her, looking impatient, Alec and Isabelle already a block ahead. "What's wrong?" Jace asked, and she could tell he was about to add something sarcastic. He must have seen the look on her face, though, because he didn't. "Clary?"

"He's gone," she whispered. "Simon. He was in my back-pack—"

"Did he climb out?"

It wasn't an unreasonable question, but Clary, exhausted and panic-stricken, reacted unreasonably. *"Of course he didn't!"* she screamed. "What, you think he wants to get smashed under someone's car, killed by a cat—"

"Clary—"

"Shut up!" she screamed, swinging the pack at him. "You were the one who said not to bother changing him back—"

Deftly he caught the pack as she swung it. Taking it out of her hand, he examined it. "The zipper's torn," he said. "From the outside. Someone ripped this bag open."

Shaking her head numbly, Clary could only whisper, "I didn't..."

"I know." His voice was gentle. He cupped his hands around his mouth. "Alec! Isabelle! You go on ahead! We'll catch up."

The two figures, already far ahead, paused; Alec hesitated, but his sister caught hold of his arm and pushed him firmly toward the subway entrance. Something pressed against Clary's back: It was Jace's hand, turning her gently around. She let him lead her forward, stumbling over the cracks in the sidewalk, until they were back in the entryway of Magnus's building. The stench of stale alcohol and the sweet, uncanny smell Clary had come to associate with Downworlders filled the tiny space. Taking his hand away from her back, Jace pressed the buzzer over Magnus's name.

"Jace," she said.

He looked down at her. "What?"

She searched for words. "Do you think he's all right?"

"Simon?" He hesitated then, and she thought of Isabelle's words: *Don't ask him a question unless you know you can stand the answer.* Instead of saying anything, he pressed the buzzer again, harder this time.

This time Magnus answered it, his voice booming through the tiny entryway. "WHO DARES DISTURB MY REST?"

Jace looked almost nervous. "Jace Wayland. Remember? I'm from the Clave."

"Oh, yes." Magnus seemed to have perked up. "Are you the one with the blue eyes?"

"He means Alec," Clary said helpfully.

"No. My eyes are usually described as golden," Jace told the intercom. "And luminous."

"Oh, you're *that* one." Magnus sounded disappointed. If Clary hadn't been so upset, she would have laughed. "I suppose you'd better come up."

The warlock answered his door wearing a silk kimono printed with dragons, a gold turban, and an expression of barely controlled annoyance.

"I was sleeping," he said loftily.

Jace looked as if he were about to say something rude, possibly about the turban, so Clary interrupted him. "Sorry to bother you—"

Something small and white peered around the warlock's ankles. It had zigzag gray stripes and tufted pink ears that made it look more like a large mouse than a small cat.

"Chairman Meow?" Clary guessed.

Magnus nodded. "He has returned."

Jace regarded the small tabby kitten with some scorn. "That's not a cat," he observed. "It's the size of a hamster."

"I am kindly going to forget you said that," said Magnus, using his foot to nudge Chairman Meow behind him. "Now, exactly what did you come here for?"

Clary held out the torn pack. "It's Simon. He's missing."

"Ah," said Magnus, delicately, "missing what, exactly?"

"*Missing,*" Jace repeated, "as in gone, absent, notable for his lack of presence, disappeared."

"Maybe he's gone and hidden under something," Magnus suggested. "It can't be easy getting used to being a rat, especially for someone so dim-witted in the first place."

"Simon's not dim-witted," Clary protested angrily.

"It's true," Jace agreed. "He just *looks* dim-witted. Really his intelligence is quite average." His tone was light but his shoulders were tense as he turned to Magnus. "When we were leaving, one of your guests brushed up against Clary. I think he tore her bag open and took the rat. Simon, I mean."

Magnus looked at him. "And?"

"And I need to find out who it was," said Jace steadily. "I'm guessing you know. You *are* the High Warlock of Brooklyn. I'm thinking not much happens in your own apartment that you don't know about."

Magnus inspected a glittery nail. "You're not wrong."

"Please tell us," Clary said. Jace's hand tightened on her wrist. She knew he wanted her to be quiet, but that was impossible. "Please."

Magnus dropped his hand with a sigh. "Fine. I saw one

of the vampire bike kids from the uptown lair leave with a brown rat in his hands. Honestly, I figured it was one of their own. Sometimes the Night Children turn into rats or bats when they get drunk."

Clary's hands were shaking. "But now you think it was *Simon?*"

"It's just a guess, but it seems likely."

"There's one more thing." Jace spoke calmly enough, but he was on alert now, the way he had been in the apartment before they'd found the Forsaken. "Where's their lair?"

"Their what?"

"The vampires' lair. That's where they went, isn't it?"

"I would imagine so." Magnus looked as if he'd rather be anywhere else.

"I need you to tell me where it is."

Magnus shook his turbaned head. "I'm not setting myself on the bad side of the Night Children for a mundane I don't even know."

"Wait," Clary interrupted. "What would they want with Simon? I thought they weren't allowed to hurt people..."

"My guess?" said Magnus, not unkindly. "They assumed he was a tame rat and thought it would be funny to kill a Shadowhunter's pet. They don't like you much, whatever the Accords might say—and there's nothing in the Covenant about not killing animals."

"They're going to kill him?" Clary said, staring.

"Not necessarily," said Magnus hastily. "They might have thought he was one of their own."

"In which case, what'll happen to him?" Clary said.

"Well, when he turns back into a human, they'll *still* kill him. But you might have a few more hours."

"Then you have to help us," Clary said to the warlock. "Otherwise Simon will die."

Magnus looked her up and down with a sort of clinical sympathy. "They all die, dear," he said. "You might as well get used to it."

He began to shut the door. Jace stuck out a foot, wedging it open. Magnus sighed. "What now?"

"You still haven't told us where the lair is," Jace said.

"And I'm not going to. I told you—"

It was Clary who cut him off, pushing herself in front of Jace. "You messed with my brain," she said. "Took my memories. Can't you do this one thing for me?"

Magnus narrowed his gleaming cat's eyes. Somewhere in the distance Chairman Meow was crying. Slowly the warlock lowered his head and struck it once, none too gently, against the wall. "The old Hotel Dumont," he said. "Uptown."

"I know where that is." Jace looked pleased.

"We need to get there right away. Do you have a Portal?" Clary demanded, addressing Magnus.

"No." He looked annoyed. "Portals are quite difficult to construct and pose no small risk to their owner. Nasty things can come through them if they're not warded properly. The only ones I know of in New York are the one at Dorothea's and the one at Renwick's, but they're both too far away to be worth the bother of trying to get there, even if you were sure their owners would let you use them, which they probably wouldn't. Got that? Now go away." Magnus stared pointedly at Jace's foot, still blocking the door. Jace didn't move.

"One more thing," Jace said. "Is there a holy place around here?"

"Good idea. If you're going to take on a lair of vampires by yourself, you'd better pray first."

"We need weapons," Jace said tersely. "More than what we've got on us."

Magnus pointed. "There's a Catholic church down on Diamond Street. Will that do?"

Jace nodded, stepping back. "That's—"

The door slammed in their faces. Clary, breathing as if she'd been running, stared at it until Jace took her arm and steered her down the steps and into the night.

14

The Hotel Dumort

At night the Diamond Street church looked spectral, its Gothic arched windows reflecting the moonlight like silvery mirrors. A wrought iron fence surrounded the building and was painted a matte black. Clary rattled the front gate, but a sturdy padlock held it closed. "It's locked," she said, glancing at Jace over her shoulder.

He brandished his stele. "Let me at it."

She watched him as he worked at the lock, watched the lean curve of his back, the swell of muscles under the short sleeves of his T-shirt. The moonlight washed the color out of his hair, turning it more silver than gold.

The padlock hit the ground with a clang, a twisted lump of metal. Jace looked pleased with himself. "As usual," he said, "I'm amazingly good at that."

Clary felt suddenly annoyed. "When the self-congratulatory part of the evening is over, maybe we could get back to saving my best friend from being exsanguinated to death?"

"Exsanguinated," said Jace, impressed. "That's a big word."

"And you're a big—"

"Tsk tsk," he interrupted. "No swearing in church."

"We're not *in* the church yet," Clary muttered, following him up the stone path to the double front doors. The stone arch above the doors was beautifully carved, an angel looking down from its highest point. Sharply pointed spires were silhouetted black against the night sky, and Clary realized that this was the church she had glimpsed earlier that night from McCarren Park. She bit her lip. "It seems wrong to pick the lock on a church door, somehow."

Jace's profile in the moonlight was serene. "We're not going to," he said, sliding his stele into his pocket. He placed a thin brown hand, marked all over with delicate white scars like a veiling of lace, against the wood of the door, just above the latch. "In the name of the Clave," he said, "I ask entry to this holy place. In the name of the Battle That Never Ends, I ask the use of your weapons. And in the name of the Angel Raziel, I ask your blessings on my mission against the darkness."

Clary stared at him. He didn't move, though the night wind blew his hair into his eyes; he blinked, and just as she was about to speak, the door opened with a click and a creak of hinges. It swung inward smoothly before them, opening onto a cool dark empty space, lit by points of fire.

Jace stepped back. "After you."

When Clary stepped inside, a wave of cool air enveloped her, along with the smell of stone and candle wax. Dim rows of pews stretched toward the altar, and a bank of candles glowed like a bed of sparks against the far wall. She realized that, apart from the Institute, which didn't really count, she'd never actually been inside a church before. She'd seen pictures, and seen the insides of churches in movies and in anime shows, where they turned up regularly. A scene in one of her favorite anime series took place in a church with a monstrous vampire priest. You were supposed to feel safe inside a church, but she didn't. Strange shapes seemed to loom up at her out of the shadows. She shivered.

"The stone walls keep out the heat," said Jace, noticing.

"It's not that," she said. "You know, I've never been in a church before."

"You've been in the Institute."

"I mean in a real church. For services. That sort of thing."

"Really. Well, this is the nave, where the pews are. It's where people sit during services." They moved forward, their voices echoing off the stone walls. "Up here is the apse. That's where we're standing. And this is the altar, where the priest performs the Eucharist. It's always at the east side of the church." He knelt down in front of the altar, and she thought for a moment that he was praying. The altar itself was high, made of a dark granite, and draped with a red cloth. Behind it loomed an ornate gold screen, etched with the figures of saints and martyrs, each with a flat gold disk behind his head representing a halo.

"Jace," she whispered. "What are you doing?"

He had placed his hands on the stone floor and was moving them back and forth rapidly, as if searching for something, his fingertips stirring up dust. "Looking for weapons."

"Here?"

"They'd be hidden, usually around the altar. Kept for our use in case of emergencies."

"And this is what, some kind of deal you have with the Catholic Church?"

"Not specifically. Demons have been on Earth as long as we have. They're all over the world, in their different forms—Greek daemons, Persian *daevas*, Hindu *asuras*, Japanese *oni*. Most belief systems have some method of incorporating both their existence and the fight against them. Shadowhunters cleave to no single religion, and in turn all religions assist us in our battle. I could as easily have gone for help to a Jewish synagogue or a Shinto temple, or—Ah. Here it is." He brushed dust aside as she knelt down beside him. Carved into one of the octagonal stones before the altar was a rune. Clary recognized it, almost as easily as if she were reading a word in English. It was the rune that meant *Nephilim*.

Jace took out his stele and touched it to the stone. With a grinding noise it moved back, revealing a dark compartment underneath. Inside the compartment was a long wooden box; Jace lifted the lid, and regarded the neatly arranged objects inside with satisfaction.

"What are all these?" Clary asked.

"Vials of holy water, blessed knives, steel and silver blades," Jace said, piling the weapons on the floor beside him, "electrum wire—not much use at the moment, but it's always good to have spare—silver bullets, charms of protection, crucifixes, stars of David—"

"Jesus," said Clary.

"I doubt he'd fit."

"*Jace*." Clary was appalled.

"What?"

"I don't know, it seems wrong to make jokes like that in a church."

He shrugged. "I'm not really a believer."

Clary looked at him in surprise. "You're not?"

He shook his head. Hair fell over his face, but he was examining a vial of clear liquid and didn't reach up to push it back. Clary's fingers itched with the desire to do it for him. "You thought I was religious?" he said.

"Well." She hesitated. "If there are demons, then there must be..."

"Must be what?" Jace slid the vial into his pocket. "Ah," he said. "You mean if there's this"—and he pointed down, toward the floor—"there must be this." He pointed up, toward the ceiling.

"It stands to reason. Doesn't it?"

Jace lowered his hand and picked up a blade, examining the hilt. "I'll tell you," he said. "I've been killing demons for a third of my life. I must have sent five hundred of them back to whatever hellish dimension they crawled out of. And in all that time—in *all* that time—I've never seen an angel. Never even heard of anyone who has."

"But it was an angel who created Shadowhunters in the first place," Clary said. "That's what Hodge said."

"It makes a nice story." Jace looked at her through eyes slitted like a cat's. "My father believed in God," he said. "I don't."

"At all?" She wasn't sure why she was needling him—she'd never given any thought to whether she believed in God and angels and so forth herself, and if asked, would have said she didn't. There was something about Jace, though, that made her want to push him, crack that shell of cynicism and make him admit he believed in *something*, felt something, cared about anything at all.

"Let me put it this way," he said, sliding a pair of knives into his belt. The faint light that filtered through the stained-glass windows threw squares of color across his face. "My father believed in a righteous God. *Deus volt*, that was his motto—'because God wills it.' It was the Crusaders' motto, and they went out to battle and were slaughtered, just like my father. And when I saw him lying dead in a pool of his own blood, I knew then that I hadn't stopped believing in God. I'd just stopped believing God cared. There might be a God, Clary, and there might not, but I don't think it matters. Either way, we're on our own."

They were the only passengers in their train car heading back uptown. Clary sat without speaking, thinking about Simon. Every once in a while Jace would look over at her as if he were about to say something, before lapsing back into an uncharacteristic silence.

When they climbed out of the subway, the streets were deserted, the air heavy and metal-tasting, the bodegas and Laundromats and check-cashing centers silent behind their nighttime doors of corrugated steel. They found the hotel, finally, after an hour of looking, on a side street off 116th. They'd walked past it twice, thinking it was just another abandoned apartment building, before Clary saw the sign. It had come loose from a nail and it dangled hidden behind a stunted tree. HOTEL DUMONT, it should have said, but someone had painted out the N and replaced it with an R.

"Hotel Dumort," Jace said when she pointed it out to him. "Cute."

Clary had only had two years of French, but it was enough to get the joke. "*Du mort*," she said. "Of death."

Jace nodded. He had gone alert all over, like a cat who sees a mouse whisking behind a sofa.

"But it can't be the hotel," Clary said. "The windows are all boarded up, and the door's been bricked over—Oh," she finished, catching his look. "Right. Vampires. But how do they get inside?"

"They fly," Jace said, and indicated the upper floors of the building. It had once, clearly, been a graceful and luxurious hotel. The stone facade was elegantly decorated with carved curlicues and fleur-de-lis, dark and eroded from years of exposure to polluted air and acid rain.

"We don't fly," Clary felt impelled to point out.

"No," Jace agreed. "We don't fly. We break and enter." He started across the street toward the hotel.

"Flying sounds like more fun," Clary said, hurrying to catch up with him.

"Right now everything sounds like more fun." She wondered if he meant it. There was an excitement about him, an anticipation of the hunt that didn't look to her as if he were as unhappy as he claimed. *He's killed more demons than anyone else his age.* You didn't kill that many demons by hanging back reluctantly from a fight.

A hot wind had come up, stirring the leaves on the stunted trees outside the hotel, sending the trash in the gutters and on the sidewalk skittering across the cracked pavement. The area was oddly deserted, Clary thought—usually, in Manhattan, there was always someone else on the street, even at four in the morning. Several of the streetlights lining the sidewalk were out, though the one closest to the hotel cast a dim yellow glow across the cracked pathway that led up to what had once been the front door.

"Stay out of the light," Jace said, pulling her toward him by her sleeve. "They might be watching from the windows. And don't look up," he added, but it was too late. Clary had already glanced up at the shattered windows of the higher floors. For a moment she half-thought she glimpsed a flicker of movement at one of the windows, a flash of whiteness that could have been a face, or a hand drawing back a heavy drape—

"Come *on*." Jace drew her with him to melt into the shadows closer to the hotel. She felt her heightened nervousness in her spine, in the pulse in her wrists, in the hard beat of blood in her ears. The faint drone of distant cars seemed very far away, the only sound the crunch of her own shoes on the garbagestrewn pavement. She wished she could walk soundlessly, like a Shadowhunter. Maybe someday she'd ask Jace to teach her.

They slipped around the corner of the hotel into an alley that had probably once been a service lane for deliveries. It was narrow, choked with garbage: moldy cardboard boxes, empty glass bottles, shredded plastic, scattered things that Clary thought at first were toothpicks, but up close looked like—

"Bones," Jace said flatly. "Dog bones, cat bones. Don't look too closely; going through vampires' trash is rarely a pretty picture."

She swallowed down her nausea. "Well," she said, "at

least we know we're in the right place," and was rewarded by the glint of respect that showed, briefly, in Jace's eyes.

"Oh, we're in the right place," he said. "Now we just have to figure out how to get inside."

There had clearly been windows here once, now bricked up. There was no door and no sign of a fire escape. "When this was a hotel," Jace said slowly, "they must have gotten their deliveries here. I mean, they wouldn't have brought things through the front door, and there's no place else for trucks to pull up. So there must be a way in."

Clary thought of the little shops and bodegas near her house in Brooklyn. She'd seen them get their deliveries, early in the morning while she was walking to school, seen the Korean deli owners opening the metal doors set into the pavement outside their front doors, so they could carry boxes of paper towels and cat food into their supply cellars. "I bet the doors are in the ground. Probably buried under all this garbage."

Jace, a beat behind her, nodded. "That's what I was thinking." He sighed. "I guess we'd better move the trash. We can start with the Dumpster." He pointed at it, looking distinctly unenthusiastic.

"You'd rather face a ravening horde of demons, wouldn't you?" Clary said.

"At least they wouldn't be crawling with maggots. Well," he added thoughtfully, "not most of them, anyway. There was this one demon, once, that I tracked down to the sewers under Grand Central—"

"Don't." Clary raised a warning hand. "I'm not really in the mood right now."

"That's got to be the first time a girl's ever said that to me," Jace mused.

"Stick with me and it won't be the last."

The corner of Jace's mouth twitched. "This is hardly the time for idle banter. We have garbage to haul." He stalked over to the Dumpster and took hold of one side of it. "You get the other. We'll tip it."

"Tipping it will make too much noise," Clary argued, taking up her station on the other side of the huge container. It was a standard city trash bin, painted dark green, splotched with strange stains. It stank, even more than most Dumpsters, of garbage and something else, something thick and sweet that filled her throat and made her want to gag. "We should push it."

"Now, look—" Jace began, when a voice spoke, suddenly, out of the shadows behind them.

"Do you really think you should be doing that?" it asked.

Clary froze, staring into the shadows at the mouth of the alley. For a panicked moment she wondered if she'd imagined the voice, but Jace was frozen too, astonishment on his face. It was rare that anything surprised him, rarer that anyone snuck up on him. He stepped away from the Dumpster, his hand sliding toward his belt, his voice flat. "Is there someone there?"

"Dios mío." The voice was male, amused, speaking a liquid Spanish. "You're not from this neighborhood, are you?"

He stepped forward, out of the thickest of the shadows. The shape of him evolved slowly: a boy, not much older than Jace and probably six inches shorter. He was thin-boned, with the big dark eyes and honey-colored skin of a Diego Rivera painting. He wore black slacks and an open-necked white shirt, and a gold chain around his neck that sparked faintly as he moved closer to the light.

"You could say that," Jace said carefully, not moving his hand away from his belt.

"You shouldn't be here." The boy raked a hand through the thick black curls that spilled over his forehead. "This place is dangerous."

He means it's a bad neighborhood. Clary almost wanted to laugh, even though it wasn't at all funny. "We know," she said. "We just got a little lost, that's all."

The boy gestured to the Dumpster. "What were you doing with that?"

I'm no good at lying on the spot, Clary thought, and looked at Jace, who, she hoped, would be excellent at it.

He disappointed her immediately. "We were trying to get into the hotel. We thought there might be a cellar door behind the trash bin."

The boy's eyes widened in disbelief. "*Puta madre*—why would you want to do something like that?"

Jace shrugged. "For a prank, you know. Just a little fun."

"You don't understand. This place is haunted, cursed. Bad luck." He shook his head vigorously and said several things in Spanish that Clary suspected had to do with the stupidity of spoiled white kids in general and their stupidity in particular. "Walk with me, I'll take you to the subway."

"We know where the subway is," said Jace.

The boy laughed a soft, vibrant laugh. "*Claro*. Of course you do, but if you go with me, no one will bother you. You do not want trouble, do you?"

"That depends," Jace said, and moved so that his jacket opened slightly, showing the glint of the weapons thrust through his belt. "How much are they paying you to keep people away from the hotel?"

The boy glanced behind him, and Clary's nerves twanged as she imagined the narrow alley mouth filling up with other shadowy figures, white-faced, red-mouthed, the glint of fangs as sudden as metal striking sparks from pavement. When he looked back at Jace, his mouth was a thin line. "How much are who paying me, *chico?*"

"The vampires. How much are they paying you? Or is it something else—did they tell you they'd make you one of them, offer you eternal life, no pain, no sickness, you get to live forever? Because it's not worth it. Life stretches out very long when you never see the sunlight, *chico*," said Jace.

The boy was expressionless. "My name is Raphael. Not *chico*."

"But you know what we're talking about. You know about the vampires?" Clary said.

Raphael turned his face to the side and spit. When he looked back at them, his eyes were full of a glittering hate. "*Los vampiros, sí,* the blood-drinking animals. Even before the hotel was boarded up, there were stories, the laughter late at night, the small animals disappearing, the sounds—" He stopped, shaking his head. "Everyone in the neighborhood knows to stay away, but what can you do? You cannot call the police and tell them your problem is vampires."

"Have you ever seen them?" Jace asked. "Or known anyone who has?"

Raphael spoke slowly. "There were some boys, once, a

group of friends. They thought they had a good idea, to go into the hotel and kill the monsters inside. They took guns with them, knives too, all blessed by a priest. They never came out. My aunt, she found their clothes later, in front of the house."

"Your aunt's house?" said Jace.

"*Sí*. One of the boys was my brother," said Raphael flatly. "So now you know why I walk by here in the middle of the night sometimes, on the way home from my aunt's house, and why I warned you away. If you go in there, you will not come out again."

"My friend is in there," said Clary. "We came to get him."

"Ah," said Raphael, "then perhaps I cannot warn you away."

"No," Jace said. "But don't worry. What happened to your friends won't happen to us." He took one of the angel blades from his belt and held it up, the faint light emanating from it lit the hollows under his cheekbones, shadowed his eyes. "I've killed plenty of vampires before. Their hearts don't beat, but they can still die."

Raphael inhaled sharply and said something in Spanish too low and rapid for Clary to understand. He came toward them, almost stumbling over a pile of crumpled plastic wrappers in his haste. "I know what you are—I have heard about your kind, from the old padre at St. Cecilia's. I thought that was just a story."

"All the stories are true," Clary said, but so quietly that he didn't seem to hear her. He was looking at Jace, his fists clenched.

"I want to go with you," he said.

Jace shook his head. "No. Absolutely not."

"I can show you how to get inside," Raphael said.

Jace wavered, temptation plain on his face. "We can't bring you."

"Fine." Raphael stalked by him and kicked aside a heap of trash piled against a wall. There was a metal grating there, thin bars filmed with a brownish red coating of rust. He knelt down, took hold of the bars, and lifted the grating away. "This is how my brother and his friends got in. It goes down to the basement, I think." He looked up as Jace and Clary joined him. Clary half-held her breath; the smell of the garbage was overwhelming, and even in the darkness she could see the darting shapes of cockroaches crawling over the piles.

A thin smile had formed, just at the corners of Jace's mouth. He still had the angel blade in his hand. The witch-light that came from it lent his face a ghostly cast, reminding her of the way Simon had held a flashlight under his chin while telling her horror stories when they were both eleven. "Thanks," he said to Raphael. "This will work just fine."

The other boy's face was pale. "You go in there and do for your friend what I could not do for my brother."

Jace slipped the seraph blade back into his belt and glanced at Clary. "Follow me," he said, and slid through the grating in a single smooth move, feet first. She held her breath, waiting for a shout of agony or amazement, but there was only the soft thump of feet landing on solid ground. "It's fine," he called up, his voice muffled. "Jump down and I'll catch you."

She looked at Raphael. "Thanks for your help."

He said nothing, only held out his hand. She used it to steady herself while she maneuvered into position. His fingers were cold. He let go as she dropped down through the grating. It was only a second's fall and Jace caught her, her dress rucking up around her thighs and his hand grazing her bare legs as she slid into his arms. He let her go almost immediately. "You all right?"

She pulled her dress down, glad he couldn't see her in the dark. "I'm fine."

Jace pulled the dimly glowing angel blade out of his belt and lifted it, letting its growing illumination wash over their surroundings. They were standing in a shallow, low-ceilinged space with a cracked concrete floor. Squares of dirt showed where the floor was broken, and Clary could see that black vines had begun to twine up the walls. A doorway, missing its door, opened onto another room.

A loud thump made her start, and she turned to see Raphael landing, knees bent, just a few feet from her. He had followed them through the grating. He straightened up and grinned manically.

Jace looked furious. "I told you—"

"And I heard you." Raphael waved a dismissive hand. "What are you going to do about it? I can't get back out the way we came in, and you can't just leave me here for the dead to find ... can you?"

"I'm thinking about it," Jace said. He looked tired, Clary saw with some surprise, the shadows under his eyes more pronounced.

Raphael pointed. "We must go that way, toward the stairs. They are up on the higher floors of the hotel. You will see." He pushed past Jace and through the narrow doorway. Jace looked after him, shaking his head.

"I'm really starting to hate mundanes," he said.

* * *

The lower floor of the hotel was a warren of mazelike corridors opening onto empty storage rooms, a deserted laundry—moldy stacks of linen towels piled high in rotted wicker baskets—even a ghostly kitchen, banks of stainless steel counters stretching away into the shadows. Most of the staircases leading upstairs were gone; not rotted but deliberately chopped away, reduced to stacks of kindling shoved against walls, bits of once-luxurious Persian carpet clinging to them like blossoms of furry mold.

The missing stairs baffled Clary. What did vampires have against stairs? They finally found an unharmed set, tucked away behind the laundry. Maids must have used it to carry linens up and down the stairs in the days before elevators. Dust lay thick on the steps now, like a layer of powdery gray snow that made Clary cough.

"Shh," hissed Raphael. "They will hear you. We are close to where they sleep."

"How do *you* know?" she whispered back. He wasn't even supposed to *be* there. What gave him the right to lecture her about noise?

"I can feel it." The corner of his eye twitched, and she saw that he was as scared as she was. "Can't you?"

She shook her head. She felt nothing, other than strangely cold; after the stifling heat of the night outside, the chill inside the hotel was intense.

At the top of the stairs was a door on which the painted word LOBBY was barely legible beneath years of accumulated dirt. The door sprayed rust when Jace pushed it open. Clary braced herself—

But the room beyond was empty. They were in a large

foyer, its rotting carpeting torn back to show the splintered floorboards beneath. Once the centerpiece of this room had been a grand staircase, gracefully curving, lined with gilt banisters and richly carpeted in gold and scarlet. Now all that remained were the higher steps, leading up into blackness. The remainder of the staircase ended just above their heads, in midair. The sight was as surreal as one of the abstract Magritte paintings Jocelyn had loved. This one, Clary thought, would be called *The Stairs to Nowhere*.

Her voice sounded as dry as the dust that coated everything. "What do vampires have against stairs?"

"Nothing," said Jace. "They just don't need to use them."

"It is a way of showing that this place is one of *theirs*." Raphael's eyes were bright. He seemed almost excited. Jace glanced at him sideways.

"Have you ever actually seen a vampire, Raphael?" he asked.

Raphael glanced at him almost absently. "I know what they look like. They are paler, thinner than human beings, but very strong. They walk like cats and spring with the swiftness of serpents. They are beautiful and terrible. Like this hotel."

"You think it's beautiful?" Clary asked, surprised.

"You can see where it was, years ago. Like an old woman who was once beautiful, but time has taken her beauty away. You must imagine this staircase the way it was once, with the gas lamps burning all up and down the steps, like fireflies in the dark, and the balconies full of people. Not the way it is now, so—" He broke off, searching for a word.

"Truncated?" Jace suggested dryly.

Raphael looked almost startled, as if Jace had broken him

out of a reverie. He laughed shakily and turned away.

Clary turned to Jace. "Where are they, anyway? The vampires, I mean."

"Upstairs, probably. They like to be high up when they sleep, like bats. And it's nearly sunrise."

Like puppets with their heads attached to strings, Clary and Raphael both looked up at the same time. There was nothing above them but the frescoed ceiling, cracked and black in places as if it had been burned in a fire. An archway to their left led farther into darkness; the pillars on either side were engraved with a motif of leaves and flowers. As Raphael glanced back down, a scar at the base of his throat, very white against his brown skin, flashed like a winking eye. She wondered how he'd gotten it.

"I think we should go back to the servants' stairs," she whispered. "I feel too exposed out here."

Jace nodded. "You realize, once we get there, you'll have to call out for Simon and hope he can hear you?"

She wondered if the fear she felt showed on her face. "I—"

Her words were cut short by a bloodcurdling scream. Clary whirled.

Raphael. He was gone, no marks in the dust showing where he might have walked—or been dragged. She reached for Jace, reflexively, but he was already moving, running toward the gaping arch in the far wall and the shadows beyond. She couldn't see him but followed the darting witchlight he carried, like a traveler being led through a swamp by a treacherous will-o'-the-wisp.

Beyond the arch was what had once been a grand ballroom. The ruined floor was white marble, now so badly cracked that it resembled a sea of floating arctic ice. Curved balconies ran along the walls, their railings veiled in rust. Gold-framed mirrors hung at intervals between them, each crowned with a gilded cupid's head. Spiderwebs drifted in the clammy air like ancient wedding veils.

Raphael was standing in the center of the room, his arms at his sides. Clary ran to him, Jace following more slowly behind her. "Are you all right?" she asked breathlessly.

He nodded slowly. "I thought I saw a movement in the shadows. It was nothing."

"We've decided to head back to the servants' stairs," Jace said. "There's nothing on this floor."

Raphael nodded. "Good idea."

He headed for the door, not looking to see if they followed. He had gotten only a few steps when Jace said, "Raphael?"

Raphael turned, eyes widening inquisitively, and Jace threw his knife.

Raphael's reflexes were quick, but not quick enough. The blade struck home, the force of the impact knocking him over. His feet went out from under him and he fell heavily to the cracked marble floor. In the dim witchlight his blood looked black.

"Jace," Clary hissed in disbelief, shock pounding through her. He'd said he hated mundanes, but he'd never—

As she turned to go to Raphael, Jace shoved her brutally aside. He flung himself on the other boy and grabbed for the knife sticking out of Raphael's chest.

But Raphael was faster. He seized the knife, then screamed as his hand came in contact with the cross-shaped hilt. It clattered to the marble floor, blade smeared black. Jace had one hand fisted in the material of Raphael's shirt, Sanvi in the other. It was glowing with such a bright light that Clary could see colors again: the peeling royal blue of the wallpaper, the gold flecks in the marble floor, the red stain spreading across Raphael's chest.

But Raphael was laughing. "You missed," he said, and grinned for the first time, showing pointed white incisors. "You missed my heart."

Jace tightened his grip. "You moved at the last minute," he said. "That was very inconsiderate."

Raphael frowned and spit, red. Clary stepped back, staring in dawning horror.

"When did you figure it out?" he demanded. His accent had faded, his words more precise and clipped now.

"I guessed in the alley," Jace said. "But I figured you'd get us inside the hotel, then turn on us. Once we'd trespassed, we'd have been out of the protection of the Covenant. Fair game. When you didn't, I thought I might have been wrong. Then I saw that scar on your throat." He sat back a little, still holding the blade at Raphael's throat. "I thought when I first saw that chain that it looked like the sort you'd hang a cross from. And you did, didn't you, when you went out to see your family? What's the scar of a little burn when your kind heal so quickly?"

Raphael laughed. "Was that all? My scar?"

"When you left the foyer, your feet didn't leave marks in the dust. Then I knew."

"It wasn't your brother who went in here looking for monsters and never came out, was it?" Clary said, realizing. "It was you."

"You are both very clever," Raphael said. "Although not quite clever enough. Look up," he said, and lifted a hand to point at the ceiling.

Jace knocked the hand away without moving his glance from Raphael. "Clary. What do you see?"

She raised her head slowly, dread curdling in the pit of her stomach.

You must imagine this staircase the way it was once, with the gas lamps burning all up and down the steps, like fireflies in the dark, and the balconies full of people. They were filled with people now, row on row of vampires with their dead white faces, their red stretched mouths, staring bemusedly downward.

Jace was still looking at Raphael. "You called them. Didn't you?"

Raphael was still grinning. The blood had stopped spreading from the wound in his chest. "Does it matter? There are too many of them, even for you, Wayland."

Jace said nothing. Though he hadn't moved, he was breathing in short quick pants, and Clary could almost feel the strength of his desire to kill the vampire boy, to shove the knife through his heart and wipe that grin off his face forever. "Jace," she said warningly. "Don't kill him."

"Why not?"

"Maybe we can use him as a hostage."

Jace's eyes widened. "A *hostage?*"

She could see them, more of them, filling the arched doorway, moving as silently as the Brothers of the Bone City. But the Brothers had not had skin so white and colorless, nor teeth as sharp as needles...

Clary licked her dry lips. "I know what I'm doing. Get him on his feet, Jace."

Jace looked at her, then shrugged. "All right."

Raphael snapped, "This isn't funny."

"That's why no one's laughing." Jace stood, hauling Raphael upright, jamming the tip of his knife between Raphael's shoulder blades. "I can pierce your heart just as easily through your back," he said. "I wouldn't move if I were you."

Clary turned away from them to face the oncoming dark shapes. She flung out a hand. "Stop right there," she said. "Or he' ll put that blade through Raphael's heart."

A sort of murmur ran through the crowd that could have been whispering or laughter. *"Stop,"* Clary said again, and this time Jace did something, she didn't see what, that made Raphael cry out in surprised pain.

One of the vampires flung an arm out to hold back his companions. Clary recognized him as the thin blond boy with the earring that she'd seen at Magnus's party. "She means it," he said. "They are Shadowhunters."

Another vampire pushed her way through the crowd to stand at his side—a pretty blue-haired Asian girl in a silver foil skirt. Clary wondered if there were any ugly vampires, or maybe any fat ones. Maybe they didn't make vampires out of ugly people. Or maybe ugly people just didn't want to live forever. "Shadowhunters trespassing on our territory," she said. "They are out of the protection of the Covenant. I say we kill them—they have killed enough of ours."

"Which of you is the master of this place?" Jace said, his voice very flat. "Let him step forward."

The girl bared her pointed teeth. "Do not use Clave language on us, Shadowhunter. You have broken your precious Covenant, coming in here. The Law will not protect you."

"That's enough, Lily," said the blond boy sharply. "Our master is not here. She is in Idris."

"Someone must rule you in her stead," Jace observed.

There was a silence. The vampires up in the balconies were hanging off the railings, leaning down to hear what was being said. Finally, "Raphael leads us," said the blond vampire.

The blue-haired girl, Lily, let out a hiss of disapproval. "Jacob—"

"I propose a trade," Clary said quickly, cutting off Lily's tirade and Jacob's retort. "By now you must know you took home too many people from the party tonight. One of them was my friend Simon."

Jacob raised his eyebrows. "You're friends with a vampire?"

"He's not a vampire. And not a Shadowhunter, either," she added, seeing Lily's pale eyes narrow. "Just an ordinary human boy."

"We didn't take any human boys home with us from Magnus's party. That would have been a violation of the Covenant."

"He'd been transformed into a rat. A small brown rat," said Clary. "Someone might have thought he was a pet, or..."

Her voice trailed off. They were staring at her as if she were insane. Cold despair seeped into her bones.

"Let me get this straight," Lily said. "You're offering to trade Raphael's life for a *rat*?"

Clary looked helplessly back at Jace. He gave her a look

that said, *This was your idea. You're on your own.*

"Yes," she said, turning back to the vampires. "That's the trade we're offering."

They stared at her, white faces nearly expressionless. In another context Clary would have said that they looked baffled.

She could *feel* Jace standing behind her, hear the rasp of his breathing. She wondered if he was racking his brain trying to figure out why he'd let her drag them both here in the first place. She wondered if he was starting to hate her.

"Do you mean this rat?"

Clary blinked. Another vampire, a thin black boy with dreadlocks, had pushed his way to the front of the crowd. He was holding something in his hands, something brown that squirmed feebly. "Simon?" she whispered.

The rat squeaked and started to thrash wildly in the boy's grip. He looked down at the captive rodent with an expression of distaste. "Man, I thought he was Zeke. I wondered why he was copping such an attitude." He shook his head, dreadlocks bouncing. "I say she can have him, dude. He's already bitten me five times."

Clary reached out for Simon, her hands aching to hold him. But Lily stepped in front of her before she could take more than a step in his direction. "Wait," Lily said. "How do we know you won't just take the rat and kill Raphael anyway?"

"We'll give our word," Clary said immediately, then tensed, waiting for them to laugh.

Nobody laughed. Raphael swore softly in Spanish. Lily looked curiously at Jace.

"Clary," he said. There was an undercurrent of exasperated desperation in his voice. "Is this really a—"

"No oath, no trade," said Lily immediately, seizing on his uncertain tone. "Elliott, hold on to that rat."

The dreadlocked boy tightened his grip on Simon, who sank his teeth savagely into Elliott's hand. "Man," he said glumly. "That hurt."

Clary took the opportunity to whisper to Jace. "Just swear! What can it hurt?"

"Swearing for us isn't like it is for you mundanes," he snapped back angrily. "I'll be bound forever to any oath I make."

"Oh, yeah? What would happen if you broke it?"

"I *wouldn't* break it, that's the point—"

"Lily is right," said Jacob. "An oath is required. Swear that you won't hurt Raphael. Even if we give you the rat back."

"I won't hurt Raphael," Clary said immediately. "No matter what."

Lily smiled at her tolerantly. "It isn't you we're worried about." She shot a pointed look at Jace, who was holding Raphael so tightly that his knuckles were white. A patch of sweat darkened the cloth of his shirt, just between his shoulder blades.

He said, "All right. I swear it."

"Speak the Oath," Lily said swiftly. "Swear on the Angel. Say it all."

Jace shook his head. "You swear first."

His words fell into the silence like stones, sending a rippling murmur through the crowd. Jacob looked concerned; Lily furious. "Not a chance, Shadowhunter."

"We have your leader." The tip of Jace's knife dug farther into Raphael's throat. "And what have you got there? A rat."

Simon, pinned in Elliott's hands, squeaked furiously.

Clary longed to snatch him up, but held herself back. "Jace—"

Lily looked toward Raphael. "Master?"

Raphael had his head down, his dark curls falling to hide his face. Blood stained the collar of his shirt, trickled down the bare brown skin underneath. "A pretty important rat," he said, "for you to come all the way here for him. It is you, Shadowhunter, I think, who will swear first."

Jace's grip on him tightened convulsively. Clary saw the swell of the muscles under his skin, the whitening of his fingers and at the sides of his mouth as he fought his anger. "The rat's a mundane," he said sharply. "If you kill him, you'll be subject to the Law—"

"He is on our territory. Trespassers are not protected by the Covenant, you know that—"

"You *brought* him here," Clary interjected. "He didn't trespass."

"Technicalities," said Raphael, grinning at her despite the knife at his throat. "Besides. You think we do not hear the rumors, the news that is running through Downworld like blood through veins? Valentine is back. There will be no Accords and no Covenant soon enough."

Jace's head jerked up. "Where did you hear that?"

Raphael frowned scornfully. "All Downworld knows it. He paid a warlock to raise a pack of Raveners only a week ago. He has brought his Forsaken to seek the Mortal Cup. When he finds it, there will be no more false peace between us, only war. No Law will prevent me from tearing your heart out on the street, Shadowhunter—"

That was enough for Clary. She dove for Simon, shouldering Lily aside, and snatched the rat out of Elliott's hands.

Simon scrabbled up her arm, gripping her sleeve with frantic paws.

"It's okay," she whispered, "it's okay." Though she knew it wasn't. She turned to run, and felt hands catch at her jacket, holding her. She struggled, but her efforts to tear herself free of the hands that held her—Lily's, narrow and bony with black fingernails—were hampered by her fear of dislodging Simon, who clung to her with paws and teeth. "Let *go*!" she screamed, kicking out at the vampire girl. Her booted toe connected, hard, and Lily shouted in pain and rage. She whipped her hand forward, striking Clary's cheek with enough force to rock her head back.

Clary staggered and nearly fell. She heard Jace shout her name, and turned to see that he had let go of Raphael and was racing toward her. Clary tried to go to him, but her shoulders were gripped by Jacob, his fingers digging into her skin.

Clary cried out—and the noise was lost in a larger shriek as Jace, snatching one of the glass vials from his jacket, flung its contents toward her. She felt cool wetness splash her face, and heard Jacob scream as the water touched his skin. Smoke rose from his fingers and he released Clary, howling a high animal howl. Lily darted toward him, crying out his name, and in the pandemonium, Clary felt someone seize her wrist. She struggled to yank herself away.

"Stop it—you idiot—it's *me*," Jace panted in her ear.

"Oh!" She relaxed momentarily, then tensed again, seeing a familiar shape loom up behind Jace. She cried out and Jace ducked and spun just as Raphael leaped at him, teeth bared, quick as a cat. His fangs caught Jace's shirt near the shoulder and tore the fabric lengthwise as Jace staggered.

Raphael clung on like a gripping spider, teeth snapping at Jace's throat. Clary fumbled in her pack for the dagger Jace had given her—

A small brown shape streaked across the floor, shot between Clary's feet, and launched itself at Raphael.

Raphael screamed. Simon hung grimly from his forearm, his sharp rat-teeth sunk deep into the flesh. Raphael let go of Jace, flailing backward, blood spurting as a stream of Spanish obscenities poured from his mouth.

Jace gaped, his mouth open. "Son of a—"

Regaining his balance, Raphael tore the rat free from his arm and flung him to the marble floor. Simon squeaked once in pain, then dashed over to Clary. She bent down and snatched him up, holding him against her chest as tightly as she could without hurting him. She could feel the hammering beat of his tiny heart against her fingers. "Simon," she whispered. "Simon—"

"There's no time for that. Hold on to him." Jace had caught at her right arm, gripping with painful force. In the other hand he held a glowing seraph blade. "Move."

He began to half-pull her, half-push her, to the edge of the crowd. The vampires winced away from the light of the seraph blade as it swept over them, all of them hissing like scalded cats.

"Enough standing around!" It was Raphael. His arm was streaming blood, his lips curled back from his pointed incisors. He glared at the teeming mass of vampires milling in confusion. "Seize the trespassers," he shouted. "Kill them *both*—the rat as well!"

The vampires started toward Jace and Clary, some of them

walking, others gliding, others swooping down from the balconies above like flapping black bats. Jace increased his pace as they broke free of the crowd, heading toward the far wall. Clary squirmed, half-turning to look up at him. "Shouldn't we stand back to back or something?"

"What? Why?"

"I don't know. In movies that's what they do in this kind of ... situation."

She felt him shake. Was he frightened? No, he was laughing. "You," he breathed. "You are the most—"

"The most what?" she demanded indignantly. They were still backing up, stepping carefully to avoid the broken bits of furniture and smashed marble that littered the floor. Jace held the angel blade high above both their heads. She could see how the vampires circled around the edges of the glimmering circle it cast. She wondered how long it would hold them off.

"Nothing," he said. "This isn't a situation, okay? I save that word for when things get really bad."

"*Really* bad? This isn't really bad? What do you want, a nuclear—"

She broke off with a scream as Lily, braving the light, launched herself at Jace, her teeth bared in a searing snarl. Jace seized the second blade from his belt and hurled it through the air; Lily fell back screeching, a long gash sizzling down her arm. As she staggered, the other vampires surged forward around her. There were so many of them, Clary thought, so many—

She fumbled at her belt, her fingers closing around the hilt of the dagger. It felt cold and foreign in her hand. She didn't know how to use a knife. She'd never hit anyone, let alone stabbed them. She'd even skipped gym class the day they'd learned how to ward off muggers and rapists with ordinary objects like car keys and pencils. She pulled the knife free, raised it in a shaking hand—

The windows exploded inward in a shower of broken glass. She heard herself cry out, saw the vampires—barely an arm's length from her and Jace—whirl in astonishment, shock mingling with terror on their faces. Through the shattered windows came dozens of sleek shapes, four-footed and low to the ground, their coats scattering moonlight and broken bits of glass. Their eyes were blue fire, and from their throats came a combined low growl that sounded like the roiling crash of a waterfall.

Wolves.

"Now *this*," said Jace, "is a situation."

15
High and Dry

The wolves crouched, low and snarling, and the vampires, looking stunned, backed away. Only Raphael held his ground. He still clutched his wounded arm, his shirt a smeared mess of blood and dirt. *"Los Niños de la Luna,"* he hissed. Even Clary, whose Spanish was almost nonexistent, knew what he had said. The Moon's Children—werewolves. "I thought they hated each other," she whispered to Jace. "Vampires and werewolves."

"They do. They never come to each other's lairs. Never. The Covenant forbids it." He sounded almost indignant. "Something must have happened. This is bad. Very bad."

"How can it be worse than it was before?"

"Because," he said, "we're about to be in the middle of a war."

"HOW DARE YOU ENTER OUR PLACE? " Raphael screamed. His face was scarlet, suffused with blood.

The largest of the wolves, a brindled gray monster with

teeth like a shark's, gave a panting doglike chuckle. As he moved forward, between one step and the next he seemed to shift and change like a wave rising and curling. Now he was a tall heavily muscled man with long hair that hung in gray ropelike tangles. He wore jeans and a thick leather jacket, and there was still something wolfish in the cast of his lean, weathered face. "We didn't come for a blooding," he said. "We came for the girl."

Raphael managed to look furious and astounded at once. "Who?"

"The human girl." The werewolf flung out a stiff arm, pointing at Clary.

She was too shocked to move. Simon, who had been squirming in her grasp, went still. Behind her Jace muttered something that sounded distinctly blasphemous. "You didn't tell me you knew any werewolves." She could hear the slight catch under his flat tone—he was as surprised as she was.

"I don't," she said.

"This is bad," said Jace.

"You said that before."

"It seemed worth repeating."

"Well, it wasn't." Clary shrank back against him. "*Jace*. They're all looking at me."

Every face was turned to her; most looked astonished. Raphael's eyes were narrowed. He turned back to the werewolf, slowly. "You can't have her," he said. "She trespassed on our ground; therefore she's ours."

The werewolf laughed. "I'm so glad you said that," he said, and launched himself forward. In midair his body rippled, and he was again a wolf, coat bristling, jaws gaping, ready to tear. He struck Raphael square in the chest, and the two went over in a writhing, snarling tangle. With answering howls of rage, the vampires charged the werewolves, who met them head-on in the center of the ballroom.

The noise was like nothing Clary had ever heard. If Bosch's paintings of hell had come with a soundtrack, they would have sounded like this.

Jace whistled. "Raphael is really having an exceptionally bad night."

"So what?" Clary had no sympathy for the vampire. "What are *we* going to do?"

He glanced around. They were pinned in a corner by the churning mass of bodies; though they were being ignored for now, it wouldn't be for long. Before Clary could voice this thought, Simon suddenly squirmed violently free of her grasp and leaped to the floor. "Simon!" she screamed as he dashed for the corner and a moldering pile of rotted velvet drapes. "Simon, *stop*!"

Jace's eyebrows made quizzical peaks. "What is he—" He grabbed for her arm, jerking her back. "Clary, don't chase the rat. He's fleeing. That's what rats do."

She shot him a furious look. "He's not a rat. He's Simon. And he bit Raphael for you, you ungrateful cretin." She yanked her arm free and dashed after Simon, who was crouched in the folds of the drapes, chittering excitedly and pawing at them. Belatedly realizing what he was trying to tell her, she yanked the drapes aside. They were slimy with mold, but behind them was—

"A door," she breathed. "You genius rat."

Simon squeaked modestly as she snatched him up. Jace

was right behind her. "A door, eh? Well, does it open?"

She grabbed for the knob and turned to him, crestfallen. "It's locked. Or stuck."

Jace threw himself against the door. It didn't budge. He cursed. "My shoulder will never be the same. I expect you to nurse me back to health."

"Just break the door down, will you?"

He looked past her with wide eyes. "Clary—"

She turned. A huge wolf had broken away from the melee and was racing toward her, ears flattened to its narrow head. It was huge, gray-black and brindled, with a long lolling red tongue. Clary screamed. Jace threw himself against the door again, still cursing. She reached for her belt, grabbed the dagger, and threw it.

She'd never thrown a weapon before, never even thought of throwing one. The closest she'd come to weaponry before this week was drawing pictures of them, so Clary was more surprised than anyone else, she suspected, when the dagger flew, wobbly but true, and sank into the werewolf's side.

It yelped, slowing, but three of its comrades were already racing toward them. One paused at the side of the wounded wolf, but the others charged for the door. Clary screamed again as Jace hurled his body against the door a third time. It gave with an explosive shriek of grinding rust and tearing wood. "Three times the charm," he panted, holding his shoulder. He ducked into the dark space that gaped beyond the broken door, and turned to hold out an impatient hand. "Clary, come *on*."

With a gasp she darted after him and flung the door shut, just as two heavy bodies thudded against it. She fumbled for the bolt, but it was gone, torn away where Jace had broken through it.

"Duck," he said, and as she did, the stele whipped over her head, slicing dark lines into the moldering wood of the door. She craned her neck to see what he'd carved: a curve like a sickle, three parallel lines, a rayed star: *To hold against pursuit.*

"I lost your dagger," she confessed. "I'm sorry."

"It happens." He pocketed the stele. She could hear the faint thuds as the wolves hurled themselves against the door again and again, but it held. "The rune will keep them back, but not for long. We'd better hurry."

She looked up. They were in a dank passageway; a narrow set of stairs led up into darkness. The steps were wood, the banisters filmy with dust. Simon thrust his nose out of her jacket pocket, his black button eyes glittering in the dim light. "All right," she nodded at Jace. "You go first."

Jace looked as if he wanted to grin but was too tired. "You know how I like to be first. But slowly," he added. "I'm not sure the stairs can hold our weight."

Clary wasn't sure either. The steps creaked and groaned as they ascended, like an old woman complaining about her aches and pains. Clary gripped the banister for balance, and a chunk of it snapped off in her hand, making her squeak and wringing an exhausted chuckle out of Jace. He took her hand. "Here. Steady."

Simon made a sound that, for a rat, sounded a lot like a snort. Jace didn't seem to hear it. They were stumbling up the steps as rapidly as they dared. The flight rose in a high spiral, up through the building. They passed landing after landing, but no doors. They had reached the fourth featureless turn when a muffled explosion rocked the stairwell, and a cloud of dust billowed upward.

"They've gotten past the door," Jace said grimly. "Damn—I thought it would hold for longer."

"Do we run now?" Clary inquired.

"*Now* we run," he said, and they thundered up the stairs, which shrieked and wailed under their weight, nails popping like gunfire. They were at the fifth landing now—she could hear the soft *thud-thud* of the wolves' paws on the steps far below, or perhaps it was just her imagination. She knew there wasn't really hot breath on the back of her neck, but the snarls and howls, getting louder as they came closer, were real and terrifying.

The sixth landing rose in front of them and they half-flung themselves onto it. Clary was gasping, her breath sawing painfully in her lungs, but she managed a weak cheer when she saw the door. It was heavy steel, riveted with nails, and propped open with a brick. She barely had time to wonder why when Jace kicked it open, pushed her though, and, following, slammed it shut. She heard a definitive click as it locked behind them. *Thank God*, she thought.

Then she turned around.

The night sky wheeled above her, scattered with stars like a handful of loose diamonds. It was not black but a clear dark blue, the color of oncoming dawn. They were standing on a bare slate roof turreted with brick chimneys. An old water tower, black with neglect, stood on a raised platform at one end; a heavy tarpaulin concealed a lumpy pile of lumber at the other. "This must be how they get in and out," Jace said, glancing back at the door. Clary could see him properly now in the pale light, the lines of strain around his eyes like shallow cuts. The blood on his clothes, mostly Raphael's, looked black. "They fly up here. Not that that does us much good."

"There might be a fire escape," Clary suggested. Together they picked their way gingerly to the edge of the roof. Clary had never liked heights, and the ten-floor drop to the street made her stomach spin. So did the sight of the fire escape, a twisted, unusable hunk of metal still clinging to the side of the hotel's stone facade. "Or not," she said. She glanced back at the door they had emerged from. It was set into a cabinlike structure in the center of the roof. It was vibrating, the knob jerking wildly. It would only hold for a few more minutes, perhaps less.

Jace pressed the backs of his hands against his eyes. The leaden air bore down on them, making the back of Clary's neck prickle. She could see the sweat trickling into his collar. She wished, irrelevantly, that it would rain. Rain would burst this heat bubble like a pricked blister.

Jace was muttering to himself. "Think, Wayland, *think*—"

Something began to take shape in the back of Clary's mind. A rune danced against the backs of her eyelids: two downward triangles, joined by a single bar—a rune like a pair of wings...

"That's *it*," Jace breathed, dropping his hands, and for a startled moment Clary wondered if he had read her mind. He looked feverish, his gold-flecked eyes very bright. "I can't believe I didn't think of it before." He dashed to the far end of the roof, then paused and looked back at her. She was still standing dazed, her thoughts full of glimmering shapes. "Come *on*, Clary."

She followed him, pushing thoughts of runes from her mind. He had reached the tarpaulin and was tugging at the edge of it. It came away, revealing not junk but sparkling chrome, tooled leather, and gleaming paint. "*Motorcycles?*"

Jace reached for the nearest one, an enormous dark red Harley with gold flames on the tank and fenders. He swung a leg over it and looked over his shoulder at her. "Get on."

Clary stared. "Are you kidding? Do you even know how to drive that thing? Do you have keys?"

"I don't need keys," he explained with infinite patience. "It runs on demon energies. Now, are you going to get on, or do you want to ride your own?"

Numbly Clary slid onto the bike behind him. Somewhere, in some part of her brain, a tiny voice was screaming about what a bad idea this was.

"Good," Jace said. "Now put your arms around me." She did, feeling the hard muscles of his abdomen contract as he leaned forward and jammed the point of the stele into the ignition. To her amazement she felt the motorcycle thrum to life under her. In her pocket Simon squeaked loudly.

"Everything's okay," she said, as soothingly as she could. "Jace!" she shouted, over the sound of the motorcycle's engine. "What are you doing?"

He yelled back something that sounded like "Pushing in the choke!"

Clary blinked. "Well, hurry it up! The door—"

On cue, the roof door burst open with a crash, torn from its hinges. Wolves poured through the gap, racing across the roof straight at them. Above them flew the vampires, hissing and screeching, filling the night with predatory cries.

She felt Jace's arm jerk back and the motorcycle lurch forward, sending her stomach slamming into her spine. She clutched convulsively at Jace's belt as they shot forward, tires skidding along the slates, scattering the wolves, who yelped as they leaped aside. She heard Jace shout something, his words torn away by the noise of wheels and wind and engine. The edge of the roof was coming up fast, so fast, and Clary wanted to shut her eyes but something held them wide open as the motorcycle hurtled over the parapet and plummeted like a rock toward the ground, ten stories down.

If Clary screamed, she didn't remember it later. It was like the first drop on a roller coaster, where the track falls away and you feel yourself hurtling through space, your hands waving uselessly in the air and your stomach jammed up around your ears. When the cycle righted itself with a sputter and a jerk, she almost wasn't surprised. Instead of plunging downward they were now hurtling up toward the diamond-littered sky.

Clary glanced back and saw a cluster of vampires standing on the roof of the hotel, surrounded by wolves. She looked away—if she never saw that hotel again, it'd be too soon.

Jace was yelling, loud whooping shrieks of delight and relief. Clary leaned forward, her arms tight around him. "My mother always told me if I rode a motorcycle with a boy, she'd kill me," she called over the noise of the wind whipping past her ears and the deafening rumble of the engine.

She couldn't hear him laugh, but she felt his body shake. "She wouldn't say that if she knew me," he called back to her confidently. "I'm an excellent driver."

Belatedly, Clary recollected something. "I thought you

said only *some* of the vampire bikes could fly?"

Deftly, Jace steered them around a stoplight in the process of turning from red to green. Below, Clary could hear cars honking, ambulance sirens wailing, and buses puffing to their stops, but she didn't dare look down. "Only some of them can!"

"How did you know this was one of them?"

"I didn't!" he shouted gleefully, and did something that made the bike rise almost vertically into the air. Clary shrieked and grabbed for his belt again.

"You should look down!" Jace shouted. "It's awesome!"

Sheer curiosity forced its way past terror and vertigo. Swallowing hard, Clary opened her eyes.

They were higher than she had realized, and for a moment the earth swung dizzily beneath her, a blurring landscape of shadow and light. They were flying east, away from the park, toward the highway that snaked along the right bank of the city.

There was a numbness in Clary's hands, a hard pressure in her chest. It was lovely, she could see that: the city rising up beside her like a towering forest of silver and glass, the dull gray shimmer of the East River, slicing between Manhattan and the boroughs like a scar. The wind was cool in her hair, on her bare legs, delicious after so many days of heat and stickiness. Still, she'd never flown, not even in an airplane, and the vast empty space between them and the ground terrified her. She couldn't keep from squinching her eyes almost shut as they shot out over the river. Just below the Queensboro Bridge, Jace turned the bike south and headed to the foot of the island. The sky had begun to lighten, and in the distance

Clary could see the glittering arch of the Brooklyn Bridge, and beyond that, a smudge on the horizon, the Statue of Liberty.

"Are you all right?" Jace shouted.

Clary said nothing, just clutched him more tightly. He banked the cycle, and then they were sailing toward the bridge, and Clary could see stars through the suspension cables. An early morning train was rattling over it—the Q, carrying a load of sleepy dawn commuters. She thought how often she'd been on that train. A wave of vertigo swamped her, and she squeezed her eyes shut, gasping with nausea.

"Clary?" Jace called. "Clary, are you all right?"

She shook her head, eyes still shut, alone in the dark and the tearing wind with just the pounding of her heart. Something sharp scratched against her chest. She ignored it until it came again, more insistent. Barely opening an eye, she saw that it was Simon, his head poking out of her pocket, tugging her shirt with an urgent paw. "It's all right, Simon," she said with an effort, not looking down. "It was just the bridge—"

He scratched her again, then pointed an urgent paw toward the waterfront of Brooklyn, rising up on their left. Dizzy and sick, she looked and saw, beyond the outlines of the warehouses and factories, a sliver of golden sunrise just visible, like the edge of a pale gilt coin. "Yes, very pretty," Clary said, closing her eyes again. "Nice sunrise."

Jace went rigid all over, as if he'd been shot. "Sunrise?" he yelled, then jerked the cycle savagely to the right. Clary's eyes flew open as they plunged toward the water, which had begun to shimmer with the blue of oncoming dawn.

Clary leaned as close to Jace as she could get without

squashing Simon between them. "What's so bad about sunrise?"

"I told you! The bike runs on demon energies!" He pulled back so that they were level with the river, just skimming along the surface with the wheels kicking up spray. River water splashed into Clary's face. "As soon as the sun comes up—"

The bike began to sputter. Jace swore colorfully, slamming his fist into the accelerator. The bike lunged forward once, then choked, jerking under them like a bucking horse. Jace was still swearing as the sun peeked over the crumbling wharves of Brooklyn, lighting the world with devastating clarity. Clary could see every rock, every pebble under them as they cleared the river and hurtled over the narrow bank. Below them was the highway, already streaming with early traffic. They only just cleared it, the wheels grazing the roof of a passing truck. Beyond was the trash-strewn parking lot of an enormous supermarket. "Hang on to me!" Jace was shouting, as the bike jerked and sputtered underneath them. "Hang on to me, Clary, and *do not let*—"

The bike tilted and struck the asphalt of the parking lot, front wheel first. It shot forward, wobbling violently, and went into a long skid, bouncing and slamming over the uneven ground, whipping Clary's head back and forth with neck-cracking force. The air stank of burned rubber. But the bike was slowing, skidding to a halt—and then it struck a concrete parking barrier with such force that she was lifted into the air and hurled sideways, her hand tearing free of Jace's belt. She barely had time to curl herself into a protective ball, holding her arms as rigid as possible and praying Simon wouldn't be crushed, when they struck the ground.

She hit hard, agony screaming up her arm. Something splashed up in her face, and she was coughing as she flipped over, rolling onto her back. She grabbed for her pocket. It was empty. She tried to say Simon's name, but the breath had been knocked out of her. She wheezed as she gasped in air. Her face was wet and dampness was running down into her collar.

Is that blood? She opened her eyes hazily. Her face felt like one big bruise, her arms, aching and stinging, like raw meat. She had rolled onto her side and was lying half-in and half-out of a puddle of filthy water. Dawn had truly come—she could see the remains of the bike, subsiding into a heap of unrecognizable ash as the sun's rays struck it.

And there was Jace, getting painfully to his feet. He started to hurry toward her, then slowed as he approached. The sleeve of his jacket had been torn away and there was a long bloody graze along his left arm. His face, under the cap of dark gold curls matted with sweat, dust, and blood, was white as a sheet. She wondered why he looked like that. Was her torn-off leg lying across the parking lot somewhere in a pool of blood?

She started to struggle up and felt a hand on her shoulder. "Clary?"

"Simon!"

He was kneeling next to her, blinking as if he couldn't quite believe it either. His clothes were crumpled and grimy, and he had lost his glasses somewhere, but he seemed otherwise unharmed. Without the glasses he looked younger, defenseless, and a little dazed. He reached to touch her face, but she flinched back. "Ow!"

"Are you okay? You look great," he said, with a catch in

his voice. "The best thing I've ever seen—"

"That's because you don't have your glasses on," she said weakly, but if she'd expected a smart-aleck response, she didn't get one. Instead he threw his arms around her, holding her tightly to him. His clothes smelled of blood and sweat and dirt, and his heart was beating a mile a minute and he was pressing on her bruises, but it was a relief nevertheless to be held by him and to know, really know, that he was all right.

"Clary," he said roughly. "I thought—I thought you—"

"Wouldn't come back for you? But of course I did," she said. "Of course I did."

She put her arms around him. Everything about him was familiar, from the overwashed fabric of his T-shirt to the sharp angle of the collarbone that rested just under her chin. He said her name, and she stroked his back reassuringly. When she glanced back just for a moment, she saw Jace turning away as if the brightness of the rising sun hurt his eyes.

16
FALLING ANGELS

Hodge was enraged. He had been standing in the foyer, Isabelle and Alec lurking behind him, when Clary and the boys limped in, filthy and covered in blood, and had immediately launched into a lecture that would have done Clary's mother proud. He didn't forget to include the part about lying to him about where they were going—which Jace, apparently, had— or the part about never trusting Jace again, and even added extra embellishments, like some bits about breaking the Law, getting tossed out of the Clave, and bringing shame on the proud and ancient name of Wayland. Winding down, he fixed Jace with a glare. "You've endangered other people with your willfulness. This is one incident I will not allow you to shrug off!"

"I wasn't planning to," Jace said. "I can't shrug anything off. My shoulder's dislocated."

"If only I thought physical pain was actually a deterrent for you," said Hodge with grim fury. "But you'll just spend the next few days in the infirmary with Alec and Isabelle fussing around you. You'll probably even *enjoy* it."

Hodge had been two-thirds right: Jace and Simon both wound up in the infirmary, but only Isabelle was fussing over either of them when Clary—who'd gone to clean herself up—came in a few hours later. Hodge had fixed the swelling bruise on her arm, and twenty minutes in the shower had gotten most of the ground-in asphalt out of her skin, but she still felt raw and aching.

Alec, sitting on the windowsill and looking like a thundercloud, scowled as the door shut behind her. "Oh. It's you."

She ignored him. "Hodge says he's on his way and he hopes you can both manage to cling to your flickering sparks of life until he gets here," she told Simon and Jace. "Or something like that."

"I wish he'd hurry," Jace said crossly. He was sitting up in bed against a pair of fluffed white pillows, still wearing his filthy clothes.

"Why? Does it hurt?" Clary asked.

"No. I have a high pain threshold. In fact, it's less of a threshold and more of a large and tastefully decorated foyer. But I do get easily bored." He squinted at her. "Do you remember back at the hotel when you promised that if we lived, you'd get dressed up in a nurse's outfit and give me a sponge bath?"

"Actually, I think you misheard," Clary said. "It was Simon who promised you the sponge bath."

Jace looked involuntarily over at Simon, who smiled at him widely. "As soon as I'm back on my feet, handsome."

"I knew we should have left you a rat," said Jace.

Clary laughed and went over to Simon, who seemed acutely

uncomfortable surrounded by dozens of pillows and with blankets heaped over his legs.

Clary sat down on the edge of Simon's bed. "How are you feeling?"

"Like someone massaged me with a cheese grater," Simon said, wincing as he pulled his legs up. "I broke a bone in my foot. It was so swollen, Isabelle had to cut my shoe off."

"Glad she's taking good care of you." Clary let a small amount of acid creep into her voice.

Simon leaned forward, not taking his eyes off Clary. "I want to talk to you."

Clary nodded in half-reluctant agreement. "I'm going to my room. Come and see me after Hodge fixes you up, okay?"

"Sure." To her surprise he leaned forward and kissed her on the cheek. It was a butterfly kiss, a quick brush of lips on skin, but as she pulled away, she knew she was blushing. Probably, she thought, standing up, because of the way everyone else was staring at them.

Out in the hallway, she touched her cheek in bemusement. A peck on the cheek didn't mean much, but it was so out of character for Simon. Maybe he was trying to make a point to Isabelle? Men, Clary thought, they were so baffling. And Jace, doing his wounded-prince routine. She'd left before he could start complaining about the thread count of the sheets.

"Clary!"

She turned around in surprise. Alec was loping down the hall after her, hurrying to catch up. He stopped when she did. "I need to talk to you."

She looked at him in surprise. "What about?"

He hesitated. With his pale skin and dark blue eyes he was

as striking as his sister, but unlike Isabelle he did everything he could to downplay his looks. The frayed sweaters and the hair that looked as if he had cut it himself in the dark were only part of it. He looked uncomfortable in his own skin. "I think you should leave. Go home," he said.

She'd known he didn't like her, but it still felt like a slap. "Alec, the last time I was home, it was infested with Forsaken. And Raveners. With fangs. Nobody wants to go home more than I do, but—"

"You must have relatives you can stay with?" There was a tinge of desperation in his voice.

"No. Besides, Hodge wants me to stay," she said shortly.

"He can't possibly. I mean, not after what you've done—"

"What *I've* done?"

He swallowed hard. "You almost got Jace killed."

"I almost—What are you *talking* about?"

"Running off after your friend like that—do you know how much danger you put him in? Do you know—"

"Him? You mean Jace?" Clary cut him off in midsentence. "For your information the whole thing was his idea. *He* asked Magnus where the lair was. He went to the church to get weapons. If I hadn't come with him, he would have gone anyway."

"You don't understand," Alec said. "You don't know him. *I* know him. He thinks he has to save the world; he'd be glad to kill himself trying. Sometimes I think he even wants to die, but that doesn't mean you should encourage him to do it."

"I don't get it," she said. "Jace is a Nephilim. This is what you *do*, you rescue people, you kill demons, you put yourselves in danger. How was last night any different?"

Alec's control shattered. "Because he *left me behind!*" he shouted. "Normally I'd be with him, covering him, watching his back, keeping him safe. But you—you're dead weight, a *mundane*." He spit the word out as if it were an obscenity.

"No," Clary said. "I'm not. I'm Nephilim—just like you."

His lip curled up at the corner. "Maybe," he said. "But with no training, no nothing, you're still not much use, are you? Your mother brought you up in the mundane world, and that's where you belong. Not here, making Jace act like—like he isn't one of us. Making him break his oath to the Clave, making him break the Law—"

"News flash," Clary snapped. "I don't *make* Jace do anything. He does what he wants. You ought to know that."

He looked at her as if she were an especially disgusting kind of demon he'd never seen before. "You mundanes are completely selfish, aren't you? Have you no idea what he's done for you, what kind of personal risks he's taken? I'm not just talking about his safety. He could lose everything. He already lost his father and mother; do you want to make sure he loses the family he's got left as well?"

Clary recoiled. Rage rose up in her like a black wave—rage against Alec, because he was partly right, and rage against everything and everyone else: against the icy road that had taken her father away from her before she was born, against Simon for nearly getting himself killed, against Jace for being a martyr and for not caring whether he lived or died. Against Luke for pretending he cared about her when it was all a lie. And against her mother for not being the boring, normal, haphazard mother she'd always pretended to be, but someone else entirely: someone heroic and spectacular and brave whom Clary didn't know at all. Someone who wasn't there now, when Clary needed her desperately.

"You should talk about selfish," she hissed, so viciously that he took a step back. "You couldn't care less about anyone in this world except yourself, Alec Lightwood. No wonder you've never killed a single demon, because you're too afraid."

Alec looked stunned. "Who told you that?"

"Jace."

He looked as if she'd slapped him. "He wouldn't. He wouldn't say that."

"He did." She could see how she was hurting him, and it made her glad. Someone else ought to be in pain for a change. "You can rant all you want about honor and honesty and how mundanes don't have any of either, but if *you* were honest, you'd admit this tantrum is just because you're in love with him. It doesn't have anything to do with—"

Alec moved, blindingly fast. A sharp crack resounded through her head. He had shoved her against the wall so hard that the back of her skull had struck the wood paneling. His face was inches from hers, eyes huge and black. "Don't you *ever*," he whispered, mouth a blanched line, "ever, say anything like that to him or I'll kill you. I swear on the Angel, I'll kill you."

The pain in her arms where he gripped her was intense. Against her will she gasped. He blinked—as if he were waking up out of a dream—and let her go, jerking his hands away like her skin had burned him. Without a word he spun and hurried back toward the infirmary. He was lurching as he walked, like someone drunk or dizzy.

Clary rubbed her sore arms, staring after him, appalled at what she'd done. *Good job, Clary. Now you've really made him hate you.*

She should have fallen instantly into bed, but despite her exhaustion, sleep remained out of reach. Eventually she pulled her sketchpad out of her backpack and started drawing, propping the tablet against her knees. Idle scribbles at first—a detail from the crumbling facade of the vampire hotel: a fanged gargoyle with bulging eyes. An empty street, a single lamppost casting a yellow pool of illumination, a shadowy figure poised at the edge of the light. She drew Raphael in his bloody white shirt with the scar of the cross on his throat. And then she drew Jace standing on the roof, looking down at the ten-story drop below. Not afraid, but as if the fall challenged him—as if there were no empty space he could not fill with his belief in his own invincibility. As in her dream, she drew him with wings that curved out behind his shoulders in an arc like the wings of the angel statue in the Bone City.

She tried to draw her mother, last. She had told Jace she didn't feel any different after reading the Gray Book, and it was mostly true. Now, though, as she tried to visualize her mother's face, she realized there was one thing that was different in her memories of Jocelyn: She could see her mother's scars, the tiny white marks that covered her back and shoulders as if she had been standing in a snowfall.

It hurt, knowing that the way she'd always seen her mother, all her life, had been a lie. She slid the sketchpad under her pillow, eyes burning.

There was a tap on the door—soft, hesitant. She scrubbed hastily at her eyes. "Come in."

It was Simon. She hadn't really focused on what a mess he was. He hadn't showered, and his clothes were torn and stained, his hair tangled. He hesitated in the doorway, oddly formal.

She scooted sideways, making room for him on the bed. There was nothing strange about sitting in bed with Simon; they'd slept over at each other's houses for years, made tents and forts with the blankets when they were small, stayed up reading comics when they were older.

"You found your glasses," she said. One lens was cracked.

"They were in my pocket. They came through better than I would have expected. I'll have to write a nice note to LensCrafters." He settled beside her gingerly.

"Did Hodge fix you up?"

He nodded. "Yeah. I still feel like I've been worked over with a tire iron, but nothing's broken—not anymore." He turned to look at her. His eyes behind the ruined glasses were the eyes she remembered: dark and serious, ringed by the kind of lashes boys didn't care about and girls would kill for. "Clary, that you came for me—that you would risk all that—"

"Don't." She held up a hand awkwardly. "You would have done it for me."

"Of course," he said, without arrogance or pretension, "but I always thought that was the way things were, with us. You know."

She scrambled around to face him, puzzled. "What do you mean?"

"I mean," said Simon, as if he were surprised to find himself explaining something that should have been obvious, "I've always been the one who needed you more than you needed me."

"That's not true." Clary was appalled.

"It is," Simon said with the same unnerving calm. "You've never seemed to really need anyone, Clary. You've always been so ... contained. All you've ever needed is your pencils and your imaginary worlds. So many times I've had to say things six, seven times before you'd even respond, you were so far away. And then you'd turn to me and smile that funny smile, and I'd know you'd forgotten all about me and just remembered—but I was never mad at you. Half of your attention is better than all of anyone else's."

She tried to catch at his hand, but got his wrist. She could feel the pulse under his skin. "I only ever loved three people in my life," she said. "My mom and Luke, and you. And I've lost all of them except you. Don't ever imagine you aren't important to me—don't even think it."

"My mom says you only need three people you can rely on in order to achieve self-actualization," said Simon. His tone was light but his voice cracked halfway through "actualization." "She says you seem pretty self-actualized."

Clary smiled at him ruefully. "Did your mom have any other words of wisdom about me?"

"Yeah." He returned her smile with one just as crooked. "But I'm not going to tell you what they were."

"No fair keeping secrets!"

"Who ever said the world was fair?"

* * *

In the end, they lay against each other as they had when they were children: shoulder to shoulder, Clary's leg thrown over Simon's. Her toes came to just below his knee. Flat on their backs, they stared up at the ceiling as they talked, a habit left over from the time when Clary's ceiling had been covered with paste-on glow-in-the-dark stars. Where Jace had smelled like soap and limes, Simon smelled like someone who'd been rolling around the parking lot of a supermarket, but Clary didn't mind.

"The weird thing is"—Simon wound a curl of her hair around his finger—"I was joking with Isabelle about vampires right before it all happened. Just trying to get her to laugh, you know? 'What freaks out Jewish vampires? Silver stars of David? Chopped liver? Checks for eighteen dollars?'"

Clary laughed.

Simon looked gratified. "Isabelle didn't laugh."

Clary thought of a number of things she wanted to say, and didn't say them. "I'm not sure that's Isabelle's kind of humor."

Simon cut a sideways glance at her under his lashes. "Is she sleeping with Jace?"

Clary's squeak of surprise turned into a cough. She glared at him. "Ew, no. They're practically related. They wouldn't do that." She paused. "I don't *think* so, anyway."

Simon shrugged. "Not like I care," he said firmly.

"Sure you don't."

"I don't!" He rolled onto his side. "You know, initially I thought Isabelle seemed, I don't know—cool. Exciting. Different. Then, at the party, I realized she was actually crazy."

Clary slit her eyes at him. "Did she tell you to drink the blue cocktail?"

He shook his head. "That was all me. I saw you go off with Jace and Alec, and I don't know... You looked so different from usual. You *seemed* so different. I couldn't help thinking you'd changed already, and this new world of yours would leave me out. I wanted to do something that would make me more a part of it. So when the little green guy came by with the tray of drinks..."

Clary groaned. "You're an idiot."

"I've never claimed otherwise."

"Sorry. Was it awful?"

"Being a rat? No. First it was disorienting. I was suddenly at ankle-level with everyone. I thought I'd drunk a shrinking potion, but I couldn't figure out why I had this urge to chew used gum wrappers."

Clary giggled. "No. I mean the vampire hotel—was that awful?"

Something flickered behind his eyes. He looked away. "No. I don't really remember much between the party and landing in the parking lot."

"Probably better that way."

He started to say something but was arrested mid-yawn. The light in the room had slowly faded. Disentangling herself from Simon and the bedsheets, Clary got up and pushed aside the window curtains. Outside, the city was bathed in the reddish glow of sunset. The silvery roof of the Chrysler Building, fifty blocks downtown, glowed like a poker left too long in the fire. "The sun's setting. Maybe we should look for some dinner."

There was no response. Turning, she saw that Simon was asleep, his arms folded under his head, legs sprawled. She sighed, went over to the bed, plucked his glasses off, and set them on the night table. She couldn't count the times he'd fallen asleep with them on and been woken by the sound of cracking lenses.

Now where am I going to sleep? Not that she minded sharing a bed with Simon, but he hadn't exactly left her any room. She considered poking him awake, but he looked so peaceful. Besides, she wasn't sleepy. She was just reaching for the sketchpad under the pillow when a knock sounded on the door.

She padded barefoot across the room and turned the doorknob quietly. It was Jace. Clean, in jeans and a gray shirt, his washed hair a halo of damp gold. The bruises on his face were already fading from purple to faint gray, and his hands were behind his back.

"Were you asleep?" he asked. There was no contrition in his voice, only curiosity.

"No." Clary stepped out into the hallway, pulling the door shut behind her. "Why would you think that?"

He eyed her baby blue cotton tank top and sleep shorts set. "No reason."

"I was in bed most of the day," she said, which was technically true. Seeing him, her jitter level had shot up about a thousand percent, but she saw no reason to share that information. "What about you? Aren't you exhausted?"

He shook his head. "Much like the postal service, demon hunters never sleep. 'Neither snow nor rain nor heat nor gloom of night stays these—'"

"You'd be in major trouble if gloom of night did stay you," she pointed out.

He grinned. Unlike his hair, his teeth weren't perfect. An upper incisor was slightly, endearingly chipped.

She gripped her elbows. It was chilly in the hallway and she could feel goose bumps starting up her arms. "What are you doing here, anyway?"

"'Here' as in your bedroom or 'here' as in the great spiritual question of our purpose here on this planet? If you're asking whether it's all just a cosmic coincidence or there's a greater meta-ethical purpose to life, well, that's a puzzler for the ages. I mean, simple ontological reductionism is clearly a fallacious argument, but—"

"I'm going back to bed." Clary reached for the doorknob.

He slid nimbly between her and the door. "I'm here," he said, "because Hodge reminded me it was your birthday."

Clary exhaled in exasperation. "Not until tomorrow."

"That's no reason not to start celebrating now."

She eyed him. "You're avoiding Alec and Isabelle."

He nodded. "Both of them are trying to pick fights with me."

"For the same reason?"

"I couldn't tell." He glanced furtively up and down the hallway. "Hodge, too. Everyone wants to talk to me. Except you. I bet you don't want to talk to me."

"No," said Clary. "I want to eat. I'm starving."

He brought his hand out from behind his back. In it was a slightly crumpled paper bag. "I sneaked some food from the kitchen when Isabelle wasn't looking."

Clary grinned. "A picnic? It's a little late for Central Park, don't you think? It's full of—"

He waved a hand. "Faeries. I know."

“I was going to say muggers,” said Clary. “Though I pity the mugger who goes after you.”

“That is a wise attitude, and I commend you for it,” said Jace, looking gratified. “But I wasn’t thinking of Central Park. How about the greenhouse?”

“Now? At night? Won’t it be—dark?”

He smiled as if at a secret. “Come on. I’ll show you.”

17

The Midnight Flower

In the half-light the big empty rooms they passed through on their way to the roof looked as deserted as stage sets, the white-draped furniture looming up out of the dimness like icebergs through fog.

When Jace opened the greenhouse door, the scent hit Clary, soft as the padded blow of a cat's paw: the rich dark smell of earth and the stronger, soapy scent of night-blooming flowers—moonflowers, white angel's trumpet, four-o'clocks—and some she didn't recognize, like a plant bearing a star-shaped yellow blossom whose petals were medallioned with golden pollen. Through the glass walls of the enclosure she could see the lights of Manhattan burning like cold jewels.

"Wow." She turned slowly, taking it in. "It's so beautiful here at night."

Jace grinned. "And we have the place to ourselves. Alec and Isabelle hate it up here. They have allergies."

Clary shivered, though she wasn't at all cold. "What kind of flowers are these?"

Jace shrugged and sat down, carefully, next to a glossy green shrub dotted all over with tightly closed flower buds. "No idea. You think I pay attention in botany class? I'm not going to be an archivist. I don't need to know about that stuff."

"You just need to know how to kill things?"

He looked up at her and smiled. He looked like a fair-haired angel from a Rembrandt painting, except for that devilish mouth. "That's right." He took a napkin-wrapped package out of the bag and offered it to her. "Also," he added, "I make a mean cheese sandwich. Try one."

Clary smiled reluctantly and sat down across from him. The stone floor of the greenhouse was cold against her bare legs, but it was pleasant after so many days of relentless heat. Out of the paper bag Jace drew some apples, a bar of fruit and nut chocolate, and a bottle of water. "Not a bad haul," she said admiringly.

The cheese sandwich was warm and a little limp, but it tasted fine. From one of the innumerable pockets inside his jacket, Jace produced a bone-handled knife that looked capable of disemboweling a grizzly. He set to work on the apples, carving them into meticulous eighths. "Well, it's not birthday cake," he said, handing her a section, "but hopefully it's better than nothing."

"Nothing is what I was expecting, so thanks." She took a bite. The apple tasted green and cool.

"Nobody should get nothing on their birthday." He was peeling the second apple, the skin coming away in long curling strips. "Birthdays should be special. My birthday was always the one day my father said I could do or have anything I wanted."

"Anything?" She laughed. "Like what kind of anything did you want?"

"Well, when I was five, I wanted to take a bath in spaghetti."

"But he didn't let you, right?"

"No, that's the thing. He did. He said it wasn't expensive, and why not if that was what I wanted? He had the servants fill a bath with boiling water and pasta, and when it cooled down..." He shrugged. "I took a bath in it."

Servants? Clary thought. Out loud she said, "How was it?"

"Slippery."

"I'll bet." She tried to picture him as a little boy, giggling, up to his ears in pasta. The image wouldn't form. Surely Jace never giggled, not even at the age of five. "What else did you ask for?"

"Weapons, mostly," he said, "which I'm sure doesn't surprise you. Books. I read a lot on my own."

"You didn't go to school?"

"No," he said, and now he spoke slowly, almost as if they were approaching a topic he didn't want to discuss.

"But your friends—"

"I didn't have friends," he said. "Besides my father. He was all I needed."

She stared at him. "No friends at all?"

He met her look steadily. "The first time I saw Alec," he said, "when I was ten years old, that was the first time I'd ever met another child my own age. The first time I *had* a friend."

She dropped her gaze. Now an image was forming, unwelcome, in her head: She thought of Alec, the way he had looked at her. *He wouldn't say that.*

"Don't feel sorry for me," Jace said, as if guessing her thoughts, though it hadn't been him she'd been feeling sorry for. "He gave me the best education, the best training. He took me all over the world. London. Saint Petersburg. Egypt. We used to love to travel." His eyes were dark. "I haven't been anywhere since he died. Nowhere but New York."

"You're lucky," Clary said. "I've never been outside this state in my life. My mom wouldn't even let me go on field trips to D.C. I guess I know why now," she added ruefully.

"She was afraid you'd freak out? Start seeing demons in the White House?"

She nibbled a piece of chocolate. "There are demons in the White House?"

"I was kidding," said Jace. "I think." He shrugged philosophically. "I'm sure someone would have mentioned it."

"I think she just didn't want me to get too far away from her. My mom, I mean. After my dad died, she changed a lot." Luke's voice echoed in her mind. *You've never been the same since it happened, but Clary isn't Jonathan.*

Jace cocked an eyebrow at her. "Do you remember your father?"

She shook her head. "No. He died before I was born."

"You're lucky," he said. "That way you don't miss him."

From anyone else it would have been an appalling thing to say, but there was no bitterness in his voice for a change, only an ache of loneliness for his own father. "Does it go away?" she asked. "Missing him, I mean?"

He looked at her obliquely, but didn't answer. "Are you thinking of your mother?"

No. She wouldn't think of her mother that way. "Of Luke, actually."

"Not that that's actually his name." He took a thoughtful bite of apple and said, "I've been thinking about him. Something about his behavior doesn't add up—"

"He's a coward." Clary's voice was bitter. "You heard him. He won't go against Valentine. Not even for my mother."

"But that's exactly—" A long clanging reverberation interrupted him. Somewhere, a bell was tolling. "Midnight," said Jace, setting the knife down. He got to his feet, holding his hand out to pull her up beside him. His fingers were slightly sticky with apple juice. "Now, watch."

His gaze was fixed on the green shrub they'd been sitting beside, with its dozens of shiny closed buds. She started to ask him what she was supposed to be looking at, but he held up a hand to forestall her. His eyes were shining. "Wait," he said.

The leaves on the shrub hung still and motionless. Suddenly one of the tightly closed buds began to quiver and tremble. It swelled to twice its size and burst open. It was like watching a speeded-up film of a flower blooming: the delicate green sepals opening outward, releasing the clustered petals inside. They were dusted with pale gold pollen as light as talcum.

"Oh!" said Clary, and looked up to find Jace watching her. "Do they bloom every night?"

"Only at midnight," he said. "Happy birthday, Clarissa Fray."

She was oddly touched. "Thank you."

"I have something for you," he said. He dug into his pocket and brought out something, which he pressed into her hand. It was a gray stone, slightly uneven, worn to smoothness in spots.

"Huh," said Clary, turning it over in her fingers. "You know, when most girls say they want a big rock, they don't mean, you know, literally a *big rock*."

"Very amusing, my sarcastic friend. It's not a rock, precisely. All Shadowhunters have a witchlight rune-stone."

"Oh." She looked at it with renewed interest, closing her fingers around it as she'd seen Jace do in the cellar. She wasn't sure, but she thought she could see a glint of light peeking out through her fingers.

"It will always bring you light," said Jace, his voice a little rough.

She slipped it into her pocket. "Well, thanks. It was nice of you to give me anything." The tension between them seemed to press down on her like humid air. "Better than a bath in spaghetti any day."

He said darkly, "If you share that little bit of personal information with anyone, I may have to kill you."

"Well, when *I* was five, I wanted my mother to let me go around and around inside the dryer with the clothes," Clary said. "The difference is, she didn't let me."

"Probably because going around and around inside a dryer can be fatal," Jace pointed out, "whereas pasta is rarely fatal. Unless Isabelle makes it."

The midnight flower was already shedding petals. They drifted toward the floor, glimmering like slivers of starlight.

"When I was twelve, I wanted a tattoo," Clary said. "My mom wouldn't let me have that, either."

Jace didn't laugh. "Most Shadowhunters get their first Marks at twelve. It must have been in your blood."

"Maybe. Although I doubt most Shadowhunters get a tattoo of Donatello from the Teenage Mutant Ninja Turtles on their left shoulder."

Jace looked baffled. "You wanted a turtle on your shoulder?"

"I wanted to cover my chicken pox scar." She pulled the strap of the tank top aside slightly, showing the star-shaped white mark at the top of her shoulder. "See?"

He looked away. "It's getting late," he said. "We should go back downstairs."

Clary pulled her strap back up awkwardly. As if he wanted to see her stupid scars.

The next words tumbled out of her mouth without any volition on her part. "Have you and Isabelle ever—dated?"

Now he did look at her. The moonlight leached the color out of his eyes. They were more silver than gold now. "Isabelle?" he said blankly.

"I thought—" Now she felt even more awkward. "Simon was wondering."

"Maybe he should ask her."

"I'm not sure he wants to," Clary said. "Anyway, never mind. It's none of my business."

He smiled unnervingly. "The answer is no. I mean, there may have been a time when one or the other of us considered it, but she's almost a sister to me. It would be strange."

"You mean Isabelle and you never—"

"Never," said Jace.

"She hates me," observed Clary.

"No, she doesn't," he said, to her surprise. "You just make her nervous, because she's always been the only girl in a crowd of adoring boys, and now she isn't anymore."

"But she's so beautiful."

"So are you," said Jace, "and very different from how she is, and she can't help but notice that. She's always wanted to be small and delicate, you know. She hates being taller than most boys."

Clary said nothing to this, because she had nothing to say. Beautiful. He'd called her beautiful. Nobody had ever called her that before, except her mother, which didn't count. Mothers were required to think you were beautiful. She stared at him.

"We should probably go downstairs," he said again. She was sure she was making him uncomfortable with the staring, but she didn't seem to be able to stop.

"All right," she said finally. To her relief, her voice sounded normal. It was a further relief to look away from him as she turned around. The moon, directly overhead now, lit everything nearly to daylight brightness. In between one step and another she saw a white spark struck off something on the floor: It was the knife Jace had been using to cut apples, lying on its side. She jerked hastily back to avoid stepping on it, and her shoulder bumped his—he put a hand out to steady her, just as she turned to apologize, and then she was somehow in the circle of his arm and he was kissing her.

It was at first almost as if he hadn't wanted to kiss her: His mouth was hard on hers, unyielding; then he put both arms around her and pulled her against him. His lips softened. She could feel the rapid beat of his heart, taste the sweetness of apples still on his mouth. She wound her hands into his hair, as she'd wanted to do since the first time she'd seen him. His hair curled around her fingers, silky and fine. Her heart was hammering, and there was a rushing sound in her ears, like beating wings—

Jace drew away from her with a muffled exclamation, though his arms were still around her. "Don't panic, but we've got an audience."

Clary turned her head. Perched on a nearby tree branch was Hugo, watching them beadily from bright black eyes. So the sound she'd heard *had* been wings rather than demented passion. That was disappointing.

"If he's here, Hodge won't be far behind," said Jace under his breath. "We should go."

"Is he *spying* on you?" Clary hissed. "Hodge, I mean."

"No. He just likes to come up here to think. Too bad—we were having such a scintillating conversation." He laughed soundlessly.

They made their way back downstairs the way they had come, but it felt like a different journey entirely to Clary. Jace kept her hand in his, sending tiny electrical shocks traveling up and down her veins from every point where he touched her: her fingers, her wrist, the palm of her hand. Her mind was buzzing with questions, but she was too afraid of breaking the mood to ask him any of them. He'd said "too bad," so she guessed their evening was over, at least the kissing part.

They reached her door. She leaned against the wall beside it, looking up at him. "Thanks for the birthday picnic," she said, trying to keep her tone neutral.

He seemed reluctant to let go of her hand. "Are you going to sleep?"

He's just being polite, she told herself. Then again, this was Jace. He was never polite. She decided to answer the question with a question. "Aren't you tired?"

His voice was low. "I've never been more awake."

He bent to kiss her, cupping her face with his free hand. Their lips touched, lightly at first, and then with a stronger pressure. It was at precisely that moment that Simon threw open the bedroom door and stepped out into the hall.

He was blinking and tousle-haired and without his glasses, but he could see well enough. "What the *hell?*" he demanded, so loudly that Clary leaped away from Jace as if his touch burned her.

"Simon! What are you—I mean, I thought you were—"

"Asleep? I was," he said. The tops of his cheekbones had flushed dark red through his tan, the way they always did when he was embarrassed or upset. "Then I woke up and you weren't there, so I thought..."

Clary couldn't think of a thing to say. Why hadn't it occurred to her that this might happen? Why hadn't she said they should go to Jace's room? The answer was as simple as it was awful: She had forgotten about Simon completely.

"I'm sorry," she said, not sure who she was even speaking to. Out of the corner of her eye she thought she saw Jace shoot her a look of white rage—but when she glanced at him, he looked as he always did: easy, confident, slightly bored.

"In future, Clarissa," he said, "it might be wise to

mention that you already have a man in your bed, to avoid such tedious situations."

"You invited him into *bed*?" Simon demanded, looking shaken.

"Ridiculous, isn't it?" said Jace. "We would never have all fit."

"I didn't invite him into bed," Clary snapped. "We were just kissing."

"Just kissing?" Jace's tone mocked her with its false hurt. "How swiftly you dismiss our love."

"Jace..."

She saw the bright malice in his eyes and trailed off. There was no point. Her stomach felt suddenly heavy. "Simon, it's late," she said tiredly. "I'm sorry we woke you up."

"So am I." He stalked back into the bedroom, slamming the door behind him.

Jace's smile was as bland as buttered toast. "Go on, go after him. Pat his head and tell him he's still your super special little guy. Isn't that what you want to do?"

"Stop it," she said. "Stop being like that."

His smile widened. "Like what?"

"If you're angry, just say it. Don't act like nothing ever touches you. It's like you never feel anything at all."

"Maybe you should have thought about that before you kissed me," he said.

She looked at him incredulously. "*I* kissed *you?*"

He looked at her with glittering malice. "Don't worry," he said, "it wasn't that memorable for me, either."

She watched him walk away, and felt the mingled urge to burst into tears and to run after him for the express purpose of kicking him in the ankle. Knowing either action would fill him with satisfaction, she did neither, but went warily back into the bedroom.

Simon was standing in the middle of the room, looking lost. He'd put his glasses back on. She heard Jace's voice in her head, saying nastily: *Pat his head and tell him he's still your super special little guy*.

She took a step toward him, then stopped when she realized what he was holding in his hand. Her sketchpad, open to the drawing she'd been doing, the one of Jace with angel wings. "Nice," he said. "All those Tisch classes must be paying off."

Normally, Clary would have told him off for looking into her sketchpad, but now wasn't the time. "Simon, look—"

"I recognize that stalking off to sulk in *your* bedroom might not have been the smoothest move," he interrupted stiffly, tossing the sketchpad back onto the bed. "But I had to get my stuff."

"Where are you going?" she asked.

"Home. I've been here too long, I think. Mundanes like me don't belong in a place like this."

She sighed. "Look, I'm sorry, okay? I wasn't intending to kiss him; it just happened. I know you don't like him."

"No," Simon said even more stiffly. "I don't *like* flat soda. I don't *like* crappy boy band pop. I don't like being stuck in traffic. I don't *like* math homework. I *hate* Jace. See the difference?"

"He saved your life," Clary pointed out, feeling like a fraud—after all, Jace had come along to the Dumort only because he'd been worried he'd get in trouble if she got herself killed.

"Details," said Simon dismissively. "He's an asshole. I thought you were better than that."

Clary's temper flared. "Oh, and now *you're* pulling a high-and-mighty trip on me?" she snapped. "You're the one who was going to ask the girl with the most 'rockin' bod' to the Fall Fling." She mimicked Eric's lazy tone. Simon's mouth thinned out angrily. "So what if Jace is a jerk sometimes? You're not my brother, you're not my dad, you don't *have* to like him. I've never liked any of your girlfriends, but at least I've had the decency to keep it to myself."

"This," said Simon, between his teeth, "is different."

"How? How is it different?"

"Because I see the way you look at him!" he shouted. "And I never looked at any of those girls like that! It was just something to do, a way to practice, until—"

"Until what?" Clary knew dimly that she was being horrible, the whole thing was horrible; they'd never even had a fight before that was more serious than an argument about who'd eaten the last Pop-Tart from the box in the tree house, but she didn't seem able to stop. "Until Isabelle came along? I can't believe you're lecturing me about Jace when you made a complete fool of yourself over her!" Her voice rose to a scream.

"I was *trying to make you jealous*!" Simon screamed, right back. His hands were fists at his sides. "You're so stupid, Clary. You're so *stupid*, can't you see anything?"

She stared at him in bewilderment. What on earth did he mean? "Trying to make me jealous? Why would you try to do that?"

She saw immediately that this was the worst thing she could have asked him.

"Because," he said, so bitterly that it shocked her, "I've been in love with you for ten years, so I thought it seemed like time to find out whether you felt the same about me. Which, I guess, you don't."

He might as well have kicked her in the stomach. She couldn't speak; the air had been sucked out of her lungs. She stared at him, trying to frame a response, any response.

He cut her off sharply. "Don't. There's nothing you can say."

She watched him walk to the door as if paralyzed; she couldn't move to hold him back, much as she wanted to. What could she say? *I love you, too?* But she didn't—did she?

He paused at the door, hand on the knob, and turned to look at her. His eyes, behind the glasses, looked more tired than angry now. "You really want to know what else it was my mom said about you?" he asked.

She shook her head.

He didn't seem to notice. "She said you'd break my heart," he told her, and left. The door closed behind him with a decided click, and Clary was alone.

After he was gone, she sank down onto the bed and picked up her sketchbook. She cradled it to her chest, not wanting to draw in it, just craving the feel and smell of familiar things: ink, paper, chalk.

She thought about running after Simon, trying to catch him. But what would she say? What could she *possibly* say? *You're so stupid, Clary*, he'd said to her. *Can't you see anything?*

She thought of a hundred things he'd said or done, jokes Eric and the others had made about them, conversations hushed when she'd walked into the room. Jace had known from the beginning. *I was laughing at you because declarations of love amuse me, especially when unrequited.* She hadn't stopped to wonder what he was talking about, but now she knew.

She had told Simon earlier that she'd only ever loved three people: her mother, Luke, and him. She wondered if it was actually possible, within the space of a week, to lose everyone that you loved. She wondered if it was the sort of thing you survived or not. And yet—for those brief moments, up on the roof with Jace, she'd forgotten her mother. She'd forgotten Luke. She'd forgotten Simon. And she'd been happy. That was the worst part, that she'd been happy.

Maybe this, she thought, *losing Simon, maybe this is my punishment for the selfishness of being happy, even for just a moment, when my mother is still missing.* None of it had been real, anyway. Jace might be an exceptional kisser, but he didn't care about her at all. He'd said as much.

She lowered the sketchbook slowly into her lap. Simon had been right; it was a good picture of Jace. She'd caught the hard line of his mouth, the incongruously vulnerable eyes. The wings looked so real she imagined that if she brushed her fingers across them, they'd be soft. She let her hand trail across the page, her mind wandering...

And jerked her hand back, staring. Her fingers had touched not dry paper but the soft down of feathers. Her eyes flashed up to the runes she'd scrawled in the corner of the page. They were shining, the way she'd seen the runes Jace drew with his stele shine.

Her heart had begun to beat with a rapid, steady sharpness. If a rune could bring a painting to life, then maybe—

Not taking her eyes off the drawing, she fumbled for her pencils. Breathless, she flipped to a new, clean page and hastily began to draw the first thing that came to mind. It was the coffee mug sitting on the nightstand next to her bed. Drawing on her memories of still life class, she drew it in every detail: the smudged rim, the crack in the handle. When she was done, it was as exact as she could make it. Driven by some instinct she didn't quite understand, she reached for the cup and set it down on top of the paper. Then, very carefully, she began to sketch the runes beside it.

18

The Mortal Cup

Jace was lying on his bed pretending to be asleep—for his own benefit, not anyone else's—when the banging on the door finally got to be too much for him. He hauled himself off the bed, wincing. Much as he'd pretended to be fine up in the greenhouse, his whole body still ached from the beating it had taken last night.

He knew who it was going to be before he opened the door. Maybe Simon had managed to get himself turned into a rat again. This time Simon could stay a goddamned rat forever, for all he, Jace Wayland, was prepared to do about it.

She was clutching her sketchpad, her bright hair escaping out of its braids. He leaned against the door frame, ignoring the kick of adrenaline the sight of her produced. He wondered why, not for the first time. Isabelle used her beauty like she used her whip, but Clary didn't know she was beautiful at all. Maybe that *was* why.

He could think of only one reason for her to be there,

though it made no sense after what he'd said to her. Words were weapons, his father had taught him that, and he'd wanted to hurt Clary more than he'd ever wanted to hurt any girl. In fact, he wasn't sure he had ever wanted to hurt a girl before. Usually he just wanted them, and then wanted them to leave him alone.

"Don't tell me," he said, drawing his words out in that way he knew she hated. "Simon's turned himself into an ocelot and you want me to do something about it before Isabelle makes him into a stole. Well, you'll have to wait till tomorrow. I'm out of commission." He pointed at himself—he was wearing blue pajamas with a hole in the sleeve. "Look. Jammies."

Clary seemed barely to have heard him. "Jace," she said. "This is important."

"Don't tell me," he said. "You've got a drawing emergency. You need a nude model. Well, I'm not in the mood. You could ask Hodge," he added, as an afterthought. "I hear he'll do anything for a—"

"JACE!" she interrupted him, her voice rising to a scream. "JUST SHUT UP FOR A SECOND AND LISTEN, WILL YOU?"

He blinked.

She took a deep breath and looked up at him. Her eyes were full of uncertainty. An unfamiliar urge rose inside him: the urge to put his arms around her and tell her it was all right. He didn't. In his experience, things were rarely all right. "Jace," she said, so softly that he had to lean forward to catch her words, "I think I know where my mother hid the Mortal Cup. It's inside a painting."

***

"What?" Jace was still staring at her as if she'd told him she'd found one of the Silent Brothers doing nude cartwheels in the hallway. "You mean she hid it *behind* a painting? All the paintings in your apartment were torn out of the frames."

"I know." Clary glanced past him into his bedroom. It didn't look like there was anyone else in there, to her relief. "Look, can I come in? I want to show you something."

He slouched back from the door. "If you must."

She sat down on the bed, balancing her sketchpad on her knees. The clothes he'd been wearing earlier were flung across the covers, but the rest of the room was neat as a monk's chamber. There were no pictures on the walls, no posters or photos of friends or family. The blankets were white and pulled tight and flat across the bed. Not exactly a typical teenage boy's bedroom. "Here," she said, flipping the pages until she found the coffee cup drawing. "Look at this."

Jace sat down next to her, shoving his discarded T-shirt out of the way. "It's a coffee cup."

She could hear the irritation in her own voice. "I *know* it's a coffee cup."

"I can't wait till you draw something really complicated, like the Brooklyn Bridge or a lobster. You'll probably send me a singing telegram."

She ignored him. "Look. This is what I wanted you to see." She passed her hand over the drawing; then, with a quick darting motion, reached *into* the paper. When she drew her hand back a moment later, there was the coffee cup, dangling from her fingers.

She had imagined Jace leaping from the bed in astonishment and gasping something like "Egad!" This didn't happen—

largely, she suspected, because Jace had seen much stranger things in his life, and also because nobody used the word "Egad!" anymore. His eyes widened, though. "You did that?"

She nodded.

"When?"

"Just now, in my bedroom, after—after Simon left."

His glance sharpened, but he didn't pursue it. "You used runes? Which ones?"

She shook her head, fingering the now blank page. "I don't know. They came into my head and I drew them exactly how I saw them."

"Ones you saw earlier in the Gray Book?"

"I don't know." She was still shaking her head. "I couldn't tell you."

"And no one ever showed you how to do this? Your mother, for instance?"

"No. I told you before, my mother always told me there was no such thing as magic—"

"I bet she did teach you," he interrupted. "And made you forget it afterward. Magnus did say your memories would come back slowly."

"Maybe."

"Of course." Jace got to his feet and started to pace. "It's probably against the Law to use runes like that unless you've been licensed. But that doesn't matter right now. You think your mother put the Cup into a painting? Like you just did with that mug?"

Clary nodded. "But not one of the paintings in the apartment."

"Where else? A gallery? It could be anywhere—"

"Not a painting at all," Clary said. "In a card."

Jace paused, turning toward her. "A card?"

"You remember that tarot deck of Madame Dorothea's? The one my mother painted for her?"

He nodded.

"And remember when I drew the Ace of Cups? Later when I saw the statue of the Angel, the Cup looked familiar to me. It was because I'd seen it before, on the Ace. My mother *painted the Mortal Cup into Madame Dorothea's tarot deck*."

Jace was a step behind her. "Because she knew that it would be safe inside those wards, and it was a way she could give it to Dorothea without actually telling her what it was or why she had to keep it hidden."

"Or even that she had to keep it hidden at all. Dorothea never goes out, she'd never give it away—"

"And your mother was ideally placed to keep an eye on both it and her." Jace sounded almost impressed. "Not a bad move."

"I guess so." Clary fought to control the waver in her voice. "I wish she hadn't been so good at hiding it."

"What do you mean?"

"I mean if they'd found it, maybe they would have left her alone. If all they wanted was the Cup—"

"They would have killed her, Clary," Jace said. She knew he was telling the truth. "These are the same men who killed my father. The only reason she may still be alive now is that they can't find the Cup. Be glad she hid it so well."

"I don't really see what any of this has to do with us," Alec said, looking blearily through his hair. Jace had woken the rest of the Institute's residents at the crack of dawn and dragged them to the library to, as he said, "devise battle strategies." Alec was still in his pajamas, Isabelle in a pink peignoir set. Hodge, in his usual sharp tweed suit, was drinking coffee out of a chipped blue ceramic mug. Only Jace, bright-eyed despite fading bruises, looked really awake. "I thought the search for the Cup was in the hands of the Clave now."

"It's just better if we do this ourselves," said Jace impatiently. "Hodge and I already discussed it and that's what we decided."

"Well." Isabelle tucked a pink-ribboned braid behind her ear. "I'm game."

"I'm not," Alec said. "There are operatives of the Clave in this city right now looking for the Cup. Pass the information on to them and let them get it."

"It's not that simple," said Jace.

"It is simple." Alec sat forward, frowning. "This has nothing to do with us and everything to do with your—your addiction to danger."

Jace shook his head, clearly exasperated. "I don't understand why you're fighting me on this."

Because he doesn't want you to get hurt, Clary thought, and wondered at his total inability to see what was really going on with Alec. Then again, she'd missed the same thing in Simon. Who was she to talk? "Look, Dorothea doesn't trust the Clave. Hates them, in fact. She does trust us."

"She trusts me," said Clary. "I don't know about you. I'm not sure she likes you at all."

Jace ignored her. "Come on, Alec. It'll be fun. And think of the glory if we bring the Mortal Cup back to Idris! Our names will never be forgotten."

"I don't care about glory," said Alec, his eyes never leaving Jace's face. "I care about not doing anything stupid."

"In this case, however, Jace is right," said Hodge. "If the Clave were to come to the sanctuary, it would be a disaster. Dorothea would flee with the Cup and would probably never be found. No, Jocelyn clearly wanted only one person to be able to find the Cup, and that is Clary, and Clary alone."

"Then let her go alone," said Alec.

Even Isabelle gave a little gasp at that. Jace, who had been leaning forward with his hands on the back of a chair, stood up straight and looked at Alec coolly. Only Jace, Clary thought, could look cool in pajama bottoms and an old T-shirt, but he pulled it off, probably through sheer force of will. "If you're afraid of a few Forsaken, by all means stay home," he said softly.

Alec went white. "I'm not afraid," he said.

"Good," said Jace. "Then there's no problem, is there?" He looked around the room. "We're all in this together."

Alec mumbled an affirmative, while Isabelle shook her head in a vigorous nod. "Sure," she said. "It sounds fun."

"I don't know about fun," said Clary. "But I'm in, of course."

"But Clary," Hodge said quickly. "If you are concerned about the danger, you don't need to go. We can notify the Clave—"

"No," Clary said, surprising herself. "My mom wanted me to find it. Not Valentine, and not them, either." *It wasn't the monsters she was hiding from*, Magnus had said. "If she really spent her whole life trying to keep Valentine away from this thing, this is the least I can do."

Hodge smiled at her. "I think she knew you would say that," he said.

"Don't worry, anyway," Isabelle said. "You'll be fine. We can handle a couple of Forsaken. They're crazy, but they're not very smart."

"And a lot easier to deal with than demons," said Jace. "Not so tricksy. Oh, and we're going to need a car," he added. "Preferably a big one."

"Why?" said Isabelle. "We've never needed a car before."

"We've never had to worry about having an immeasurably precious object with us before. I don't want to haul it on the L train," Jace explained.

"There's taxis," said Isabelle. "And rental vans."

Jace shook his head. "I want an environment we control. I don't want to deal with taxi drivers or mundane rental companies when we're doing something this important."

"Don't you have a driver's license or a car?" Alec asked Clary, looking at her with veiled loathing. "I thought all mundanes had those."

"Not when they're fifteen," Clary said crossly. "I was supposed to get one this year, but not yet."

"Fat lot of use you are."

"At least my friends can drive," she shot back. "Simon's got a license."

She instantly regretted saying it.

"*Does* he?" said Jace, in an aggravatingly thoughtful tone.

"But he hasn't got a car," she added quickly.

"So does he drive his parents' car?" Jace asked.

Clary sighed. "No. Usually he drives Eric's van. Like, to gigs and stuff. Sometimes Eric lets him borrow it for other stuff. Like if he has a date."

Jace snorted. "He picks up his dates in a van? No wonder

he's such a hit with the ladies."

"It's a car," Clary said. "You're just mad Simon has something you haven't got."

"He has many things I haven't got," said Jace. "Like nearsightedness, bad posture, and an appalling lack of coordination."

"You know," Clary said, "most psychologists agree that hostility is really just sublimated sexual attraction."

"Ah," said Jace blithely, "that might explain why I so often run into people who seem to dislike me."

"I don't dislike you," said Alec quickly.

"That is because we share a brotherly affection," said Jace, striding over to the desk. He took the black telephone and held it out to Clary. "Call him."

"Call who?" Clary said, stalling for time. "Eric? He'd never lend me his car."

"Simon," said Jace. "Call Simon and ask him if he'll drive us to your house."

Clary made a last effort. "Don't you know any Shadowhunters who have cars?"

"In New York?" Jace's grin faded. "Look, everyone's in Idris for the Accords, and anyway, they'd insist on coming with us. It's this or nothing."

She met his eyes for a moment. There was a challenge in them, and something more, as if he were daring her to explain her reluctance. With a scowl she stalked over to the desk and snatched the telephone out of his hand.

She didn't have to think before dialing. Simon's number was as familiar to her as her own. She braced herself to deal with his mother or sister, but he picked up on the second ring. "Hello?"

"Simon?"

Silence.

Jace was looking at her. Clary squeezed her eyes shut, trying to pretend he wasn't there. "It's me," she said. "Clary."

"I *know* who it is." He sounded irritated. "I was asleep, you know."

"I know. It's early. I'm sorry." She twirled the phone cord around her finger. "I need to ask you for a favor."

There was another silence before he laughed bleakly. "You're kidding."

"I'm not kidding," she said. "We know where the Mortal Cup is, and we're prepared to go get it. The only thing is, we need a car."

He laughed again. "Sorry, are you telling me that your demon-slaying buddies need to be driven to their next assignation with the forces of darkness by *my mom*?"

"Actually, I thought you could ask Eric if you could borrow the van."

"Clary, if you think that I—"

"If we get the Mortal Cup, I'll have a way to get my mom back. It's the only reason Valentine hasn't killed her or let her go."

Simon let out a long, whistling breath. "You think it's going to be that easy to make a trade? Clary, I don't know."

"I don't know either. I just know it's a chance."

"This thing is powerful, right? In D&D it's usually better not to mess with powerful objects until you know what they do."

"I'm not going to mess with it. I'm just going to use it to get my mom back."

"That doesn't make any sense, Clary."

"This isn't D&D, Simon!" she half-screamed. "It's not a funny game where the worst thing that happens is you get a bad dice roll. This is my *mom* we're talking about, and Valentine could be torturing her. He could *kill* her. I have to do anything I can to get her back—just like I did for you."

Pause. "Maybe you're right. I don't know, this isn't really my world. Look, where are we driving to, exactly? So I can tell Eric."

"Don't *bring* him," she said quickly.

"I know," he replied with exaggerated patience. "I'm not stupid."

"We're driving to my house. It's in my house."

There was a short silence—bewilderment this time. "In your *house*? I thought your house was full of zombies."

"Forsaken warriors. They're not zombies. Anyway, Jace and the others can take care of them while I get the Cup."

"Why do *you* have to get the Cup?" He sounded alarmed.

"Because I'm the only one who can," she said. "Pick us up at the corner as soon as you can."

He muttered something nearly inaudible, then: "Fine."

She opened her eyes. The world swam before her in a blur of tears. "Thanks, Simon," she said. "You're a—"

But he had hung up.

"It occurs to me," said Hodge, "that the dilemmas of power are always the same."

Clary glanced at him sideways. "What do you mean?"

She sat on the window seat in the library, Hodge in his chair with Hugo on the armrest. The remains of breakfast—sticky jam, toast crumbs, and smears of butter—clung to a stack of plates on the low table that no one had seemed inclined to clear away. After breakfast they had scattered to prepare themselves, and Clary had been the first one back. This was hardly surprising, considering that all she had to do was pull on jeans and a shirt and run a brush through her hair, while everyone else had to arm themselves heavily. Having lost Jace's dagger in the hotel, the only remotely supernatural object she had on her was the witchlight stone in her pocket.

"I was thinking of your Simon," Hodge said, "and of Alec and Jace, among others."

She glanced out the window. It was raining, thick fat drops spattering against the panes. The sky was an impenetrable gray. "What do they have to do with each other?"

"Where there is feeling that is not requited," said Hodge, "there is an imbalance of power. It is an imbalance that is easy to exploit, but it is not a wise course. Where there is love, there is often also hate. They can exist side by side."

"Simon doesn't hate me."

"He might grow to, over time, if he felt you were using him." Hodge held up a hand. "I know you do not intend to, and in some cases necessity trumps nicety of feeling. But the situation has put me in mind of another. Do you still have that photograph I gave you?"

Clary shook her head. "Not on me. It's back in my room. I could go get it—"

"No." Hodge stroked Hugo's ebony feathers. "When your mother was young, she had a best friend, just as you have Simon. They were as close as siblings. In fact, they were often mistaken for brother and sister. As they grew older, it became clear to everyone around them that he was in love with her, but she never saw it. She always called him a 'friend.'"

Clary stared at Hodge. "Do you mean Luke?"

"Yes," said Hodge. "Lucian always thought he and Jocelyn would be together. When she met and loved Valentine, he could not bear it. After they were married, he left the Circle, disappeared—and let us all think that he was dead."

"He never said—never even hinted at anything like that," Clary said. "All these years, he could have asked her—"

"He knew what the answer would be," said Hodge, looking past her toward the rain-spattered skylight. "Lucian was never the sort of man who would have deluded himself. No, he contented himself with being near her—assuming, perhaps, that over time her feelings might change."

"But if he loved her, why did he tell those men he didn't care what happened to her? Why did he refuse to let them tell him where she was?"

"As I said before, where there is love, there is also hatred," said Hodge. "She hurt him badly all those years ago. She turned her back on him. And yet he has played her faithful lapdog ever since, never remonstrating, never accusing, never confronting her with his feelings. Perhaps he saw an opportunity to turn the tables. To hurt her as he'd been hurt."

"Luke wouldn't do that." But Clary was remembering his icy tone as he told her not to ask him for favors. She saw the hard look in his eyes as he faced Valentine's men. That wasn't the Luke she'd known, the Luke she'd grown up with. That Luke would never have wanted to punish her mother for not loving him enough or in the right way. "But she did love him," Clary said, speaking aloud without realizing it. "It just wasn't the same way he loved her. Isn't that enough?"

"Perhaps he didn't think so."

"What will happen after we get the Cup?" she said. "How will we reach Valentine to let him know we have it?"

"Hugo will find him."

The rain smashed against the windows. Clary shivered. "I'm going to get a jacket," she said, slipping off the window seat.

She found her green and pink hoodie stuffed down at the bottom of her backpack. When she pulled it out, she heard something crinkle. It was the photograph of the Circle, her mother and Valentine. She looked at it for a long moment before slipping it back into the bag.

When she returned to the library, the others were all gathered there: Hodge sitting watchfully with Hugo on his shoulder, Jace all in black, Isabelle with her demon-stomping boots and gold whip, and Alec with a quiver of arrows strapped across his shoulder and a leather bracer sheathing his right arm from wrist to elbow. Everyone but Hodge was covered in freshly applied Marks, every inch of bare skin inked with swirling patterns. Jace had his left sleeve pulled up, chin on his shoulder, and was frowning as he scrawled an octagonal Mark on the skin of his upper arm.

Alec looked over at him. "You're messing it up," he said. "Let me do that."

"I'm left-handed," Jace pointed out, but he spoke mildly and held his stele out. Alec looked relieved as he took it, as if he hadn't been sure until now that he was forgiven for his earlier behavior. "It's a basic *iratze*," Jace said as Alec bent his dark head over Jace's arm, carefully tracing the lines of the healing rune. Jace winced as the stele slid over his skin, his eyes half-closing and his fist tightening until the muscles of his left arm stood out like cords. "By the Angel, Alec—"

"I'm trying to be careful," said Alec. He let go of Jace's arm and stepped back to admire his handiwork. "There."

Jace unclenched his fist, lowering his arm. "Thanks." He seemed to sense Clary's presence then, glancing over at her, his gold eyes narrowing. "Clary."

"You look ready," she said as Alec, suddenly flushed, moved away from Jace and busied himself with his arrows.

"We are," Jace said. "Do you still have that dagger I gave you?"

"No. I lost it in the Dumort, remember?"

"That's right." Jace looked at her, pleased. "Nearly killed a werewolf with it. I remember."

Isabelle, who had been standing by the window, rolled her eyes. "I forgot that's what gets you all hot and bothered, Jace. Girls killing things."

"I like anyone killing things," he said equably. "Especially me."

Clary glanced anxiously toward the clock on the desk. "We should go downstairs. Simon will be here any minute."

Hodge stood up from his chair. He looked very tired, Clary thought, as if he hadn't slept in days.

"May the Angel watch over you all," he said, and Hugo rose up from his shoulder into the air cawing loudly, just as the noon bells began to ring.

It was still drizzling when Simon pulled the van up at the corner and honked twice. Clary's heart leaped—some part of her had been worried that he wasn't going to show up.

Jace squinted through the dripping rain. The four of them had taken shelter under a carved stone cornice. "*That's* the van? It looks like a rotting banana."

This was undeniable—Eric had painted the van a neon shade of yellow, and it was blotched with dings and rust like splotches of decay. Simon honked again. Clary could see him, a blurred shape through the wet windows. She sighed and pulled her hood up to cover her hair. "Let's go."

They splashed through the filthy puddles that had collected on the pavement, Isabelle's enormous boots making a satisfying noise every time she put her feet down. Simon, leaving the motor idling, crawled into the back to pull the door aside, revealing seats whose upholstery had half-rotted through. Dangerous-looking springs poked through the gaps. Isabelle wrinkled her nose. "Is it safe to sit?"

"Safer than being strapped to the roof," said Simon pleasantly, "which is your other option." He nodded a greeting to Jace and Alec, ignoring Clary completely. "Hey."

"Hey indeed," said Jace, and lifted the rattling canvas duffel bag that held their weapons. "Where can we put these?"

Simon directed him to the back, where the boys usually kept their musical instruments, while Alec and Isabelle crawled into the van's interior and perched on the seats. "Shotgun!" announced Clary as Jace came back around the side of the van.

Alec grabbed for his bow, strapped across his back. "Where?"

"She means she wants the front seat," said Jace, pushing wet hair out of his eyes.

"That's a nice bow," said Simon, with a nod toward Alec.

Alec blinked, rain running off his eyelashes. "Do you

know much about archery?" he asked, in a tone that suggested that he doubted it.

"I did archery at camp," said Simon. "Six years running."

The response to this was three blank stares and a supportive smile from Clary, which Simon ignored. He glanced up at the lowering sky. "We should go before it starts pouring again."

The front seat of the car was covered in Doritos wrappers and Pop-Tart crumbs. Clary brushed away what she could. Simon put his foot down on the gas pedal before she'd finished, flinging her back against the seat. "Ouch," she said reprovingly.

"Sorry." He didn't look at her.

Clary could hear the others talking softly in the back amongst themselves—probably discussing battle strategies and the best way to behead a demon without getting ichor on your new leather boots. Though there was nothing separating the front seat from the rest of the van, Clary felt the awkward silence between her and Simon as if they were alone.

"So what's with that 'hey' thing?" she asked as Simon maneuvered the car onto the FDR parkway, the highway that ran alongside the East River.

"What 'hey' thing?" he replied, cutting off a black SUV whose occupant, a suited man with a cell phone in his hand, made an obscene gesture at them through the tinted windows.

"The 'hey' thing that guys always do. Like when you saw Jace and Alec, you said 'hey,' and they said 'hey' back. What's wrong with 'hello'?"

She thought she saw a muscle twitch in his cheek. "'Hello' is girly," he informed her. "Real men are terse. Laconic."

"So the more manly you are, the less you say?"

"Right." Simon nodded. Past him she could see the humid fog lowering over the East River, shrouding the waterfront in feathery gray mist. The water itself was the color of lead, churned to a whipped cream consistency by the steady wind. "That's why when major badasses greet each other in movies, they don't say anything, they just nod. The nod means, 'I am a badass, and I recognize that you, too, are a badass,' but they don't say anything because they're Wolverine and Magneto and it would mess up their vibe to explain."

"I have no idea what you're talking about," said Jace, from the backseat.

"Good," Clary said, and was rewarded by the smallest of smiles from Simon as he turned the van onto the Manhattan Bridge, heading toward Brooklyn and home.

By the time they reached Clary's house, it had finally stopped raining. Threaded beams of sunlight were burning away the remnants of mist, and the puddles on the sidewalk were drying. Jace, Alec, and Isabelle made Simon and Clary wait by the van while they went to check, as Jace said, the "demonic activity levels."

Simon watched as the three Shadowhunters headed up the rose-lined walkway to the house. "Demonic activity levels? Do they have a device that measures whether the demons inside the house are doing power yoga?"

"No," Clary said, pushing her damp hood back so she could enjoy the feel of the sunlight on her draggled hair. "The Sensor tells them how powerful the demons are—if there are any demons."

Simon looked impressed. "That *is* useful."

She turned to him. "Simon, about last night—"

He held up a hand. "We don't have to talk about it. In fact, I'd rather not."

"Just let me say one thing." She spoke quickly. "I know that when you said you loved me, what I said back wasn't what you wanted to hear."

"True. I'd always hoped that when I finally said 'I love you' to a girl, she'd say 'I know' back, like Leia did to Han in *Return of the Jedi*."

"That is *so geeky*," Clary said, unable to help herself.

He glared at her.

"Sorry," she said. "Look, Simon, I—"

"No," he said. "*You* look, Clary. Look at me, and really see me. Can you do that?"

She looked at him. Looked at the dark eyes, flecked with lighter color toward the outside edge of the iris, at the familiar, slightly uneven eyebrows, the long lashes, the dark hair and hesitating smile and graceful musical hands that were all part of Simon, who was part of her. If she had to tell the truth, would she really say that she'd never known that he loved her? Or just that she'd never known what she would do about it if he did?

She sighed. "Seeing through a glamour is easy. It's people that are hard."

"We all see what we want to see," he said quietly.

"Not Jace," she said, unable to help herself, thinking of those clear, impassive eyes.

"Him more than anyone."

She frowned. "What do you—"

"All right," came Jace's voice, interrupting them. Clary turned hastily. "We've checked all four corners of the house—nothing. Low activity. Probably just the Forsaken, and they might not even bother us unless we try getting into the upstairs apartment."

"And if they do," said Isabelle, her grin as glittering as her whip, "we'll be ready for them."

Alec dragged the heavy canvas bag out of the back of the van, dropping it on the sidewalk. "Ready to go," he announced. "Let's kick some demon butt!"

Jace looked at him a little oddly. "You all right?"

"Fine." Not looking at him, Alec discarded his bow and arrow in favor of a polished wooden featherstaff, with two glittering blades that appeared at a light touch from his fingers. "This is better."

Isabelle looked at her brother with concern. "But the bow..."

Alec cut her off. "I know what I'm doing, Isabelle."

The bow lay across the backseat, gleaming in the sunlight. Simon reached for it, then drew his hand back as a laughing group of young women pushing strollers headed up the street in the direction of the park. They took no notice of the three heavily armed teenagers crouched by the yellow van. "How come I can see you guys?" Simon asked. "What happened to that invisibility magic of yours?"

"You can see us," said Jace, "because now you know the truth of what you're looking at."

"Yeah," said Simon. "I guess I do."

He protested a little when they asked him to stay by the van, but Jace impressed upon him the importance of having a getaway vehicle idling by the curb. "Sunlight's fatal to demons, but it won't hurt the Forsaken. What if they chase us? What if the car gets *towed?*"

The last Clary saw of Simon as she turned to wave from the front porch was his long legs propped up on the dashboard as he sorted through Eric's CD collection. She breathed a sigh of relief. At least Simon was safe.

The smell hit her the moment they walked through the front door. It was almost indescribable, like spoiled eggs and maggoty meat and seaweed rotting on a hot beach. Isabelle wrinkled her nose and Alec turned greenish, but Jace looked as if he were inhaling rare perfume. "Demons have been here," he announced, with cold delight. "Recently, too."

Clary looked at him anxiously. "But they're not still—"

"No." He shook his head. "We would have sensed it. Still." He jerked his chin at Dorothea's door, tightly shut without a wisp of light peeking from underneath. "She might have some questions to answer if the Clave hears she's been entertaining demons."

"I doubt the Clave will be too pleased about any of this," said Isabelle. "On balance, she'll probably come out of it better than we do."

"They won't care as long as we get the Cup in the end." Alec was glancing around, blue eyes taking in the sizeable foyer, the curved staircase leading upstairs, the stains on the walls. "Especially if we slaughter a few Forsaken while we do it."

Jace shook his head. "They're in the upstairs apartment. My guess is that they won't bother us unless we try to get in."

Isabelle blew a sticky strand of hair out of her face and

frowned at Clary. "What are you waiting for?"

Clary glanced involuntarily at Jace, who gave her a sideways smile. *Go ahead*, said his eyes.

She moved across the foyer toward Dorothea's door, stepping carefully. With the skylight blackened with dirt and the entryway lightbulb still out, the only illumination came from Jace's witchlight. The air was hot and close, and the shadows seemed to rise up before her like magically fast-growing plants in a nightmare forest. She reached up to knock on Dorothea's door, once lightly and then again with more force.

It swung open, spilling a great wash of golden light into the foyer. Dorothea stood there, massive and imposing in swaths of green and orange. Today her turban was neon yellow, adorned with a stuffed canary and rickrack trim. Chandelier earrings bobbed against her hair, and her big feet were bare. Clary was surprised—she'd never seen Dorothea barefoot before, or wearing anything other than her faded carpet slippers.

Her toenails were a pale, and very tasteful, shell pink.

"Clary!" she exclaimed, and swept Clary into an overwhelming embrace. For a moment Clary struggled, embroiled in a sea of perfumed flesh, swaths of velvet, and the tasseled ends of Dorothea's shawl. "Good Lord, girl," said the witch, shaking her head until her earrings swung like wind chimes in a storm. "The last time I saw you, you were disappearing through my Portal. Where'd you end up?"

"Williamsburg," said Clary, catching her breath.

Dorothea's eyebrows shot skyward. "And they say there's no convenient public transportation in Brooklyn." She swung the door open and gestured for them to come in.

The place looked unchanged from the last time Clary had seen it: There were the same tarot cards and crystal ball scattered on the table. Her fingers itched for the cards, itched to snatch them up and see what might lie hidden inside their slickly painted surfaces.

Dorothea sank gratefully into an armchair and regarded the Shadowhunters with a stare as beady as the eyes of the stuffed canary on her hat. Scented candles burned in dishes on either side of the table, which did little to dispel the thick stench pervading every inch of the house. "I take it you haven't located your mother?" she asked Clary.

Clary shook her head. "No. But I know who took her."

Dorothea's eyes darted past Clary to Alec and Isabelle, who were examining the Hand of Fate on the wall. Jace, looking supremely unconcerned in his role of bodyguard, lounged against a chair arm. Satisfied that none of her belongings were being destroyed, Dorothea returned her gaze to Clary. "Was it—"

"Valentine," Clary confirmed. "Yes."

Dorothea sighed. "I feared as much." She settled back against the cushions. "Do you know what he wants with her?"

"I know she was married to him—"

The witch grunted. "Love gone wrong. The worst."

Jace made a soft, almost inaudible noise at that—a chuckle. Dorothea's ears pricked like a cat's. "What's so funny, boy?"

"What would you know about it?" he said. "Love, I mean."

Dorothea folded her soft white hands in her lap. "More than you might think," she said. "Didn't I read your tea leaves, Shadowhunter? Have you fallen in love with the wrong person yet?"

Jace said, "Unfortunately, my one true love remains myself."

Dorothea roared at that. "At least," she said, "you don't have to worry about rejection, Jace Wayland."

"Not necessarily. I turn myself down occasionally, just to keep it interesting."

Dorothea roared again. Clary interrupted her. "You must be wondering why we're here, Madame Dorothea."

Dorothea subsided, wiping at her eyes. "I assumed," she said, "that you came for the pleasure of my company. Was I wrong?"

"I don't have time for the pleasure of anyone's company. I have to help my mother, and to do that there's something I need."

"And what's that?"

"It's something called the Mortal Cup," Clary said, "and Valentine thought my mother had it. That's why he took her."

Dorothea looked well and truly astonished. "The Cup of the Angel?" she said, disbelief coloring her voice. "Raziel's Cup, in which he mixed the blood of angels and the blood of men and gave of this mixture to a man to drink, and created the first Shadowhunter?"

"That would be the one," said Jace, a little dryness in his tone.

"Why on earth would he think she had it?" Dorothea demanded. "Jocelyn, of all people?" Realization dawned on her face before Clary could speak. "Because she wasn't Jocelyn Fray at all, of course," she said. "She was Jocelyn Fairchild, his wife. The one everyone thought had died. She took the Cup and fled, didn't she?"

Something flickered in the back of the witch's eyes then, but she lowered her lids so quickly that Clary thought she might have imagined it. "So," Dorothea said, "do you know what you're going to do now? Wherever she's hidden it, it can't be easy to find—if you even want it found. Valentine could do terrible things with his hands on that Cup."

"I want it found," said Clary. "We want to—"

Jace cut her off smoothly. "We know where it is," he said. "It's only a matter of retrieving it."

Dorothea's eyes widened. "Well, where is it?"

"Here," said Jace, in a tone so smug that Isabelle and Alec wandered over from their perusal of the bookcase to see what was going on.

"Here? You mean you have it with you?"

"Not exactly," said Jace, who was, Clary felt, enjoying himself in a truly appalling manner. "I meant that *you* have it."

Dorothea's mouth snapped shut. "That's not funny," she said, so sharply that Clary became worried that this was all going terribly wrong. Why did Jace always have to antagonize everyone?

"You do have it," Clary interrupted hurriedly, "but not—"

Dorothea rose from the armchair to her full, magnificent height, and glowered down at them. "You are mistaken," she said coldly. "Both in imagining that I have the Cup, and in daring to come here and call me a liar."

Alec's hand went to his featherstaff. "Oh, boy," he said under his breath.

Baffled, Clary shook her head. "No," she said quickly, "I'm not calling you a liar, I promise. I'm saying the Cup is here, but *you never knew it.*"

Madame Dorothea stared at her. Her eyes, nearly hidden in the folds of her face, were hard as marbles. "Explain yourself," she said.

"I'm saying my mother hid it here," said Clary. "Years ago. She never told you because she didn't want to involve you."

"So she gave it to you disguised," Jace explained, "in the form of a gift."

Dorothea looked at him blankly.

Doesn't she remember? Clary thought, puzzled. "The tarot deck," she said. "The cards she painted for you."

The witch's gaze went to the cards, lying in their silk wrappings on the table. "The cards?" As her gaze widened, Clary stepped to the table and picked up the deck. They were warm to the touch, almost slippery. Now, as she had not been able to before, she felt the power from the runes painted on their backs pulsing through the tips of her fingers. She found the Ace of Cups by touch and pulled it out, setting the rest of the cards back down on the table.

"Here it is," she said.

They were all looking at her, expectant, perfectly still. Slowly she turned the card over and looked again at her mother's artwork: the slim painted hand, its fingers wrapped around the gold stem of the Mortal Cup.

"Jace," she said. "Give me your stele."

He pressed it, warm and alive-feeling, into her palm. She turned the card over and traced over the runes painted on its back—a twist here and a line there and they meant something entirely different. When she turned the card back over, the picture had subtly changed: The fingers had released their grip on the Cup's stem, and the hand seemed almost to be offering the Cup to her as if to say, *Here, take it*.

She slid the stele into her pocket. Then, though the painted square was no bigger than her hand, she reached into it as if through a wide gap. Her hand wrapped around the base of the Cup—her fingers closed on it—and as she drew her hand back, the Cup gripped firmly in it, she thought she heard the smallest of sighs before the card, now blank and empty, turned to ash that sifted away between her fingers to the carpeted floor.

19

Abbadon

Clary wasn't sure what she'd expected—exclamations of delight, perhaps a smattering of applause. Instead there was silence, broken only when Jace said, "Somehow, I thought it would be bigger."

Clary looked at the Cup in her hand. It was the size, perhaps, of an ordinary wineglass, only much heavier. Power thrummed through it, like blood through living veins. "It's a perfectly nice size," she said indignantly.

"Oh, it's big enough," he said patronizingly, "but somehow I was expecting something ... you know." He gestured with his hands, indicating something roughly the size of a house cat.

"It's the Mortal Cup, Jace, not the Mortal Toilet Bowl," said Isabelle. "Are we done now? Can we go?"

Dorothea had her head cocked to one side, her beady eyes bright and interested. "But it's damaged!" she exclaimed. "How did that happen?"

"Damaged?" Clary looked at the Cup in bewilderment. It looked fine to her.

"Here," said the witch, "let me show you," and she took a step toward Clary, holding her long red-nailed hands out for the Cup. Clary, without knowing why, shrank back. Suddenly Jace was between them, his hand hovering near the sword at his waist.

"No offense," he said calmly, "but nobody touches the Mortal Cup except us."

Dorothea looked at him for a moment, and that same strange blankness returned to her eyes. "Now," she said, "let's not be hasty. Valentine would be displeased if anything were to happen to the Cup."

With a soft *snick*, the sword at Jace's waist came free. The point hovered just below Dorothea's chin. Jace's look was steady. "I don't know what this is about," he said. "But we're leaving."

The old woman's eyes gleamed. "Of course, Shadowhunter," she said, backing up to the curtained wall. "Would you like to use the Portal?"

The point of Jace's sword wavered as he stared in momentary confusion. Then Clary saw his jaw tighten. "Don't touch that—"

Dorothea chuckled, and quick as a flash she jerked down the curtains hanging along the wall. They fell with a sound of soft collapse. The Portal behind them was open.

Clary heard Alec, behind her, suck in his breath. "What is that?" Clary had caught only a glimpse of what was visible through the door—red roiling clouds shot through with black lightning, and a terrible dark, rushing shape that hurtled toward them—when Jace shouted for them to get down. He dropped to the floor, yanking Clary down with him. Flat on her stomach on the carpet, she lifted her head in time to see the rushing dark thing strike Madame Dorothea, who screamed, thrusting her arms upward. Rather than knocking her down, the dark thing wrapped her like a shroud, its blackness seeming to seep into her like ink sinking into paper. Her back humped monstrously, her whole shape elongating as she rose and rose into the air, her bulk stretching and reforming. A sharp rattle of objects striking the floor made Clary look down: They were Dorothea's bracelets, twisted and broken. Scattered among the jewels were what looked like small white stones. It took Clary a moment to realize that they were teeth.

Beside her Jace whispered something. It sounded like an exclamation of disbelief. Next to him, Alec in a choked voice said, "But you said there wasn't much demonic activity—you *said* the levels were low!"

"They *were* low," Jace growled.

"Your version of low must be different from mine!" Alec shouted, as the thing that had once been Dorothea howled and twisted. It seemed to be spreading, humped and knobbled and grotesquely misshapen—

Clary tore her eyes away as Jace stood, pulling her after him. Isabelle and Alec stumbled to their feet, gripping their weapons. The hand holding Isabelle's whip was trembling slightly.

"*Move!*" Jace shoved Clary toward the apartment door. When she tried to look back over her shoulder, she saw only a thickly swirling grayness, like storm clouds, a dark shape at its center...

The four of them burst out into the foyer, Isabelle in the lead. She raced toward the front door, tried it, and turned with a stricken face: "It's resistant. Must be a spell—"

Jace swore and fumbled in his jacket. "Where the hell is my stele?"

"I have it," Clary said, remembering. As she reached for her pocket, a noise like thunder exploded through the room. The floor heaved under her feet. She stumbled and nearly fell, catching at the banister for support. When she looked up, she saw a gaping new hole in the wall separating the foyer from Dorothea's apartment, lined all around its ragged edges with wood and plaster rubble, through which *something* was climbing—almost oozing—

"Alec!" It was Jace, shouting: Alec was standing in front of the hole, white-faced and horrified-looking. Swearing, Jace ran up and grabbed him, dragging him back just as the oozing thing pulled itself free of the wall and into the foyer.

Clary heard her breath catch. The creature's flesh was livid and bruised-looking. Through the seeping skin, bones protruded—not new white bones, but bones that looked as if they had been in the earth a thousand years, black and cracked and filthy. Its fingers were stripped and skeletal, its thin-fleshed arms pocked with dripping black sores through which more yellowing bone was visible. Its face was a skull, its nose and eyes caved-in holes. Its taloned fingers brushed the floor. Tangled around its wrists and shoulders were bright swatches of cloth: all that remained of Madame Dorothea's silk scarves and turban. It was at least nine feet tall.

It looked down at the four teenagers with empty eye sockets. "Give me," it said, in a voice like the wind blowing trash across empty pavement, "the Mortal Cup. Give it to me, and I will let you live."

Panicked, Clary stared at the others. Isabelle looked as if the sight of the thing had hit her like a punch to the stomach. Alec was motionless. It was Jace, as always, who spoke. "What are you?" he asked, voice steady, though he looked more rattled than Clary had ever seen him.

The thing inclined its head. "I am Abbadon. I am the Demon of the Abyss. Mine are the empty places between the worlds. Mine is the wind and the howling darkness. I am as unlike those mewling things you call *demons* as an eagle is unlike a fly. You cannot hope to defeat me. Give me the Cup or die."

Isabelle's whip trembled. "It's a Greater Demon," she said. "Jace, if we—"

"What about Dorothea?" Clary's voice came shrilly out of her mouth before she could stop it. "What happened to her?"

The demon's empty eyes swung to regard her. "She was a vessel only," it said. "She opened the Portal and I took possession of her. Her death was swift." Its gaze moved to the Cup in her hand. "Yours will not be."

It began to move toward her. Jace blocked its way, the glittering sword in one hand, a seraph blade appearing in the other. Alec was watching him, his expression sick with horror.

"By the Angel," Jace said, looking the demon up and down. "I knew Greater Demons were meant to be ugly, but no one ever warned me about the smell."

Abbadon opened its mouth and hissed. Inside its mouth were two rows of jagged glass-sharp teeth.

"I'm not so sure about this wind and howling darkness business," Jace went on, "smells more like landfill to me. You sure you're not from Staten Island?"

The demon leaped at him. Jace whipped his blades up and outward with an almost frightening speed; both sank into the fleshiest part of the demon, its abdomen. It howled and struck at him, knocking him aside the way a cat might bat aside a kitten. Jace rolled and got to his feet, but Clary could see from the way he was holding his arm that he'd been hurt.

That was enough for Isabelle. Darting forward, she lashed out at the demon with her whip. It struck the demon's gray hide, and a red weal appeared, welling blood. Abbadon ignored her, moving toward Jace.

With his uninjured hand Jace drew out a second seraph blade. He whispered to it and it sprung free, bright and gleaming. He raised it as the demon loomed up before him; he looked impossibly small in front of it, a child dwarfed by a monster. And he was grinning, even as the demon reached for him. Isabelle, screaming, lashed at it, sending blood in a thick spray across the floor—

The demon struck, its razored hand lashing down at Jace. Jace staggered back, but he was unharmed. Something had thrown itself between him and the demon, a slim black shadow with a gleaming blade in its hand. Alec. The demon shrieked— Alec's featherstaff had pierced its skin. With a snarl it struck again, bone-talons catching Alec a vicious blow that lifted him off his feet and hurled him against the far wall. He struck with a sickening crunch and slid to the floor.

Isabelle screamed her brother's name. He didn't move. Lowering the whip, she started to run to him. The demon, turning, caught her a backhanded blow that sent her spinning to the ground. Coughing blood, Isabelle started to get to her feet; Abbadon knocked her down again, and this time she lay still.

The demon moved toward Clary.

Jace stood frozen, staring at Alec's crumpled body like someone caught in a dream. Clary screamed as Abbadon neared her. She began to back up the stairs, stumbling on the broken steps. The stele burned against her skin. If only she had a weapon, anything—

Isabelle had clawed her way into a sitting position. Pushing her bloody hair back, she screamed at Jace. Clary heard her own name in Isabelle's screams and saw Jace, blinking as if slapped awake, spin toward her. He began to run. The demon was close enough now that Clary could see the black sores on its skin, could see that there were *things* crawling inside them. It reached for her—

But Jace was there, knocking Abbadon's hand aside. He flung the seraph blade at the demon; it stuck in the creature's chest, next to the two blades already there. The demon snarled as if the blades were no more than an annoyance.

"Shadowhunter," it snarled. "I shall take pleasure in killing you, in hearing your bones crunch as your friend's did—"

Springing onto the banister, Jace flung himself at Abbadon. The force of the jump knocked the demon backward; it staggered, Jace clinging to its back. He seized a seraph blade out of its chest, sending up a spray of ichor, and brought the blade down, again and again, into the demon's back, its shoulders running with black fluid.

Snarling, Abbadon backed toward the wall. Jace had to

drop or be crushed. He fell to the ground, landed lightly, and raised the blade again. But Abbadon was too swift for him; its hand lashed out, knocking Jace into the stairs. Jace went down, a circle of talons at his throat.

"Tell them to give me the Cup," Abbadon snarled, talons hovering just above Jace's skin. "Tell them to give it to me and I will let them live."

Jace swallowed. *"Clary—"*

But Clary would never know what he would have said, because at that moment the front door flew open. For a moment all she saw was brightness. Then, blinking away the fiery afterimage, she saw Simon standing in the open doorway. *Simon.* She had forgotten he was outside, had almost forgotten he existed.

He saw her, crouched on the stairs, and his gaze moved past her and over Abbadon and Jace. He reached back over his shoulder. He was holding Alec's bow, she realized, and the quiver was strapped across his back. He drew an arrow from it, fitted it to the string, and lifted the bow expertly, as if he'd done the same thing a hundred times before.

The arrow sprang free. It made a hot buzzing sound, like a huge bumblebee, as it shot over Abbadon's head, plunged toward the roof—

And shattered the skylight. Dirty black glass fell like rain, and through the broken pane streamed sunlight, quantities of sunlight, great golden bars of it stabbing downward and flooding the foyer with light.

Abbadon screamed and staggered back, shielding its misshapen head with its hands. Jace put a hand to his unharmed throat, staring in disbelief as the demon crumpled, howling, to the floor. Clary half-expected it to burst into flames, but instead it began to fold in on itself. Its legs collapsed toward its torso, its skull crumpling like burning paper, and within the span of a minute it had vanished entirely, leaving only scorch marks behind.

Simon lowered the bow. He was blinking behind his glasses, his mouth slightly open. He looked as astonished as Clary felt.

Jace lay on the stairs where the demon had thrown him. He was struggling to sit up as Clary slid down the steps and fell to her knees beside him. "Jace—"

"I'm all right." He sat up, wiping blood from his mouth. He coughed and spit red. "Alec—"

"Your stele," she interrupted, reaching for her pocket. "Do you need it to fix yourself?"

He looked at her. The sunlight pouring through the shattered skylight lit his face. He looked as if he were holding himself back from something with a terrible effort. "I'm all *right*," he said again, and pushed her aside, none too gently. He got to his feet, staggered, and nearly fell—the first ungraceful thing she'd ever seen him do. "Alec?"

Clary watched him as he limped across the foyer toward his unconscious friend. Then she zipped the Mortal Cup into the pocket of her hoodie and got to her feet. Isabelle had crawled to her brother's side and was cradling his head in her lap, stroking his hair. His chest rose and fell—slowly, but he was breathing. Simon, leaning against the wall watching them, looked utterly drained. Clary squeezed his hand as she passed him. "Thank you," she whispered. "That was amazing."

"Don't thank me," he said, "thank the archery program at B'nai B'rith summer camp."

"Simon, I don't—"

"Clary!" It was Jace, calling her. "Bring my stele."

Simon let her go reluctantly. She knelt down next to the Shadowhunters, the Mortal Cup thumping heavily against her side. Alec's face was white, freckled with drops of blood, his eyes unnaturally blue. His grip on Jace's wrist left bloody smears. "Did..." he started, then seemed to see Clary, as if for the first time. There was something in his look she hadn't expected. Triumph. "Did I kill it?"

Jace's face twisted painfully. "You—"

"Yes," Clary said. "It's dead."

Alec looked at her and laughed. Blood bubbled up in his mouth. Jace pulled his wrist free, touched his fingers to either side of Alec's face. "Don't," he said. "Hold still, just hold still."

Alec closed his eyes. "Do what you have to," he whispered.

Isabelle held her stele out to Jace. "Take it."

He nodded, and drew the tip of the stele down the front of Alec's shirt. The material parted as if he'd sliced it with a knife. Isabelle watched him through frantic eyes as he yanked the shirt open, leaving Alec's chest bare. His skin was very white, marked here and there with old translucent scars. There were other injuries there too: a darkening lattice of claw marks, each hole red and oozing. Jaw set, Jace set the stele to Alec's skin, moving it back and forth with the ease of long practice. But there was something wrong. Even as he drew the healing marks, they seemed to vanish as if he were writing on water.

Jace threw the stele aside. "Damn it."

Isabelle's voice was shrill. "What's going on?"

"It cut him with its talons," Jace said. "There's demon poison in him. The Marks can't work." He touched Alec's face again, gently. "Alec," he said. "Can you hear me? "

Alec didn't move. The shadows under his eyes looked blue and as dark as bruises. If it weren't for his breathing, Clary would have thought he was already dead.

Isabelle bent her head, her hair covering Alec's face. Her arms were around him. "Maybe," she whispered, "we could—"

"Take him to the hospital." It was Simon, standing over them, the bow dangling in his hand. "I'll help you carry him to the van. There's Methodist down on Seventh Avenue—"

"No hospitals," said Isabelle. "We need to get him to the Institute."

"But—"

"They won't know how to treat him in a hospital," said Jace. "He's been cut by a Greater Demon. No mundane doctor would know how to heal those wounds."

Simon nodded. "All right. Let's get him to the car."

In a stroke of good luck, the van hadn't been towed. Isabelle draped a dirty blanket across the backseat and they laid Alec down across it, his head on Isabelle's lap. Jace crouched down on the floor beside his friend. His shirt was stained dark across the sleeves and chest with blood, demon and human. When he looked at Simon, Clary saw that all the gold seemed washed out of his eyes by something she had never seen in them before. Panic.

"Drive fast, mundane," he said. "Drive like hell was following you."

Simon drove.

***

They careened down Flatbush and rocketed onto the bridge, keeping pace with the Q train as it roared over the blue water. The sun was painfully bright in Clary's eyes, striking hot sparks off the river. She clutched at her seat as Simon took the curving ramp off the bridge at fifty miles an hour.

She thought about the awful things she'd said to Alec, the way he'd thrown himself at Abbadon, the look of triumph on his face. When she turned her head now, she saw Jace kneeling next to his friend as blood seeped through the blanket. She thought of the little boy with the dead falcon. *To love is to destroy*.

Clary turned back around, a hard lump lodged in the back of her throat. Isabelle was visible in the badly angled rearview mirror, wrapping the blanket around Alec's throat. She looked up and met Clary's eyes. "How much farther?"

"Maybe ten minutes. Simon's driving as fast as he can."

"I know," Isabelle said. "Simon—what you did, that was incredible. You moved so fast. I wouldn't have thought a mundane could have thought of something like that."

Simon didn't seem fazed by praise from such an unexpected quarter; his eyes were on the road. "You mean shooting out the skylight? It hit me after you guys went inside. I was thinking about the skylight and how you'd said demons couldn't stand direct sun. So, actually, it took me a while to act on it. Don't feel bad," he added, "you can't even see that skylight unless you know it's there."

I knew it was there, Clary thought. *I should have acted on it. Even if I didn't have a bow and arrow like Simon, I could have thrown something at it or told Jace about it.* She felt stupid and useless and thick, as though her head were full of cotton. The truth was that she'd been frightened. Too frightened to think straight. She felt a bright surge of shame that burst behind her eyelids like a small sun.

Jace spoke then. "It was well done," he said.

Simon's eyes narrowed. "So, if you don't mind telling me—that thing, the demon—where did it come from?"

"It was Madame Dorothea," said Clary. "I mean, it was sort of her."

"She was never exactly a pinup, but I don't remember her looking *that* bad."

"I think she was possessed," said Clary slowly, trying to piece it together in her own mind. "She wanted me to give her the Cup. Then she opened the Portal..."

"It was clever," said Jace. "The demon possessed her, then hid the majority of its ethereal form just outside the Portal, where the Sensor wouldn't register it. So we went in expecting to fight a few Forsaken. Instead we found ourselves facing a Greater Demon. Abbadon—one of the Ancients. The Lord of the Fallen."

"Well, it looks like the Fallen will just have to learn to get along without him from now on," said Simon, turning onto the street.

"He's not dead," Isabelle said. "Hardly anyone's ever killed a Greater Demon. You have to kill them in their physical *and* ethereal forms before they'll die. We just scared him off."

"Oh." Simon looked disappointed. "What about Madame Dorothea? Will she be all right now that—"

He broke off, because Alec had begun to choke, his breath rattling in his chest. Jace swore under his breath with vicious precision. *"Why aren't we there yet?"*

"We *are* here. I just don't want to crash into a wall." As Simon pulled up carefully at the corner, Clary saw that the door of the Institute was open, Hodge standing framed in the arch. The van jerked to a halt and Jace leaped out, reaching back to lift Alec as if he weighed no more than a child. Isabelle followed him up the walk, holding her brother's bloody featherstaff. The Institute door slammed shut behind them.

Tiredness washing over her, Clary looked at Simon. "I'm sorry. I don't know how you're going to explain all the blood to Eric."

"Screw Eric," he said with conviction. "Are *you* all right?"

"Not a scratch. Everyone else got hurt, but not me."

"It's their job, Clary," he said gently. "Fighting demons—it's what they do. Not what you do."

"What do I do, Simon?" she asked, searching his face for an answer. "What do *I* do?"

"Well—you got the Cup," he said. "Didn't you?"

She nodded, and tapped her pocket. "Yes."

He looked relieved. "I almost didn't want to ask," he said. "That's good, right?"

"It is," she said. She thought of her mother, and her hand tightened on the Cup. "I know it is."

Church met her at the top of the stairs, yowling like a foghorn, and led her to the infirmary. The double doors were open, and through them she could see Alec's still figure, motionless on one of the white beds. Hodge was bent over him; Isabelle, beside the older man, held a silver tray in her hands.

Jace was not with them. He was not with them because he was standing outside the infirmary, leaning against the wall, his bare, bloody hands curled at his sides. When Clary stopped in front of him, his lids flew open, and she saw that the pupils of his eyes were dilated, all the gold swallowed up in black.

"How is he?" she asked, as gently as she could.

"He's lost a lot of blood. Demon poisonings are common, but since it was a Greater Demon, Hodge isn't sure if the antidotes he usually employs will be viable."

She reached to touch his arm. "Jace—"

He flinched away. "Don't."

She sucked in her breath. "I never would have wanted anything to happen to Alec. I'm so sorry."

He looked at her as if seeing her there for the first time. "It's not *your* fault," he said. "It's mine."

"Yours? Jace, no it isn't—"

"Oh, but it is," he said, his voice as fragile as a sliver of ice. "*Mea culpa, mea maxima culpa.*"

"What does that mean?"

"'My fault,'" he said, "'my own fault, my most grievous fault.' It's Latin." He brushed a lock of her hair back from her forehead absently, as if unaware he was doing it. "Part of the Mass."

"I thought you didn't believe in religion."

"I may not believe in sin," he said, "but I do feel guilt. We Shadowhunters live by a code, and that code isn't flexible. Honor, fault, penance, those are real to us, and they have nothing to do with religion and everything to do with who we are. This is who I *am*, Clary," he said desperately. "I am one of the Clave. It's in my blood and bones. So tell me, if you're so sure this wasn't my fault, why is it that the first thought in my mind when I saw Abbadon wasn't for my fellow warriors but for *you?*" His other hand came up; he was holding her face, prisoned between his palms. "I know—I *knew*—Alec wasn't acting like himself. I knew something was wrong. But all I could think about was you..."

He bent his head forward, so their foreheads touched. She could feel his breath stir her eyelashes. She closed her eyes, letting the nearness of him wash over her like a tide. "If he dies, it will be like I killed him," he said. "I let my father die, and now I've killed the only brother I ever had."

"That's not true," she whispered.

"Yes, it *is*." They were close enough to kiss. And still he held her tightly, as if nothing could reassure him that she was real. "Clary," he said. "What's happening to me?"

She searched her mind for an answer—and heard someone clear his throat. She opened her eyes. Hodge stood by the infirmary door, his neat suit stained with patches of rust. "I have done what I can. He is sedated, not in pain, but..." He shook his head. "I must contact the Silent Brothers. This is beyond my abilities."

Jace drew slowly away from Clary. "How long will it take them to get here?"

"I don't know." Hodge started down the corridor, shaking his head. "I'll send Hugo immediately, but the Brothers come at their own discretion."

"But for *this*—" Even Jace was scrambling to keep up with Hodge's long strides; Clary had fallen hopelessly behind the two of them and had to strain her ears to hear what he was saying. "He might die otherwise."

"He might," was all Hodge said in response.

The library was dark and smelled like rain: One of the windows had been left open, and a puddle of water had collected under the curtains. Hugo chirruped and bounced on his perch as Hodge strode over to him, pausing only to light the lamp on his desk. "It is a pity," Hodge said, reaching for paper and a fountain pen, "that you did not retrieve the Cup. It would, I think, bring some comfort to Alec and certainly to his—"

"But I *did* retrieve the Cup," said Clary, amazed. "Didn't you tell him, Jace?"

Jace was blinking, though whether it was because of surprise or the sudden light, Clary couldn't tell. "There wasn't time—I was bringing Alec upstairs..."

Hodge had gone very still, the pen motionless between his fingers. *"You have the Cup?"*

"Yes." Clary drew the Cup out of her pocket: It was still cold, as if contact with her body could not warm the metal. The rubies winked like red eyes. "I have it here."

The pen slipped from Hodge's hand entirely and struck the floor at his feet. The lamplight, thrown upward, was not kind to his ravaged face: It showed every etched line of harshness and worry and despair. "That is the Angel's Cup?"

"The one," said Jace. "It was—"

"Never mind that now," said Hodge. He set the paper down on the desk and moved toward Jace, catching his student by the shoulders. "Jace Wayland, do you know what you've done?"

Jace looked up at Hodge, surprised. Clary noted the contrast: the ravaged face of the older man and the boy's unlined one, the pale locks of hair falling into Jace's eyes making him look even younger. "I'm not sure what you mean," Jace said.

Hodge's breath hissed out through his teeth. "You look so much like him."

"Like who?" said Jace in astonishment; he had clearly never heard Hodge talk this way before.

"Like your father," Hodge said, and raised his eyes to where Hugo, black wings stirring the humid air, hovered just overhead.

Hodge narrowed his eyes. *"Hugin,"* he said, and with an unearthly caw the bird dived straight for Clary's face, claws outstretched.

Clary heard Jace shout, and then the world was whirling feathers and slashing beak and claws. Bright pain bloomed along her cheek and she shrieked, instinctively throwing her hands up to cover her face.

She felt the Mortal Cup yanked from her grasp. "No!" she cried, grabbing for it. An agonizing pain shot up her arm. Her legs seemed to go out from under her. She slipped and fell, striking her knees painfully against the hard floor. Claws raked her forehead.

"That's enough, Hugo," said Hodge in his quiet voice.

Obediently the bird spun away from Clary. Gagging, she blinked blood out of her eyes. Her face felt shredded.

Hodge had not moved; he stood where he was, holding the Mortal Cup. Hugo was circling him in wide, agitated rounds, cawing softly. And Jace—Jace lay on the floor at Hodge's feet, very still, as if he had fallen suddenly asleep.

All other thoughts were driven from her mind. *"Jace!"* Speaking hurt—the pain in her cheek was startling and she could taste blood in her mouth. Jace didn't move.

"He's not hurt," said Hodge. Clary started to her feet, meaning to fling herself at him—then reeled back as she struck something invisible but as hard and strong as glass. Infuriated, she struck against the air with her fist.

"Hodge!" she shouted. She kicked out, nearly bruising her feet on the same invisible wall. "Don't be stupid. When the Clave finds out what you've done—"

"I'll be long gone by then," he said, kneeling over Jace.

"But—" A shock ran through her, a jolt of electric realization. "You never sent a message to the Clave, did you? That's why you were so weird when I asked you about it. You wanted the Cup for yourself."

"Not," said Hodge, "for myself."

Clary's throat was dry as dust. "You work for Valentine," she whispered.

"I do not work *for* Valentine," said Hodge. He lifted Jace's hand and drew something from it. It was the engraved ring Jace always wore. Hodge slipped it onto his own finger. "But I am Valentine's man, it is true."

With a swift movement he twisted the ring three times around his finger. For a moment nothing happened; then Clary heard the sound of a door opening and turned instinctively to see who was coming into the library. When she turned back, she saw that the air beside Hodge was shimmering, like the surface of a lake seen from a distance. The shimmering wall of air parted like a silver curtain, and then a tall man was standing next to Hodge, as if he had coalesced out of the humid air.

"Starkweather," he said. "You have the Cup?"

Hodge raised the Cup in his hands, but said nothing. He appeared paralyzed, whether with fear or astonishment, it was impossible to tell. He had always seemed tall to Clary, but now he looked hunched and small. "My Lord Valentine," he said, finally. "I had not expected you so quickly."

Valentine. He bore little resemblance to the handsome boy in the photograph, though his eyes were still black. His face was not what she had expected: It was a restrained, closed, interior face, the face of a priest, with sorrowful eyes. Creeping out beneath the black cuffs of his tailored suit were the ridged white scars that spoke of years of the stele. "I told you I would come to you through a Portal," he said. His voice was resonant, and strangely familiar. "Didn't you believe me?"

"Yes. It's just—I thought you'd send Pangborn or Blackwell, not come yourself."

"You think I would send them to collect the Cup? I am not a fool. I know its lure." Valentine held out his hand, and Clary saw, gleaming on his finger, a ring that was the twin of Jace's. "Give it to me."

But Hodge held the Cup fast. "I want what you promised me first."

"First? You don't trust me, Starkweather? " Valentine smiled, a smile not without humor in it. "I'll do as you asked. A bargain is a bargain. Though I must say I was astonished to get your message. I wouldn't have thought you'd mind a life of hidden contemplation, so to speak. You never were much for the battlefield."

"You don't know what it's like," Hodge said, letting out his breath with a hissing gasp. "Being afraid all the time—"

"That's true. I don't." Valentine's voice was as sorrowful as his eyes, as if he pitied Hodge. But there was dislike in his eyes too, a trace of scorn. "If you did not intend to give the Cup to me," he said, "you should not have summoned me here."

Hodge's face worked. "It is not easy to betray what you believe in—those who trust you."

"Do you mean the Lightwoods, or their children?"

"Both," said Hodge.

"Ah, the Lightwoods." Valentine reached out, and with a hand caressed the brass globe that stood on the desk, his long fingers tracing the outlines of continents and seas. "But what do you owe them, really? Yours is the punishment that should have been theirs. If they had not had such high connections in the Clave, they would have been cursed along with you. As it is, they are free to come and go, to walk in the sunlight like ordinary men. They are free to go home." His voice as he said "home" thrilled with all the meaning of the word. His finger had stopped moving over the globe; Clary was sure he was touching the place where Idris would be.

Hodge's eyes darted away. "They did what anyone would do."

"You would not have done it. I would not have done it. To let a friend suffer in my place? And surely it must engender some bitterness in you, Starkweather, to know that they so easily left this fate to you..."

Hodge's shoulders shook. "But it is not the children's fault. They have done nothing—"

"I never knew you to be so fond of children, Starkweather," Valentine said, as if the idea entertained him.

The breath rattled in Hodge's chest. "Jace—"

"You will not speak of Jace." For the first time Valentine

sounded angry. He glanced at the still figure on the floor. "He is bleeding," he observed. "Why?"

Hodge held the Cup against his heart. His knuckles were white. "It's not his blood. He's unconscious, but not injured."

Valentine raised his head with a pleasant smile. "I wonder," he said, "what he will think of you when he wakes. Betrayal is never pretty, but to betray a child—that's a double betrayal, don't you think?"

"You won't hurt him," whispered Hodge. "You swore you wouldn't hurt him."

"I never did that," said Valentine. "Come, now." He moved away from the desk, toward Hodge, who flinched away like a small, trapped animal. Clary could see his misery. "And what would you do if I said I did plan to hurt him? Would you fight me? Keep the Cup from me? Even if you could kill me, the Clave will never lift your curse. You'll hide here till you die, terrified to do so much as open a window too widely. What wouldn't you trade away, not to be afraid any longer? What wouldn't you give up, to go home again?"

Clary tore her eyes away. She could no longer bear the look on Hodge's face. In a choked voice he said, "Tell me you won't hurt him, and I'll give it to you."

"No," said Valentine, even more softly. "You'll give it to me anyway." And he reached out his hand.

Hodge closed his eyes. For a moment his face was the face of one of the marble angels beneath the desk, pained and grave and crushed beneath a terrible weight. Then he swore, pathetically, under his breath, and held the Mortal Cup out for Valentine to take, though his hand shook like a leaf in a high wind.

"Thank you," said Valentine. He took the Cup, and eyed it thoughtfully. "I do believe you've dented the rim."

Hodge said nothing. His face was gray. Valentine bent down and gathered up Jace; as he lifted him up lightly, Clary saw the impeccably cut jacket tighten over his arms and back, and she realized that he was a deceptively massive man, with a torso like the trunk of an oak tree. Jace, limp in his arms, looked like a child by comparison.

"He'll be with his father soon," said Valentine, looking down at Jace's white face. "Where he belongs."

Hodge flinched. Valentine turned away from him and walked back toward the shimmering curtain of air that he had come through. He must have left the Portal door open behind him, Clary realized. Looking at it was like looking at sunlight bouncing off the surface of a mirror.

Hodge reached out an imploring hand. "Wait!" he cried. "What of your promise to me? You swore to end my curse."

"That is true," said Valentine. He paused, and looked hard at Hodge, who gasped and stepped back, his hand flying to his chest as if something had struck him in the heart. Black fluid seeped out around his splayed fingers and trickled to the floor. Hodge lifted his scarred face to Valentine. "Is it done?" he asked wildly. "The curse—it is lifted?"

"Yes," said Valentine. "And may your bought freedom bring you joy." And with that he stepped through the curtain of glowing air. For a moment he himself seemed to shimmer, as if he stood underwater. Then he vanished, taking Jace with him.

20

In Rat's Alley

Hodge, gasping, stared after him, his fists clenching and unclenching at his sides. His left hand was gloved with the wet dark fluid that had seeped from his chest. The look on his face was a mixture of exultation and self-loathing.

"Hodge!" Clary slammed her hand into the invisible wall between them. Pain shot up her arm, but it was nothing compared to the searing pain inside her chest. She felt as if her heart were going to slam its way out of her rib cage. *Jace, Jace, Jace*—the words echoed in her mind, wanting to be screamed out loud. She bit them back. "Hodge, let me out!"

Hodge turned, shaking his head. "I can't," he said, using his immaculately folded handkerchief to rub at his stained hand. He sounded genuinely regretful. "You'll only try to kill me."

"I won't," she said. "I promise."

"But you were not raised a Shadowhunter," he said, "and your promises mean nothing." The edge of his handkerchief was smoking now, as if he'd dipped it in acid, and his hand was no less blackened. Frowning, he abandoned the project.

"But Hodge," she said desperately, "didn't you hear him? He's going to kill Jace."

"He didn't say that." Hodge was at the desk now, opening a drawer, taking out a piece of paper. He drew a pen from his pocket, tapping it sharply against the edge of the desk to make the ink flow. Clary stared at him. Was he writing a *letter*?

"Hodge," she said carefully, "Valentine said Jace would be with his father soon. Jace's father is *dead*. What else could he have meant?"

Hodge didn't look up from the paper he was scribbling on. "It's complicated. You wouldn't understand."

"I understand enough." Her bitterness felt like it might burn through her tongue. "I understand that Jace trusted you and you traded him away to a man who hated his father and probably hates Jace, too, just because you're too cowardly to live with a curse you deserved."

Hodge's head jerked up. "Is that what you think?"

"It's what I know."

He laid his pen down, shaking his head. He looked tired, and so old, so much older than Valentine had looked, though they were the same age. "You only know bits and fragments, Clary. And you're better off that way." He folded the paper he'd been writing on into a neat square and tossed it into the fire, which flared up a bright acidic green before subsiding.

"What are you *doing*?" Clary demanded.

"Sending a message." Hodge turned away from the fire. He was standing close to her, separated only by the invisible wall. She pressed her fingers against it, wishing she could dig them into his eyes—though they were as sad as

Valentine's had been angry. "You are young," he said. "The past is nothing to you, not even another country as it is to the old, or a nightmare as it is to the guilty. The Clave laid this curse on me because I aided Valentine. But I was hardly the only member of the Circle to serve him—were the Lightwoods not as guilty as I was? Were not the Waylands? Yet I was the only one cursed to live out my life without being able to set so much as a foot outdoors, not so much as a hand through the window."

"That's not my fault," said Clary. "It's not Jace's fault. Why punish him for what the Clave did? I can understand giving Valentine the Cup, but Jace? He'll kill Jace, just like he killed Jace's father—"

"Valentine," said Hodge, "did not kill Jace's father."

A sob broke free from Clary's chest. "I don't believe you! All you do is tell lies! Everything you've ever said was a lie!"

"Ah," he said, "the moral absolutism of the young, which allows for no concessions. Can't you see, Clary, that in my own way I'm trying to be a good man?"

She shook her head. "It doesn't work that way. The good things you do don't cancel out the bad ones. But—" She bit her lip. "If you told me where Valentine was—"

"*No.*" He breathed the word. "It is said that the Nephilim are the children of men and angels. All that this angelic heritage has given to us is a longer distance to fall." He touched the invisible surface of the wall with his fingertips. "You were not raised as one of us. You have no part of this life of scars and killing. You can still get away. Leave the Institute, Clary, as soon as you can. Leave, and never come back."

She shook her head. "I can't," she said. "I can't do that."

"Then you have my condolences," he said, and walked out of the room.

The door closed behind Hodge, leaving Clary in silence. There was only her own harsh breathing and the scrabble of her fingertips against the ungiving transparent barrier between her and the door. She did exactly what she'd told herself she wouldn't do, and flung herself against it, again and again, until she was exhausted and her sides ached. Then she sank to the floor and tried not to cry.

Somewhere on the other side of this barrier Alec was dying, while Isabelle waited for Hodge to come and save him. Somewhere beyond this room Jace was being shaken roughly awake by Valentine. Somewhere her mother's chances were ebbing away, moment by moment, second by second. And she was trapped here, as useless and helpless as the child she was.

She sat bolt upright then, remembering the moment at Madame Dorothea's when Jace had pressed the stele into her hand. Had she ever given it *back* to him? Holding her breath, she felt in her left jacket pocket; it was empty. Slowly her hand crept into the right pocket, her sweaty fingers picking up lint and then skidding across something hard, smooth, and round—the stele.

She bounded to her feet, her heart pounding, and felt with her left hand for the invisible wall. Finding it, she braced herself, inching the tip of the stele forward with her other hand until it rested against the smooth, level air. Already an image was forming in her mind, like a fish rising up through cloudy water, the pattern of its scales growing clearer and clearer as it neared the surface. Slowly at first, and then more confidently, she moved the stele across the wall, leaving searingly bright ash-white lines hovering in the air before her.

She *felt* when the rune was done, and lowered her hand, breathing hard. For a moment everything was motionless and silent and the rune hung like glowing neon, burning her eyes. Then came a sound like the loudest shattering she had ever heard, as if she were standing under a waterfall of stones listening to them crash to the ground all around her. The rune she had drawn turned black and sifted away like ash; the floor trembled under her feet; then it was over, and she knew, without a doubt, that she was free.

Still holding the stele, she raced to the window and pushed the curtain aside. Twilight was falling and the streets below were bathed in a reddish purple glow. She caught a clear glimpse of Hodge crossing a street, his gray head bobbing above the crowd.

She dashed out of the library and down the stairs, pausing only to shove the stele back into her jacket pocket. She took the stairs running and hit the street with a stitch already forming in her side. People walking their dogs in the humid twilight jumped aside as she barreled down the walkway alongside the East River. She caught sight of herself in the darkened window of an apartment building as she careened around a corner. Her sweaty hair was plastered to her forehead, her face crusted with dried blood.

She reached the intersection where she had seen Hodge. For a moment she thought she'd lost him. She darted through the crowd near the subway entrance, shouldering people aside, using her knees and elbows as weapons. Sweaty and bruised, Clary pulled free of the crowd just in time to see a flash of tweed suit disappear around the corner of a narrow service alley between two buildings.

She wriggled around a Dumpster and into the mouth of the alley. The back of her throat felt like it was burning every time she breathed. Though it had been twilight on the street, here in the alley it was as dark as nightfall. She could just see Hodge, standing at the far end of the alley, where it dead-ended into the back of a fast-food restaurant. Restaurant trash was piled outside: heaping bags of food, dirty paper plates, and plastic cutlery that crunched unpleasantly under his boots as he turned to look at her. She remembered a poem she'd read in English class: *I think we are in rats' alley / Where the dead men lost their bones*.

"You followed me," he said. "You shouldn't have."

"I'll leave you alone if you just tell me where Valentine is."

"I can't do that," he said. "He'll know I told you, and my freedom will be as short as my life."

"It will be anyway when the Clave finds out that you gave the Mortal Cup to Valentine," Clary pointed out. "After tricking us into finding it for you. How can you live with yourself, knowing what he plans to do with it?"

He cut her off with a short laugh. "I fear Valentine more than the Clave, and so would you, if you were wise," he said. "He would have found the Cup eventually, whether I helped him or not."

"And you don't care that he's going to use it to kill people?"

A spasm crossed his face as he took a step forward; she saw something shine in his hand. "Does all this really matter to you this much?"

"I told you before," she said. "I can't just walk away."

"That's too bad," he said, and she saw him raise his arm—and remembered suddenly Jace saying that Hodge's weapon had been the *chakhram*, the flying disk. She ducked even before she saw the bright circle of metal spin singing toward her head; it passed, humming, inches from her face and embedded itself in the metal fire escape on her left.

She looked up. Hodge was gazing at her, the second metal disk held lightly in his right hand. "You can still run," he said.

Instinctively she raised her hands, though logic told her the *chakhram* would just slice them to pieces. "Hodge—"

Something hurtled in front of her, something big, gray-black, and *alive*. She heard Hodge shout in horror. Stumbling backward, Clary saw the thing more clearly as it paced between her and Hodge. It was a wolf, six feet in length, with a jet-black coat shot through with a single stripe of gray.

Hodge, the metal disc gripped in his hand, was white as a bone. "You," he breathed, and with a sense of distant astonishment Clary realized he was talking to the wolf. "I thought that you had fled—"

The wolf's lips drew back from its teeth, and she saw its lolling red tongue. There was hatred in its eyes as it looked at Hodge, a pure and human hatred.

"Did you come for me, or for the girl?" said Hodge. Sweat streamed from his temples, but his hand was steady.

The wolf paced toward him, growling low in its throat.

"There's still time," said Hodge. "Valentine would take you back—"

With a howl the wolf sprang. Hodge cried out again, then there was a flash of silver, and a sickening noise as the *chakhram* embedded itself in the wolf's side. The wolf reared back on its hind legs, and Clary saw the disk's edge jutting from the wolf 's fur, blood streaming, just as it struck Hodge.

Hodge screamed once as he went down, the wolf's jaws clamping shut over his shoulder. Blood flew into the air like the spray of paint from a broken can, splattering the cement wall with red. The wolf lifted its head from the tutor's limp body and turned its gray, lupine gaze on Clary, teeth dripping scarlet.

She didn't scream. There was no air in her lungs that she could have dragged up to make a sound; she scrambled to her feet and ran, ran for the mouth of the alley and the familiar neon lights of the street, ran for the safety of the real world. She could hear the wolf growling behind her, feel its hot breath on the bare backs of her legs. She put on one last burst of speed, flinging herself toward the street—

The wolf 's jaws closed on her leg, jerking her backward. Just before her head struck the hard pavement, plunging her into blackness, she discovered that she did have enough air to scream, after all.

The sound of dripping water woke her. Slowly Clary peeled her eyes open. There wasn't much to see. She lay on a wide cot that had been placed on the floor of a small dingy-walled room. There was a rickety table propped against one wall. On it was a cheap-looking brass candleholder sporting a fat red candle that cast the only light in the room. The ceiling was cracked and damp, wetness seeping down through the fissures in the stone. Clary felt a vague sense that something was missing from the room, but this concern was overwhelmed by the strong smell of wet dog.

She sat up and immediately wished she hadn't. Hot pain drove through her head like a spike, followed by a racking wave of nausea. If there had been anything in her stomach, she would have thrown it up.

A mirror hung over the cot, dangling from a nail driven between two stones. She glanced in it and was appalled. No wonder her face hurt—long parallel scratches ran from the corner of her right eye down to the edge of her mouth. Her right cheek was crusted with blood, and blood was smeared on her neck and all down the front of her shirt and jacket. In a sudden panic she grabbed for her pocket, then relaxed. The stele was still there.

It was then that she realized what was odd about the room. One wall of it was bars: thick iron floor-to-ceiling bars. She was in a jail cell.

Veins surging with adrenaline, Clary staggered to her feet. A wave of dizziness washed over her, and she caught at the table to steady herself. *I will not faint,* she told herself grimly. Then she heard the footsteps.

Someone was coming down the hallway outside the cell. Clary backed up against the table.

It was a man. He was carrying a lamp, its light brighter than the candle, which made her blink and turned him into a back-lit shadow. She saw height, square shoulders, ragged hair; it was only when he pushed the door of the cell open and came inside that she realized who he was.

He looked the same: worn jeans, denim shirt, work boots, same uneven hair, same glasses pushed down to the bridge of his nose. The scars she'd noticed along the side of his throat last time she'd seen him were healing patches of shiny skin now.

Luke.

It was all too much for Clary. Exhaustion, lack of sleep and food, terror and blood-loss, caught up with her in a rushing wave. She felt her knees buckle as she slid toward the ground.

In seconds Luke was across the room. He moved so fast, she didn't have time to hit the floor before he caught her, swinging her up the way he'd done when she was a little girl. He set her down on the cot and stepped back, eyes anxious. "Clary?" he said, reaching for her. "Are you all right?"

She flinched away, throwing up her hands to ward him off. "Don't touch me."

An expression of profound hurt crossed his face. Wearily he drew a hand across his forehead. "I guess I deserve that."

"Yeah. You do."

The look on his face was troubled. "I don't expect you to trust me—"

"That's good. Because I don't."

"Clary..." He began to pace the length of the cell. "What I did... I don't expect you to understand. I know you feel that I abandoned you—"

"You *did* abandon me," she said. "You told me never to call you again. You never cared about me. You never cared about my mother. You lied about everything."

"Not," he said, "about everything."

"So your name really is Luke Garroway?"

His shoulders drooped perceptibly. "No," he said, then glanced down. A dark red patch was spreading across the front of his blue denim shirt.

Clary sat up straight. "Is that *blood*?" she demanded. She forgot for a moment to be furious.

"Yes," said Luke, his hand against his side. "The wound must have torn open when I lifted you."

"What wound?" Clary couldn't help asking.

He said with deliberation: "Hodge's discs are still sharp, though his throwing arm is not what it once was. I think he may have nicked a rib."

"Hodge?" Clary said. "When did you...?"

He looked at her, not saying anything, and she remembered suddenly the wolf in the alley, all black except for that one gray streak down its side, and she remembered the disc hitting it, and she realized.

"You're a *werewolf*."

He took his hand away from his shirt; his fingers were stained red. "Yep," he said laconically. He moved to the wall and rapped sharply on it: once, twice, three times. Then he turned back to her. "I am."

"You killed Hodge," she said, remembering.

"No." He shook his head. "I hurt him pretty badly, I think, but when I went back for the body, it was gone. He must have dragged himself away."

"You tore at his shoulder," she said. "I saw you."

"Yes. Though it's worth noting that he was trying to kill you at the time. Did he hurt anyone else?"

Clary sank her teeth into her lip. She tasted blood, but it was old blood from where Hugo had attacked her. "Jace," she said in a whisper. "Hodge knocked him out and handed him over to ... to Valentine."

"To *Valentine*?" Luke said, looking astonished. "I knew Hodge had given Valentine the Mortal Cup, but I hadn't realized—"

"How did you know that?" Clary began, before remembering.

"You heard me talking to Hodge in the alley," she said. "Before you jumped him."

"I jumped him, as you put it, because he was about to slice your head off," Luke said, then looked up as the cell door opened again and a tall man came in, followed by a tiny woman, so short she looked like a child. Both of them wore plain, casual clothes: jeans and cotton shirts, and both had the same untidy, flyaway hair, though the woman's was fair and the man's was a badgery gray and black. Both had the same young-old faces, unlined but with tired eyes. "Clary," said Luke, "meet my second and third, Gretel and Alaric."

Alaric inclined his massive head to her. "We have met."

Clary stared, alarmed. "Have we?"

"At the Hotel Dumort," he said. "You put your knife in my ribs."

She shrank against the wall. "I, ah ... I'm sorry?"

"Don't be," he said. "It was an excellent throw." He slid a hand into his breast pocket and removed Jace's dagger, with its winking red eye. He held it out to her. "I think this is yours?"

Clary stared. "But—"

"Don't worry," he assured her. "I cleaned the blade."

Wordlessly, she took it. Luke was chuckling under his breath. "In retrospect," he said, "perhaps the raid on the Dumort was not as well-planned as it might have been. I had set a group of my wolves to watch you, and go after you if you seemed to be in any danger. When you went into the Dumort..."

"Jace and I could have handled it." Clary slid the dagger into her belt.

Gretel aimed a tolerant smile at her. "Is that what you summoned us for, sir?"

"No," said Luke. He touched his side. "My wound's opened up, and Clary here has some injuries of her own that could use a bit of tending. If you wouldn't mind getting the supplies…"

Gretel inclined her head. "I will return with the healing kit," she said, and left, Alaric trailing her like an outsize shadow.

"She called you 'sir,'" said Clary, the moment the cell door closed behind them. "And what do you mean by your second and your third? Second and third what?"

"In command," said Luke slowly. "I am the leader of this particular wolf pack. That's why Gretel called me 'sir.' Believe me, it took a fair bit of work to break her of the habit of calling me 'master.'"

"Did my mother know?"

"Know what?"

"That you're a werewolf."

"Yes. She's known since it happened."

"Neither of you, of course, thought to mention this to me."

"I would have told you," said Luke. "But your mother was adamant that you know nothing of Shadowhunters or the Shadow World. I couldn't explain away my being a werewolf as some kind of isolated incident, Clary. It's all part of the larger pattern that your mother didn't want you to see. I don't know what you've learned—"

"A lot," Clary said flatly. "I know my mother was a Shadowhunter. I know she was married to Valentine and that she stole the Mortal Cup from him and went into hiding. I know that after she had me, she took me to Magnus Bane every two years to have my Sight taken away. I know that when Valentine tried to get you to tell him where the Cup was in exchange for my mom's life, you told him she didn't matter to you."

Luke stared at the wall. "I didn't know where the Cup was," he said. "She'd never told me."

"You could have tried to bargain—"

"Valentine doesn't bargain. He never has. If the advantage isn't his, he won't even come to the table. He's entirely single-minded and totally without compassion, and though he may have loved your mother once, he wouldn't hesitate to kill her. No, I wasn't going to bargain with Valentine."

"So you just decided to *abandon* her?" Clary demanded furiously. "You're the leader of a whole pack of werewolves and you just decided she didn't even really need your help? You know, it was bad enough when I thought you were another Shadowhunter and you'd turned your back on her because of some stupid Shadowhunter vow or something, but now I know you're just a slimy Downworlder who didn't even care that all those years she treated you like a friend—like an equal—and this is how you paid her back!"

"Listen to you," Luke said quietly. "You sound like a Lightwood."

She narrowed her eyes. "Don't talk about Alec and Isabelle like you know them."

"I meant their parents," said Luke. "Whom I did know, very well in fact, when we were all Shadowhunters together."

She felt her lips part in surprise. "I know you were in the

Circle, but how did you keep them from finding out you were a werewolf ? Didn't they know?"

"No," said Luke. "Because I wasn't born a werewolf. I was made one. And I can already see that if you're going to be persuaded to listen to anything I have to say, you're going to have to hear the whole story. It's a long tale, but I think we have the time for it."

Part Three

The Descent Beckons

The descent beckons
as the ascent beckoned.
—William Carlos Williams, *The Descent*

21
The Werewolf's Tale

The truth is, I've known your mother since we were children. We grew up in Idris. It's a beautiful place, and I've always regretted that you've never seen it: You would love the glossy pines in winter, the dark earth and cold crystal rivers. There's a small network of towns and a single city, Alicante, where the Clave meets. They call it the Glass City because its towers are shaped from the same demon-repelling substance as our steles; in the sunlight they sparkle like glass.

When Jocelyn and I were old enough, we were sent to Alicante to school. It was there that I met Valentine.

He was older than I was by a year. By far the most popular boy in school. He was handsome, clever, rich, dedicated, an incredible warrior. I was nothing—neither rich nor brilliant, from an unremarkable country family. And I struggled in my studies. Jocelyn was a natural Shadowhunter; I was not. I could not bear the lightest Marks or learn the simplest techniques. I thought sometimes about running away, returning home in shame. Even becoming a mundane. I was that miserable.

It was Valentine who saved me. He came to my room—I'd never even thought he knew my name. He offered to train me. He said he knew that I was struggling, but he saw in me the seeds of a great Shadowhunter. And under his tutelage I did improve. I passed my exams, bore my first Marks, killed my first demon.

I worshipped him. I thought the sun rose and set on Valentine Morgenstern. I wasn't the only misfit he'd rescued, of course. There were others. Hodge Starkweather, who got along better with books than he did with people; Maryse Trueblood, whose brother had married a mundane; Robert Lightwood, who was terrified of the Marks—Valentine brought them all under his wing. I thought it was kindness, then; now I am not so sure. Now I think he was building himself a cult.

Valentine was obsessed with the idea that in every generation there were fewer and fewer Shadowhunters—that we were a dying breed. He was sure that if only the Clave would more freely use Raziel's Cup, more Shadowhunters could be made. To the teachers this idea was sacrilege—it is not for just anyone to choose who can and cannot become a Shadowhunter. Flippantly, Valentine would ask, Why not make all men Shadowhunters, then? Why not gift them all with the ability to see the Shadow World? Why keep that power selfishly to ourselves?

When the teachers answered that most humans cannot survive the transition, Valentine claimed they were lying, trying to keep the power of the Nephilim limited to an elite few.

That was his claim, at the time—now I think he probably felt the collateral damage was worth the end result. In any case, he convinced our little group of his rightness. We formed the Circle, with our stated intent being to save the race of Shadowhunters from extinction. Of course, being seventeen, we weren't quite sure how we would do it, but we were sure we'd eventually accomplish something significant.

Then came the night that Valentine's father was killed in a routine raid on a werewolf encampment. When Valentine returned to school, after the funeral, he wore the red Marks of mourning. He was different in other ways. His kindness was now interspersed with flashes of rage that bordered on cruelty. I put this new behavior down to grief and tried harder than ever to please him. I never answered his anger with anger of my own. I felt only the sick sense that I had disappointed him.

The only one that could calm his rages was your mother. She had always stood a little apart from our group, sometimes mockingly calling us Valentine's fan club. That changed when his father died. His pain awakened her sympathy. They fell in love.

I loved him too: He was my closest friend, and I was happy to see Jocelyn with him. When we left school, they married and went to live on her family's estate. I also returned home, but the Circle continued. It had started as a sort of school adventure, but it grew in scale and power, and Valentine grew with it. Its ideals had changed as well. The Circle still clamored for the Mortal Cup, but since the death of his father, Valentine had become an outspoken proponent of war against all Downworlders, not just those who broke the Accords. This world was for humans, he argued, not part-demons. Demons could never be fully trusted.

I was uncomfortable with the Circle's new direction, but I stuck with it—partly because I still couldn't bear to let Valentine down, partly because Jocelyn had asked me to continue. She had some hope that I would be able to bring moderation to the Circle, but that was impossible. There was no moderating Valentine, and Robert and Maryse Lightwood—now married— were almost as bad. Only Michael Wayland was unsure, as I was, but despite our reluctance we followed still; as a group we hunted Downworlders tirelessly, seeking those who had committed even the slightest infraction. Valentine never killed a creature who had not broken the Accords, but he did other things. I saw him fasten silver coins to the eyelids of a werewolf child, blinding her, in an attempt to get the girl to tell him where her brother was… I saw him—but you don't need to hear this. No. I'm sorry.

What happened next was that Jocelyn became pregnant. The day she told me that, she also confessed that she had grown afraid of her husband. His behavior had turned weird, erratic. He would disappear into their cellars for nights at a time. Sometimes she would hear screams through the walls…

I went to him. He laughed, dismissing her fears as the jitters of a woman carrying her first child. He invited me to hunt with him that night. We were still trying to clean out the nest of werewolves who had killed his father years before. We were *parabatai*, a perfect hunting team of two, warriors who would die for each other. So when Valentine told me he would guard my back that night, I believed him. I didn't see the wolf until it was on me. I remember its teeth fastened in my shoulder, and nothing else of that night. When I awoke, I was lying in Valentine's house, my shoulder bandaged, and Jocelyn was there.

Not all werewolf bites result in lycanthropy. I healed of the injury and passed the next weeks in a torment of waiting. Waiting for the full moon. The Clave would have locked me in an observation cell, had they known. But Valentine and Jocelyn kept silent. Three weeks later the moon rose full and bright, and I began to change. The first Change is always the hardest. I remember a bewilderment of agony, a blackness, and waking up hours later in a meadow miles from the city. I was covered in blood, the torn body of some small woodland animal at my feet.

I made my way back to the manor, and they met me at the door. Jocelyn fell on me, weeping, but Valentine pulled her away. I stood, bloody and shaking on my feet. I could scarcely think, and the taste of raw meat was still in my mouth. I don't know what I had expected, but I suppose I should have known.

Valentine dragged me down the steps and into the woods with him. He told me that he ought to kill me himself, but seeing me then, he could not bring himself to do it. He gave me a *kindjal* dagger that had once belonged to his father. He said I should do the honorable thing and end my own life. He kissed the dagger when he handed it to me, and went back inside the manor house, and barred the door.

I ran through the night, sometimes as a man, sometimes as a wolf, until I crossed the border. I burst into the midst of the werewolf encampment, brandishing my dagger, and demanded to meet in combat the lycanthrope who had bitten me and turned me into one of them. Laughing, they pointed me toward the clan leader. Hands and teeth still bloody from the hunt, he rose to face me.

I had never been much for single combat. The crossbow was my weapon; I had excellent sight and aim. But I had never been very good at close range; it was Valentine who was skilled in fighting hand to hand. But I wanted only to die, and to take with me the creature who had ruined me. I suppose I thought if I could avenge myself, and kill the wolves who had murdered his father, Valentine would mourn me. As we grappled, sometimes as men, sometimes as wolves, I saw that he was surprised by my fierceness. As the night faded into day, he began to tire, but my rage never abated. And as the sun began to set again, I sank my dagger into his neck and he died, soaking me with his blood.

I expected the pack to set on me and tear me apart. But they knelt at my feet and bared their throats in submission. The wolves have a law: Whoever kills the clan leader takes his place. I had come to the place of the wolves, and instead of finding death and vengeance there, I found a new life.

I left my old self behind and almost forgot what it was like to be a Shadowhunter. But I did not forget Jocelyn. The thought of her was a constant companion. I feared for her in the company of Valentine, but knew that if I came near the manor house, the Circle would hunt me down and kill me.

In the end she came to me. I was asleep in the camp when my second in command came to tell me that there was a young Shadowhunter woman waiting to see me. I knew immediately who it must be. I could see the disapproval in his eyes as I raced to meet her. They all knew I had once been a Shadowhunter, of course, but it was considered a shameful secret, never spoken of. Valentine would have laughed.

She was waiting for me just outside the encampment. She was no longer pregnant, and looked drawn and pale. She had had her child, she said, a boy, and had named him Jonathan Christopher. She cried when she saw me. She was angry that I had not let her know I was still alive. Valentine had told the Circle I had taken my own life, but she had not believed it. She knew that I would never do such a thing. I felt her faith in me was unwarranted, but I was so relieved to see her again that I didn't contradict her.

I asked how she had found me. She said that there were rumors in Alicante of a werewolf who had once been a Shadowhunter. Valentine had heard the rumors too, and she had ridden to warn me. He came soon after, but I hid from him, as werewolves can, and he left without bloodshed.

After that I began to meet Jocelyn in secret. It was the year of the Accords, and all of Downworld was abuzz about them and Valentine's probable plans for disrupting them. I heard that he had argued passionately in the Clave against the Accords, but with no success. So the Circle made a new plan, steeped in secrecy. They allied themselves with demons—the greatest enemies of Shadowhunters—in order to procure weapons that could be smuggled undetected into the Great Hall of the Angel, where the Accords would be signed. And with the aid of a demon, Valentine stole the Mortal Cup. He left in its place a facsimile. It was months before the Clave realized the Cup was missing, and by then it was too late.

Jocelyn tried to learn what Valentine intended to do with the Cup, but could not. But she knew that the Circle planned to fall upon the unarmed Downworlders and murder them in the

Hall. After such wholesale slaughter, the Accords would fail.

Despite the chaos, in a strange way those were happy days. Jocelyn and I sent messages covertly to the faeries, the warlocks, and even to those age-old enemies of wolfkind, the vampires, warning them of Valentine's plans and bidding them prepare for battle. We worked together, werewolf and Nephilim.

On the day of the Accords, I watched from a hidden place as Jocelyn and Valentine left the manor house. I remember how she bent to kiss the white-blond head of her son. I remember the way the sun shone on her hair; I remember her smile.

They rode into Alicante by carriage; I followed running on four feet, and my pack ran with me. The Great Hall of the Angel was crowded with all the assembled Clave and score upon score of Downworlders. When the Accords were presented for signing, Valentine rose to his feet, and the Circle rose with him, sweeping back their cloaks to lift their weapons. As the Hall exploded into chaos, Jocelyn ran to the great double doors of the Hall and flung them open.

My pack were the first at the door. We burst into the Hall, tearing the night with our howls, and were followed by faerie knights with weapons of glass and twisted thorns. After them came the Night Children with bared fangs, and warlocks wielding flame and iron. As the panicked masses fled the Hall, we fell upon the members of the Circle.

Never had the Hall of the Angel seen such bloodshed. We tried not to harm those Shadowhunters who were not of the Circle; Jocelyn marked them out, one by one, with a warlock's spell. But many died, and I fear we were responsible for some. Certainly, afterward, we were blamed for many. As for the

Circle, there were far more of them than we had imagined, and they clashed fiercely with the Downworlders. I fought through the crowd to Valentine. My only thought had been of him—that I might be the one to kill him, that I might have that honor. I found him at last by the great statue of the Angel, dispatching a faerie knight with a broad stroke of his blood-stained dagger. When he saw me, he smiled, fierce and feral. "A werewolf who fights with sword and dagger," he said, "is as unnatural as a dog who eats with a fork and a knife."

"You know the sword, you know the dagger," I said. "And you know who I am. If you must address me, use my name."

"I do not know the names of half men," said Valentine. "Once I had a friend, a man of honor who would have died before he let his blood be polluted. Now a nameless monster with his face stands before me." He raised his blade. "I should have killed you while I had the chance," he cried, and lunged for me.

I parried the blow, and we fought up and down the dais, while the battle raged around us and one by one the members of the Circle fell. I saw the Lightwoods drop their weapons and flee; Hodge was already gone, having fled at the outset. And then I saw Jocelyn racing up the stairs toward me, her face a mask of fear. "Valentine, stop!" she cried out. "This is Luke, your friend, almost your brother—"

With a snarl Valentine seized her and dragged her in front of him, his dagger to her throat. I dropped my blade. I would not risk his harming her. He saw what was in my eyes. "You always wanted her," he hissed. "And now the two of you have plotted my betrayal together. You will regret what you have done, all the rest of your lives."

With that, he snatched the locket from Jocelyn's throat and hurled it at me. The silver cord burned me like a lash. I screamed and fell back, and in that moment he vanished into the melee, dragging her with him. I followed, burned and bleeding, but he was too fast, cutting a path through the thick of the crowd and over the dead.

I staggered out into the moonlight. The Hall was burning and the sky was lit with fire. I could see all down the green lawns of the capital to the dark river, and the road along the riverbank where people were fleeing into the night. I found Jocelyn by the banks of the river, at last. Valentine was gone and she was terrified for Jonathan, desperate to get home. We found a horse, and she plunged away. Dropping into wolf form, I followed at her heels.

Wolves are fast, but a rested horse is faster. I fell far behind, and she arrived at the manor house before I did.

I knew even as I neared the house that something was terribly wrong. Here too the smell of fire hung heavy in the air, and there was something overlaying it, something thick and sweet—the stench of demonic witchcraft. I became a man again as I limped up the long drive, white in the moonlight, like a river of silver leading ... to ruins. For the manor house had been reduced to ashes, layer upon layer of sifting whiteness, strewn across the lawns by the night wind. Only the foundations, like burned bones, were still visible: here a window, there a leaning chimney—but the substance of the house, the bricks and the mortar, the priceless books and ancient tapestries handed down through generations of Shadowhunters, were dust blowing across the face of the moon.

Valentine had destroyed the house with demon fire. He

must have. No fire of this world burns so hot, nor leaves so little behind.

I made my way into the still-smoldering ruins. I found Jocelyn kneeling on what had perhaps once been the front doorsteps. They were blackened by fire. And, there were bones. Charred to blackness, but recognizably human, with scraps of cloth here and there, and bits of jewelry the fire had not taken. Red and gold threads still clung to the bones of Jocelyn's mother, and the heat had melted her father's dagger to his skeletal hand. Among another pile of bones gleamed Valentine's silver amulet, with the insignia of the Circle still burning white-hot upon its face ... and among the remains, scattered as if they were too fragile to hold together, were the bones of a child.

You will regret what you have done, Valentine had said. And as I knelt with Jocelyn on the burned paving stones, I knew that he was right. I did regret it and have regretted it every day since.

We rode back through the city that night, among the still-burning fires and shrieking people, and then out into the darkness of the country. It was a week before Jocelyn spoke again. I took her out of Idris. We fled to Paris. We had no money, but she refused to go to the Institute there and ask for help. She was done with Shadowhunters, she told me, done with the Shadow World.

I sat in the tiny, cheap hotel room we had rented and tried to reason with her, but it did no good. She was obstinate. At last she told me why: She was carrying another child, and had known it for weeks. She would make a new life for herself and her baby, and she wanted no whisper of Clave or Covenant ever to taint her future. She showed me the amulet she had taken from the pile of bones; in the flea market at Clignancourt she sold it, and with that money purchased an airplane ticket. She wouldn't tell me where she was going. The farther away she could get from Idris, she said, the better.

I knew that leaving her old life behind meant leaving me behind as well, and I argued with her, but to no avail. I knew that if not for the child she carried, she would have taken her own life, and since to lose her to the mundane world was better than to lose her to death, I at last reluctantly agreed to her plan. And so it was that I bid her good-bye at the airport. The last words Jocelyn spoke to me in that dreary departure hall chilled me to the bone: "Valentine is not dead."

After she was gone, I returned to my pack, but I found no peace there. Always there was a hollow aching inside me, and always I woke with her name unspoken on my lips. I was not the leader I had once been; I knew that much. I was just and fair, but remote; I could not find friends among the wolfpeople, nor a mate. I was, in the end, too much human—too much Shadowhunter—to be at rest among the lycanthropes. I hunted, but the hunt brought no satisfaction; and when it came time for the Accords to be signed at last, I went into the city to sign them.

In the Hall of the Angel, scrubbed free of blood, the Shadowhunters and the four branches of half humans sat down again to sign the papers that would bring peace among us. I was astonished to see the Lightwoods, who seemed equally astonished that I wasn't dead. They themselves, they said, along with Hodge Starkweather and Michael Wayland, were the only members of the former Circle to have escaped death that night in the Hall. Michael, wracked with grief over the loss of his wife, had hidden himself away at his country estate with his young son. The Clave had punished the other three with exile: They were leaving for New York, to run the Institute there. The Lightwoods, who had connections to the highest families in the Clave, got off with a far lighter sentence than Hodge. A curse had been laid on him: He would go with them, but if ever he were to leave the hallowed ground of the Institute, he would be instantly slain. He was devoting himself to his studies, they said, and would make a fine tutor for their children.

When we had signed the Accords, I rose from my chair and went from the hall, down to the river where I had found Jocelyn on the night of the Uprising. Watching the dark waters flow, I knew I could never find peace in my homeland: I had to be with her or nowhere at all. I determined to look for her.

I left my pack, naming another in my stead; I think they were relieved to see me go. I traveled as the wolf without a pack travels: alone, at night, keeping to the byways and country roads. I went back to Paris, but found no clue there. Then I went to London. From London I took a boat to Boston.

I stayed awhile in the cities, then in the White Mountains of the frozen north. I traveled a good deal, but more and more I found myself thinking of New York, and the exiled Shadowhunters there. Jocelyn, in a way, was an exile too. At length I arrived in New York with a single duffel bag and no idea where to look for your mother. It would have been easy enough for me to find a wolf pack and join it, but I resisted. As I had done in other cities, I sent out messages through

Downworld, searching for any sign of Jocelyn, but there was nothing, no word at all, as if she had simply disappeared into the mundane world without a trace. I began to despair.

In the end I found her by chance. I was prowling the streets of SoHo, randomly. As I stood on the cobblestones of Broome Street, a painting hanging in a gallery window caught my eye.

It was the study of a landscape I recognized immediately: the view from the windows of her family's manor house, the green lawns sweeping down to the line of trees that hid the road beyond. I recognized her style, her brushwork, everything. I banged on the door of the gallery, but it was closed and locked. I returned to the painting, and this time saw the signature. It was the first time I had seen her new name: Jocelyn Fray.

By that evening, I had found her, living in a fifth-floor walkup in that artists' haven, the East Village. I walked up the grimy half-lit stairs with my heart in my throat, and knocked on her door. It was opened by a little girl with dark red braids and inquisitive eyes. And then, behind her, I saw Jocelyn walking toward me, her hands stained with paint and her face just the same as it had been when we were children...

The rest you know.

22

Renwick's Ruin

For a long moment after Luke finished speaking, there was silence in the room. The only sound was the faint drip of water down the stone walls. Finally, he said:

"Say something, Clary."

"What do you want me to say?"

He sighed. "Maybe that you understand?"

Clary could hear her blood pounding in her ears. She felt as if her life had been built on a sheet of ice as thin as paper, and now the ice was beginning to crack, threatening to plunge her into the icy darkness below. Down into the dark water, she thought, where all her mother's secrets drifted in the currents, the forgotten remains of a shipwrecked life.

She looked up at Luke. He seemed wavering, indistinct, as if she looked through a blurred glass. "My father," she said. "That picture my mother always kept on the mantel—"

"That wasn't your father," said Luke.

"Did he ever even exist?" Clary's voice rose. "Was there

ever a John Clark, or did my mother make him up too?"

"John Clark existed. But he wasn't your father. He was the son of two of your mother's neighbors when you lived in the East Village. He died in a car crash, just like your mother told you, but she never knew him. She had his photo because the neighbors commissioned her to paint a portrait of him in his Army uniform. She gave them the portrait but kept the photo, and pretended the man in it had been your father. I think she thought it was easier that way. After all, if she'd claimed he'd run off or disappeared, you'd have wanted to look for him. A dead man—"

"Won't contradict your lies," Clary finished for him bitterly. "Didn't she think it was wrong, all those years, letting me think my father was dead, when my real father—"

Luke said nothing, letting her find the end of the sentence herself, letting her think the unthinkable thought on her own.

"Is *Valentine*." Her voice shook. "That's what you're telling me, right? That Valentine was—is—my father?"

Luke nodded, his knotted fingers the only sign of the tension he felt. "Yes."

"Oh, my *God*." Clary leaped to her feet, no longer able to sit still. She paced to the bars of the cell. "That's not possible. It's just not possible."

"Clary, please don't get upset—"

"Don't get upset? You're telling me that my dad is a guy who's basically an evil overlord, and you want me not to get upset?"

"He wasn't evil to begin with," Luke said, sounding almost apologetic.

"Oh, I beg to differ. I think he was *clearly* evil. All that stuff he was spouting about keeping the human race pure and the importance of untainted blood—he was like one of those creepy white power guys. And you two totally fell for it."

"I wasn't the one talking about 'slimy' Downworlders just minutes ago," Luke said quietly. "Or about how they couldn't be trusted."

"That's not the same thing!" Clary could hear the tears in her voice. "I had a brother," she went on, her voice catching. "Grandparents, too. They're dead?"

Luke nodded, looking down at his big hands, open on his knees. "They're dead."

"Jonathan," she said softly. "He would have been older than me? A year older?"

Luke said nothing.

"I always wanted a brother," she said.

"Don't," he said wretchedly. "Don't torture yourself. You can see why your mother kept all this from you, can't you? What good would it have done you to know what you had lost before you were even born?"

"That box," Clary said, her mind working feverishly. "With the J. C. on it. Jonathan Christopher. That was what she was always crying over, that was his lock of hair—my brother's, not my father's."

"Yes."

"And when you said 'Clary isn't Jonathan,' you meant my brother. My mom was so overprotective of me because she'd already had one child who died."

Before Luke could reply, the cell door clanged open and

Gretel entered. The "healing kit," which Clary had been envisioning as a hard plastic-sided box with the Red Cross insignia on it, turned out to be a big wooden tray, stacked with folded bandages, steaming bowls of unidentified liquids, and herbs that gave off a pungent lemony odor. Gretel set the tray down beside the cot and gestured for Clary to sit down, which she did unwillingly.

"That's a good girl," said the wolf-woman, dipping a cloth into one of the bowls and lifting it to Clary's face. Gently she cleaned away the dried blood. "What happened to you?" she asked disapprovingly, as if she suspected Clary of taking a cheese grater to her face.

"I was wondering that myself," said Luke, watching the goings-on with folded arms.

"Hugo attacked me." Clary tried not to wince as the astringent liquid stung her wounds.

"Hugo?" Luke blinked.

"Hodge's bird. I think it was his bird, anyway. Maybe it was Valentine's."

"Hugin," Luke said softly. "Hugin and Munin were Valentine's pet birds. Their names mean 'Thought' and 'Memory.'"

"Well, they should mean 'Attack' and 'Kill,'" said Clary. "Hugo almost tore my eyes out."

"That's what he's trained to do." Luke was tapping the fingers of one hand against his other arm. "Hodge must have taken him in after the Uprising. But he'd still be Valentine's creature."

"Just like Hodge was," Clary said, wincing as Gretel cleaned the long slash along her arm, which was crusted with dirt and dried blood. Then Gretel began bandaging it up neatly.

"Clary—"

"I don't want to talk about the past anymore," she said fiercely. "I want to know what we're going to do now. Now Valentine's got my mom, Jace—and the Cup. And we've got nothing."

"I wouldn't say we have nothing," said Luke. "We have a powerful wolf pack. The problem is that we don't know where Valentine is."

Clary shook her head. Lank strings of hair fell into her eyes, and she tossed them back impatiently. God, she was filthy. The one thing she wanted more than anything else—*almost* anything else—was a shower. "Doesn't Valentine have some kind of hideout? A secret lair?"

"If he does," said Luke, "he has kept it secret indeed."

Gretel released Clary, who moved her arm gingerly. The greenish ointment Gretel had smeared on the cut had minimized the pain, but the arm still felt stiff and wooden. "Wait a second," Clary said.

"I never understand why people say that," Luke said, to no one in particular. "I wasn't going anywhere."

"Could Valentine be somewhere in New York?"

"Possibly."

"When I saw him at the Institute, he came through a Portal. Magnus said there are only two Portals in New York. One at Dorothea's, and one at Renwick's. The one at Dorothea's was destroyed, and I can't really see him hiding out there anyway, so—"

"Renwick's? " Luke looked baffled. "Renwick isn't a

Shadowhunter name."

"What if Renwick isn't a person, though?" said Clary. "What if it's a place? *Renwick's*. Like a restaurant, or ... or a hotel or something."

Luke's eyes went suddenly wide. He turned to Gretel, who was advancing on him with the medical kit. "Get me a phone book," he said.

She stopped in her tracks, holding the tray out toward him in an accusatory manner. "But, sir, your *wounds*—"

"Forget my wounds and get me a phone book," he snapped. "We're in a police station. You'd think there'd be plenty of old ones around."

With a look of disdainful exasperation Gretel set the tray down on the ground and marched out of the room. Luke looked at Clary over his spectacles, which had slid partway down his nose. "Good thinking."

She didn't reply. There was a hard knot at the center of her stomach. She found herself trying to breathe around it. The beginning of a thought tickled at the edge of her mind, wanting to resolve itself into a full-blown realization. But she pushed it firmly down and away. She couldn't afford to give her resources, her energy, to anything but the issue immediately at hand.

Gretel returned with damp-looking yellow pages and thrust them at Luke. He read the book standing up while the wolf-woman attacked his injured side with bandages and sticky pots of ointment. "There are seven Renwicks in the phone book," he said finally. "No restaurants, hotels, or other locations." He pushed his spectacles up; they slid down again instantly. "They are not Shadowhunters," he said, "and it seems unlikely to me that Valentine would set up headquarters in the home of a mundane or a Downworlder. Though, perhaps—"

"Do you have a phone?" Clary interrupted.

"Not on me." Luke, still holding the phone book, peered under it at Gretel. "Could you get the telephone?"

With a disgusted snort she tossed the wad of bloody cloths she'd been holding onto the floor, and stalked out of the room a second time. Luke set the phone book down on the table, picked up the roll of bandaging, and began winding it around the diagonal cut across his ribs. "Sorry," he said, as Clary stared. "I know it's disgusting."

"If we catch Valentine," she asked abruptly, "can we kill him?"

Luke nearly dropped the bandages. "What?"

She fiddled with a stray thread poking out of the pocket of her jeans. "He killed my older brother. He killed my grandparents. Didn't he?"

Luke set the bandages on the table and pulled his shirt down. "And you think killing him will what? Erase those things?"

Gretel returned before Clary could say anything to that. She wore a martyred expression and handed Luke a clunky-looking old-fashioned cell phone. Clary wondered who paid the phone bills.

Clary held her hand out. "Let me make a call."

Luke seemed hesitant. "Clary…"

"It's about Renwick's. It'll only take a second."

He handed her the phone warily. She punched in the number, and half-turned away from him to give herself the illusion of privacy.

Simon picked up on the third ring. "Hello?"

"It's me."

His voice climbed an octave. "Are you all right?"

"I'm fine. Why? Have you heard anything from Isabelle?"

"No. What would I have heard from Isabelle? *Is* there something wrong? Is it Alec?"

"No," Clary said, not wanting to lie and say that Alec was fine. "It's not Alec. Look, I just need you to Google something for me."

Simon snorted. "You're kidding. Don't they have a computer there? You know what, don't answer that." She heard the sounds of a door opening and the thump-meow as Simon's mother's cat was banished from his perch on the keyboard of his computer. She could picture Simon quite clearly in her head as he sat down, his fingers moving quickly over the keyboard. "What do you want me to look up?"

She told him. She could feel Luke's worried eyes on her as she talked. It was the same way he'd looked at her when she was eleven years old and had the flu with a spiking fever. He'd brought her ice cubes to suck on and had read to her out of her favorite books, doing all the voices.

"You're right," Simon said, snapping her out of her reverie. "It's a place. Or at least, it was a place. It's abandoned now."

Her sweaty hand slipped on the phone, and she tightened her grip. "Tell me about it."

"The most famous of the lunatic asylums, debtor's prisons, and hospitals built on Roosevelt Island in the 1800s," Simon read dutifully. *"Renwick Smallpox Hospital was designed by architect Jacob Renwick and intended to quarantine the poorest victims of Manhattan's uncontrollable smallpox epidemic. Most who entered*

the macabre Gothic structure would die within its walls. During the next century the hospital was abandoned to disrepair. Public access to the ruin is forbidden."

"Okay, that's enough," said Clary, her heart pounding. "That's *got* to be it. Roosevelt Island? Don't people *live* there?"

"Not everyone lives in the Slope, princess," said Simon, with a fair degree of mock sarcasm. "Anyway, do you need me to give you a ride again or something?"

"No! I'm fine, I don't need anything. I just wanted the information."

"All right." He sounded a little hurt, Clary thought, but told herself it didn't matter. He was safe at home, and that was what was important.

She hung up, turning to Luke. "There's an abandoned hospital at the south end of Roosevelt Island called Renwick's. I think Valentine's there."

Luke shoved his glasses up again. "Blackwell's Island. Of course."

"What do you mean, Blackwell's? I said—"

He cut her off with a gesture. "That's what Roosevelt Island used to be called. Blackwell's. It was owned by an old Shadowhunter family. I should have guessed." He turned to Gretel. "Get Alaric. We're going to need everyone back here as soon as possible." His lips were curled into a half smile that reminded Clary of the cold grin Jace wore during fights. "Tell them to ready themselves for battle."

They made their way up to the street via a circuitous maze of cells and corridors that eventually opened out into what had once been the lobby of a police station. The building was abandoned now, and the slanting light of late afternoon cast strange shadows over the empty desks, the padlocked cabinets pocked with black termite holes, the cracked floor tiles spelling out the motto of the NYPD: *Fidelis ad Mortem*.

"Faithful unto death," said Luke, following her gaze.

"Let me guess," said Clary. "On the inside it's an abandoned police station; from the outside, mundanes only see a condemned apartment building, or a vacant lot, or..."

"Actually it looks like a Chinese restaurant from the outside," Luke said. "Takeout only, no table service."

"A Chinese restaurant?" Clary echoed in disbelief.

He shrugged. "Well, we are in Chinatown. This was the Second Precinct building once."

"People must think it's weird that there's no phone number to call for orders."

Luke grinned. "There is. We just don't answer it much. Sometimes, if they're bored, some of the cubs will deliver someone some mu shu pork."

"You're kidding."

"Not at all. The tips come in handy." He pushed the front door open, letting in a stream of sunlight.

Still not sure whether he was kidding or not, Clary followed Luke across Baxter Street to where his car was parked. The inside of the pickup truck was comfortingly familiar. The faint smell of wood chips and old paper and soap, the faded pair of plush gold dice that she'd given him when she was ten because they looked like the gold dice hanging from the rearview mirror of the *Millennium Falcon*. The discarded gum wrappers and empty coffee cups rolling around on the floor. Clary hauled herself up into the passenger seat, settling back against the headrest with a sigh. She was more tired than she would have liked to admit.

Luke shut the door after her. "Stay right here."

She watched as he talked to Gretel and Alaric, who were standing on the steps of the old police station, waiting patiently. Clary amused herself by letting her eyes fade in and out of focus, watching the glamour appear and disappear. First it was an old police station, then it was a dilapidated storefront sporting a yellow awning that read JADE WOLF CHINESE CUISINE.

Luke was gesturing to his second and third, pointing down the street. His pickup was the first in a line of vans, motorcycles, Jeeps, and even a wrecked-looking old school bus. The vehicles stretched in a line down the block and around the corner. A convoy of werewolves. Clary wondered how they'd begged, borrowed, stolen, or commandeered so many vehicles on such short notice. On the plus side, at least they wouldn't all have to go on the aerial tram.

Luke accepted a white paper bag from Gretel, and with a nod, bounded back to the pickup. Folding his lanky body behind the wheel, he handed her the bag. "You're in charge of this."

Clary peered at it suspiciously. "What is it? Weapons?"

Luke's shoulders shook with soundless laughter. "Steamed bao buns, actually," he said, pulling the truck out into the street. "And coffee."

Clary ripped the bag open as they headed uptown, her stomach growling furiously. She tore a bun apart, savoring the rich savory-salt taste of the pork, the chewiness of the white dough. She washed it down with a swig of black supersweet coffee, and offered a bun to Luke. "Want one?"

"Sure." It was almost like old times, she thought, as they swung onto Canal Street, when they had picked up bags of hot dumplings from the Golden Carriage Bakery and eaten half of them on the drive home over the Manhattan Bridge.

"So tell me about this Jace," said Luke.

Clary nearly choked on a bun. She reached for the coffee, drowning her coughs with hot liquid. "What about him?"

"Do you have any idea what Valentine might want with him?"

"No."

Luke frowned into the setting sun. "I thought Jace was one of the Lightwood kids?"

"No." Clary bit into a third bun. "His last name is Wayland. His father was—"

"Michael Wayland?"

She nodded. "And when Jace was ten years old, Valentine killed him. Michael, I mean."

"That sounds like something he would do," said Luke. His tone was neutral, but there was something in his voice that made Clary look at him sideways. Did he not believe her?

"Jace saw him die," she added, as if to bolster her claim.

"That's awful," said Luke. "Poor messed-up kid."

They were driving over the Fifty-ninth Street Bridge. Clary glanced down and saw the river turned all to gold and blood by the setting sun. She could glimpse the south end of Roosevelt Island from here, though it was just a smudge to the north. "He's not so bad," she said. "The Lightwoods have taken good care of him."

"I can imagine. They were always close with Michael,"

observed Luke, swerving into the left lane. In the side mirror Clary could see the caravan of following vehicles alter its course to mimic his. "They would want to look after his son."

"So what happens when the moon comes up?" she asked. "Are you all going to suddenly wolf out, or what?"

Luke's mouth twitched. "Not exactly. Only the young ones, the ones who've just Changed, can't control their transformations. Most of the rest of us have learned how to, over the years. Only the moon at its fullest can force a Change on me now."

"So when the moon's only partly full, you only feel a little wolfy?" Clary asked.

"You could say that."

"Well, you can go ahead and hang your head out the car window if you feel like it."

Luke laughed. "I'm a werewolf, not a golden retriever."

"How long have you been the clan leader?" she asked abruptly.

Luke hesitated. "About a week."

Clary swung around to stare at him. "A *week?*"

He sighed. "I knew Valentine had taken your mother," he said without much inflection. "I knew I had little chance against him by myself and that I could expect no assistance from the Clave. It took me a day to track down the location of the nearest lycanthrope pack."

"You killed the clan leader so you could take his place?"

"It was the fastest way I could think of to acquire a sizeable number of allies in a short period of time," said Luke, without any regret in his tone, though without any pride either. She remembered spying on him in his house, how she'd noticed the deep scratches on his hands and face and the way he'd winced when he moved his arm. "I had done it before. I was fairly sure I could do it again." He shrugged. "Your mother was gone. I knew I'd made you hate me. I had nothing to lose."

Clary braced her green sneakers against the dashboard. Through the cracked windshield, above the tips of her toes, the moon was rising over the bridge. "Well," she said. "You do now."

The hospital at the southern end of Roosevelt Island was floodlit at night, its ghostly outlines curiously visible against the darkness of the river and the greater illumination of Manhattan. Luke and Clary fell silent as the pickup skirted the tiny island, as the paved road they were on turned to gravel and finally to packed dirt. The road followed the curve of a high chain-link fence, the top of which was strung with curlicues of razor wire like festive loops of ribbon.

When the road grew too bumpy for them to drive any farther, Luke pulled the truck to a stop and killed the lights. He looked at Clary. "Any chance if I asked you to wait here for me, you would?"

She shook her head. "It wouldn't necessarily be any safer in the car. Who knows what Valentine's got patrolling his perimeter?"

Luke laughed softly. "*Perimeter*. Listen to you." He swung himself out of the truck and came around to her side to help her down. She could have jumped down from the truck herself, but it was nice to have him help, the way he'd done since she was too small to climb down on her own.

Her feet hit the dry-packed dirt, sending up puffs of dust.

The cars that had been following them were pulling up, one by one, forming a sort of circle around Luke's truck. Their headlights swept across her view, lighting the chain-link fence to white-silver. Beyond the fence, the hospital itself was a ruin bathed in harsh light that pointed out its dilapidated state: the roofless walls jutting up from the uneven ground like broken teeth, the crenellated stone parapets overgrown with a green carpet of ivy. "It's a wreck," she heard herself say softly, a flicker of apprehension in her voice. "I don't see how Valentine could possibly be hiding here."

Luke glanced past her at the hospital. "It's a strong glamour," he said. "Try to look past the lights." Alaric was walking over to them along the road, the light breeze making his denim jacket flutter open, showing the scarred chest underneath. The werewolves walking behind him looked like completely ordinary people, Clary thought. If she'd seen them all together in a group somewhere, she might have thought they knew each other somehow—there was a certain nonphysical resemblance, a bluntness to their gazes, a forcefulness to their expressions. She might have thought they were farmers, since they looked more sunburned, lean, and rawboned than your average citydweller, or maybe she would have taken them for a biker gang. But they looked nothing like monsters.

They came together in a quick conference by Luke's truck, like a football huddle. Clary, feeling very much on the outside, turned to look at the hospital again. This time she tried to stare around the lights, or through them, the way you could sometimes look past a thin topcoat of paint to see what was underneath. As it usually did, thinking of how she would draw it helped. The lights seemed to fade, and now she was looking across an oak-dusted lawn to an ornate Gothic Revival structure that seemed to loom up above the trees like the bulwark of a great ship. The windows of the lower floors were dark and shuttered, but light poured through the mitred arches of the third-story windows, like a line of flame burning along the ridge of a distant mountain range. A heavy stone porch faced outward, hiding the front door.

"You see it?" It was Luke, who had come up behind her with the padding grace of—well, a wolf.

She was still staring. "It looks more like a castle than a hospital."

Taking her by the shoulders, Luke turned her to face him. "Clary, listen to me." His grip was painfully tight. "I want you to stay next to me. Move when I move. Hold on to my sleeve if you have to. The others are going to stay around us, protecting us, but if you get outside the circle, they won't be able to guard you. They're going to move us toward the door." He dropped his hands from her shoulders, and when he moved, she saw the glint of something metal just inside his jacket. She hadn't realized he was carrying a weapon, but then she remembered what Simon had said about what was in Luke's old green duffel bag and supposed it made sense. "Do you promise you'll do what I say?"

"I promise."

The fence was real, not part of the glamour. Alaric, still in front, rattled it experimentally, then raised a lazy hand. Long claws sprouted from beneath his fingernails, and he slashed at the chain-link with them, slicing the metal to ribbons. They fell in a clattering pile, like Tinkertoys.

"Go." He gestured the others through. They surged forward like one person, a coordinated sea of movement. Gripping Clary's arm, Luke pushed her ahead of him, ducking to follow. They straightened up inside the fence, looking up toward the smallpox hospital, where gathered dark shapes, massed on the porch, were beginning to move down the steps.

Alaric had his head up, sniffing the wind. "The stench of death lies heavy on the air."

Luke's breath left his lungs in a hissing rush. *"Forsaken."*

He shoved Clary behind him; she went, stumbling slightly on the uneven ground. The pack began to move toward her and Luke; as they neared, they dropped to all fours, lips snarling back from their lengthening fangs, limbs extending into long, furred extremities, clothes overgrown by fur. Some tiny instinctual voice in the back of Clary's brain was screaming at her: *Wolves! Run away!* But she fought it and stayed where she was, though she could feel the jump and tremble of nerves in her hands.

The pack encircled them, facing outward. More wolves flanked the circle on either side. It was as if she and Luke were the center of a star. Like that, they began to move toward the front porch of the hospital. Still behind Luke, Clary didn't even see the first of the Forsaken as they struck. She heard a wolf howl as if in pain. The howl went up and up, turning quickly into a snarl. There was a thudding sound, then a gurgling cry and a sound like ripping paper—

Clary found herself wondering if the Forsaken were edible.

She glanced up at Luke. His face was set. She could see them now, beyond the ring of wolves, the scene lit to brilliance by floodlights and the shimmering glow of Manhattan:

dozens of Forsaken, their skin corpse-pale in the moonlight, seared by lesionlike runes. Their eyes were vacant as they hurled themselves at the wolves, and the wolves met them head-on, claws tearing, teeth gouging and rending. She saw one of the Forsaken warriors—a woman—fall back, throat torn out, arms still twitching. Another hacked at a wolf with one arm while the other arm lay on the ground a meter away, blood pulsing from the stump. Black blood, brackish as swamp water, ran in streams, slicking the grass so that Clary's feet slipped out from under her. Luke caught her before she could fall. "Stay with me."

I'm here, she wanted to say, but no words would come out of her mouth. The group was still moving up the lawn toward the hospital, agonizingly slowly. Luke's grip was rigid as iron. Clary couldn't tell who was winning, if anyone. The wolves had size and speed on their side, but the Forsaken moved with a grim inevitability and were surprisingly hard to kill. She saw the big brindled wolf who was Alaric take one down by tearing its legs out from under it, then leaping for its throat. It kept moving even as he ripped it apart, its slashing axe opening up a long red cut along Alaric's glinting coat.

Distracted, Clary hardly noticed the Forsaken that broke through the protective circle, until it loomed up in front of her, as if it had sprung up from the grass at her feet. White-eyed, with matted hair, it raised a dripping knife.

She screamed. Luke whirled, dragging her sideways, and caught the thing's wrist, and twisted. She heard the snap of bone, and the knife fell to the grass. The Forsaken's hand dangled limply, but it kept coming on toward them, evincing no sign of pain. Luke was shouting hoarsely for Alaric. Clary tried to reach the dagger in her belt, but Luke's grip on her arm was too strong. Before she could shout at him to let go of her, a lick of slim silver fire hurtled between them. It was Gretel. She landed with her front paws against the Forsaken's chest, knocking it to the ground. A fierce whine of rage rose from Gretel's throat, but the Forsaken was stronger; it flung her aside like a rag doll and rolled to its feet.

Something lifted Clary off her feet. She shouted, but it was Alaric, half in and half out of wolf form, his hands taloned with sharp claws. Still, they held her gently as he swung her up into his arms.

Luke was motioning at them. "Get her out of here! Get her to the doors!" he was shouting.

"Luke!" Clary twisted in Alaric's grasp.

"Don't look," Alaric said in a growl.

But she did look. Long enough to see Luke start toward Gretel, a blade in his hand, but he was too late. The Forsaken seized up its knife, which had fallen into the blood-wet grass, and sank it into Gretel's back, again and again as she clawed and struggled and finally collapsed, the light in her silvery eyes fading into darkness. With a shout Luke swung his blade at the Forsaken's throat—

"I told you not to look," Alaric growled, turning so that her line of sight was blocked by his looming bulk. They were racing up the steps now, the sound of his clawed feet scraping the granite like nails on a blackboard.

"Alaric," Clary said.

"Yes?"

"I'm sorry I threw a knife at you."

"Don't be. It was a well-placed blow."

She tried to look past him. "Where's Luke?"

"I'm here," Luke said. Alaric turned. Luke was coming up the steps, sliding his sword back into its sheath, which was strapped to his side, beneath his jacket. The blade was black and sticky.

Alaric let Clary slide to the porch. She landed, turning. She couldn't see Gretel or the Forsaken who had killed her, only a mass of heaving bodies and flashing metal. Her face was wet. She reached up with a free hand to see if she was bleeding but realized that she was crying instead. Luke looked at her curiously. "She was only a Downworlder," he said.

Clary's eyes burned. "Don't *say* that."

"I see." He turned to Alaric. "Thank you for taking care of her. While we go on—"

"I'm going with you," said Alaric. He had made most of the transformation to man-form, but his eyes were still wolf's eyes, and his lips were drawn back from teeth as long as toothpicks. He flexed his long-nailed hands.

Luke's eyes were troubled. "Alaric, no."

Alaric's growling voice was flat. "You are the pack leader. I am your second now that Gretel is dead. It would not be right to let you go alone."

"I—" Luke looked at Clary, and then back out at the field in front of the hospital. "I need you out here, Alaric. I'm sorry. That's an order."

Alaric's eyes flashed resentfully, but he stepped aside. The hospital door was ornate heavy carved wood, patterns familiar to Clary, the roses of Idris, curling runes, rayed suns. It gave with the popping noise of a burst latch when Luke kicked at it. He pushed Clary forward as the door swung wide. "Get inside."

She stumbled past him, turned on the threshold. She caught a single brief glimpse of Alaric looking after them, his wolf eyes gleaming. Behind him the lawn in front of the hospital was strewn with bodies, the dirt stained with blood, black and red. When the door slammed shut behind her, cutting off her view, she was grateful.

She and Luke stood in half-lit dimness, in a stone entryway lit by a single torch. After the din of battle the silence was like a smothering cloak. Clary found herself gasping in breaths of air, air that wasn't thick with humidity and the smell of blood.

Luke gripped her shoulder with his hand. "Are you all right?"

She wiped at her cheeks. "You shouldn't have said that. About Gretel being just a Downworlder. I don't think that."

"I'm glad to hear it." He reached for the torch in its metal holder. "I hated the idea of the Lightwoods turning you into a copy of them."

"Well, they haven't."

The torch would not come away in Luke's hand; he frowned. Digging into her pocket, Clary removed the smooth rune-stone Jace had given her for her birthday, and raised it high. Light burst between her fingers, as if she'd cracked a seed of darkness, letting out the illumination trapped inside. Luke let go of the torch.

"Witchlight?" he said.

"Jace gave it to me." She could feel it pulse in her hand, like the heartbeat of a tiny bird. She wondered where Jace was in this gray stone pile of rooms, if he was frightened, if he had wondered whether he'd see her again.

"It's been years since I fought by witchlight," Luke said, and started up the stairs. They creaked loudly under his boots. "Follow me."

The flaring glow of the witchlight cast their shadows, weirdly elongated, against the smooth granite walls. They paused at a stone landing that curved around in an arc. Above them she could see light. "Is this what the hospital used to look like, hundreds of years ago?" Clary whispered.

"Oh, the bones of what Renwick built are still here," said Luke. "But I would imagine Valentine, Blackwell, and the others had the place renovated to be a bit more to their taste. Look here." He scraped a boot along the floor: Clary glanced down and saw a rune carved into the granite beneath their feet: a circle, in the center of which was a Latin motto: *In Hoc Signo Vinces*.

"What does that mean?" she asked.

"It means 'By this sign we will conquer.' It was the motto of the Circle."

She glanced up, toward the light. "So they're here."

"They're here," said Luke, and there was anticipation in the narrow edge of his tone. "Come."

They went up the winding staircase, circling under the light until it was all around them and they were standing at the entrance to a long and narrow corridor. Torches blazed along the passage. Clary closed her hand over the witchlight, and it blinked out like a doused star.

There were doors set at intervals along the corridor, all of them closed tight. She wondered if they had been wards when this had once been a hospital, or perhaps private rooms. As they moved down the corridor, Clary saw the marks of boot-prints, muddy from the grass outside, criss-crossing the passage. Someone had walked here recently.

The first door they tried swung open easily, but the room beyond was empty: only polished wood floor and stone walls, lit to eeriness by the moonlight spilling through the window. The dim roar of the battle outside filled the room, as rhythmic as the sound of the ocean. The second room was full of weapons: swords, maces, and axes. Moonlight ran like silver water over row upon row of cold unsheathed steel. Luke whistled under his breath. "Quite a collection."

"You think Valentine uses all these?"

"Unlikely. I suspect they're for his army." Luke turned away.

The third room was a bedroom. The hangings around the four-poster bed were blue, the Persian carpet patterned in blue, black, and gray, and the furniture was painted white, like the furnishings in a child's room. A thin and ghostly layer of dust covered it all, glinting faintly in the moonlight.

In the bed lay Jocelyn, asleep.

She was on her back, one hand thrown carelessly across her chest, her hair spread across the pillow. She wore a sort of white nightdress Clary had never seen, and she was breathing regularly and quietly. In the piercing moonlight Clary could see the flutter of her mother's eyelids as she dreamed.

With a little scream Clary hurled herself forward—but Luke's outflung arm caught her across the chest like a bar of iron, holding her back. "Wait," he said, his own voice tense with effort. "We have to be careful."

Clary glared at him, but he was looking past her, his expression angry and pained. She followed the line of his gaze and saw what she had not wanted to see before. Silver manacles closed around Jocelyn's wrists and feet, the ends of their chains sunk deep into the stone floor on either side of the bed. The table beside the bed was covered in a weird array of tubes and bottles, glass jars and long, wickedly tipped instruments glinting with surgical steel. A rubberized tube ran from one of the glass jars to a vein in Jocelyn's left arm.

Clary jerked herself away from Luke's restraining hand and lunged toward the bed, wrapping her arms around her mother's unresponsive body. But it was like trying to hug a badly jointed doll. Jocelyn remained motionless and stiff, her slow breathing unaltered.

A week ago Clary would have cried as she had that first terrible night she had discovered her mother missing, cried and called out. But no tears came now, as she let her mother go and straightened up. There was no terror in her now, and no self-pity: only a bitter rage and a need to find the man who'd done this, the one responsible for all of it.

"Valentine," she said.

"Of course." Luke was beside her, touching her mother's face lightly, raising her eyelids. The eyes beneath were as blank as marbles. "She's not drugged," he said. "Some kind of spell, I expect."

Clary let her breath out in a tight half sob. "How do we get her out of here?"

"I can't touch the manacles," said Luke. "Silver. Do you have—"

"The weapons room," Clary said, standing up. "I saw an axe there. Several. We could cut the chains—"

"Those chains are unbreakable." The voice that spoke

from the door was low, gritty, and familiar. Clary spun and saw Blackwell. He was grinning now, wearing the same clotted-blood-colored robes as before, the hood pushed back, muddy boots visible under the hem. "Graymark," he said. "What a nice surprise."

Luke stood up. "If you're surprised, you're an idiot," he said. "I didn't exactly arrive quietly."

Blackwell's cheeks flushed a darker purple, but he didn't move toward Luke. "Clan leader again, are you?" he said, and gave an unpleasant laugh. "Can't break yourself of the habit of getting Downworlders to do your dirty work? Valentine's troops are busy strewing pieces of them all over the lawn, and you're up here safe with your girlfriends." He sneered in Clary's direction. "That one looks a little young for you, Lucian."

Clary flushed angrily, her hands balling into fists, but Luke's voice, when he replied, was polite. "I wouldn't exactly call those *troops*, Blackwell," he said. "They're Forsaken. Tormented once-human beings. If I recall properly, the Clave looks pretty darkly on all that—torturing people, performing black magic. I can't imagine they'll be too pleased."

"Damn the Clave," growled Blackwell. "We don't need them and their half-breed-tolerating ways. Besides, the Forsaken won't be Forsaken much longer. Once Valentine uses the Cup on them, they'll be Shadowhunters as good as the rest of us—better than what the Clave is passing off as warriors these days. Downworlder-loving milksops." He bared his blunt teeth.

"If that is his plan for the Cup," said Luke, "why hasn't he done it already? What's he waiting for?"

Blackwell's eyebrows went up. "Didn't you know? He's got his—"

A silky laugh interrupted him. Pangborn had appeared at his elbow, all in black with a leather strap across his shoulder. "Enough, Blackwell," he said. "You talk too much, as usual." He flashed his pointed teeth at Luke. "Interesting move, Graymark. I didn't think you'd have the stomach for leading your newest clan on a suicide mission."

A muscle twitched in Luke's cheek. "Jocelyn," he said. "What has he done to her?"

Pangborn chuckled musically. "I thought you didn't care."

"I don't see what he wants with her now," Luke went on, ignoring the jibe. "He's got the Cup. She can't be of further use. Valentine was never one for pointless murder. Murder with a point. Now, that might be a different story."

Pangborn shrugged indifferently. "It makes no difference to us what he does with her," he said. "She was his wife. Perhaps he hates her. That's a point."

"Let her go," said Luke, "and we'll leave with her, call the clan off. I'll owe you one."

"No!" Clary's furious outburst made Pangborn and Blackwell swing their stares to her. Both looked faintly incredulous, as if she were a talking cockroach. She turned to Luke. "There's still Jace. He's here somewhere."

Blackwell was chuckling. "Jace? Never heard of a Jace," he said. "Now, I could ask Pangborn to let her out. But I'd rather not. She was always a bitch to me, Jocelyn was. Thought she was better than the rest of us, with her looks and her lineage. Just a pedigreed bitch, that's all. She only married him so she could turn it around on us all—"

"Disappointed you didn't get to marry him yourself,

Blackwell?" was all Luke said in reply, though Clary could hear the cold rage in his voice.

Blackwell, his face purpling, took an angry step forward into the room.

And Luke, moving so swiftly that Clary almost did not see him do it, seized a scalpel from the bedside table and flung it. It flipped twice in the air and sank point-first into Blackwell's throat, cutting off his growling retort. He gagged, eyes rolling up to the whites, and fell to his knees, hands at his throat. Scarlet liquid pulsed between his spread fingers. He opened his mouth as if to speak, but only a thin line of blood dribbled out. His hands slipped from his throat, and he crashed to the ground like a tree falling.

"Oh, dear," said Pangborn, gazing at the fallen body of his comrade with fastidious distaste. "How unpleasant."

Blood from Blackwell's cut throat was spreading across the floor in a viscous red pool. Luke, taking Clary's shoulder, whispered something in her ear. It meant nothing. Clary was aware only of a numb buzzing in her head. She remembered another poem from English class, something about how after the first death you saw, no other deaths mattered. That poet hadn't known what he was talking about.

Luke let her go. "The keys, Pangborn," he said.

Pangborn nudged Blackwell with a foot, and glanced up. He looked irritable. "Or what? You'll throw a syringe at me? There was only one blade on that table. No," he added, reaching behind him and drawing from his shoulder a long and wicked-looking sword, "I'm afraid that if you want the keys, you'll have to come and get them. Not because I care about Jocelyn Morgenstern one way or the other, you understand, but only because I, for one, have been looking forward to killing you ... for years."

He drew the last word out, savoring it with a delicious exultation as he moved forward into the room. His blade flashed, a spear of lightning in the moonlight. Clary saw Luke thrust a hand out toward her—a strangely elongated hand, tipped with nails like tiny daggers—and she realized two things: that he was about to Change, and that what he had whispered in her ear was a single word.

Run.

She ran. She zigzagged around Pangborn, who barely glanced at her, skirted Blackwell's body, and was out the door and in the corridor, heart pounding, before Luke's transformation was complete. She didn't glance back, but she heard a howl, long and piercing, the sound of metal on metal, and a shattering fall. *Breaking glass,* she thought. Perhaps they had knocked over the bedside table.

She dashed down the hall to the weapons room. Inside, she reached for a weathered steel-hafted axe. It stuck firmly to the wall, no matter how hard she yanked at it. She tried a sword, and then a featherstaff—even a small dagger—but not a single blade would come free in her hand. At last, nails torn and fingers bloodied with effort, she had to give up. There was magic in this room, and not runic magic either: something wild and strange, something *dark*.

She backed out of the room. There was nothing on this floor that could help her. She limped down the corridor—she was beginning to feel the ache of true exhaustion in her legs and arms—and found herself at the junction of the stairs. Up or down? Down, she recalled, had been lightless, empty. Of course, there was the witchlight in her pocket, but something in her quailed at the thought of entering those black spaces alone. Upstairs she saw the blaze of more lights, caught a flicker of something that might have been movement.

She went up. Her legs hurt, her feet hurt, everything hurt. Her cuts had been bandaged, but that didn't stop them from stinging. Her face ached where Hugo had slashed her cheek, and her mouth tasted metallic and bitter.

She reached the last landing. It was curved gently like the bow of a ship, as silent here as it had been downstairs; no sound of the fighting outside reached her ears. Another long corridor stretched out in front of her, with the same multiple doors, but here some were open, spilling even more light out into the hallway. She went forward, and some instinct drew her to the last door on her left. Cautiously she glanced inside.

At first the room reminded her of one of the period reconstruction displays in the Metropolitan Museum of Art. It was as if she had stepped into the past—the paneled walls gleamed as if recently polished, as did the endlessly long dining table set with delicate china. An ornate gold-framed mirror adorned the far wall, between two oil portraits in heavy frames. Everything glittered under the torchlight: the plates on the table, heaped with food, the fluted glasses shaped like calla lilies, the linens so white they were blinding. At the end of the room were two wide windows, draped with swags of heavy velvet. Jace stood at one of the windows, so still that for a moment she imagined he was a statue, until she realized she could see the light shining on his hair. His left hand held the curtain aside, and in the dark window she saw the reflection of the dozens of candles inside the room, trapped in the glass like fireflies.

"Jace," she said. She heard her own voice as if from a distance: astonishment, gratitude, longing so sharp it was painful. He turned, dropping the curtain, and she saw the wondering look on his face.

"Jace!" she said again, and ran toward him. He caught her as she flung herself at him. His arms wrapped tightly around her.

"Clary." His voice was almost unrecognizable. "Clary, what are you doing here?"

Her voice was muffled against his shirt. "I came for you."

"You shouldn't have." His grip on her loosened suddenly; he stepped back, holding her a little away from him. "My God," he said, touching her face. "You idiot, what a thing to do." His voice was angry, but the gaze that swept her face, the fingers that gently brushed her hair back, were tender. She had never seen him look like this; there was a sort of fragility about him, as if he might be not just touched but hurt, even. "Why don't you ever *think*?" he whispered.

"I *was* thinking," she said. "I was thinking about you."

He closed his eyes for a moment. "If anything had happened to you..." His hands traced the line of her arms gently, down to her wrists, as if to reassure himself that she was really there. "How did you find me?"

"Luke," she replied. "I came with Luke. To rescue you."

Still holding her, he glanced from her face to the window, a slight frown curling the edge of his mouth. "So those are—you came with the wolf clan?" he asked, an odd tone in his voice.

"Luke's," she said. "He's a werewolf, and—"

"I know." Jace cut her off. "I should have guessed—the manacles." He glanced toward the door. "Where is he?"

"Downstairs," said Clary slowly. "He killed Blackwell. I came up to look for you—"

"He's going to have to call them off," said Jace.

She looked at him uncomprehendingly. "What?"

"Luke," said Jace. "He's going to have to call off his pack. There's been a misunderstanding."

"What, you kidnapped yourself ?" She'd meant to sound teasing, but her voice was too thin. "Come on, Jace."

She yanked at his wrist, but he resisted. He was looking at her intently, and she realized with a jolt what she had not noticed in her first rush of relief.

The last time she had seen him, he'd been cut and bruised, clothes stained with dirt and blood, his hair filthy with ichor and dust. Now he was dressed in a loose white shirt and dark pants, his scrubbed hair falling all around his face, pale gold and flyaway. He swept a few strands out of his eyes with a slim hand, and she saw that his heavy silver ring was back on his finger.

"Are those your clothes?" she asked, baffled. "And—you're all bandaged up..." Her voice trailed off. "Valentine seems to be taking awfully good care of you."

He smiled at her with a weary affection. "If I told you the truth, you'd say I was crazy," he said.

She felt her heart flutter hard against the inside of her chest, like a hummingbird's rapid wing beat. "No, I wouldn't."

"My father gave me these clothes," he said.

The flutter became a rapid pounding. "Jace," she said carefully, "your father is dead."

"No." He shook his head. She had the sense that he was holding back some enormous feeling, like horror or delight—or both. "I thought he was, but he isn't. It's all been a mistake."

She remembered what Hodge had said about Valentine and his ability to tell charming and convincing lies. "Is this something Valentine told you? Because he's a liar, Jace. Remember what Hodge said. If he's telling you your father is alive, it's a lie to get you to do what he wants."

"I've seen my father," said Jace. "I've talked to him. He gave me this." He tugged on the new, clean shirt, as if it were ineluctable proof. "My father isn't dead. Valentine didn't kill him. Hodge lied to me. All these years I thought he was dead, but he wasn't."

Clary glanced around wildly, at the room with its shining china and guttering torches and empty, glaring mirrors. "Well, if your father's really in this place, then where is he? Did Valentine kidnap him, too?"

Jace's eyes were shining. The neck of his shirt was open and she could see the thin white scars that covered his collarbone, like cracks in the smooth golden skin. "My father—"

The door of the room, which Clary had shut behind her, opened with a creak, and a man walked into the room.

It was Valentine. His silvery close-cropped hair gleamed like a polished steel helmet and his mouth was hard. He wore a waist sheath on his thick belt and the hilt of a long sword protruded from the top of it. "So," he said, resting a hand on the hilt as he spoke, "have you gathered your things? Our Forsaken can hold off the wolf-men for only so—"

Seeing Clary, he broke off midsentence. He was not the sort of man who was ever really caught off guard, but she saw the flicker of astonishment in his eyes. "What is this?" he asked, turning his glance to Jace.

But Clary was already fumbling at her waist for the dagger. She seized it by the hilt, jerking it out of its scabbard, and drew her hand back. Rage pounded behind her eyes like a drumbeat. She could kill this man. She *would* kill him.

Jace caught at her wrist. "No."

She could not contain her disbelief. "But, Jace—"

"Clary," he said firmly. "This is my father."

23
VALENTINE

"I see I've interrupted something," said Valentine, his voice as dry as a desert afternoon. "Son, would you care to tell me who this is? One of the Lightwood children, perhaps?"

"No," said Jace. He sounded tired and unhappy, but the hand on her wrist didn't loosen. "This is Clary. Clarissa Fray. She's a friend of mine. She—"

Valentine's black eyes raked her slowly, from the top of her disheveled head to the toes of her scuffed sneakers. They fastened on the dagger still gripped in her hand.

An indefinable look passed over his face—part amusement, part irritation. "Where did you come by that blade, young lady?"

Clary answered coldly. "Jace gave it to me."

"Of course he did," said Valentine. His tone was mild. "May I see it?"

"No!" Clary took a step back, as if she thought he might lunge at her, and felt the blade plucked neatly out of her fingers. Jace, holding the dagger, looked at her with an apologetic expression. "*Jace*," she hissed, putting every ounce of the betrayal she felt into the single syllable of his name.

All he said was, "You still don't understand, Clary." With a sort of deferential care that made her feel sick to her stomach, he went to Valentine and handed him the dagger. "Here you go, Father."

Valentine took the dagger in his big, long-boned hand and examined it. "This is a *kindjal*, a Circassian dagger. This particular one used to be one of a matched pair. Here, see the star of the Morgensterns, carved into the blade." He turned it over, showing it to Jace. "I'm surprised the Lightwoods never noticed it."

"I never showed it to them," said Jace. "They let me have my own private things. They didn't pry."

"Of course they didn't," said Valentine. He handed the *kindjal* back to Jace. "They thought you were Michael Wayland's son."

Jace, sliding the red-hilted dagger into his belt, looked up. "So did I," he said softly, and in that moment Clary saw that this was no joke, that Jace was not just playing along for his own purposes. He really thought Valentine was his father returned to him.

A cold despair was spreading through Clary's veins. Jace angry, Jace hostile, furious, she could have dealt with, but this new Jace, fragile and shining in the light of his own personal miracle, was a stranger to her.

Valentine looked at her over Jace's tawny head; his eyes were cool with amusement. "Perhaps," he said, "it would be a good idea for you to sit down now, Clary?"

She crossed her arms stubbornly over her chest. "No."

"As you like." Valentine pulled out a chair and seated himself at the head of the table. After a moment Jace sat down as well, beside a half-filled bottle of wine. "But you are going to be hearing some things that might make you wish you had taken a chair."

"I'll let you know," Clary told him, "if that happens."

"Very well." Valentine sat back, his hands behind his head. The neck of his shirt gaped open a little, showing his scarred collarbones. Scarred, like his son's, like all the Nephilim. *A life of scars and killing*, Hodge had said. "Clary," he said again, as if tasting the sound of her name. "Short for Clarissa? Not a name I would have chosen."

There was a grim curl to his lips. *He knows I'm his daughter*, Clary thought. *Somehow, he knows. But he isn't saying it. Why isn't he* saying *it?*

Because of Jace, she realized. Jace would think—she couldn't imagine what he would think. Valentine had seen them embracing when he'd walked in the door. He must know he held a devastating piece of information in his hands. Somewhere behind those fathomless black eyes, his sharp mind was clicking away rapidly, trying to decide how best to use what he knew.

She cast another beseeching glance at Jace, but he was staring down at the wineglass by his left hand, half-full of purplish red liquid. She could see the rapid rise and fall of his chest as he breathed; he was more upset than he was letting on.

"I don't really care what you would have chosen," Clary said.

"I am sure," replied Valentine, leaning forward, "that you don't."

"You're not Jace's father," she said. "You're trying to trick us. Jace's father was Michael Wayland. The Lightwoods know it. Everyone knows it."

"The Lightwoods were misinformed," said Valentine. "They truly believed—*believe* that Jace is the son of their friend Michael. As does the Clave. Even the Silent Brothers do not know who he really is. Although soon enough, they will."

"But the Wayland ring—"

"The ring," said Valentine, looking at Jace's hand, where the ring glittered like snake scales. "I see you've begun wearing it again, Jonathan, just in the last few days. Funny, isn't it, how an *M* worn upside down resembles a *W*? Of course, if you'd bothered to think about it, you'd probably have thought it a little strange that the symbol of the Wayland family would be a falling star. But not at all strange that it would be the symbol of the Morgensterns."

Clary stared. "I have no idea what you mean."

"I forget how regrettably lax mundane education is," Valentine said. "Morgenstern means 'morning star.' As in '*How are thou fallen from heaven, O Lucifer, son of the morning! How art thou cut down to the ground, which didst weaken the nations!*'"

A small shiver passed over Clary. "You mean Satan."

"Or any great power lost," said Valentine, "out of a refusal to serve. As mine was. I would not serve a corrupt government, and for that I lost my family, my lands, almost my life—"

"The Uprising was your *fault*!" snapped Clary. "People died in it! Shadowhunters like you!"

"Clary." Jace leaned forward, nearly knocking over the glass at his elbow. "Just listen to him, will you? It's not like you thought. Hodge lied to us."

"I know," said Clary. "He betrayed us to Valentine. He was Valentine's pawn."

"No," said Jace. "No, Hodge was the one who wanted the Mortal Cup all along. He was the one who sent the Raveners after your mother. My father—Valentine only found out about it afterward, and came to stop him. He brought your mother here to heal her, not to hurt her."

"And you believe that crap?" Clary said in disgust. "It isn't true. Hodge was working for Valentine. They were in it together, getting the Cup. He set us up, it's true, but he was just a tool."

"But he was the one who needed the Mortal Cup," said Jace. "So he could get the curse off him and flee before my father told the Clave about everything he'd done."

"I know that isn't true!" said Clary hotly. "I was there!" She turned on Valentine. "I was in the room when you came to get the Cup. You couldn't see me, but I was there. I saw you. You took the Cup and you lifted the curse off Hodge. He couldn't have done it by himself. He said so."

"I did lift his curse," said Valentine measuredly, "but I was moved by pity. He seemed so pathetic."

"You didn't feel pity. You didn't feel anything."

"That's enough, Clary!" It was Jace. She stared at him. His cheeks were flushed as if he'd been drinking the wine at his elbow, his eyes too bright. "Don't talk to my father like that."

"He's *not your father*!"

Jace looked as if she had slapped him. "Why are you so determined not to believe us?"

"Because she loves you," said Valentine.

Clary felt the blood drain out of her face. She looked at him, not knowing what he might say next, but dreading it. She felt as if she were edging toward a precipice, some terrible hurtling fall into nothing and nowhere. Vertigo gripped her stomach.

"What?" Jace looked surprised.

Valentine was looking at Clary with amusement, as if he could tell he had her pinned there like a butterfly to a board. "She fears I am taking advantage of you," he said. "That I have brainwashed you. It isn't so, of course. If you looked into your own memories, Clary, you would know it."

"Clary." Jace started to get to his feet, his eyes on her. She could see the circles beneath them, the strain he was under. "I—"

"Sit down," said Valentine. "Let her come to it on her own, Jonathan."

Jace subsided instantly, sinking back into the chair. Through the dizziness of vertigo, Clary groped for understanding. *Jonathan*? "I thought your name was Jace," she said. "Did you lie about that, too?"

"No. Jace is a nickname."

She was very near to the precipice now, so close she could almost look down. "For what?"

He looked at her as if he couldn't understand why she was making so much of something so small. "It's my initials," he said. "J. C."

The precipice opened before her. She could see the long

fall into darkness. "Jonathan," she said faintly. "Jonathan Christopher."

Jace's eyebrows drew together. "How did you—?"

Valentine cut in. His voice was soothing. "Jace, I had thought to spare you. I thought a story of a mother who died would hurt you less than the story of a mother who abandoned you before your first birthday."

Jace's slim fingers tightened convulsively around the glass's stem. Clary thought for a moment that it might shatter. "My mother is alive?"

"She is," said Valentine. "Alive, and asleep in one of the downstairs rooms at this very moment. Yes," he said, cutting off Jace before he could speak, "Jocelyn is your mother, Jonathan. And Clary—Clary is your sister."

Jace jerked his hand back. The wineglass tipped, spilling frothing scarlet liquid across the white tablecloth.

"Jonathan," said Valentine.

Jace had gone an awful color, a sort of greenish white. "That's not true," he said. "There's been a mistake. It couldn't possibly be true."

Valentine looked steadily at his son. "A cause for rejoicing," he said in a low, contemplative voice, "I would have thought. Yesterday you were an orphan, Jonathan. And now a father, a mother, a sister, you never knew you had."

"It isn't possible," said Jace again. "Clary isn't my sister. If she were..."

"Then what?" Valentine said.

Jace did not reply, but his sick look of nauseous horror was enough for Clary. Stumbling a little, she came around the table and knelt beside his chair, reaching for his hand. "Jace—"

He jerked away from her, his fingers knotting in the sodden tablecloth. *"Don't."*

Hatred for Valentine burned in her throat like unshed tears. He had held back, and by not saying what he knew—that she was his daughter—made her complicit in his silence. And now, having dropped the truth on them with the weight of a crushing boulder, he sat back to watch the results with a cool consideration. How could Jace not see how hateful he was?

"Tell me it's not true," Jace said, staring at the tablecloth.

Clary swallowed against the burning in her throat. "I can't do that."

Valentine sounded as if he were smiling. "So you admit now that I've been telling the truth all this time?"

"No," she shot back without looking at him. "You're telling lies with a little bit of the truth mixed in, is all."

"This grows tiresome," said Valentine. "If you want to hear the truth, Clarissa, this is the truth. You have heard stories of the Uprising and so you think I am a villain. Is that correct?"

Clary said nothing. She was looking at Jace, who seemed as if he might be about to throw up. Valentine went on relentlessly. "It is simple, really. The story you heard was true in some of its parts, but not in others—lies mixed in with a little truth, as you said. The fact is that Michael Wayland is not and has never been Jace's father. Wayland was killed during the Uprising. I assumed Michael's name and place when I fled the Glass City with my son. It was easy enough; Wayland had no real relations, and his closest friends, the Lightwoods, were in exile. He himself would have been in disgrace for his part in the Uprising, so I lived that disgraced life, quietly enough, alone with Jace on the Waylands' estate. I read my books. I raised my son. And I bided my time." He fingered the filigreed edge of a glass thoughtfully. He was left-handed, Clary saw. Like Jace.

"Ten years on, I received a letter. The writer of the letter indicated that he knew my true identity, and if I were not prepared to take certain steps, he would reveal it. I did not know who the letter was from, but it did not matter. I was not prepared to give the writer of it what he wanted. Besides, I knew my safety was compromised, and would be unless he thought me dead, beyond his reach. I staged my death a second time, with the help of Blackwell and Pangborn, and for Jace's own safety made sure that my son would be sent here, to the protection of the Lightwoods."

"So you let Jace think you were dead? You just let him think you were dead, all these years? That's despicable."

"Don't," said Jace again. He had raised his hands to cover his face. He spoke against his own fingers, voice muffled. "Don't, Clary."

Valentine looked at his son with a smile Jace couldn't see. "Jonathan had to think I was dead, yes. He had to think he was Michael Wayland's son, or the Lightwoods would not have protected him as they did. It was Michael they owed a debt to, not me. It was on Michael's account that they loved him, not mine."

"Maybe they loved him on his own account," said Clary.

"A commendably sentimental interpretation," said Valentine, "but unlikely. You do not know the Lightwoods as

I once did." He did not seem to see Jace's flinch, or if he did, he ignored it. "It hardly matters, in the end," Valentine added. "The Lightwoods were intended as protection for Jace, not as a replacement family, you see. He has a family. He has a father."

Jace made a noise in his throat, and moved his hands away from his face. "My mother—"

"Fled after the Uprising," said Valentine. "I was a disgraced man. The Clave would have hunted me down had they thought I lived. She could not bear her association with me, and ran." The pain in his voice was palpable—and faked, Clary thought bitterly. The manipulative creep. "I did not know she was pregnant at the time. With Clary." He smiled a little, running his finger slowly down the wineglass. "But blood calls to blood, as they say," he went on. "Fate has borne us to this convergence. Our family, together again. We can use the Portal," he said, turning his gaze to Jace. "Go to Idris. Back to the manor house."

Jace shivered a little but nodded, still staring numbly at his hands.

"We'll be together there," said Valentine. "As we should be."

That sounds terrific, thought Clary. *Just you, your comatose wife, your shell-shocked son, and your daughter who hates your guts. Not to mention that your two kids may be in love with each other. Yeah, that sounds like a perfect family reunion.* Aloud, she said only, "I am not going anywhere with you, and neither is my mother."

"He's right, Clary," said Jace hoarsely. He flexed his hands; the fingertips were stained red. "It's the only place for us to go. We can sort things out there."

"You can't be serious—"

An enormous crash came from downstairs, so loud that it sounded as if a wall of the hospital had collapsed in on itself. *Luke*, Clary thought, springing to her feet.

Jace, despite his look of nauseous horror, responded automatically, half-rising from his chair, his hand going to his belt. "Father, they're—"

"They're on their way." Valentine rose to his feet. Clary heard footsteps. A moment later the door of the room was flung open, and Luke stood on the threshold.

Clary bit back a cry. He was covered in blood, his jeans and shirt dark and clotted, the lower half of his face bearded with it. His hands were red to the wrists, the blood that coated them still wet and running. She had no idea if any of the blood was his. She heard herself cry out his name, and then she was running across the room to him and nearly tripping over herself in her eagerness to grab at his shirt-front and hang on, the way she hadn't done since she was eight years old.

For a moment his big hand came up and cupped the back of her head, holding her against him in a one-armed bear hug. Then he pushed her away gently. "I'm all over blood," he said. "Don't worry—it isn't mine."

"Then whose is it?" It was Valentine's voice, and Clary turned, Luke's arm protectively across her shoulders. Valentine was watching them both, his eyes narrow and calculating. Jace had risen to his feet and come around the table and was standing hesitantly behind his father. Clary could not remember him ever doing anything hesitantly before.

"Pangborn's," said Luke.

Valentine passed a hand over his face, as if the news pained him. "I see. Did you tear out his throat with your teeth?"

"Actually," said Luke, "I killed him with this." With his free hand he held out the long thin dagger he had killed the Forsaken with. In the light she could see the blue stones in the hilt. "Do you remember it?"

Valentine looked at it, and Clary saw his jaw tighten. "I do," he said, and Clary wondered if he, too, were remembering their earlier conversation.

This is a kindjal, *a Circassian dagger. This particular one used to be one of a matched pair.*

"You handed it to me seventeen years ago and told me to end my life with it," said Luke, the weapon gripped tightly in his hand. The blade of it was longer than the blade of the red-hilted *kindjal* in Jace's belt; it was somewhere between a dagger and a sword, and its blade was needle-tipped. "And I nearly did."

"Do you expect me to deny it?" There was pain in Valentine's voice, the memory of an old grief. "I tried to save you from yourself, Lucian. I made a grave mistake. If only I'd had the strength to kill you myself, you could have died a man."

"Like you?" asked Luke, and in that moment Clary saw something in him of the Luke she'd always known, who could tell when she was lying or pretending, who called her on it when she was being arrogant or untruthful. In the bitterness of his voice she heard the love he'd once had for Valentine, curdled into a weary hatred. "A man who chains his unconscious wife to a bed in the hopes of torturing her for information when she wakes up? That's your *bravery*?"

Jace was staring at his father. Clary saw the seizure of

anger that momentarily twisted Valentine's features; then it was gone, and his face was smooth. "I didn't torture her," he said. "She is chained for her own protection."

"Against *what?*" Luke demanded, stepping farther into the room. "The only thing endangering her is you. The only thing that ever endangered her was you. She's spent her life running to get away from you."

"I loved her," said Valentine. "I never would have hurt her. It was you who turned her against me."

Luke laughed. "She didn't need me to turn her against you. She learned to hate you on her own."

"That is a *lie!*" Valentine roared with sudden savagery, and drew his sword from the sheath at his waist. The blade was flat and matte black, patterned with a design of silver stars. He leveled the blade at Luke's heart.

Jace took a step toward Valentine. "Father—"

"Jonathan, *be silent!*" shouted Valentine, but it was too late; Clary saw the shock on Luke's face as he stared at Jace.

"Jonathan?" he whispered.

Jace's mouth twisted. "Don't you call me that," he said fiercely, his gold eyes blazing. "I'll kill you myself if you call me that."

Luke, ignoring the blade pointed at his heart, didn't take his eyes off Jace. "Your mother would be proud," he said, so quietly that even Clary, standing beside him, had to strain to hear it.

"I don't have a mother," said Jace. His hands were shaking. "The woman who gave birth to me walked away from me before I learned to remember her face. I was nothing to her, so she is nothing to me."

"Your mother is not the one who walked away from you," said Luke, his gaze moving slowly to Valentine. "I would have thought even you," he said slowly, "were above using your own flesh and blood as bait. I suppose I was wrong."

"That's enough." Valentine's tone was almost languid, but there was fierceness in it, a hungry threat of violence. "Let go of my daughter, or I'll kill you where you stand."

"I'm not your daughter," said Clary fiercely, but Luke pushed her away from him, so hard that she nearly fell.

"Get out of here," he said. "Get to where it's safe."

"I'm not leaving you!"

"Clary, I mean it. *Get out of here.*" Luke was already lifting his dagger. "This is not your fight."

Clary stumbled away from him, toward the door that led to the landing. Maybe she could run for help, for Alaric—

Then Jace was in front of her, blocking her way to the door. She had forgotten how fast he moved, soft as a cat, quick as water. "Are you insane?" he hissed. "They've broken down the front door. This place will be full of Forsaken."

She shoved at him. "Let me out—"

Jace held her back with a grip like iron. "So they can tear you apart? Not a chance."

A loud clash of metal sounded behind her. Clary pulled away from Jace and saw that Valentine had struck at Luke, who had met his blow with an ear-shattering parry. Their blades ground apart, and now they were moving across the floor in a blur of feints and slashes. "Oh, my God," she whispered. "They're going to kill each other."

Jace's eyes were nearly black. "You don't understand," he said. "This is how it's done—" He broke off and sucked in a breath as Luke slipped past Valentine's guard, catching him a blow across the shoulder. Blood flowed freely, staining the cloth of his white shirt.

Valentine threw back his head and laughed. "A true hit," he said. "I hardly thought you had it in you, Lucian."

Luke stood very straight, the knife blocking his face from Clary's view. "You taught me that move yourself."

"But that was years ago," said Valentine in a voice like raw silk, "and since then, you've hardly had need of a knife, have you? Not when you have claws and fangs at your disposal."

"All the better to tear your heart out with."

Valentine shook his head. "You tore my heart out years ago," he said, and even Clary could not tell if the sorrow in his voice was real or feigned. "When you betrayed and deserted me." Luke struck at him again, but Valentine was moving swiftly back across the floor. For a big man he moved surprisingly lightly. "It was you who turned my wife against her own kind. You came to her when she was weakest, with your piteousness, your helpless need. I was distant and she thought you loved her. She was a fool."

Jace was taut as a wire beside Clary. She could feel his tension, like the sparks given off by a downed electrical cable. "That's your mother Valentine's talking about," she said.

"She abandoned me," said Jace. "Some mother."

"She thought you were *dead*. You want to know how I know that? Because she kept a box in her bedroom. It had your initials on it. J. C."

"So she had a box," said Jace. "Lots of people have boxes. They keep things in them. It's a growing trend, I hear."

"It had a lock of your hair in it. Baby hair. And a photograph, maybe two. She used to take it out every year and cry over it. Awful brokenhearted crying—"

Jace's hand clenched at his side. "Stop it," he said between his teeth.

"Stop what? Telling you the truth? She thought you had died—she'd never have left you if she'd known you were alive. You thought your father was dead—"

"I *saw* him die! Or I thought I did. I didn't just—just hear about it and choose to believe it!"

"She found your burned bones," said Clary quietly. "In the ruins of her house. Along with the bones of her mother and father."

At last Jace looked at her. She saw the disbelief plain in his eyes, and around his eyes, the strain of maintaining that disbelief. She could see, almost as if she saw through a glamour, the fragile construct of his faith in his father that he wore like a transparent armor, protecting him from the truth. Somewhere, she thought, there was a chink in that armor; somewhere, if she could find the right words, it could be breached. "That's ridiculous," he said. "I didn't die—there weren't any bones."

"There were."

"So it was a glamour," he said roughly.

"Ask your father what happened to his mother- and father-in-law," said Clary. She reached to touch his hand. "Ask him if that was a glamour, too—"

"*Shut up!*" Jace's control cracked and he turned on her, livid. Clary saw Luke glance toward them, startled by the noise, and in that moment of distraction Valentine dove under his guard and, with a single forward thrust, drove the blade of his sword into Luke's chest, just below his collarbone.

Luke's eyes flew open as if in astonishment rather than pain. Valentine jerked his hand back, and the blade slid back, stained red to the hilt. With a sharp laugh Valentine struck again, this time knocking the weapon from Luke's hand. It hit the floor with a hollow clang and Valentine kicked it hard, sending it skittering under the table as Luke collapsed.

Valentine raised the black sword over Luke's prone body, ready to deliver the killing stroke. Inlaid silvery stars gleamed along the blade's length and Clary thought, frozen in a moment of horror, *how could anything so deadly be so beautiful?*

Jace, as if knowing what Clary was going to do before she did it, whirled on her. "Clary—"

The frozen moment passed. Clary twisted away from Jace, ducking his reaching hands, and raced across the stone floor to Luke. He was on the ground, supporting himself with one arm; Clary threw herself on him just as Valentine's sword drove downward.

She saw Valentine's eyes as the sword hurtled toward her; it seemed like eons, though it could only have been a split second. She saw that he could stop the blow if he wanted. Saw that he knew it might well strike her if he didn't. Saw that he was going to do it anyway.

She threw her hands up, squeezing her eyes shut—

There was a clang. She heard Valentine cry out, and she looked up to see him holding his empty sword hand, which was bleeding. The red-hilted *kindjal* lay several feet away on the stone floor, next to the black sword. Turning in astonishment, she saw Jace by the door, his arm still raised, and realized he must have flung the dagger with enough force to knock the black sword out of his father's hand.

Very pale, he slowly lowered his arm, his eyes on Valentine—wide and pleading. "Father..."

Valentine looked at his bleeding hand, and for a moment, Clary saw a spasm of rage cross his face, like a light flickering out. His voice, when he spoke, was mild. "That was an excellent throw, Jace."

Jace hesitated. "But your hand. I just thought—"

"I would not have hurt your sister," said Valentine, moving swiftly to retrieve both his sword and the red-hilted *kindjal*, which he stuck through his belt. "I would have stopped the blow. But your family concern is commendable."

Liar. But Clary had no time for Valentine's prevarications. She turned to look at Luke and felt a sharp nauseous pang. Luke was lying on his back, eyes half-closed, his breathing ragged. Blood bubbled up from the hole in his torn shirt. "I need a bandage," Clary said in a choked voice. Some cloth, anything."

"Don't move, Jonathan," said Valentine in a steely voice, and Jace froze where he was, hand already reaching toward his pocket. "Clarissa," her father said, in a voice as oily as steel slicked with butter, "this man is an enemy of our family, an enemy of the Clave. We are hunters, and that means sometimes we are killers. Surely you understand that."

"*Demon* hunters," said Clary. "*Demon* killers. Not *murderers*. There's a difference."

"He is a demon, Clarissa," said Valentine, still in the same soft voice. "A demon with a man's face. I know how deceptive such monsters can be. Remember, I spared him once myself."

"*Monster?*" echoed Clary. She thought of Luke, Luke pushing her on the swings when she was five years old, higher, always higher; Luke at her graduation from middle school, camera clicking away like a proud father's; Luke sorting through each box of books as it arrived at his store, looking for anything she might like and putting it aside. Luke lifting her up to pull apples down from the trees near his farmhouse. Luke, whose place as her father this man was trying to take. "Luke isn't a monster," she said in a voice that matched Valentine's, steel for steel. "Or a murderer. You are."

"Clary!" It was Jace.

Clary ignored him. Her eyes were fixed on her father's cold black ones. "You murdered your wife's parents, not in battle but in cold blood," she said. "And I bet you murdered Michael Wayland and his little boy, too. Threw their bones in with my grandparents' so that my mother would think you and Jace were dead. Put your necklace around Michael Wayland's neck before you burned him so everyone would think those bones were yours. After all your talk about the untainted blood of the Clave—you didn't care at all about their blood or their innocence when you killed them, did you? Slaughtering old people and children in cold blood, *that's* monstrous."

Another spasm of rage contorted Valentine's features. "That's *enough*!" Valentine roared, raising the black-star sword again, and Clary heard the truth of who he was in his voice, the rage that had propelled him all his life. The unending seething rage. "Jonathan! Drag your sister out of my way, or by the Angel, I'll knock her down to kill the monster she's protecting!"

For the briefest moment Jace hesitated. Then he raised

his head. "Certainly, Father," he said, and crossed the room to Clary. Before she could throw up her hands to ward him off, he had caught her up roughly by the arm. He yanked her to her feet, pulling her away from Luke.

"Jace," she whispered, appalled.

"Don't," he said. His fingers dug painfully into her arms. He smelled of wine and metal and sweat. "Don't talk to me."

"But—"

"I said, don't *talk*." He shook her, hard. She stumbled, regained her footing, and looked up to see Valentine standing, gloating over Luke's crumpled body. He reached out a fastidious booted toe and shoved Luke, who made a choking sound.

"Leave him alone!" Clary shouted, trying to yank herself out of Jace's grasp. It was useless—he was much too strong.

"Stop it," he hissed in her ear. "You'll just make it worse for yourself. It's better if you don't look."

"Like you do?" she hissed back. "Shutting your eyes and pretending something's not happening doesn't make it not true, Jace. You ought to know better—"

"Clary, *stop*." His tone almost brought her up short. He sounded desperate.

Valentine was chuckling. "If only I had thought," he said, "to bring with me a blade of real silver, I could have dispatched you in the true manner of your kind, Lucian."

Luke snarled something Clary couldn't hear. She hoped it was rude. She tried to twist away from Jace. Her feet slipped and he caught her, yanking her back with agonizing force. He had his arms around her, she thought, but not the way she had once hoped, not as she had ever imagined.

"At least let me get up," said Luke. "Let me die on my feet."

Valentine looked at him along the length of the blade, and shrugged. "You can die on your back or on your knees," he said. "But only a man deserves to die standing, and you are not a man."

"NO!" Clary shouted as, not looking at her, Luke began to pull himself painfully into a kneeling position.

"Why do you have to make it worse for yourself ?" Jace demanded in a low, tense whisper. "I told you not to look."

She was panting with exertion and pain. "Why do you have to *lie* to yourself ?"

"I'm not lying!" His grip on her tightened savagely, though she hadn't tried to pull away. "I just want what's good in my life—my father—my family—I can't lose it all again."

Luke was kneeling upright now. Valentine had raised the bloodstained sword. Luke's eyes were closed, and he was murmuring something: words, a prayer, Clary didn't know. She twisted in Jace's arms, wrenching around so that she could look up into his face. His lips were drawn thin, his jaw set, but his eyes—

The fragile armor was breaking. It needed only a last push from her. She struggled for the words.

"You have a family," she said. "Family, those are just the people who love you. Like the Lightwoods love you. Alec, Isabelle—" Her voice cracked. "Luke is my family, and you're going to make me watch him die just like you thought you watched your father die when you were ten years old? Is this what you want, Jace? Is this the kind of man you want to be? Like—"

She broke off, suddenly terrified that she had gone too far.

"Like my father," he said.

His voice was icy, distant, flat as the blade of a knife.

I've lost him, she thought despairingly.

"Get down," he said, and pushed her, hard. She stumbled, fell to the ground, rolled onto one knee. Kneeling upright, she saw Valentine raise his sword high over his head. The glow from the chandelier overhead exploding off the blade sent brilliant points of light stabbing into her eyes. *"Luke!"* she shrieked.

The blade slammed home—into the floor. Luke was no longer there. Jace, having moved faster than Clary would have thought possible even for a Shadowhunter, had knocked him out of the way, sending him sprawling to the side. Jace stood facing his father over the quivering hilt of the sword, his face white, but his gaze steady.

"I think you should leave," Jace said.

Valentine stared incredulously at his son. *"What did you say?"*

Luke had pulled himself into a sitting position. Fresh blood stained his shirt. He stared as Jace reached out a hand and gently, almost disinterestedly, caressed the hilt of the sword that had been driven into the floor. "I think you heard me, Father."

Valentine's voice was like a whip. "Jonathan Morgenstern—"

Quick as lightning, Jace seized the hilt of the sword, tore it free from the floorboards, and raised it. He held it lightly, level and flat, the point hovering a few inches below his father's chin. "That's not my name," he said. "My name is Jace Wayland."

Valentine's eyes were still fixed on Jace; he barely seemed to notice the sword at his throat. "*Wayland?*" he roared. "You have no Wayland blood! Michael Wayland was a stranger to you—"

"So," said Jace calmly, "are you." He jerked the sword to the left. "Now move."

Valentine was shaking his head. "Never. I will not take orders from a child."

The tip of the sword kissed Valentine's throat. Clary stared in fascinated horror. "I am a very well-trained child," Jace said. "You instructed me yourself in the precise art of killing. I only need to move two fingers to cut your throat, did you know that?" His eyes were steely. "I suppose you did."

"You're skilled enough," said Valentine. His tone was dismissive, but, Clary noticed, he was standing very still indeed. "But you could not kill me. You have always been softhearted."

"Perhaps he couldn't." It was Luke, on his feet now, pale and bloody but upright. "But I could. And I'm not entirely sure he could stop me."

Valentine's feverish eyes flicked to Luke, and back to his son. Jace hadn't turned when Luke spoke, but stood still as a statue, the sword unmoving in his hand. "You hear the monster threatening me, Jonathan," said Valentine. "You side with *it?*"

"It has a point," said Jace mildly. "I'm not entirely sure I could stop him if he wanted to do you damage. Werewolves heal so fast."

Valentine's lip curled. "So," he spat, "like your mother,

you prefer this creature, this half-bred demon thing to your own blood, your own family?"

For the first time the sword in Jace's hand seemed to tremble. "You left me when I was a child," he said in a measured voice. "You let me think you were dead and you sent me away to live with strangers. You never told me I had a mother, a sister. You left me *alone*." The word was a cry.

"I did it for you—to keep you safe," Valentine protested.

"If you cared about Jace, if you cared about blood, you wouldn't have killed his grandparents. You murdered innocent people," Clary cut in, furious.

"Innocent?" snapped Valentine. "No one is innocent in a war! They sided with Jocelyn against me! They would have let her take my son from me!"

Luke let out a hissing breath. "You knew she was going to leave you," he said. "You knew she was going to run, even before the Uprising?"

"Of course I knew!" roared Valentine. His icy control had cracked and Clary could see the molten rage seething underneath, coiling the tendons in his neck, clenching his hands into fists. "I did what I had to to protect my own, and in the end I gave them more than they ever deserved: the funeral pyre awarded only to the greatest warriors of the Clave!"

"You burned them," said Clary flatly.

"Yes!" shouted Valentine. *"I burned them."*

Jace made a strangled noise. "My grandparents—"

"You never knew them," said Valentine. "Don't pretend to a grief you do not feel."

The point of the sword was trembling more rapidly now. Luke put a hand on Jace's shoulder. "Steady," he said.

Jace didn't look at him. He was breathing as if he had been running. Clary could see the sweat shimmering on the sharp divide of his collarbones, sticking his hair to his temples. The veins were visible along the backs of his hands. *He's going to kill him*, she thought. *He's going to kill Valentine*.

She stepped forward hastily. "Jace—we need the Cup. Or you know what he'll do with it."

Jace licked his dry lips. "The Cup, Father. Where is it?"

"In Idris," said Valentine calmly. "Where you will never find it."

Jace's hand was shaking. "Tell me—"

"Give me the sword, Jonathan." It was Luke, his voice calm, even kind.

Jace sounded as if he were speaking from the bottom of a well. "What?"

Clary took a step forward. "Give Luke the sword. Let him have it, Jace."

He shook his head. "I can't do that."

She took another step forward; one more, and she'd be close enough to touch him. "Yes, you can," she said gently. "Please."

He didn't look at her. His eyes were locked on his father's. The moment stretched out and out, interminable. At last he nodded, curtly, without lowering his hand. But he did let Luke move to stand beside him, and place his hand over Jace's, on the hilt of the blade. "You can let go now, Jonathan," Luke said— and then, seeing Clary's face, amended himself. "Jace."

Jace seemed not to have heard him. He released the hilt and moved away from his father. Some of Jace's color had come back, and he was now a shade more like putty, his lip bloody where he'd bitten it. Clary ached to touch him, put her arms around him, knew he'd never let her.

"I have a suggestion," said Valentine to Luke, in a surprisingly even tone.

"Let me guess," said Luke. "It's 'Don't kill me,' isn't it?"

Valentine laughed, a sound without any humor in it. "I would hardly lower myself to ask you for my life," he said.

"Good," said Luke, nudging the other man's chin with his blade. "I'm not going to kill you unless you force my hand, Valentine. I draw the line at murdering you in front of your own children. What I want is the Cup."

The roaring downstairs was louder now. Clary could hear what sounded like footsteps in the corridor outside. "Luke—"

"I hear it," he snapped.

"The Cup's in Idris, I told you," said Valentine, his eyes shifting past Luke.

Luke was sweating. "If it's in Idris, you used the Portal to bring it there. I'll go with you. Bring it back." Luke's eyes were darting. There was more movement in the corridor outside now, sounds of shouting, of something shattering. "Clary, stay with your brother. After we go through, you use the Portal to take you to a safe place."

"I won't leave here," said Jace.

"Yes, you will." Something thudded against the door. Luke raised his voice, "Valentine, the Portal. Move."

"Or what?" Valentine's eyes were fixed on the door with a considering look.

"I'll kill you if you force my hand," Luke said. "In front of them, or not. The Portal, Valentine. Now."

Valentine spread his hands wide. "If you wish."

He stepped lightly backward, just as the door exploded inward, hinges scattering across the floor. Luke ducked out of the way to avoid being crushed by the falling door, turning as he did so, the sword still in his hand.

A wolf stood in the doorway, a mountain of growling, brindled fur, shoulders hunched forward, lips curled back over snarling teeth. Blood ran from innumerable gashes in his pelt.

Jace was swearing softly, a seraph blade already in his hand. Clary caught at his wrist. "Don't—he's a friend."

Jace shot her an incredulous glance, but lowered his arm.

"Alaric—" Luke shouted something then, in a language Clary didn't understand. Alaric snarled again, crouching closer to the floor, and for a confused moment she thought he was going to hurl himself at Luke. Then she saw Valentine's hand at his belt, the flash of red jewels, and realized that she had forgotten that he still had Jace's dagger.

She heard a voice shout Luke's name, thought it was her own—then realized that her throat seemed glued shut, and that it was Jace who had shouted.

Luke slewed around, excruciatingly slowly, it seemed, as the knife left Valentine's hand and flew toward him like a silver butterfly, turning over and over in the air. Luke raised his blade—and something huge and tawny gray hurtled between him and Valentine. She heard Alaric's howl, rising, suddenly cut off; heard the sound as the blade struck. She gasped and tried to run forward, but Jace pulled her back.

The wolf crumpled at Luke's feet, blood spattering his

fur. Feebly, with his paws, Alaric clawed at the hilt of the knife protruding from his chest.

Valentine laughed. "And this is how you repay the unquestioning loyalty you bought so cheaply, Lucian," he said. "By letting them die for you." He was backing up, his eyes still on Luke.

Luke, white-faced, looked at him, and then down at Alaric; shook his head once, and dropped to his knees, leaning over the fallen werewolf. Jace, still holding Clary by the shoulders, hissed, "Stay here, you hear me? Stay *here*," and set off after Valentine, who was hurrying, inexplicably, toward the far wall. Did he plan to throw himself out the window? Clary could see his reflection in the big, gold-framed mirror as he neared it, and the expression on his face—a sort of sneering relief—filled her with a murderous rage.

"Like hell I will," she muttered, moving to follow Jace. She paused only to grab the blue-hilted *kindjal* from the floor beneath the table, where Valentine had kicked it. The weapon in her hand felt comfortable now, reassuring, as she pushed a fallen chair out of her way and approached the mirror.

Jace had the seraph blade out, its light casting a hard illumination upward, darkening the circles under his eyes, the hollows of his cheeks. Valentine had turned and stood outlined in its light, his back against the mirror. In its surface Clary could also see Luke behind them; he had set his sword down, and was pulling the red-hilted *kindjal* out of Alaric's chest, gently and carefully. She felt sick and gripped her own blade more tightly. "Jace—" she began.

He didn't turn to look at her, though of course he could

see her in the mirror's reflection. "Clary, I told you to wait."

"She's like her mother," said Valentine. One of his hands was behind him; he was running it along the edge of the mirror's heavy gilt frame. "Doesn't like to do what she's told."

Jace wasn't shaking as he had been earlier, but Clary could sense how thin his control had been stretched, like the skin over a drum. "I'll go with him to Idris, Clary. I'll bring the Cup back."

"No, you can't," Clary began, and saw, in the mirror, how his face twisted.

"Do you have a better idea?" he demanded.

"But Luke—"

"Lucian," said Valentine in a voice like silk, "is attending to a fallen comrade. As for the Cup, and Idris, they are not far. Through the looking glass, one might say."

Jace's eyes narrowed. "The mirror is the Portal?"

Valentine's lips thinned and he dropped his hand, moving back from the mirror as the image in it swirled and changed like watercolors running in a painting. Instead of the room with its dark wood and candles, now Clary could see green fields, the thick emerald leaves of trees, and a wide meadow sweeping down to a large stone house in the distance. She could hear the buzzing sound of bees and the rustle of leaves in wind, and smell the honeysuckle carried on the wind.

"I told you it was not far." Valentine stood in what was now a gilt-arched doorway, his hair stirring in the same wind that ruffled the leaves on the distant trees. "Is it as you remember it, Jonathan? Has nothing changed?"

Clary's heart clenched inside her chest. She had no doubt

this was Jace's childhood home, presented to tempt him as you might tempt a child with candy or a toy. She looked toward Jace, but he didn't seem to see her at all. He was staring at the Portal, and the view beyond it of the green fields and the manor house. She saw his face soften, the wistful curve of his mouth, as if he were looking at someone he loved.

"You can still come home," said his father. The light from the seraph blade that Jace held threw his shadow backward so it seemed to move across the Portal, darkening the bright fields, the meadow beyond.

The smile faded from Jace's mouth. "That's not my home," he said. "This is my home now."

A spasm of fury twisting his features, Valentine looked at his son. She would never forget that look—it made her feel a sudden wild longing for her mother. Because no matter how angry her mother had been with her, Jocelyn had never looked at her like that. She had always looked at her with love.

If she could have felt more pity for Jace than she already did, she would have felt it then.

"Very well," said Valentine, and took a swift step back through the Portal so that his feet struck the earth of Idris. His lips curved into a smile. "Ah," he said, "home."

Jace stumbled to the edge of the Portal before stopping, a hand against the gilt frame. A strange hesitation seemed to have taken hold of him, even as Idris shimmered before his eyes like a mirage in the desert. It would only take a step—

"Jace, don't," Clary said quickly. "Don't go after him."

"But the Cup," said Jace. She could not tell what he was thinking, but the blade in his hand was shaking violently as his hand shook.

"Let the Clave get it! Jace, please." *If you go through that Portal, you might never come back. Valentine will kill you. You don't want to believe it, but he will.*

"Your sister is right." Valentine was standing amid green grass and wildflowers, the blades waving around his feet, and Clary realized that though he and they were inches away from each other, they stood in different countries. "Do you really think you can win this? Though you have a seraph blade and I am unarmed? Not only am I stronger than you, but I doubt you have it in you to kill me. And you will have to kill me, Jonathan, before I'll give the Cup to you."

Jace tightened his grip on the angel blade. "I can—"

"No, you can't." Valentine reached out, *through* the Portal, and seized Jace's wrist in his hand, dragging it forward until the tip of the seraph blade touched his chest. Where Jace's hand and wrist passed through the Portal, they seemed to shimmer as if they had been cast in water. "Do it, then," said Valentine. "Drive the blade in. Three inches—maybe four." He jerked the blade forward, the dagger's tip slicing the fabric of his shirt. A red circle like a poppy bloomed just over his heart. Jace, with a gasp, yanked his arm free and staggered back.

"As I thought," said Valentine. "Too softhearted." And with a shocking suddenness he swung his fist toward Jace. Clary cried out, but the blow never connected: instead it struck the surface of the Portal between them with a sound like a thousand fragile shattering things. Spiderwebbing cracks fissured the glass-that-was-not-glass; the last thing Clary heard before the Portal dissolved into a deluge of ragged shards was Valentine's derisive laughter.

***

Glass surged across the floor like a shower of ice, a strangely beautiful cascade of silver shards. Clary stepped back, but Jace stood very still as the glass rained around him, staring at the empty frame of the mirror.

Clary had expected him to swear, to shout or curse at his father, but instead he only waited for the shards to stop falling. When they did, he knelt down silently and carefully in the welter of broken glass and picked up one of the larger pieces, turning it over in his hands.

"Don't." Clary knelt down next to him, setting down the knife she'd been holding. Its presence no longer comforted her. "There wasn't anything you could have done."

"Yes, there was." He was still looking down at the glass. Broken slivers of it powdered his hair. "I could have killed him." He turned the shard toward her. "Look," he said.

She looked. In the bit of glass she could still see a piece of Idris—a bit of blue sky, the shadow of green leaves. She exhaled painfully. "Jace—"

"Are you all right?"

Clary looked up. It was Luke, standing over them. He was weaponless, his eyes sunk into blue circles of exhaustion. "We're fine," she said. She could see a crumpled figure on the ground behind him, half-covered in Valentine's long coat. A hand protruded from beneath the fabric's edge; it was tipped with claws. "Alaric...?"

"Is dead," said Luke. There was a wealth of controlled pain in his voice; though he had barely known Alaric, Clary knew the crushing weight of guilt would stay with him forever. *And this is how you repay the unquestioning loyalty you bought so cheaply, Lucian. By letting them die for you.*

"My father got away," said Jace. "With the Cup." His voice was dull. "We delivered it right to him. I failed."

Luke let one of his hands fall on Jace's head, brushing the glass from his hair. His claws were still out, his fingers stained with blood, but Jace suffered his touch as if he didn't mind it, and said nothing at all. "It's not your fault," Luke said, looking down at Clary. His blue eyes were steady. They said: *Your brother needs you; stay with him.*

She nodded, and Luke left them and went to the window. He threw it open, sending a draft of air through the room that guttered the candles. Clary could hear him shouting, calling down to the wolves below.

She knelt down next to Jace. "It's all right," she said haltingly, though clearly it wasn't, and might never be again, and she put her hand on his shoulder. The cloth of his shirt was rough under her fingertips, damp with sweat, strangely comforting. "We have my mom back. We have you. We have everything that matters."

"He was right. That's why I couldn't make myself go through the Portal," Jace whispered. "I couldn't do it. I couldn't kill him."

"The only way you would have failed," she said, "is if you had."

He said nothing, only whispered something under his breath. She couldn't quite hear the words, but she reached out and took the bit of glass out of his hand. He was bleeding where he'd held it, from two fine and narrow gashes. She put the shard down and took his hand, closing his fingers over the injured palm. "Honestly, Jace," she said, as gently as she'd touched him, "don't you know better than to play with broken glass?"

He made a sound like a choked laugh before he reached out and pulled her into his arms. She was aware of Luke watching them from the window, but she shut her eyes resolutely and buried her face against Jace's shoulder. He smelled of salt and blood, and only when his mouth came close to her ear did she understand what he was saying, what he had been whispering before, and it was the simplest litany of all: her name, just her name.

Epilogue
The Ascent Beckons

The hospital hallway was blindingly white. After so many days living by torchlight, gaslight, and eerie witchlight, the fluorescent lighting made things look sallow and unnatural. When Clary signed herself in at the front desk, she noticed that the nurse handing her the clipboard had skin that looked strangely yellowish under the bright lights. *Maybe she's a demon,* Clary thought, handing the clipboard back. "Last door at the end of the hall," said the nurse, flashing a kind smile. *Or I could be going crazy.*

"I know," said Clary. "I was here yesterday." *And the day before, and the day before that.* It was early evening, and the hallway wasn't crowded. An old man shuffled along in carpet slippers and a robe, dragging a mobile oxygen unit behind him. Two doctors in green surgical scrubs carried Styrofoam cups of coffee, steam rising from the surface of the liquid into the frigid air. Inside the hospital it was aggressively air-conditioned, though outside the weather had finally begun to turn toward fall.

Clary found the door at the end of the hall. It was open. She peered inside, not wanting to wake Luke up if he was asleep in the chair by the bed, as he had been the last two times she'd come. But he was up and conferring with a tall man in the parchment-colored robes of the Silent Brothers. He turned, as if sensing Clary's arrival, and she saw that it was Brother Jeremiah.

She crossed her arms over her chest. "What's going on?"

Luke looked exhausted, with three days' worth of scruffy beard growth, his glasses pushed up to the top of his head. She could see the bulk of the bandages that still wrapped his upper chest under his loose flannel shirt. "Brother Jeremiah was just leaving," he said.

Raising his hood, Jeremiah moved toward the door, but Clary blocked his way. "So?" she challenged him. "Are you going to help my mother?"

Jeremiah came closer to her. She could feel the cold that wafted off his body, like the steam from an iceberg. *You cannot save others until you first save yourself*, said the voice in her mind.

"This fortune-cookie stuff is getting really old," Clary said. "What's wrong with my mother? Do you know? Can the Silent Brothers help her like you helped Alec?"

We helped no one, said Jeremiah. *Nor is it our place to assist those who have willingly separated themselves from the Clave.*

She drew back as Jeremiah moved past her into the hallway. She watched him walk away, mingling with the crowd, none of whom gave him a second glance. When she let her own eyes fall half-shut, she saw the shimmering aura of glamour that surrounded him, and wondered what they were seeing: Another patient? A doctor hurrying along in surgical scrubs? A grieving visitor?

"He was telling the truth," said Luke from behind her. "He didn't cure Alec; that was Magnus Bane. And he doesn't know what's wrong with your mother either."

"I know," said Clary, turning back into the room. She approached the bed warily. It was hard to connect the small white figure in the bed, snaked over and under by a nest of tubes, with her vibrant flame-haired mother. Of course, her hair was still red, spread out across the pillow like a shawl of coppery thread, but her skin was so pale that she reminded Clary of the wax Sleeping Beauty in Madame Tussauds, whose chest rose and fell only because it was animated by clockwork.

She took her mother's thin hand and held it, as she'd done yesterday and the day before. She could feel the pulse beating in Jocelyn's wrist, steady and insistent. *She wants to wake up*, Clary thought. *I know she does.*

"Of course she does," said Luke, and Clary started in the realization that she had spoken aloud. "She has everything to get better for, even more than she could know."

Clary laid her mother's hand gently back down on the bed. "You mean Jace."

"Of course I mean Jace," said Luke. "She's mourned him for seventeen years. If I could tell her that she no longer needed to mourn—" He broke off.

"They say people in comas can sometimes hear you," Clary offered. Of course, the doctors had also said that this was no ordinary coma—no injury, no lack of oxygen, no sudden failure of heart or brain had caused it. It was as if she were simply asleep, and could not be woken up.

"I know," said Luke. "I've been talking to her. Almost non-stop." He flashed a tired smile. "I've told her how brave you've been. How she'd be proud of you. Her warrior daughter."

Something sharp and painful rose up the back of her throat. She swallowed it down, looking away from Luke toward the window. Through it she could see the blank brick wall of the building opposite. No pretty views of trees or river here. "I did the shopping you asked," she said. "I got peanut butter and milk and cereal and bread from Fortunato Brothers." She dug into her jeans pocket. "I've got change—"

"Keep it," said Luke. "You can use it for cab fare back."

"Simon's driving me back," said Clary. She checked the butterfly watch dangling from her key chain. "In fact, he's probably downstairs now."

"Good, I'm glad you'll be spending some time with him." Luke looked relieved. "Keep the money anyway. Get some takeout tonight."

She opened her mouth to argue, then closed it. Luke was, as her mother had always said, a rock in times of trouble—solid, dependable, and totally immovable. "Come home eventually, okay? You need to sleep too."

"Sleep? Who needs sleep?" he scoffed, but she saw the tiredness in his face as he went back to sit down by her mother's bed. Gently he reached to brush a strand of hair away from Jocelyn's face. Clary turned away, her eyes stinging.

Eric's van was idling at the curb when she walked out of the hospital's main exit. The sky arced overhead, the perfect blue of a china bowl, darkening to sapphire over the Hudson River, where the sun was going down. Simon leaned over to pop the door for her, and she scrambled up into the seat beside him. "Thanks."

"Where to? Back home?" he asked, pulling the van out into the traffic on First.

Clary sighed. "I don't even know where that is anymore."

Simon glanced at her sideways. "Feeling sorry for yourself, Fray?" His tone was mocking, but gentle. If she looked past him, she could still see the dark stains on the backseat where Alec had lain, bleeding, across Isabelle's lap.

"Yes. No. I don't know." She sighed again, tugging on a wayward curl of copper hair. "Everything's changed. Everything's different. I wish sometimes it could all go back to the way it was before."

"I don't," said Simon, to her surprise. "Where are we going again? Tell me uptown or downtown at least."

"To the Institute," said Clary. "Sorry," she added, as he executed a terrifically illegal U-turn. The van, turning on two wheels, screeched in protest. "I should have told you that before."

"Huh," said Simon. "You haven't been back yet, right? Not since—"

"No, not since," said Clary. "Jace called me and told me Alec and Isabelle were okay. Apparently their parents are racing back from Idris, now that someone finally *actually* told them what's going on. They'll be here in a couple of days."

"Was it weird, hearing from Jace?" asked Simon, his voice carefully neutral. "I mean, since you found out..."

His voice trailed off.

"Yes?" said Clary, her voiced sharply edged. "Since I found out what? That he's a killer transvestite who molests cats?"

"No wonder that cat of his hates everyone."

"Oh, shut up, Simon," Clary said crossly. "I know what you mean, and no, it wasn't weird. Nothing ever happened between us anyway."

"Nothing?" echoed Simon, disbelief plain in his tone.

"Nothing," Clary repeated firmly, glancing out the window so that he wouldn't see the blood staining her cheeks. They were passing a row of restaurants, and she could see Taki's, brightly lit in the gathering twilight.

They turned the corner just as the sun disappeared behind the rose window of the Institute, flooding the street below with seashell light that only they could see. Simon pulled up in front of the door and killed the engine, jittering the keys in his hand. "Do you want me to go up with you?"

She hesitated. "No. I should do this on my own."

She saw the look of disappointment flicker across his face, but it vanished quickly. Simon, she thought, had grown up a lot in these past two weeks, just as she had. Which was good, since she wouldn't have wanted to leave him behind. He was part of her, as much as her drawing talent, the dusty air of Brooklyn, her mother's laughter, and her own Shadowhunter blood. "All right," he said. "Are you going to need a ride later?"

She shook her head. "Luke gave me money for a cab. Want to come over tomorrow, though?" she added. "We could watch some *Trigun*, pop some corn. I could use some couch time."

He nodded. "That sounds good." He leaned forward then, and brushed a kiss along her cheekbone. It was a kiss as light as a blown leaf, but she felt a shiver far down in her bones. She looked at him.

"Do you think that it was a coincidence?" she asked.

"Do I think what was a coincidence?"

"That we wound up in Pandemonium the same night that Jace and the others just happened to be there, pursuing a demon? The night before Valentine came for my mother?"

Simon shook his head. "I don't believe in coincidences," he said.

"Neither do I."

"But I have to admit," Simon added, "coincidence or not, it turned out to be a fortuitous occurrence."

"The Fortuitous Occurrences," said Clary. "Now there's a band name for you."

"It's better than most of the ones we've come up with," Simon admitted.

"You bet." She jumped down out of the van, slamming the door behind her. She heard him honk as she ran up the path to the door between the slabs of overgrown grass, and waved without turning around.

The interior of the cathedral was cool and dark, and smelled of rain and damp paper. Her footsteps echoed loudly on the stone floor, and she thought of Jace in the church in Brooklyn: *There might be a God, Clary, and there might not. Either way, we're on our own.*

In the elevator she stole a look at herself in the mirror as the door clanged shut behind her. Most of her bruises and scrapes had healed to invisibility. She wondered if Jace had ever seen her looking as prim as she did today—she'd dressed for the hospital in a black pleated skirt, pink lip gloss, and a vintage sailor-collared blouse. She thought she looked about eight.

Not that it mattered what Jace thought about how she looked, she reminded herself, now or ever. She wondered if they'd ever be the way Simon was with his sister: a mixture of boredom and loving irritation. She couldn't imagine it.

She heard the loud meows before the elevator door even opened. "Hey, Church," she said, kneeling down by the wriggling gray ball on the floor. "Where is everyone?"

Church, who clearly wanted his stomach rubbed, muttered ominously. With a sigh Clary gave in. "Demented cat," she said, rubbing with vigor. "Where—"

"Clary!" It was Isabelle, swooping into the foyer in a long red skirt, her hair piled on top of her head with jeweled clips. "It's so great to see you!"

She descended on Clary with a hug that nearly overbalanced her.

"Isabelle," Clary gasped. "It's good to see you, too," she added, letting Isabelle pull her up to a standing position.

"I was so worried about you," said Isabelle brightly. "After you guys went off to the library with Hodge, and I was with Alec, I heard the most terrific banging explosion, and when I got to the library, of course, you were gone, and everything was strewn all over the floor. And there was blood and sticky black goo everywhere." She shuddered. "What was that stuff?"

"A curse," Clary said quietly. "Hodge's curse."

"Oh, right," Isabelle said. "Jace told me about Hodge."

"He did?" Clary was surprised.

"That he got the curse taken off him and left? Yeah, he did. I would have thought he'd have stayed to say goodbye." Isabelle added, "I'm kind of disappointed in him. But I guess he was scared of the Clave. He'll get in touch eventually, I bet."

So Jace hadn't told them that Hodge had betrayed them, Clary thought, not sure how she felt about that. Then again, if Jace was trying to spare Isabelle confusion and disappointment, maybe she shouldn't interfere.

"Anyway," Isabelle went on, "it was horrible, and I don't know what we would have done if Magnus hadn't showed up and magicked Alec back to health. Is that a word, 'magicked'?" She crinkled her eyebrows. "Jace told us all about what happened on the island afterward. Actually, we knew about it even before, because Magnus was on the phone about it all night. Everyone in Downworld was buzzing about it. You're famous, you know."

"Me?"

"Sure. Valentine's daughter."

Clary shuddered. "So I guess Jace is famous too."

"You're both famous," said Isabelle in the same overbright voice. "The famous brother and sister."

Clary looked at Isabelle curiously. "I didn't expect you to be this glad to see me, I have to admit."

The other girl put her hands on her hips indignantly. "Why not?"

"I didn't think you liked me all that much."

Isabelle's brightness faded and she looked down at her silvery toes. "I didn't think I did either," she admitted. "But when I went to look for you and Jace, and you were gone..." Her voice trailed off. "I wasn't just worried about him; I was worried about you, too. There's something so ... reassuring about you. And Jace is so much better when you're around."

Clary's eyes widened. "He is?"

"He is, actually. Less sharp-edged, somehow. It's not so

much that he's kinder, but that he lets you see the kindness in him." She paused. "And I guess I resented you at first, but I realize now that was stupid. Just because I've never had a friend who was a girl doesn't mean I couldn't learn how to have one."

"Me too, actually," said Clary. "And, Isabelle?"

"Yeah?"

"You don't have to pretend to be nice. I like it better when you just act like yourself."

"Bitchy, you mean?" Isabelle said, and laughed.

Clary was about to protest when Alec swung into the entryway on a pair of crutches. One of his legs was bandaged, his jeans rolled up to the knee, and there was another bandage on his temple, under the dark hair. Otherwise he looked remarkably healthy for someone who'd nearly died four days before. He waved a crutch in greeting.

"Hi," Clary said, surprised to see him up and around. "Are you..."

"All right? I'm fine," Alec said. "I won't even need these in a few days."

Guilt swelled her throat. If it hadn't been for her, Alec wouldn't be on crutches at all. "I'm really glad you're okay, Alec," she said, putting every ounce of sincerity into her voice that she could muster.

Alec blinked. "Thanks."

"So Magnus fixed you?" Clary said. "Luke said—"

"He did!" said Isabelle. "It was so awesome. He showed up and ordered everyone out of the room and shut the door. Blue and red sparks kept exploding out into the hallway from underneath the door."

"I don't remember any of it," said Alec.

"Then he sat by Alec's bed all night and into the morning to make sure he woke up okay," Isabelle added.

"I don't remember that, either," Alec added hastily.

Isabelle's red lips curved into a smile. "I wonder how Magnus knew to come? I asked him, but he wouldn't say."

Clary thought of the folded paper Hodge had thrown into the fire after Valentine had gone. He was a strange man, she thought, who'd taken the time to do what he could to save Alec even while betraying everyone—and everything—he'd ever cared about. "I don't know," she said.

Isabelle shrugged. "I guess he heard about it somewhere. He does seem to be hooked into an enormous gossip network. He's such a *girl*."

"He's the High Warlock of Brooklyn, Isabelle," Alec reminded her, but not without some amusement. He turned to Clary. "Jace is up in the greenhouse if you want to see him," he said. "I'll walk you."

"You will?"

"Sure." Alec looked only slightly uncomfortable. "Why not?"

Clary glanced at Isabelle, who shrugged. Whatever Alec was up to, he hadn't shared it with his sister. "Go on," said Isabelle. "I've got stuff to do anyway." She waved a hand at them. "Shoo."

They set off down the hallway together. Alec's pace was fast, even on crutches. Clary had to jog to keep up. "I have short legs," she reminded him.

"Sorry." He slowed down, contrite. "Look," he began. "Those things you said to me, when I yelled at you about Jace..."

"I remember," she said in a small voice.

"When you told me that you, you know, that I was just—that it was because—" He seemed to be having trouble forming a complete sentence. He tried again. "When you said I was..."

"Alec, don't."

"Sure. Never mind." He clamped his lips together. "You don't want to talk about it."

"It's not that. It's that I feel awful about what I said. It was horrible. It wasn't true at all—"

"But it was true," said Alec. "Every word."

"That doesn't make it okay," she said. "Not everything that's true needs to be said. It was mean. And when I said Jace had told me you'd never killed a demon, he said it was because you were always protecting him and Isabelle. It was a good thing he was saying about you. Jace can be a jerk, but he—" *Loves you*, she was about to say, and stopped. "Never said a bad word about you to me, ever. I swear."

"You don't have to swear," he said. "I know already." He sounded calm, even confident in a way she'd never heard him sound before. She looked at him, surprised. "I know I didn't kill Abbadon either. But I appreciate you telling me I had."

She laughed shakily. "You appreciate me lying to you?"

"You did it out of kindness," he said. "That means a lot, that you would be kind to me, even after how I treated you."

"I think Jace would have been pretty pissed at me for lying if he hadn't been so upset at the time," said Clary. "Not as mad as he would be if he knew what I'd said to you before, though."

"I've got an idea," said Alec, his mouth turning up at the corners. "Let's not tell him. I mean, maybe Jace *can* behead a Du'sien demon from a distance of fifty feet with just a corkscrew and a rubber band, but sometimes I think he doesn't know much about people."

"I guess so." Clary grinned.

They'd reached the bottom of the spiral staircase that led to the roof. "I can't go up." Alec tapped his crutch against a metal step. It rang tinnily.

"It's okay. I can find my way."

He made as if to turn away, then glanced back at her. "I should have guessed you were Jace's sister," he said. "You both have the same artistic talent."

Clary paused, her foot on the lowest stair. She was taken aback. "Jace can draw?"

"Nah." When Alec smiled, his eyes lit like blue lamps, and Clary could see what Magnus had found so captivating about him. "I was just kidding. He can't draw a straight line." Chuckling, he swung away on his crutches. Clary watched him go, bemused. An Alec who cracked jokes and poked fun at Jace was something she could get used to, even if his sense of humor was somewhat inexplicable.

The greenhouse was just as she'd remembered it, though the sky above the glass roof was sapphire now. The clean, soapy smell of the flowers cleared her head. Breathing in deeply, she pushed her way through the tightly woven leaves and branches.

She found Jace sitting on the marble bench in the middle of the greenhouse. His head was bent, and he seemed to be turning an object over in his hands, idly. He looked up as she ducked under a branch, and quickly closed his hand around the object. "Clary." He sounded surprised. "What are you doing here?"

"I came to see you," she said. "I wanted to know how you were."

"I'm fine." He was wearing jeans and a white T-shirt. She could see his still-fading bruises, like the dark spots on the white flesh of an apple. Of course, she thought, the real injuries were internal, hidden from every eye but his own.

"What is that?" she asked, pointing to his closed hand.

He opened his fingers. A jagged shard of silver lay in his palm, glimmering blue and green at the edges. "A piece of the Portal mirror."

She sat down on the bench next to him. "Can you see anything in it?"

He turned it a little, letting the light run over it like water. "Bits of sky. Trees, a path... I keep angling it, trying to see the manor house. My father."

"Valentine," she corrected. "Why would you want to see him?"

"I thought maybe I could see what he was doing with the Mortal Cup," he said reluctantly. "Where it was."

"Jace, that's not our responsibility anymore. Not our problem. Now that the Clave finally knows what happened, the Lightwoods are rushing back. Let them deal with it."

Now he did look at her. She wondered how it was that they could be brother and sister and look so little alike. Couldn't she at least have gotten the curling dark lashes or the angular cheekbones? It hardly seemed fair. He said, "When I looked through the Portal and saw Idris, I knew exactly what Valentine was trying to do, that he wanted to see if I'd break.

And it didn't matter—I still wanted to go home more badly than I could have imagined."

She shook her head. "I don't see what's so great about Idris. It's just a place. The way you and Hodge talk about it—" She broke off.

He closed his hand over the shard again. "I was happy there. It was the only place I was ever happy like that."

Clary plucked a stem from a nearby bush and began to denude it of its leaves. "You felt sorry for Hodge. That's why you didn't tell Alec and Isabelle what he really did."

He shrugged.

"They'll find out eventually, you know."

"I know. But I won't be the one who told them."

"Jace..." The surface of the pond was green with fallen leaves. "How could you have been happy there? I know what you thought, but Valentine was a terrible father. He killed your pets, lied to you, and I know he hit you—don't even try to pretend he didn't."

A flicker of a smile ghosted across Jace's face. "Only on alternate Thursdays."

"Then how could—"

"It was the only time I ever felt sure about who I was. Where I belonged. It sounds stupid, but..." He shrugged. "I kill demons because it's what I'm good at and what I was taught to do, but it isn't who I am. And I'm partly good at it because after I thought my father had died, I was—cut free. No consequences. No one to grieve. No one who had a stake in my life because they'd been part of giving it to me." His face looked as if it had been carved out of something hard. "I don't feel that way anymore."

The stem was entirely denuded of leaves; Clary threw it aside. "Why not?"

"Because of you," he said. "If it weren't for you, I would have gone with my father through the Portal. If it weren't for you, I would go after him right now."

Clary stared down into the clogged pond. Her throat burned. "I thought I made you feel unsettled."

"It's been so long," he said simply, "that I think I was unsettled by the idea of feeling like I belonged anywhere. But you made me feel like I belong."

"I want you to go somewhere with me," she said abruptly.

He looked at her sideways. Something about the way his light gold hair fell into his eyes made her feel unbearably sad. "Where?"

"I was hoping you'd come to the hospital with me."

"I knew it." His eyes narrowed until they looked like the edges of coins. "Clary, that woman—"

"She's your mother too, Jace."

"I know," he said. "But she's a stranger to me. I only ever had one parent, and he's gone. Worse than dead."

"I know. And I know there's no point in telling you how great my mom is, what an amazing, terrific, wonderful person she is and that you'd be lucky to know her. I'm not asking this for you, I'm asking for me. I think if she heard your voice..."

"Then what?"

"She might wake up." She looked at him steadily.

He held her gaze, then broke it with a smile—crooked and a little battered, but a real smile. "Fine. I'll go with you." He stood up. "You don't have to tell me good things about your mother," he added. "I already know them."

"Do you?"

He shrugged slightly. "She raised you, didn't she?" He glanced toward the glass roof. "The sun's almost set."

Clary got to her feet. "We should head out to the hospital. I'll pay for the cab," she added, as an afterthought. "Luke gave me some cash."

"That won't be necessary." Jace's smile widened. "Come on. I've got something to show you."

"But where did you get it?" Clary demanded, staring at the motorcycle perched at the edge of the cathedral's roof. It was a shiny poison green, with silver-rimmed wheels and bright flames painted on the seat.

"Magnus was complaining that someone had left it outside his house the last time he had a party," said Jace. "I convinced him to give it to me."

"And you flew it up here?" She was still staring.

"Uh-huh. I'm getting pretty good at it." He swung a leg over the seat, and beckoned her to come and sit behind him. "Come on, I'll show you."

"Well, at least you know it works this time," she said, getting on behind him. "If we crash into the parking lot of a Key Food, I'll kill you, you know that?"

"Don't be ridiculous," said Jace. "There are no parking lots on the Upper East Side. Why drive when you can get your groceries delivered?" The bike started with a roar, drowning out his laugh. Shrieking, Clary grabbed hold of his belt as the bike hurtled down the slanted roof of the Institute and launched itself into space.

The wind tore her hair as they rose up, up over the cathedral, up above the roofs of the nearby high-rises and apartment buildings. And there it was spread out before her like a carelessly opened jewelry box, this city more populous and more amazing than she had ever imagined: There was the emerald square of Central Park, where the faerie courts met on midsummer evenings; there were the lights of the clubs and bars downtown, where the vampires danced the nights away at Pandemonium; there the alleys of Chinatown down which the werewolves slunk at night, their coats reflecting the city's lights. There walked warlocks in all their bat-winged, cat-eyed glory, and here, as they swung out over the river, she saw the darting flash of multicolored tails under the silvery skin of the water, the shimmer of long, pearl-strewn hair, and heard the high, rippling laughter of the mermaids.

Jace turned to look over his shoulder, the wind whipping his hair into tangles. "What are you thinking?" he called back to her.

"Just how different everything down there is now, you know, now that I can *see*."

"Everything down there is exactly the same," he said, angling the cycle toward the East River. They were heading toward the Brooklyn Bridge again. "You're the one that's different."

Her hands tightened convulsively on his belt as they dipped lower and lower over the river. "Jace!"

"Don't worry." He sounded maddeningly amused. "I know what I'm doing. I won't drown us."

She squinted her eyes against the tearing wind. "Are you

testing what Alec said about some of these bikes being able to go underwater?"

"No." He leveled the bike out carefully as they rose from the river's surface. "I think that's just a story."

"But Jace," she said. "All the stories are true."

She didn't hear him laugh, but she felt it, vibrating through his rib cage and into her fingertips. She held on tightly as he angled the cycle up, gunning it so that it shot forward and darted up the side of the bridge like a bird freed from a cage. Her stomach dropped out from under her as the silver river spun away and the spires of the bridge slid under her feet, but this time Clary kept her eyes open, so that she could see it all.

Acknowledgments

I would like to thank my writing group, the Massachusetts All-Stars: Ellen Kushner, Delia Sherman, Kelly Link, Gavin Grant, Holly Black, and Sarah Smith. Also, Tom Holt and Peg Kerr for encouraging me before there ever was a book, and Justine Larbalestier and Eve Sinaiko for giving me their thoughts on it once it was. My mother and father for their dedication, affection, and unswerving belief that I would eventually produce something publishable. Jim Hill and Kate Connor for their encouragement and support. Eric for vampire motorbikes that run on demon energies and Elka for looking better in black than the widows of her enemies. Theo and Val for creating beautiful images to go with my prose. My glamorous agent, Barry Goldblatt, and my talented editor, Karen Wojtyla. Holly for living through this book with me, and Josh for making it all worthwhile.

READ ALL THE BOOKS

IN THE BREATHTAKING

THE MORTAL INSTRUMENTS

Clary Fray just wishes her life would go back to normal. But what's normal when you're a demon-slaying Shadow-hunter, your mother is in a magically induced coma and you can suddenly see Downworlders like werewolves, vampires and fairies? As Clary searches for a way to help her mother, she is forced to confront her past and her feelings for a boy who can never be hers...

Read the first chapter of *City of Ashes*.

www.ukshadowhunters.com

eBook
available